OUTLAWED MYTH SERIES

BOOK 4

FLOOD

OF THE

FIRE

EVELYN
PUERTO

FLOOD OF THE FIRE

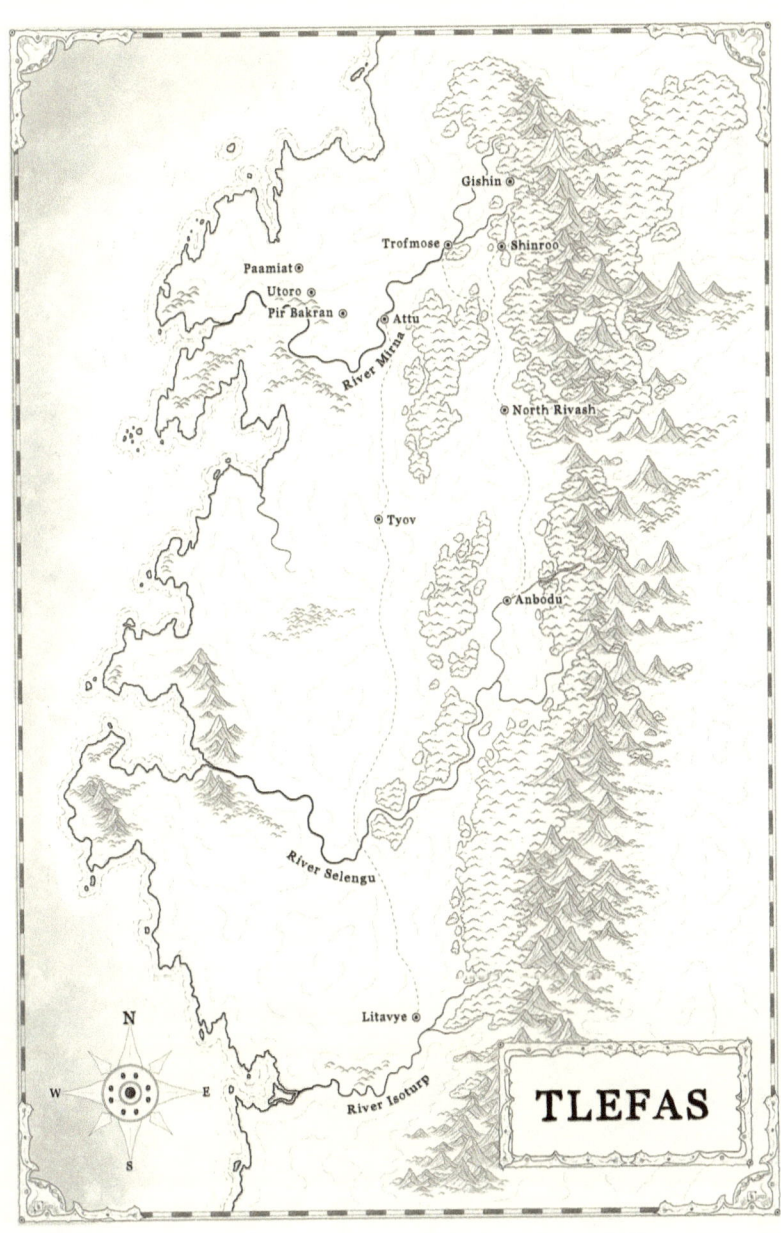

Gishin ⊚

Trofmose ⊚   ⊚ Shinroo

Paamiat ⊚
Utoro ⊚
Pif Bakran ⊚   ⊚ Attu

River Mizna

⊚ North Rivash

⊚ Tyov

⊚ Anbodu

River Selengu

Litavye ⊚

River Isoturp

N
W   E
S

TLEFAS

CONTENTS

1

Tereka wasn't sure about many things, but she knew this. She had no idea how to start a revolution.

Nor did she have a clue how to keep her fellow fugitives in line. Some accepted her leadership willingly, others grudgingly, never missing an opportunity to challenge her.

Angry shouts filled the brisk spring air. Relio and Sebezh were at it again. All winter long, they'd maneuvered for dominance, the former prison brigade boss against his second. Usually, their fights were simply annoying. Today, their animosity could get someone killed.

Leaning against the parapet, Tereka surveyed the mountain slope tumbling away below her, the fresh green of early summer finally overtaking the gray, barren branches of birch and maple trees. An eagle soared beneath her, then dove into the canopy. If only she could gaze on the tranquil forest all afternoon. With a sigh, she turned and walked to the south side of the wide courtyard.

Naco was standing on the edge of the cliff, a rope twisted around his muscular forearm and tied around his waist, the breeze tousling his dark hair. Alikse picked up the rest of the rope and strode to a pine tree. He looped the rope around the thick trunk. With a smooth motion, he shifted the coiled rope to his massive shoulder and returned to Naco's side.

At least those two worked well together, Tereka thought. Cheery Naco and silent Alikse were a good pair and could always be relied on. Even in the worst of times, like when the prison guards were plotting to execute them. She shuddered at how easily Alikse grabbed a guard's head and snapped his neck. *Good thing he likes me.*

A few feet from Naco, thick-set Hinat sidled toward the edge of the cliff, whistling tunelessly through the gap in his front teeth. But while Naco stood with his face tipped to the sky, Hinat peered over the edge of the precipice, frowning doubtfully.

"Why are you making this harder than it is?" Sebezh shouted at Relio. He scratched his red, scruffy beard.

"Because I'm no *durak*." Relio spat on the ground.

"No, just the spawn of a *durak* mated to a *yanshyr*."

Tereka rolled her eyes and approached them. "What seems to be the problem now?"

Sebezh poked a finger at Relio's chest. "Do you think I can't hold him?"

Hinat's eyes darted from Sebezh to the precipice and back. He didn't look too confident in Sebezh's strength.

"I'm the one going over the cliff," Naco said. "If it's all the same to you, I'd rather have a little assurance I won't end the day in a broken heap at the bottom."

Alikse chuckled. "Can't say I blame you."

Who would have thought building a pulley to help bring supplies up the mountain would have caused such a ruckus? "No one needs to die today," Tereka said. "Why would they?"

"Great, now girly thinks she's the expert," Sebezh said.

Relio scowled at him, deep ridges forming in jowls covered with black and gray stubble. He motioned for Tereka to join him at the cliff's edge. "The pulley goes here."

"If her uncles get around to bringing it," put in Sebezh.

Ignoring Sebezh as if he were no more than a buzzing insect, Relio continued. "Your uncles thought this was the best place. Here the cliff edge is hard rock. The problem is the rock juts out in a few spots on the way down. They suggested we chip some of it away, so anything we're hoisting up won't get caught."

"If there's one thing we know how to do, it's chip stone," Naco said, flashing a grin at Tereka.

He was right, but just thinking about their days mining for copper in the Prime Konamei's prison camp made Tereka's heart pound and her skin crawl. Shaking off the sensation, she surveyed the scowling faces. "So?"

Sebezh scratched under his arm. "That one"—he spit in Relio's direction— "wants to loop the rope around a tree."

"It will make it easier to hold the men chipping the rock. And it's only a loop. You'll still be able to let out more rope if you need to." Relio crossed his arms.

"But it uses up twenty yards," Sebezh shot back. "What if we need that length to send them lower?

"We can worry about that then." Relio's glare would frighten a warboar, but Sebezh didn't seem to be intimidated.

"And you call me a *durak*," he said, twisting his mouth into a sneer. "If you're so smart, why don't you hold the rope?"

Tereka stepped forward. No sense reminding Sebezh about Relio's back pain. It was hard enough to get him to accept any direction from Relio. The last thing she needed was Sebezh deciding to exploit Relio's weakness. "I think we should let Naco and Hinat decide." She shrugged. "They're the ones taking the risk."

"I'd rather use the tree," Naco said. "Anything to help the person holding the rope."

Hinat nodded vigorously. "That will be safer."

He must really be scared, Tereka thought as she surveyed Hinat's pale face. He didn't usually oppose Sebezh.

"Well, since that's settled, let's get on with it," Relio said. A gust of wind blew down the slope and he cursed. "The day's not getting any warmer. And we don't want to wait until the wind picks up more."

Sebezh stalked to another pine tree and wrapped his rope around the trunk. Wearing a sullen frown, he took his place near Hinat. Tereka noted the end of each rope was tied in a loop with a big knot. Probably to help Sebezh and Alikse hold on to it if they had to let the whole length out.

Naco stepped to the edge. He fixed his eyes on Alikse. "Ready?"

The big man nodded. He took a step back and gripped the rope.

Seizing his end of the rope, Naco lowered himself to the ground. Then he slid off the cliff.

Tereka's heart raced. Would Alikse be able to hold him? The man's biceps bulged as he slowly let out the rope. He seemed able to control how fast Naco was descending.

Hinat crept to the rim of the cliff. He glowered at Sebezh. "Don't drop me." He tied the rope snugly around his waist and wrapped it around his left forearm, then slid off the edge.

Sebezh took a few steps forward, then pulled back. He let more rope out. "See? This is easy. Even girly could do this."

Shouts from below drew Tereka's attention. She crouched on the rim of the cliff and gingerly peered over. Sweat dampened her palms. Naco and Hinat were brave to let themselves dangle over the precipice, high over the jagged rocks at the mountain's feet. She shivered. She was relieved no one had suggested she do the job.

Both Naco and Hinat had reached the rock that jutted out like an accusing fist. They braced their feet against the face of the cliff. Naco wiped his forehead and pulled a chisel and hammer from his belt. Hinat clung to the rope for several moments before he did the same.

The gentle tap-tap of the hammers made Tereka wince. The chipping sound was a painful reminder of their days as the Prime Konamei's prisoners, laboring in his copper mines. She shook off the dreadful memory, eased away from the cliff's edge, and approached Alikse.

He glanced at her and grunted. "Good thing I've got skinny Naco and not that brute Hinat."

Tereka grinned. Hinat and Alikse never had a kind word for each other. "Good thing, indeed. You'd be tempted to let him go."

"Nah, just scare him a little."

"Like this?" Sebezh dropped his coiled rope. Immediately, it began to unwind, pulled by Hinat's weight. Hinat's shriek cut through the air. Sebezh lunged for the rope and tripped, landing face-first on the ground.

By reflex, Tereka grabbed the looped end. Sebezh was groaning, his chin scraped and bloody. He'd never get up in time. She wasn't strong enough to support Hinat's weight. If she tried, they'd both plunge to their deaths. She thrust an arm through the loop, grasped the rope, and sprinted for the cliff's edge. She held her breath, closed her eyes, and jumped.

2

Tereka's breath caught as she plummeted toward the jagged rocks below. With a jerk, her descent stopped, and she clung to the rope. Her arm felt as it had been wrenched from her shoulder. Sharp pain burned where the rope dug into her flesh through the coarse fabric of her tunic's sleeve. She took a few gasping breaths, her eyes watering from the shock.

She peeked down. Fifty feet below her, Hinat dangled, his fall arrested by her weight on the other end of the rope. *Now if only the tree that's supporting us holds.* Hinat hung three hundred feet or more above the jagged rocks at the bottom. If he fell...

"What were you thinking?" Naco swayed ten feet below her, his tawny eyes wide in his coppery face. She tried to give him a smile and failed.

"That I had to save Hinat." Her rope jerked, and she dropped a few feet. Her breath caught. "What was that?"

"Girly," Relio shouted at her. "Don't move. You broke the tree."

Tereka heard only snatches of Relio's next words. She hoped they had more to do with hoisting them all back to the top than chastising Sebezh for his recklessness.

"Heave!" Relio barked the order. Tereka's rope didn't move. Then she noticed Hinat had shifted a few feet up.

"Heave!"

She dropped two feet. Her heart pounded in her ears. "What was that?"

"I think as they pull Hinat up, they are letting your side of the rope go down," Naco said calmly. "My guess is both Relio and Sebezh are pulling Hinat up together, to be faster. They don't have anyone to hold your end of the rope."

It took only a few more jerky downward motions for Tereka to draw level with Naco. "Are you alright?" she asked.

"I'm fine." He frowned. "I'd like to finish the job while I'm here. But I don't want to hit Hinat with any falling rock."

"Hmm." A gust of wind spun her away from him. She closed her eyes to shut out the spiky rocks far below, jutting into the air like sharpened swords.

Tereka clenched the rope tighter with her sweaty hands, her knuckles whitening. The rope cut into the flesh under her arm like it was digging a canal. Stinging pain ran along her neck. She wasn't sure how much longer she'd be able to endure it.

She glanced below. "Why wouldn't they pull me up first? I'm closer." She gasped as she dropped another few feet.

"But you're lighter. Makes it easier for them to pull you up later when they're tired."

"I'm not sure I want my life in Sebezh's hands."

By this time, Hinat had nearly reached her level. His face was pale, his eyes half closed. The arm he'd twisted in the rope was bent at an odd angle. Tereka winced. Had he broken it in the fall?

"Hinat," she said, trying to keep the pain from her voice.

He opened his eyes. With a frown, he shook his head. "What're you doing, girly?"

Before she could answer, she dropped again and Hinat's rope jerked him upwards. His knees were now level with her nose. She tilted her head up to concentrate on Naco's tawny eyes, forcing herself to focus on his gaze. She stifled her thoughts of falling to the rocks below, hoping they'd all survive this ordeal.

A few more jerks downward, then scuffling noises at the top of the cliff told her Hinat was pulled to safety.

"Hang on, girly." Relio's voice sounded strained and tired. Tereka rose a few feet, then a few more, ascending much faster than Hinat had.

As she neared the top, she heard a crack and dropped about six feet. Pain shot through her arm and shoulder. She screwed her eyes shut. Surely, they wouldn't drop her now. A few shouts, and a long pull on the rope.

Tereka stretched out her hand to grab a rock near the top of the cliff. A dark brown hand reached for hers and pulled her over the edge. Her stomach scraped along the rocks right before she looked up into Alikse's flushed and sweaty face. "Who's holding Naco?" she asked.

"The tree, with some help from Poales. Relio's done for."

She crawled away from the lip of the cliff. "Thank you." She turned and sat on the stone pavement, panting, unable to believe she was no longer suspended hundreds of feet in the air.

Savinnia and Poales must have heard all the commotion and come running. He was assisting Sebezh and Alikse haul Naco up, while Relio lay moaning on the ground. Savinnia was helping Relio drink from a dipper, her dark hair tumbling around her face.

The tree they'd wrapped the rope around was cracked and bent, some of its roots pulled from the soil. Had the rope not caught on a branch, she and Hinat would have fallen to the rocks below. She rubbed her sore shoulder, wincing at the sting of the rope burn on her neck.

The pine tree supporting Naco's rope creaked. Her heart skipped a beat, and she clenched her shaking hands. Would they manage to get Naco up before the tree gave way? She didn't want to imagine life without Naco.

When Alikse pulled Naco over the edge, she let out a breath. They'd all survived. She shakily got to her feet and stumbled to Hinat.

He lay on the ground, clutching his damaged forearm.

Tereka knelt beside him. "Hinat."

With a moan, he opened one eye. "My shoulder—"

With a few strides, Naco reached him and helped him sit up. When Hinat's arm flopped uselessly, Naco grabbed his elbow. "I'll fix it. Ready?" Without waiting for an answer, he jerked the arm. With a pop that made Tereka flinch, the arm snapped into place.

Hinat yelled, then groaned. "That's better."

"Good," said Tereka. "Now for the bone."

Savinnia handed her some strips of cloth, a short piece of wood, and a pot of water. Tereka gently removed Hinat's torn sleeve from his arm. Angry red stripes scored the flesh of his forearm, which canted at an awkward angle a little below the elbow.

Naco held Hinat's other arm down while Tereka pushed the bone back in place. She washed the wounds and bound the splint to the arm. "Better?"

"Some." Hinat opened one eye. "Can't you do some of your magic, girly?"

She shrugged. "I'll try once we get you inside. But you know I can't promise anything."

And she couldn't. The sky-god was the power behind the amulets, and she couldn't dictate what he would do. She'd found over the winter that usually she could count on her amulets to relieve aches and pains and to speed up healing. Rarely did the amulets allow her to heal instantly and completely.

Now, she became more aware of her own hurts—the rope burn on her neck, the chafing under her arm, her scraped hands. She lifted her shoulder and hissed at the stabbing pain. Cautiously, she moved her arm. The pain was bearable, so her shoulder wasn't out of joint like Hinat's.

Staggering to her feet, she turned to Naco. He was coiling the ropes and appeared to be unscathed. Relio was sitting up, drinking water. Alikse and Sebezh were glaring at each other like two dogs about to fight.

"C-could someone tell me what happened?" Poales asked.

Relio, Sebezh, and Alikse all spoke at once. Naco opened his mouth, closed it, and shook his head.

Hinat's face turned purple. His voice rose above the others' as he shook his fist in Sebezh's face. "This *yanshyr* nearly got me killed!" Tereka figured his injured arm was the only reason he didn't fling himself on Sebezh.

"Right, blame me," Sebezh snarled. "I wasn't the *yanshyr* who wanted both of them to go down at once. Had you listened to me, none of this would have happened."

"Right," said Relio. "Because you wouldn't have been holding a rope, so it wouldn't have mattered if you let it go or not."

Sebezh spat. "That's what you think."

Tereka sighed. How was she going to contain this? Tensions had risen over the winter, with Relio and Sebezh coming to blows at least twice a month. What had she been thinking to want to start a revolution? If she couldn't convince a few unruly men to follow her directions, how would she possibly lead the numbers needed to overthrow the Prime Konamei?

"Stop it, all of you." She tried to make her voice commanding. Hinat stopped shouting, at least. Tereka strode up to Relio and Sebezh and forced her way between them. "Stop. Now." This time, they listened. "We're not going to survive if we're at each others' throats."

"We won't survive if we listen to that *durak*," Sebezh said.

"I'm not the *yanshyr* who dropped the rope." Relio glared at Sebezh, his voice rising.

Putting a hand on Relio's chest, Tereka pushed him backward. Then she spun to face Sebezh. She tipped her chin up to look him in the eye. "Now hear this. Even if Relio's plan was no good, you were the one who nearly ruined it."

"I don't have to take this from you, girly."

"What are you going to do? Leave?"

Sebezh narrowed his eyes. "I just might do that."

Relio and Alikse cursed, but Tereka stifled her reaction. This was no time to let Sebezh believe his threat held any weight.

"You need to think long and hard about that, Sebezh," she said. "In case you've forgotten, I promised my uncles that I'd kill you if you tried to leave. And if I don't succeed in stopping you, they'll hunt you down and finish the job."

"Bah. You and your uncles. You tell us they're savages, but they do nothing but help." He waved a hand at the mount Tereka's Risker uncles had built for the pulley. "And they have wonders the villages never dreamed of. Some barbarians they are. I don't believe they'd have the stomach to kill me in cold blood."

She clenched her jaw. "If you left, they'd see that as a threat to me. And they'd do anything to prevent you from putting me in danger." She paused, staring into his beady brown eyes.

Five heartbeats passed before he dropped his gaze. "Fine. Have it your way." He slouched away down the steps.

Tereka's heart pounded, her pulse loud in her ears. He'd backed down. This time.

3
___

A gust of chilly air puffed through the pine trees and nipped Tereka's ears. She pulled her hood over her head. Even though by the calendar it was summer, the breeze nipped her ears like early spring.

Last autumn's leaves swirled near the ground, tumbling and scattering with each breath of wind that hissed through the woods. She pressed her lips together, wishing the hard feelings that lingered a full week after the accident on the cliff's edge could dissipate as easily.

The explosive anger from that afternoon had receded into simmering tension. Sebezh had subsided into grumbling under his breath whenever someone tried to tell him what to do. Relio cursed every time his eyes fell on Sebezh.

The other two members of their band had been horrified and angered when they'd heard of Sebezh's nearly fatal joke. Poales muttered that he'd feel safer with the pirates. Savinnia refused to remain anywhere near Sebezh.

Then there was Naco. Outwardly, he seemed to be his usual cheerful self, but something had changed.

Tereka rubbed the back of her head and ran her fingers through her hair, now grown out a few inches since being shaved in the prison camp seven months before. Why was Naco being so aloof? She could always count on him to back her up or to shield her from Sebezh's unwanted advances, but now he treated her the same way he treated his sister Savinnia. Had she imagined he felt something for her?

Another gust of wind tugged at her tattered gray cloak. She pulled it closer. Surely the sun should be stronger this far south. All her memories of North Rivash were of a hot and dusty town. Not this damp cold that seeped into her feet through the thin leather of her boots. The waiting wasn't making her feel any warmer. This was no way to start a revolution.

Added to the challenge of keeping her unruly followers in line was Hinat's injury. While his shoulder was on the mend and his broken arm seemed to be healing properly, he wasn't able to join them on this mission. With the risk they were about to take, she didn't like being short a man.

Breathing deeply to get her thoughts under control, Tereka fumbled with the bag tied into her pocket and fingered her amulets. The stones were smooth, cold, and motionless, like puddles on the road when there was no breeze. No vibration. She tapped her fingers against her lips. Her amulets had vibrated the night Sebezh got drunk and tried to assault her, as if they were warning her of lurking peril. Did no vibration today mean no danger? It was hard to tell. Learning to use the dragonfly amulets was like walking through a mist. She could only see a few steps ahead, blind to any obstacle she was about to trip over.

Idly, she watched a squirrel leap from one bare branch of a birch tree to the curving limb of a maple. The small animal had no problem taking a chance to get what it wanted.

If only she could be as sure of her risky plan for starting the revolt. So much hinged on their success today. If all went well, they would be one step closer to dislodging Juquila, the syndic of Trofmose, from power. That would be their first blow against the Prime Konamei. If they could topple Juquila, they could work on undermining Kaberco, Trofmose's ephor. Hopefully, as word of their rebellion spread, it would inspire others to stand against the oppressive, corrupt regime that ruled Tlefas.

And perhaps, once they began to act against their common enemies, Sebezh and the others would put aside their differences long enough to see the revolution through. Tereka didn't want to consider what would happen if they didn't.

She shook her head, remembering how her uncles had laughed when she told them about the accident on the cliff. Of course, Chen and Lilio would find it amusing. They'd spent their childhoods dangling from ropes, harvesting honey off the cliffs. That grown men couldn't handle a rope job that didn't involve dodging angry bees was quite a joke for them.

When they'd stopped chuckling, they made quick work of chipping the stone and setting up the pulley. Sebezh and Relio wore shamed expressions, but Tereka knew they were as glad as she was to be liberated from the drudgery of lugging supplies up the mountain.

Revolution was far less amusing, evidently. Her uncles hadn't laughed when she explained her plan to dislodge Juquila and Kaberco from power. "Once a prejudice takes root, it's like pulling up a tree stump to get rid of it," Chen told her.

Tereka leaned against the rough bark of a pine tree and blew on her icy fingers. Chen might be right. But she had to try something. At least action had made Sebezh a bit more agreeable.

But the waiting was so hard. Alikse had gone to look for the overdue caravan. Naco, Relio, and Sebezh were squatting in the center of the clearing, gambling over a game played with pebbles and little pits they'd dug in a circle. She inhaled a deep breath. They had the right idea. No sense letting nerves take over. She ambled toward them, hoping to get caught up in their competition.

Naco moved one of his pebbles and laughed. "And with that, I win." She liked how his face softened when he smiled, happiness smoothing the creases that years of labor in the mines had carved into his copper-colored face. He glanced at her and winked. Relio cursed and Sebezh spat. The three men arranged their pebbles and started another game.

At the sound of soft rustling in the undergrowth, Tereka spun and reached for her bow. Alikse ducked under a pine branch and pushed his way into the clearing. She let her muscles relax. "Any sign of them?"

Alikse shrugged his massive shoulders. "None. I went as far as the next bend, but nothing."

Just her luck. The first time she tried her plan, the caravan was delayed. Or maybe it hadn't left Shinroo at all. She rubbed the back of her neck. "Perhaps we should just walk down the road to meet them."

Relio barked out a laugh. "That's what I like about you, girly. Always ready to make a bold move."

"I'm game." Naco scrambled to his feet.

Sebezh snorted. "That's because I was about to win." He stood up. "But girly's right. Anything's better than just sitting here."

They readied their weapons and slung rucksacks on their backs. Tereka stepped out from the trees onto the road. Clouds scurried across the pale blue sky, hurried along by the brisk wind. A few birds chirped, and a squirrel chittered. No sound of a caravan's creaking wagon wheels or the gentle clopping of horses' hooves on the road. She pulled three arrows from the quiver at her hip and held them next to her bow. "Shall we?"

She set off, heading south toward Shinroo. Naco fell into place beside her, with Relio on her other side. Sebezh and Alikse followed.

Heartbeat after heartbeat, they walked, until Tereka's scalp was prickling. Something wasn't right. They should have met the caravan long ago.

Quickening her stride, she rounded one bend, then another. With a gasp, she halted. Fifty yards ahead of them, five ragged men were pillaging the wagons, while another ten were fighting traders. The bandits wielded swords while the traders were armed with only whips and whatever they could throw at their assailants. A few brown-clad traders lay scattered on the ground, red splotches staining their tunics and trousers.

"I think we're just in time, don't you, girly?" Relio drew his sword.

Tereka nodded. "Look, the guards aren't even fighting back." She pointed at six men wearing black leather seated on horses. Three held bows with nocked arrows. The other three brandished long swords that gleamed in the sunlight. None of them engaged the bandits.

Her pulse sped up and her face heated. Cowards. They'd rather watch traders die than risk injury. "I'll shoot from the right. You four take the left. Ready?" She nocked an arrow. "Here we go."

She ran a few steps to the right side of the road, hoping the trees would shelter her from the wind. Then she aimed, held her breath, and released her arrow. It struck a bandit in the neck. Within three heartbeats, she'd shot two more.

Sprinting toward the caravan, Tereka readied another trio of arrows. Relio and Alikse had already taken down two outlaws—Relio with a few swings of his sword and Alikse by grabbing a bandit by the head and breaking his neck.

A few heartbeats more, and most of the robbers lay dead. The rest fled into the trees on the north side of the road.

Relio and Alikse stood panting next to Sebezh, whose face was red and beaded with sweat. Tereka and Naco dashed over. "Anyone hurt?" she asked.

Before they could answer, the captain of the guardsmen strode up to them, his sword outstretched. "Who are you? What are you doing? You know full well that weapons are illegal."

Good, Tereka thought. We were right to wear gray clothing. He thinks we're villagers.

Five or six traders crowded around. One stepped forward. "Thank you, whoever you are."

That gave Tereka the opening she was looking for. "Friends, we were glad to assist you. But think. Why did you need help?" She pointed her bow at the guardsmen. "Your guards, who are paid to protect you, failed in their task. You've been told that you should trust them for your safety. But they sat on their horses while you were attacked. You've been told weapons are dangerous. But it's more dangerous to venture onto the roads unarmed."

The traders murmured. Tereka wondered if it was in approval or disdain.

"And who made you these promises?" She held up her arm, pointing toward the northwest, roughly in the direction of Trofmose. "Do you rely on the word of that leaning fence, Juquila, who will gladly collapse under any force that will give her more power? Or that tottering wall, Kaberco, who will do anything to protect himself but has nothing left for you?"

The captain waved his sword at Tereka, his black eyes cold. "I don't know who you are, but if you don't stop talking, I'll have you taken."

Tereka and her crew burst into laughter.

Naco grinned. "You don't scare us, coward."

Relio chuckled. "It's a little late for that, don't ya think?"

"I wouldn't keep threatening us, my friend," Tereka said to the captain. "And you, traders. What other lies have they told you?" She reached into her rucksack and pulled out a loaf of bread. "Have you ever seen bread like this? Why do they force you to eat hard, black bread?" She tossed the loaf to a trader.

Alikse, Naco, and Relio reached into their sacks and flung loaves into the group of traders. Relio pitched one into the face of the captain. Sebezh's sack held a small basket of tomatoes and cucumbers, and he simply placed it in the middle of the road in front of the gathered traders.

"Who are you to question the Prime Konamei?" yelled a trader.

Turning the loaf over in his hands, the captain stared as if he held a great treasure. His eyes flicked to the basket. "Where did you get fresh tomatoes this time of year?" His eyes narrowed. "That's only possible through Risker magic."

Tereka opened her mouth to explain about the Riskers' greenhouses, but a guard cut her off, hefting the bread in his hands. "This is Risker bread." He dropped the loaf in the dust of the road. "Are you trying to get us taken?"

The captain jerked, then hurled his bread at Tereka. "You are unsafe and have broken many of the Prime Konamei's laws. We're going to have you taken."

Many of the traders murmured in approval. "Don't you see how they've lied?" Tereka said to them. "How they are still lying?" She forced the words out through clenched teeth. "Do you have any wounded?"

Naco put a hand on her arm. She shook it off. Yes, the plan was to talk and distribute food. Her uncles had been adamant that she not use the amulets. But these people wouldn't listen.

Two men carried a third to Tereka. Blood pulsed from a wound on his tanned neck. She winced. Had it sliced any deeper, he would have already bled out and died. She pulled out one of her dragonfly amulets and held it up for all to see. "You've been told these are dangerous. Or that they are mere remnants of old myths and fairy tales. That they hold no power. None of that is true."

She held the amulet over the man's neck and murmured to

the sky-god. Green light flared and the bleeding stopped. The edges of the wound drew together.

The man's jaw dropped. "What evil is this? I have no pain."

The eyes of the two men next to him widened. They backed away, pulling their friend with them.

Tereka's mouth fell open. They didn't believe her. They refused to see what was in front of their own eyes. Her shoulders drooped and she let out a sigh.

The captain pointed his sword at Tereka. "Take them."

None of the guards moved. Tereka used their hesitation to run back, pulling three arrows from her quiver. She spun and nocked one. Holding her breath, she released the arrows, one after the other. The first knocked the captain's hat from his head. The second struck his sword just below the man's grip on its hilt. A heartbeat later, the third scraped his earlobe.

"Next time, I won't try to miss." She glared at him. "Think about what you've heard," Tereka told the traders. "Consider what you have seen, and what you will taste if you dare to eat the bread and vegetables we brought. And decide for yourselves what is truth and what is a lie." She gestured with her head to the south. "You'll be late getting to North Rivash if you don't hurry." She smirked at the captain. "And don't try to follow us." She took off at a trot, running past the halted caravan, heading north for home.

4

Tereka loped down the road, puffs of dust rising with each step. She ignored the snarled insults the traders tossed her way as she passed the halted wagons. A stone struck her between the shoulder blades. She huffed and kept running. The leather vest concealed by her gray cloak had dulled the impact. "Keep going," she shouted to the men following her.

Warmth flooded her face, a heat not solely driven by her exertion. How could the traders be so blind? When confronted with evidence they'd been lied to, they chose to ignore it. She pounded her feet on the road as if to stomp on the lies that held the people in bondage for centuries. *One, two, three, four...* She counted her footsteps. Anything to focus her mind away from their failure. Not a single trader had listened to her at all. Even the one she'd healed had been more frightened than grateful.

As she ran, she heard only the panting breath of the others behind her. No shouts commanding them to halt, no arrows to stop them. It seemed the guardsmen had enough sense to let them go, deal with the dead and wounded, and get the caravan in motion again.

When she trod on a rut, Tereka stumbled but recovered her footing after a few staggered steps. She turned more of her attention to the road ahead, but could not shake those traders out of her mind. How could they ignore the evidence in front of their eyes? She'd counted on at least a few of them listening and thinking about the lies of the Prime Konamei.

Prompted by the sharp pain in her hands, she relaxed her clenched fists. She was a fool. It wasn't that long ago she'd believed all the lies.

So why should she expect a group of traders to accept her word? The Prime Konamei's rules gave people structure. Everyone knew their place, whether they liked it or not. Raised to see everything as a source of danger, it was no surprise people wanted nothing to change. The protection the guards offered satisfied most people.

Chen, she had to admit, had been right. People wouldn't easily give up their beliefs. She felt a pang of shame, remembering how stubbornly she'd clung to her prejudice and ignorance concerning the Riskers.

But now what? It would take them two days of rugged travel to get back to their mountain hideout. At least she'd have that much time to consider her next move.

She'd asked Da why the earlier occupants of the land would build a tower in such a remote place. He had pointed west, north, and east. From the heights they could see far in any direction. Da thought the tower was used for early warnings of invasion from any of those directions. Who the builders had been afraid of, he had no idea.

Whoever they were, they'd died centuries ago. Maybe their guard tower had proved useless against the threat it had been built to meet.

And now she and her fellow escaped prisoners lived there. It was shelter, to be sure. But the seven months they'd spent there hadn't exactly been comfortable.

Relio and Sebezh never stopped sparring, trying to

achieve dominance in their little world. Savinnia had so far convinced Relio she had no intention of continuing her relationship with him. Poales served as a good buffer, but he was becoming increasingly concerned about his wife and children who lived far to the south in Litavye, and his anxiety was making him short-tempered. Alikse and Hinat were cooperative, but they still followed the lead of Relio and Sebezh.

And Naco. Strong, dependable Naco. He always supported her and helped keep the others in line. Because he was eating better, the gauntness of his prison days was fading. Dimples appeared when he grinned, and his arms bulged when he worked. And sometimes, very rarely, he gave her a smile that not only brought out the dimples but stretched all the way to his eyes, a smile he saved just for her. Sometimes when he looked at her that way, she allowed herself to hope he had feelings for her.

Of course, she'd thought Kemet had felt something for her. But when things got dicey, he proved he cared more for his own safety. No. Better to count footsteps than torture herself with hopes that were probably vain. *Twenty, twenty-one.*

Tereka jogged around a bend in the road, keeping her eyes to the right. A break in the trees marked a path that led up into the hills. She turned into the forest and slowed her pace. No sense wearing herself out charging up a slope. She turned her face to the breeze, letting the dappled shade cool her sweaty face.

When the shadows lengthened, they made camp close to a stream. After so many months together, they fell naturally into their routine. Sebezh and Alikse gathered wood. Naco and Relio hunted. Tereka built the fire, sending Alikse to stand guard. Bandits and warboars prowled the slopes of the mountains. Tereka had no intention of being eaten by either.

Naco returned with a pair of rabbits, and Relio had stumbled on a bush full of hopberries. Added to the round orange fruit Tereka had in her sack, the fruit Osip grew in his green-house, they'd have a full meal.

While the scent of stewing rabbit filled the air, Tereka counted her arrows, asking the others to do the same. Between them, they still had over fifty. Enough to see them home, as long as they didn't run into many bandits.

Relio dropped to sit beside her. "So, girly, what do you think?"

Before she could answer, Sebezh chimed in. "That could have been a disaster. I knew it wouldn't work."

Tereka wanted to pound her fist into his teeth. She swallowed hard and let her breath out slowly.

Naco answered for her. "You're right, you're still with us."

Sebezh flushed as Relio chuckled. "True," Relio said. "But I want to know what girly's thinking."

"Well, I think Sebezh is right. That could have gone very badly for us." Tereka measured every word as she spoke. "But we all came back, none of us were hurt, and we learned something important."

She looked around at them all, Alikse attentive, Sebezh sneering, Relio and Naco wary. "It's going to be harder to convince people they've been lied to than I expected."

Relio nodded. "It's hard for people to admit they've been fools."

"And they never will, not the way you're going about it," Sebezh said.

Tereka raised an eyebrow. "And what, oh wise one, do you suggest?"

"Giving them bread won't work." Sebezh scowled at her. "The Prime Konamei will tell them Risker bread is poison. The only ones who know different are the konameis who eat it and the traders who sell it. Traders aren't about to risk their lives to expose the truth."

He was right, of course. Tereka studied her hands. "You would think being rescued would make a difference."

Naco shook his head. "Maybe some of them were grateful. But no one would say so in front of the guards."

Another good point. "That's why I healed the man. How could they dismiss that?"

Relio laughed. "All you did was show them a little Risker magic. Even if they agree with you, they'd be taken if they so much as breathed a word about it." He scratched under his arm. "Keep this up, and you'll be like the *durak* who tried to get dirt from his eye and ended up blind."

Tereka rubbed her forehead. "But if talking to them is useless, if showing them the things they've been deprived of won't work, and how their leaders have lied to them, what do I do?"

The others exchanged glances. After a pause, Naco spoke up. "I know you don't want to hear this, but it's the truth. And we all agree."

"What?" Tereka frowned. She had a feeling she knew what was coming.

"You have to declare yourself the Desired One of the prophecy. Announce you are Tereka Sabidur, a trader who was taken and escaped through the power of the sky-god and the amulets you carry. Do that, and they'll have the courage to listen to you."

A lump formed in her throat. She'd hoped that Naco, at least, would understand. She crossed her arms. "I'm not the Desired One."

"That's right, girly, you keep denying it," Relio said. Tereka raked a glare over his grinning face. Why couldn't they give up this Desired One nonsense?

Sebezh spit into the fire, the wetness hissing. "You can deny it all you want. I don't care if that old myth is talking about you or not. All I know is it's the only thing that will get people to listen." He smirked. "And if they're not listening to you, who are they listening to? The Prime Konamei? Or worse, your sweet aunt Juquila."

Tereka scowled. Juquila wasn't really her aunt, and she was anything but sweet. Venomous was more like it. And as syndic in charge of trade for the northern region, Juquila held a lot of power. She was the reason Tereka had been imprisoned in the first place.

"No." Tereka jutted her chin out. "I'm not the Desired One." Couldn't they see? She was only nineteen years old, not worthy or capable of ruling the entire land. All she wanted to do was take down the corrupt powers and replace them with people who would rule with wisdom and a fair hand.

She abruptly stood up and strode away from the fire, losing herself in the shadows under the trees. She would not allow anyone to force a name on her, not even a name out of myth. Desired One. That wasn't her.

Aunt Juquila had called her "spawn." Tereka's stomach writhed and her eyes burned. Useless spawn, not worthy to sit at the same table with her cousins. How Juquila would mock at the idea that she, Tereka, was destined to bring a new order. And if she tried and failed, that would prove Juquila's taunts had been accurate. That she was incompetent and inferior.

A familiar ache tightened her throat. When she was eighteen, she learned that "Tereka" was the name given to her by the man who took her in and raised her as his own. She'd never know what her parents had called her. If she only knew that name, maybe she could shake off the shame and humiliation of being the nameless orphan who'd been scorned and abused.

She snorted. Her caravan scheme failed, not even after they rescued the traders. How could anyone expect her to govern a country? She didn't want the power, anyway. If she succeeded, would she have to move into the Prime Konamei's estate in Anbodu? She wanted to settle with her Risker relatives in the free air of the mountains, not be constrained in the towns and cities that huddled in the lowlands below. She returned to the light of the campfire. "What if the real Desired One is someone else?"

Relio shook his head and Sebezh muttered curses. As usual, Alikse kept his opinions to himself, but from the way his face fell at her repeated denials, she knew he agreed with Sebezh.

Maybe Naco would back her up now. He must be able to see she didn't want this. She faced him, hoping for the words she wanted to hear. "You should think about it," he said. "Who else is an amazing archer and carries two Amulets of Power?"

"Someone who learned a few tricks and got lucky, I suppose." Her heart sank. Even Naco wanted her to be the Desired One. That must mean she'd read him wrong. He didn't want a future with her, so he was pushing her into a destiny that would take her far away.

"Fine." She let out a huff. "I'll think about it. But unless I have proof, you can't talk me into it." She stood and stretched. "Who's taking the first watch? I'm tired." Without waiting for an answer, she spread her bedroll next to the fire and wrapped herself in the blanket.

Closing her eyes did nothing to lull her to sleep. The crackle of the fire, the rustling of the trees, and the snapping of small animals scuttling through fallen leaves left her wary. There were enough people who wanted to destroy her, one or two possibly in her own group. How many more enemies would the Desired One have?

5

———

Tereka forced her aching legs to take the final steps up the steep, rocky path. With a huff, she stepped into the courtyard of their mountain hideout. After two days of hard travel, they'd made it back without incident. That is, if she didn't count Sebezh, who needled her about becoming the Desired One every chance he got. It didn't help that the others thought her revolution was doomed if she refused to claim the role.

To forestall debate, she announced she would be the first to take a bath. That way, she'd be free of them all. Then she got everyone busy cutting wood and foraging for food to supplement the supplies Poales and Savinnia had gathered in their absence.

"Girly, you've turned into a taskmaster," Relio said. "Can't we rest now that we're home? Are you sure you were a trader, and not a prison guard before they took you?"

She chuckled. "And what? Let you take a bath now and say you don't want to work up a sweat afterwards?" She tipped her head to the side. "Are you saying Poales and Savinnia should treat us like conquering heroes and wait on us hand and foot?"

"Would be nice," Relio answered.

Sebezh snorted. "Some heroes we are."

With discouragement and weariness weighing on her shoulders, Tereka turned away, leaving the argument and the stale, sweaty odor of her companions behind. She knew she could count on Relio to hash out who would chop wood and who would go fishing. He would get them all moving.

After hanging her bow and quiver in the lean-to where they kept their weapons, she ambled into the kitchen. Her stomach rumbled and her mouth watered when the aroma of freshly baked flatbread caressed her nose. Resisting the temptation to steal a piece, she filled a large pot with water from one of the tall earthen jars that flanked the door to the storeroom like silent guards. A fire roared in the hearth, most likely Savinnia's work. She hung the pot on the trivet over the flames.

While she waited for her bath water to heat, Tereka wandered into the storeroom on the western side of the tower, the driest room that received the most sun. She surveyed the piles of dried fish on the shelves, the sacks of milled flour, the mounds of dried berries. Savinnia, Hinat, and Poales had been busy while the rest of them were away.

Tereka descended the stone steps to the storage chamber dug into the side of the mountain. Bumps rose on her skin and she shivered in the cooler air. The dim light that penetrated from the room above illuminated the white ropes of onions hung from the ceiling and jars of pickled vegetables lined up in neat rows on shelves. Large clay pots held water. She noted a pair of barrels that hadn't been there when she'd left. Her uncles must have brought wine or beer. Maybe that would sweeten Sebezh's mood.

She did a quick calculation. They had enough food for at least three months. Would that be enough? Her grandfather Osip had been adamant. No revolution without adequate supplies of food, spare clothing, and weapons.

Osip was right, of course. Once things got going, they'd have no time for hunting or to make more arrows. Over the winter, they'd amassed quite an armory, including many more bows than they could use. *But you can never have too many arrows.*

Firm footsteps on the stairs turned her attention away from their stores. She came face to face with Naco, a smile crinkling the corners of his eyes.

"I thought you'd be here," he said.

"We've done well, haven't we?" She pointed up the stairs at the upper storeroom. "I didn't remember that you'd caught so many fish."

A melodic laugh revealed Savinnia had followed her brother down the steps. "Don't give Naco the credit. While you were gone, your da showed up. Bearing a gift from your admirer who thought you could use some fish."

Tereka's face and ears heated, and she looked down at her boots. Savinnia was talking about Kemet. Tereka had loved Kemet, but he'd decided that she wasn't safe to know. Her toes curled at the memory. As much as it hurt, she couldn't blame him for not wanting to take up with a half-Risker who was tangled up in an ancient, outlawed myth. "He's not my admirer. He just feels guilty."

Savinnia snickered. "If you say so." She turned to Naco. "When you can, we could use some more water. I'm sure the rest of you will want baths once Tereka's done." She waved a hand at Tereka and skipped up the stairs.

Naco took a step after his sister, but Tereka put a hand on his arm. "Naco."

"Yes?"

"Do you really believe that—?" The words stuck in her throat.

"Water is wet and always useful."

She poked him in the hard muscle of his arm. "Not about that. About the prophecy."

In the dim light, his tawny eyes darkened to a warm

brown, the color of acorns. "Tereka, I don't think there's any question that the prophecy speaks of you." He paused. "If it makes you feel any better, I don't like it any more than you do."

That must mean he didn't think she was worthy of the role. She frowned as Naco ran a hand through his dark hair.

"I'm afraid for you," he said. "Who knows what dangers the Desired One will have to face? And what will happen after you bring the new order to the land? You'd have to live in Anbodu, in the Prime Konamei's house. I know you don't want that." He sounded wistful, almost sad. "So, I'd rather you weren't what they think you are."

"That makes two of us." She let out a sigh. "Can't I just refuse?"

He shuffled back a step. "Before I met you, I thought the whole sky-god story was a silly myth. Now I've seen too much to have doubts. If the sky-god is calling you, how can you resist?"

"But why would the sky-god choose me?"

"Other than thinking you're the right one for the job? I don't know. His plans are not my plans, that's for sure." He shook his head. "I'm just glad I'm not the Desired One. That would be a perilous and lonely life."

Her heart lurched and her limbs felt heavy, as if millstones hung from her wrists. There. He'd said it. If she was the Desired One, he wouldn't want to be part of her life.

Naco didn't seem to notice her drooping shoulders. "I just hope when this is over, when you've brought the new order, you'll have time for your old friends. That you won't be too good for escaped prisoners and companions of pirates." He pulled his eyebrows together and gave her a pitiful expression.

She laughed. "Oh, Naco, of course I'll have time for all of you."

Something flickered in his eyes. "Any of us in particular?"

Was he hinting at what she thought he was? No, it was

impossible. He'd flirted with her on and off all winter, to be sure. She'd allowed herself to hope that he could love her. After all, he was an escaped prisoner like she was, broken and battered, damaged and despised. Not like Kemet, who'd never been anything but the model safe and fair subject of the Prime Konamei.

Her breath caught. Maybe Naco thought she wanted Kemet back.

Tereka lowered her eyes. She didn't have a future with Kemet, she was sure of that. But she'd allowed herself to hope about Naco. Now she had to face the truth. For all his support and camaraderie, Naco had never acted like he foresaw a life with her. And he'd just told her he didn't want her if she was the Desired One, that he didn't want that dangerous, lonely existence.

Could she ignore the way her heart sped up when he smiled at her? The way warmth flowed through her every time he happened to touch her, a warmth that spread down to her toes? She wanted to tell him, yes, she'd be especially glad to see him and would be particularly bereft if he stayed away. But she'd let Kemet into her heart, and he'd spurned her once things got dangerous.

She didn't want to endure that again, to feel the anguish and shame of rejection. Besides, they could all die trying to unseat the Prime Konamei. Better to avoid these kinds of complications. She stepped away from Naco. "Perhaps." She smirked at him. "If you're kind to me." She turned from him and bounded up the steps to the kitchen.

6

Juquila struggled to keep from scowling. What was this idiot telling her? The trader kept babbling and repeating himself so that she couldn't make sense of what he was saying.

Even more annoying was the sticky sweat on her forehead under her gray turban. She hated wearing the stupid thing, but it was a small price to pay for her power and privilege.

She picked up her quill and used it to point to the stool in front of her writing table. "Sit."

When the man complied, she replaced the quill in her inkwell. Slowly, deliberately, she collected the documents spread out on the table and stacked them in a neat pile. Then she folded her hands and rested them on the open ledger. Staring into the man's eyes, she smiled. "Now tell me." She used the sultry voice that had served her well over the years. "From the beginning. No need to rush."

Under her gaze, a well-practiced one that tantalized with a promise of many delights, he blinked and took a deep breath. "If you please, the caravan from Shinroo was more than halfway to North Rivash. We rounded a bend and were attacked by bandits."

"Hmm." This was nothing new. Bandits attacked regularly, more now that the ebbing of the spring rains had made travel easier.

The man gulped and leaned forward. "If you please." He spoke in a whisper. "The guards did nothing."

Juquila nodded, staring into his eyes as if she was captivated by what she saw there. Guards failing to guard, that also was nothing new, and was happening more often. While she bemoaned the lost revenue, it did give her leverage over the ephor Kaberco. "I'm sorry to hear it. I'll take it up with the ephor. Then what?"

"All of a sudden, from the north, five people burst around the bend in the road. They shot arrows, a hailstorm of them that dropped the bandits where they stood. Others had swords. One killed with his bare hands."

This was interesting. She raised her eyebrows. "Were they guards from North Rivash?"

"No, if you please. They wore gray."

"Villagers who had weapons?" Juquila allowed a tiny frown to slip onto her face. This couldn't be permitted.

"I don't think they were villagers."

Juquila resisted the urge to roll her eyes. Couldn't this man just come out with it? "Then who were they?" She kept her tone soft and caressing.

"I don't know. They told us things they shouldn't have. Forbidden things."

"Really?" Juquila tipped her head to the side. The man looked down, avoiding her gaze. "Tell me," she said. "You have nothing to fear."

"They gave us bread, soft bread if you please. And fresh tomatoes and cucumbers."

Soft bread and out-of-season vegetables could only mean Riskers. But would Riskers dare violate the treaty?

"They said that we'd been lied to," the man continued.

"That we didn't have to live the way we did, and that the Prime Konamei couldn't keep us safe."

"What did the guards do?" She managed to keep her tone soft despite the anger that heated her face. *The fools should have run these outlaws through, that's what they should have done.*

"The captain threatened to have them taken." The man shivered. "They just laughed. Then the girl—"

"What girl?" Juquila couldn't keep the sharpness from her voice. She forced her face to relax and infused her tone with honey. "You didn't mention her before."

"Didn't I? She was their best archer. Shot three arrows in a row faster than any guardsman could. Took down three men in two heartbeats. Anyway, she asked if we had any wounded." The man gulped, his face flushed, his long fingers twitching. "One of the bandits had sliced my neck. Blood was everywhere. I thought I was done for. A few others pulled me over to the girl." He looked down at his trembling hands.

Juquila leaned forward. "And then?" she asked softly.

"I, I'm not sure what happened. I was feeling faint. You know, from losing so much blood. I saw a flash of green light in her hand, and she muttered something about the sky." The man shook his head. "Then the pain stopped. And the bleeding." He paused; his eyebrows pulled together. "I knew that somehow, I'd live."

"That's impossible." Juquila stared at him. "How could you bring me such a tale?"

The man jerked his head up and tugged at the neck of his ash-colored tunic. "See for yourself."

Peering at the man's neck, Juquila narrowed her eyes. She studied the wound, now dried over with a black scab that traveled from chin to chest. *Amazing that it hadn't killed the man outright.* "Is this some kind of trick?"

"No, if you please. All I know is, I was wounded and bloody. Then the bleeding stopped, and the pain vanished."

"Would others say the same?"

His eyes shifted, and he glanced down. "I think so."

She pressed her lips together. If the stories turned out not to match, either he'd told her a pack of lies or the others feared to risk telling the truth. "Assuming this is true, how did this girl heal you?"

"I don't know. You'd have to ask her. If you please." Now his voice was trembling.

Juquila leaned back in her chair and nodded. She needed to reassure the man. No sense scaring off one of her best informants. She smiled, a slow, lazy smile as if he hadn't told her anything shocking. "What did this girl look like?"

"Tall, wiry, bright blue eyes. Golden tan skin. Dark hair, a bit shorter than most village women wear it."

Her heart thumped, but she ignored it. There was nothing she could do about it, or the heat rising up the back of her neck. That blasted Tereka, her supposed niece, was back.

Picking up her quill, Juquila wrote on the parchment before her. Anything to give her a moment to collect her thoughts without the trader seeing she was rattled.

So Tereka escaped prison and survived. Did Kaberco know? That would explain why he'd been so jumpy lately. But Juquila needed to be sure.

She laid down her quill. "What else did this girl say?"

"If you please, when the captain ordered his guards to take them, she did her trick with the three arrows. Nearly took off the captain's earlobe. Gave me shivers to see her shoot so well in that breeze." The man gulped. "Then she said the next time she wouldn't miss. And that we all needed to think about what she'd said, if we were brave enough to eat the bread she'd left. She told us to get moving, or we'd be late getting to North Rivash. Then she and her gang ran off."

"Hmm." Juquila inspected her fingernails. "Did anyone eat the bread?"

"I, I don't know. I didn't see what the captain did with it.

He ordered us to attend to our wounded and to get the caravan ready to move on."

Juquila studied the man's face. Was he lying? He kept shifting in his seat and was having trouble looking her in the eye. Or was he simply nervous? *After all, sharing tales like this could get someone taken.*

"Thank you for telling me," she said. "I don't suppose I need to tell you to keep this to yourself?" She gave him a slow smile. "In the interests of keeping everyone"—she emphasized the word everyone—"safe, we need to be careful to not let this girl's lies spread. You do understand, don't you?"

The man nodded vigorously, his eyes wide.

"Good. I would hate to think that you would do anything unsafe."

He gripped his shaking hands together, still nodding.

Let's hope that frightened him enough to keep his mouth shut. Juquila waved a hand in dismissal. "Peace and safety to you."

Without waiting to see if he obeyed, she bent her head to her writing, ignoring his murmured, "Peace and safety." She scribbled a few words.

When she heard the door shut, she lifted her head and clenched her fist. What to do about that cursed Tereka? It would have been one thing if she'd stayed hidden and never came back. But no, she just had to stir up more trouble. Just like that father of hers.

She turned in her seat to survey the map of Tlefas pinned to the wall. Tereka had chosen well. A lonely stretch of road where it hugged the forest. Easy to pull her stunt and vanish among the pines and birch. Maybe she should disregard this or pass it off as a few disgruntled traders. Or blame the Riskers? Since Tereka's gang only killed a few bandits, no one would be interested in tracking down the culprits. Unless some bandits wanted to avenge their comrades' deaths.

Juquila shifted back in her chair, making the bronze chain she wore over her shoulders clink softly. She fingered the links.

Bronze for the syndic, she thought. What she really wanted was to wear the gold chain of the ephor.

Maybe I can use this against Kaberco.

A smile spread across her face. Yes, she could definitely use this incident to bring the ephor down. He must have known Tereka survived her escape from prison and he'd kept it quiet, spinning some tale that she'd probably died in the desert. Juquila snorted. The man who prided himself on being so perfectly correct had blundered. And she was the one who'd make him pay for that error.

7

F or once they had gathered on time for the konament
meeting, milling about like chickens waiting to be fed.
Kaberco, ephor of Trofmose, surveyed his four
konameis, wondering who would be cooperative and who
would be more like a fox stalking a meal.

Yavaros, the questor in charge of the courts, sat on Kaberco's right. His faded blue eyes were bloodshot, his shoulders
slumped. The man seemed more beaten down than usual.

Next to Yavaros came Birita, the adile in charge of roads
and buildings. She shuffled through her documents, her head
bent over them so only the top of her gray turban was visible.
She could be counted on to only bring up serious matters.

Kulooq the ludi occupied the seat across from Birita. He
oversaw schools and education. A huge hulking man, he was
normally quick with a joke but had been withdrawn and silent
lately, as if retreating behind his bushy eyebrows and deep-set
eyes.

Last, Kaberco turned to study Juquila, who managed
trade and commerce with a deft and heavy hand. She had
sauntered into the room with a sensual grace that was all the
more remarkable in a woman approaching forty who'd borne

five children. She assumed her place on Kaberco's left, wearing a wider smirk than usual, as if she knew some delightful secret that she wasn't quite ready to share. Whatever her game, he wasn't playing.

"Peace and safety, konameis," Kaberco said. "Let's get started. Reports first. Yavaros, what troublemakers do you have in jail?"

Kaberco heard their reports, issued some orders, then moved efficiently through the rest of his agenda. They hashed out the forecast for the year's harvest, the lack of progress on repairs to the town's house of healing, and whether or not they should allow the shoemakers to change the design of men's boots.

The last item elicited the most animated debate. Kaberco scowled at his hourglass, the sand nearly run out. One thing he despised was long, drawn-out meetings. Too much opportunity for his konameis to bicker, if not outright skewer each other with accusations and insults. He let out a sigh. Did any of them truly want to build a safe, fair, and prosperous society for all, or were they out only for their own power?

He cut off the footwear discussion by commanding Juquila to decide before the next meeting. Then he settled back in his chair, the wood creaking under his bulk. "Does anyone have anything else to add?"

Juquila leaned forward, her large dark eyes wide in her mahogany face, her head tipped to the side. Kaberco set his jaw, bracing himself. This was her guileless look, the one she put on when she was about to say something especially poisonous.

She glanced at the other three konameis before locking her eyes on Kaberco. "There was an attack on the caravan to North Rivash several days ago."

"Yes," Kaberco answered slowly. "I'm aware." Why bring this up now? Whatever her reason, he wasn't going to like it.

"If you please, I was wondering why you didn't report it

earlier when you discussed posting extra guards on the caravans." She spoke innocently enough, as if she was idly curious.

Which he knew was not true. He sensed the motive behind
her question. "Well, Juquila, it's like this." He met her gaze
head-on. "That particular attack was not the work of the
usual bandits, so it merited additional investigation. Once I
have actual facts to report, I'll share them."

"Oh, good," she replied. "I'd hate to think that the rumor
was true."

He narrowed his eyes. "What rumor?"

Juquila leaned back in her chair. "That your guards were
in league with this gang, whoever they were."

Grinding his teeth together, Kaberco mentally flung every
curse he could think of at Juquila's smirking face. He took a
deep breath. "I'm surprised at you for repeating falsehoods,
Juquila."

"And how do you know it is a lie? You just told us you were
still investigating." She turned to the questor. "Isn't that right,
Yavaros?"

Kaberco didn't allow the questor to reply. "I know it's a lie
because it's ridiculous. What would any guardsman gain from
allowing anyone to pull such a stunt?"

"A handful of stones and sheaves, perhaps?" Juquila
shrugged.

The ephor hated he had to agree with her. Yes, a pile of
silver and bronze coins could make it worth a guardsman's
trouble, but it would take a lot of money to bribe enough of
them to ensure the plot would work. "You're assuming this
gang had the means to buy off most of the guards. And the
bandits as well. That makes no sense."

She nodded. "Perhaps not. I'll wait for your investigation
then. Let's hope the investigators come back with certainties,
not lies and half-truths."

He slid his hands off the table and grasped his thighs,
gripping the hard muscle as if he were wrapping his fingers

around her neck. *Lies and half-truths are your currency.* She was most likely the source of the rumor about his guardsmen. He wondered if this would be a good time to bring up the gossip that she had taken Kulooq to her bed.

"Shouldn't the rest of us be informed?" the adile asked, tension raising the pitch of her alto voice.

"Of course, I can fill you in with what I know." Kaberco pointed at Yavaros. "We've been working together on this for several days now." He flicked his glance toward Juquila. A tightening around her lips and eyes told him she either hadn't known this, or didn't approve.

"So, for you two." He looked at the adile and ludi, willing them to believe him rather than Juquila's half-truth. "The caravan left Shinroo, heading south to North Rivash, and was past the halfway point when bandits attacked. The guards fought them off."

"If you please," said Juquila, "I heard they did not."

Kaberco tipped his head. "The accounts we've received are contradictory, which is one reason we're investigating. The guards in question are from Anbodu, out of my jurisdiction. But since this occurred in the Trofmose region, I have the right to interview them. Believe me, I have been in touch with the ephor of Anbodu to find out what really happened." He raised his eyebrows, daring her to object. She remained silent.

"So. At some point, a group of people ran to the caravan," Kaberco went on. "How many, we are not sure. Some reports say four, others seven, still others no less than a dozen, but everyone agrees they wore the gray clothing of villagers. They fought off the bandits."

"How much cargo was lost?" Juquila asked.

"I'm still trying to find out. And more importantly, how many traders were killed or injured." *Not that you care about them.* He took a deep breath and continued. "Then the leader of the group threw bread at the traders and told them a pack of lies. When the guardsmen threatened to take them, they laughed. Then they fled." He turned to Juquila. "Did I retell the story accurately enough?"

The syndic smirked and nodded. "Oh, you did a fine job as far as it goes."

She knows, he thought. She knows about the healing, the vegetables, and that the bread was Risker made. What else does she know?

Juquila looked down at her hands. "Did they offer a description of the leader?" She asked the question as casually as if she was inquiring about the appearance of a pebble.

Kaberco glanced at the questor. The man's face was drawn and tight. He had never wanted to sentence Tereka in the first place and hadn't been able to hide his relief when Kaberco informed him she'd escaped.

Yavaros' throat bobbed. "They say—"

"The description varied," Kaberco said, cutting him off. "As noted, we're investigating. And I promise you a full report when we have uncovered the truth."

The ludi and the adile nodded. At least he'd managed to keep those two in line.

"Are you sure you're telling us everything? Why are you holding back?" Juquila shook her head. "Don't you trust your own konameis?"

With great effort, Kaberco held himself rigid. He wanted to strangle Juquila with the bronze chain on her shoulders. He held her gaze for one, two, three heartbeats. Then he looked around the table. "As I said, I don't want to spread unverified facts. But given that our syndic seems to want me to repeat hearsay, I'll tell you." Without mentioning her name, Kaberco told them of Tereka's archery, how she supposedly healed the wounded trader, and her taunts about the lies of the Prime Konamei. He skipped the insults directed at him and Juquila. When he'd finished, he couldn't ignore the look of triumph on Juquila's face or the look of shame on the questor's.

The other two kept their startled eyes on the ephor. "The archer has a point," the ludi whispered.

Juquila whirled on him. "That liar has a point?"

The ludi flinched. "It sounds like the girl offered Risker bread to the traders. Bread that we all eat every day even as we deny its existence to everyone else."

The syndic snorted and waved her hand. "Just a small privilege to make up for how we toil ceaselessly to build a safe, fair, and prosperous society for all."

Kaberco put his hand to his mouth and coughed. Juquila must know how ludicrous that sounded. They'd all been repeating that fiction for years. Now, Tereka's words had exposed it, as if she'd opened the door to a dark room, allowing all to see what was inside. And the truth, Kaberco thought, isn't flattering to any of us.

"We have to contain this." Juquila slapped her hand on the wood table. "Otherwise, the rumors will cause unrest and incite people to act in unsafe ways. We can't have that."

"If you please," the questor said, "what do you suggest?"

"Every trader from that caravan should be taken. Immediately. The same for those useless guards. They should have killed that girl and her band." Juquila leaned toward the questor. "Killed her before she could make more trouble."

The questor's face blanched. Kaberco knew Yavaros was a man who truly believed in justice for all. Tereka's taking had never sat well with him, but he stood to lose as much as the rest of them.

Drumming his fingers on the table, Kaberco considered Juquila's idea. Taking the traders might stop further talk, but they'd probably already told their spouses, parents, siblings, and neighbors about their narrow escape. Tereka chose that caravan well. What better way to stir things up than to rile the capital?

He pursed his lips. How to retaliate was the question. He

didn't like Juquila's idea at all. A mass taking would only give credence to the lie.

"What do you all think?" Juquila asked. "I, for one, believe we need decisive, strong action against these hooligans. We must preserve the safety of Tlefas. That demands powerful leaders who are not afraid to do what it takes."

So that's your game, Kaberco thought. Make me look weak and you strong. For a moment he toyed with quoting Tereka's personal attack on Juquila, then discarded the idea. She'd only repeat Tereka's insult directed at him. Unless, perhaps, she didn't know about that. "Yavaros, what do you say?"

"I still believe that uncovering the facts is our best option," the questor said. "Had that caravan come to Trofmose, we could have suppressed the story one way or another. But unless the authorities in Anbodu acted promptly, the tale is already out. We can't take an entire city."

The adile nodded her agreement. The ludi, with a glance at Juquila, shook his head.

"So, it's two votes for extreme action, and two for prudence," Kaberco said, scowling at the ludi. "I side with prudence. We can't order a mass taking, especially of people in another territory. I will send a squad to Anbodu to assist with the interrogations and make sure everyone involved understands the need for silence."

Then I'm going to have to track down Tereka. And muzzle her for good.

8

Tereka grunted, the muscles of her arms and shoulders burning as she hauled the fishing net toward her. The weight told her she'd caught something, perhaps several nelmafish. She leaped to a rock in the middle of the stream, letting the mist rising from the waterfall cool her face and wash away the sweat brought out by the glare of the midsummer sun.

Maybe from this angle it will be easier. She tested various rocks and found a stable place to plant her feet. Bending her knees, she hauled on the net, straining to lift it from the water of the deep pool formed by the waterfall. With a sound like a muffled belch, the netting tore. Her foot slipped, and she sat down hard on the rock, pain shooting through her lower back. She shouted a curse, then pulled in the remnant of her net.

A gentle laugh floated on the breeze, blending with the hissing of the falling water. Tereka snapped her head up. Would she have time to retrieve her bow before whoever had mocked her attacked?

The bushes rustled, and she saw a flash of crimson and amber. A heartbeat later a woman came into view, the bright colors of her dress vivid against the dark pines.

"Cillia!" Tereka dropped the pieces of her net and bounded from rock to rock to reach her grandmother. The older woman swept her into a hug.

"You're not glad to see me?" The teasing, deep voice of her grandfather Osip caused her to release Cillia and throw her arms around him.

"I am, but why are you here? I wasn't expecting you."

Cillia frowned, but her eyes were merry. "We could tell from your language."

Tereka flushed. "Well, that. I guess I'm not much of a fisher." She pointed at her net. "I don't suppose you came here to help me mend that."

Osip laughed. "We did not." He patted Tereka's shoulder. "We'd gone to visit our girls and found out your uncles had hired your men to assist with some stonework."

"None of them wanted anything to do with chipping stone," Tereka said, flashing a smirk at her grandfather. "But offer them a barrel or two of beer…"

The smile slipped off Cillia's face. "We thought this would be a perfect chance to have a private chat with you."

That didn't sound good. "Would you like to talk here, or up in the tower?" Tereka asked.

"Here is fine." Cillia gracefully moved to one of the massive rocks on the side of the stream. Osip lowered himself to sit next to her, pointing at the rock opposite.

Her muscles tensed as she braced herself for bad news. Tereka sat and surveyed her grandparents' somber faces.

Cillia glanced at Osip, then at Tereka. "Tell us about your life."

Tereka shrugged and allowed a small smile to twitch the corners of her mouth, relieved that so far this chat didn't involve a rebuke. "What's to tell? We're surviving, thanks to all your help."

"How are you getting along?" Cillia's vivid green eyes searched Tereka's face.

With a sigh, Tereka held up her hands, then let them fall into her lap. "We're doing all right. Mostly because we have so much physical labor to do, with the farming and the hunting and the fishing and cutting wood and hauling water. Everyone's exhausted by the end of the day. That keeps Sebezh from stirring up trouble."

"And Relio?"

"He's tired, too. Which means he hasn't pushed Savinnia too hard to resume their old, uh, relationship. Yet. Naco and Poales have been able to keep him from being more aggressive with her so far. But all of them are restless. If you know what I mean."

"I surely do." Cillia tipped her head to the side. "What are you doing about it?"

"Well, I tried to start a revolution." Tereka gave her grandmother a rueful smile. "It wasn't very successful."

Cillia laughed. "Don't tell me you're giving up after one try."

"No. It's just harder than I thought. Confronting people with the truth is one thing. Inspiring them to have the courage to face it is another."

"You found it hard to accept the truth about you and your family," Osip said, his tone soft.

Tereka smiled at her grandparents, grateful for the love Osip and Cillia had shown her when she lashed out in anger after learning she was half Risker. "True." Tereka stared into the distance. "We've agreed to not do anything else until we find out how the Prime Konamei and his allies are going to react to our last action. But I can't help feeling there's something more I could be doing."

"There is," Osip said.

"Like what?"

"The amulets," Cillia said. "We think you should try to figure out how they work."

Tereka's shoulders drooped. "I've tried. But they don't always do what I want them to."

"That's because they channel the sky-god's power," her grandmother answered. "They don't work on command like some kind of magic trick."

"So what good are they?"

Cillia tipped her head back. "How have you used them in the past?"

"Well, I've been able to heal people with them. That seems to work the best."

"Right. Because healing others serves others, not just you."

"But sometimes the healing got me out of a jam." Tereka shivered, thinking of the pirates who'd threatened to kill her if she couldn't heal their wounded and ill.

"And does that mean those people weren't glad to be healed?" Osip raised an eyebrow. "Would they have said, 'No, thank you. We don't want you to heal us if you get some benefit.' "

Tereka chuckled. "It does sound ridiculous when you put it that way." She rubbed the back of her head and tugged on her hair. "Then there's the guidance the amulets give me. Like how I knew where the second Amulet of Power would be, and the way it led me to weapons when we needed them the most." She shook her head. "I could use that now. But the amulets are silent."

"There's no way to control how the power comes to you," Cillia explained. "But I think there are ways to cultivate it, to make it easier for you to sense how the amulets want to lead you or help you."

"How?" Tereka leaned forward.

"I can't tell you exactly." She rubbed her hands together. "While you perched up here all winter, I found out everything I could about the Amulets of Power. A few Riskers have made a study of the old lore and I was able to get in contact with them. You'll have to thank your Uncle Tikul for that. He spent months traveling to the other camps, seeking those sages."

"What did he find out?"

Cillia pressed her lips together. "Well, everyone agreed about the working of the lesser amulets, the ones with only one or two stones in the dragonfly's tail. They have the power to heal and protect. They also give wisdom and guidance, and amplify abilities."

Tereka nodded. "That's why I've become such a good archer."

"Right," Osip said. "Keep practicing your archery, so when the amulet enhances what you can do, your skills will be that much greater."

"That I can do. But what about the Amulets of Power?"

"Everyone had a different opinion about them." Cillia shook her head. "Some think the Amulets of Power have no additional powers."

"Wonderful." Tereka's shoulders slumped.

"It's not so bad. Others say they can be used as weapons. Just not in the same way as the scorpion amulets."

"Scorpions?"

"Yes, scorpions," Cillia said. "One woman said she'd heard about them from her grandmother, who heard from her grandmother. As she tells it, centuries ago, some people who lived beyond the mountains didn't like the idea that powerful objects could only be used as the sky-god willed. They sought to bend the power to their own will, to dictate its use, so they made the scorpion amulets. Some had one or two stones in their tails, but they also created three Amulets of Power with three stones in the tail."

"What did they use them for?"

Osip picked up a rock and jiggled it in his hand. "For war and conquest."

"The sky-god let them do that?"

"The sky-god isn't the power behind the scorpions." Osip

hurled the rock into the water. "The woman wasn't able to tell Tikul what gives them their power, only that it's a powerful evil that can destroy the user."

"So that's another myth." Tereka frowned. "Or maybe not. But how does that help me?"

Cillia leaned toward Tereka. "The scorpions are copies of the dragonflies. Which made this woman think the dragonflies could also be used as weapons. Maybe only in the service of the sky-god, at his direction, but weapons nonetheless."

Tereka's eyes widened. *A powerful, magical weapon is just what I need.* "How do they work?"

"She couldn't say, except that if misused, they could cause great harm to the user. And that to wield the amulets in this manner was probably meant only for the Desired One." She raised her eyebrows at Tereka.

"Which I'm not." Tereka spat the words out of her dry mouth a bit more sharply than she intended. With a softer tone, she continued. "I don't want to know how to use them badly enough to accept that I'm the Desired One."

The high-pitched whistle of an eagle cut through the air. Cillia watched the bird arc through the sky before she turned back to Tereka. "My dear," she said. "If you are the Desired One, there's nothing you can do about it."

"But what use are the amulets if I don't know how to wield them?"

"Have you tried?"

"What do you mean?"

Osip's next words came at a slow pace, like a traveler picking his way through uncertain terrain. "If you could employ them as a weapon, think about how that would work. Could they hurl objects at an enemy?"

Tereka pursed her lips and nodded. "That would be useful."

"Then try lifting something with your amulets."

As Tereka pulled her two Amulets of Power from the tiny

bag she kept in an inner pocket, her heart beat faster. Maybe she could harness their power. In the sunlight, the dragonflies twinkled with green and purple light. "What should I do?"

Cillia set a pebble on the rock next to Osip. "Try moving that. Do whatever you do when you use the amulets to heal."

Holding the amulets up, Tereka stared at the tiny rock. "Sky-god, lift the pebble. Please."

Nothing happened.

"Try again," Cillia said.

Tereka refocused her attention on the pebble. Nothing. Her heart dropped with a thud. She shook her head. "Enough. It's not working." She shoved the amulets into her pocket. "If I can't control their power, then they're useless as weapons."

"Oh." Cillia drew the word out. "That's your problem."

"What? What's my problem?"

"Think of it this way. How did you make the amulets work before?"

"I don't know." Tereka pulled her eyebrows together. "The archery, it just came. When I needed to make impossible shots, I did. Like someone was shooting through me."

Cillia nodded. "And the healing?"

"I asked the sky-god to heal. Sometimes the healing was complete, sometimes not."

"So the sky-god controlled the power, and the result." Cillia looked up at the clouds. "When you used the amulets, did you sense the sky-god's presence?"

"I don't know. I never thought about it."

"Maybe that's what you need to do. Use the amulets to sense the sky-god's presence, to follow his lead."

"How will that help?"

"The woman said the Desired One would know."

Tereka stared at her grandmother. "Then I'm not the Desired One."

Osip shook a finger at her. "You've only just started trying to sense the sky-god. That's what you need to ask for when you use the amulets."

Scowling, Tereka looked from one grandparent to the other.

"Listen, Tereka," Cillia said, her tone gentle. "If the Amulets of Power can only be used as the sky-god sees fit, then you must be clear on what he wants. Sensing his presence will lead you."

Before Tereka could respond with more doubt, her grandfather spoke up. "Besides, the third amulet hasn't found you yet."

Her grandmother held up a hand when Tereka opened her mouth to argue. The older woman shook her head, a stern look in her green eyes. Tereka gulped, wondering what was disturbing her.

"You don't understand," Osip said to Tereka, leaning forward. "Tikul had to explain to the other camps why he was so interested in the Amulets of Power. Some leaders were furious that we were harboring fugitives from the Prime Konamei. When they learned you were one of them, they were even more incensed."

Tereka's throat tightened. Her father's people wanted to abandon her? "Why?"

"My dear girl," Cillia said softly, "they haven't forgotten all the trouble when you were born. How Kaberco tracked your parents through every camp. How for years every trader who came to our camps was watched. No one wants to repeat that. One reason the leaders didn't demand we cut you off was because you're so isolated here." She swallowed hard. "But harboring you is a clear violation of the treaty."

"What did they suppose you should have done? Let us fend for ourselves among the bandits and warboars?"

Osip snorted. "Tikul asked them that same question. After endless debate, they all came to the same conclusion—that they'd be willing to take some risks for the Desired One, the bringer of a new order. We Riskers have long wanted changes to the treaty, to end the prejudice and mistrust. To show the villagers a better way of life. Most of us believe any effort led by the Desired One would be worth our support." Osip fixed his piercing blue eyes on Tereka. "But the actions of a bunch of troublemakers? Especially one of mixed parentage? No."

Folding her arms, Tereka met her grandfather's hard gaze. "What do they want me to do?"

"If you are the Desired One, declare yourself. If not, stay up here in your tower and don't come down. That's what they said a few months ago."

Tereka's heart skipped a beat. Osip's frown foretold some bad news. She was sure of it. "And what are they saying now?"

"Word came to us about the caravan you rescued." Osip clasped his hands together. "You gave them Risker bread in violation of the treaty. Our elder was not pleased."

"But—"

Osip held up a hand. "He thought you were starting a revolution the right way."

"So, he agrees?"

"In principle. He'd like you to try persuasion, rather than violence. 'By a sweet tongue you can drag a warboar by a hair' were his exact words."

"And?" Tereka drew out the word, suspecting she wasn't going to like her grandfather's next words.

"He said to inform you that you have three choices. Either declare yourself the Desired One and fight for what is right, cease your efforts and stay up here in your tower, or leave and fend for yourself in the wilderness."

She stared at Osip, her insides shriveling like a corpse under the summer sun.

Cillia took her hand. "The elders of Mikkeliad agree."

Tereka pressed a fist to her lips and clamped her jaw on the words that rushed to her mouth. *They're throwing me out. No one wants me.* Tears stung her eyes. She couldn't blame them. They'd taken substantial risks for her already.

"We want to help you." Osip's tone was gentle but implacable, like the towering mountain behind them. "But you must help us. Accept you are the Desired One, and you'll have all the aid the Riskers can give."

An eagle swooped to the pool, talons outstretched. It skimmed the water and rose, a thrashing fish tight in its grasp. Tereka watched the bird soar over the trees.

"But I'm not—" She just couldn't be the Desired One! She wasn't worthy. And even if she was, she was powerless to topple the Prime Konamei. She couldn't even get people to see Juquila's corruption.

"It doesn't matter how you feel about it." Cillia squeezed her fingers. "If the sky-god chooses you, it will save a lot of trouble for everyone if you just respond to the call."

Tereka frowned. "Can I think about it?" She'd have to figure out a way to convince the other Risker camps to give her more time. If the Riskers forced her band to leave their mountain home, they'd have to start over in the wilderness. She shuddered, imagining what Sebezh and the others would do if she didn't have her Risker uncles to keep them in line. "Maybe until I find the third amulet?"

Cillia and Osip exchanged glances. "They might wait a few weeks longer if you don't stir up any more trouble. But you need to decide, and soon."

The amulets in her pocket were vibrating slightly. She ignored them. Just because the amulets had been useful in the past, that didn't make her the fulfillment of some half-forgotten prophecy. And she wouldn't be if she could help it.

9

Damira's heart pounded and her fingers tingled as she leaned forward in the saddle. Eighteen years she'd labored for this moment. Eighteen long years of subduing the unruly, bickering warlords and welding the scattered pieces of Razdelia into one nation. Her people could barely believe that the Endless War had finally ceased, and they gave their undying gratitude to their new overlords, their adulation of Shagonar and her akin to worship. And now the final stage of her plan was about to commence. They would begin the conquest of the Abandoned Lands, the country the inhabitants called Tlefas. A slow smile spread across her face.

The officer leading the vanguard raised his bow in the air. That was the signal that he'd reached the top of the mountain pass. Damira sat up straighter and pulled in a long breath. At last.

Urging her mare forward, Damira wished she could break into a gallop, to surge past the riders before so she could be the first to enter the territory they were about to claim. Warm air blew her long hair back, along with the smell of hot horses and sweating men. After many years, it was her first breath of the air of Tlefas.

Her brother Syzyan rode in front of her, his back straight, head held high, wearing the spiked hat that marked him as head of a household. She shook her head. All these years commanding Shagonar's armies and he still refused to wear any symbol of power other than what any other man could bear.

She twisted to look over her shoulder at Shagonar, riding behind her. Dear Shag, loyal as ever. The finest husband she ever could have wished for.

He flashed a grin, his dimples making her smile in answer. Heat spread through her body that had nothing to do with the summer sun.

But that was for later. First, they had one more foe to subdue. She faced forward.

The people who fled to the Abandoned Lands centuries ago were no friends to Razdelia. She ground her teeth, remembering how callously those people had turned her, Shagonar, and Syzyan away when they were in desperate need. After their conquest of Razdelia, her husband and her brother had eventually come around to her way of thinking, though it had taken her years to convince them. They'd agreed to conquer Tlefas before it invaded Razdelia.

With her horse's hoofs thumping on the hard dirt of the path, she crested the pass. Before her, the mountain rolled into a plain, a land of square patches in varying shades of green and yellow, the vivid colors attesting to the fertility of the land. She wondered what crops the people grew. They'd know soon enough.

Halfway down the slope, they came to a river that widened as it flowed downhill. Syzyan called a halt, giving the soldiers time to water their horses and refresh themselves. He swung from his horse and handed the reins to a groom.

Damira and Shagonar slid from their mounts. Syzyan strode to her, a waterskin in his hand, his lips and chin wet and glistening. "Will you walk with me a little?"

The three of them strolled upstream to the place the river emerged from the towering pine trees. Damira knelt on the bank and splashed the cool water on her sweaty face.

"Dami."

She knew that tone. Syzyan was about to play big brother again. Her face grew hot. After all these years, he still seemed to forget who was the Emperor. And who wielded the Amulets of Power.

"Syz." She stood and faced him.

He held out his hands to her. "I have to ask one last time. Are you sure this is the best way?"

"Well, yes, Syz." She stuck her chin in the air. "Generally, the best way to conquer a country is to invade it with an army."

Shagonar put a hand on her shoulder. "I think what Syz is asking is, shouldn't we try to send an envoy first?"

Damira rolled her eyes. "We've been through all this. At least once a month since we defeated Wei Fang. These people wouldn't give aid to refugees. They were ready to throw us in prison. Why would they bother talking to an envoy?"

Syzyan glared at her. "Oh, I don't know, Dami. Perhaps the army we brought with us will encourage them to listen."

Kill him.

The voice in her head was no more than a whisper. If she hastened to obey its commands to conquer Tlefas, it might stay that way. She narrowed her eyes. "True. But that will just drag things out. Whether they surrender to our envoy or after our army has surrounded their city, surrender they will."

"Fine," Syzyan said, his jaw clenched. "We'll move in half an hour." He spun on his heel and stalked away.

She glanced at Shagonar, who was frowning. "What?"

Her husband wrapped his arms around her and spoke into her hair. "Let's try not to hurt too many people. We want to guarantee peace, not bring the suffering of the Endless War here."

Kill him.

Damira ignored the voice. "You're right, Shag. Now, shall we have something to eat? All this invading is making me hungry."

An hour later, they were within sight of Litavye, the southernmost city in the land. Syzyan's scouts reported that the city was situated on the north bank of one tributary of a large river.

Syzyan chose a route that would avoid trapping the army between the mountains and the river. Instead, his forces circled west to advance on the city from the north. The army then split into two groups to surround the city, hemming it in against the rushing water. Syzyan sent a small brigade of archers to approach from the south, just in case anyone tried to flee across the river.

Only a few more hours, and Litavye would be hers. All Damira needed was for the inhabitants to cooperate. She accompanied Shagonar and Syzyan as they rode in front of their army, now twice the distance an arrow could fly away from the city. She wriggled her stinging toes. How long would it be before the residents acknowledged their presence? Perhaps they should send a message. And not a written one.

She eyed the city gates. Set between high stone walls, the wooden gates rose four times the height of a tall man, with horizontal iron bars adding strength to the wood. It wouldn't take more than a moment to burn through them, not with the power she held in her hand.

The gates opened, and a delegation emerged. Five riders on horses, all wearing black, carrying a black and white flag. Did that mean they were surrendering? Or were they bearing a challenge?

Shagonar rode forward, flanked by a pair of flinty-eyed archers and two towering, bulky men who wore leather armor and carried spears and battle axes. Damira and Syzyan followed.

When he was near enough to be heard, Shagonar stopped. The only sounds were the flapping of the flag in the wind and a horse's occasional nicker.

Damira patted her mare's neck as she studied the men who'd ridden out to meet them. They all wore black leather tunics, gloomy and drab in contrast to Shagonar and his men, who wore scarlet tunics under their black leather armor.

A man from the city spoke first, his deep voice booming. "Newcomers, what do you want from us?"

"Tell us," Shagonar replied, "the name of your city."

"Litavye."

"Litavye, very good. And the name of your country?"

"Tlefas. But surely you know this?"

Shagonar tipped his head back. "What we know and don't know isn't important. What is of consequence is that you understand we came to liberate you from your chains."

"Chains?" The man glanced at his companions. One of them shook his head and shrugged.

"You live under oppression," Shagonar pointed at the city, "and don't even know it. We have come from beyond the mountains to set you free. Will you welcome us as liberators or spurn us as enemies?"

Suppressing a smile, Damira kept her expression stern. Shagonar was playing his part well. So reasonable of him to give the people a chance to surrender. Not that they expected their conquest to be easy, but things would go more quickly if they didn't have to battle for every city.

The men from Litavye leaned together. After a few moments of head shaking, whispering, and pointing, they turned to face Shagonar. "We can do nothing without orders from the Prime Konamei."

"You mean the one who holds you in bondage?"

"Yes." The man hesitated. "I mean, no. His rule keeps us safe and prosperous."

That's odd, Damira thought. They don't seem interested in being free.

"Safe? He failed to keep an army from advancing on his southernmost city," Shagonar replied. "Very well. Send messages to your Prime Konamei. Send someone to us now to discuss the future of your city."

More shaking of heads, and pointing, this time accompanied by raised voices. No one, it seemed, wanted to be the one to venture into the enemy camp. Damira couldn't blame them.

After a few moments, Shagonar spoke. "Send us an envoy now, or my army will advance on your city. You choose."

One man pointed, clearly giving some kind of order. One of the others scowled and rode toward Shagonar.

"Poor fellow," Damira said. "He lost the argument."

The other four turned and galloped back to the city, not wasting an instant. Their unfortunate comrade let his horse amble toward Shagonar. When he drew near, Shagonar leaned forward. "You have nothing to fear, as long as you behave with honor," he said. "Don't make us take your weapons."

The man's jaw dropped and Damira stifled a laugh. He wasn't expecting that. Shagonar positioned his chestnut mare alongside the Litavyan's dun gelding and led the way back to their army.

When they arrived, grooms took their horses, and they escorted the Litavyan to their command tent, a large structure erected over a wooden floor. Tall poles held the felt sides high. Inside, the servants had already arranged the seats for Damira and Shagonar and were brewing tea and arranging platters of figs, dates, and sweet buns.

Damira limped to one of the two carved wooden chairs and Shagonar took the other. Syzyan stood to the side, ever the cautious observer. Damira studied the Litavyan. He was dark-skinned like an Izolliyan but had the blue eyes of a

Vernian. Interesting. Had the refugees intermarried? That would have been one way to eliminate the old racial divisions.

Shagonar glanced at her, and she nodded for him to begin. "Tell me your name."

"Kaltan." The man tipped his chin up. "And, if you please, who are you?"

"I am Shagonar, Lord and Emperor of Razdelia, and this is my wife, Empress Damira."

"Razdelia? Where is that?"

"Have you forgotten from whence you came?" Damira asked. "Go east, over the mountains and across the desert, to the land that fought the Endless War."

The man's eyes widened. "But everyone there died centuries ago."

"No, not everyone," Shagonar said. "There was a time when it looked like that could happen. While the war dragged on, many managed to survive. And here we are."

"Why have you come?" The man's throat bobbed, and he looked at his feet.

"We told you. We are here to liberate you from your oppressors."

Damira repressed the urge to drum her fingers on the chair's arms. Patience. That's how we'll win them over.

Destroy him.

She compressed her lips, pretending she hadn't heard the voice.

The man pulled his eyebrows together and shook his head. "But we aren't oppressed."

Shagonar gestured to a servant, who poured a cup of tea. "Would you like some?" he asked Kaltan. He pointed to the fruit. "Or perhaps a fig? I like them better than the dates."

Leaning back in her chair, Damira imitated Shagonar's nonchalance. She didn't want Kaltan to notice how badly they wanted to learn about this land. They'd been able to ferret out very little about Tlefas and how it was ruled. Now was their chance.

"Tell me something," Shagonar asked Kaltan as if he really wasn't interested in the answer. "Who rules you?"

"The Prime Konamei, of course."

"Of course. And what does he do for you?"

"He keeps us safe."

Damira ran a hand over her mouth. This time Kaltan spoke with conviction, not like his half-hearted denial about being oppressed.

Shagonar smiled and enunciated as if he were talking to a child. "And yet, a large army just strolled in and surrounded one of this Prime Konamei's largest cities. Interesting way of keeping people safe."

"The Prime Konamei has kept us safe. It's the ephor who failed us."

This was new. Damira tipped her head to the side. "The ephor?" she asked. "What does he do?"

"He rules the city and commands the Prime Konamei's guards. He enforces the laws."

"What happens to lawbreakers?" Syzyan asked.

"They're brought to court. Unless they did something unsafe, then they're taken."

"Taken where?"

The man shuddered. "No one knows. They're taken and never come back."

Damira looked at Shagonar. The guards who'd turned them away years ago had threatened them with being taken. "Sounds like a horrible way to keep order. Don't you agree?"

Shagonar nodded. "Nothing fair about that. But enough of this. We are here to liberate you from the Prime Konamei and his unfair rule."

Little by little, the man had grown agitated. He opened his mouth, then closed it. He squeezed his eyes shut, then opened them. He made a few incoherent sounds, then went silent.

"Do you want to say something?" Damira snapped the words at him.

The man jerked.

Frowning, Shagonar laid a hand on Damira's arm. "Don't be afraid, Kaltan. Just speak out."

Kaltan sucked in a breath. "Are you the Desired One?"

Damira studied him, noting the beads of sweat on his upper lip, his shaking hands and hunched shoulders. He was frightened. She glanced at Shagonar, who shrugged, then leaned forward and spoke softly. "Who is this Desired One?"

"The one prophesied of in the outlawed myth. The one who will bring a new order to the land using magic amulets."

After a conscious effort to slow her breathing, Damira adopted a somber expression. At last, some information they could use. She let the corners of her mouth slide upward. "My friend, I see we can't keep the truth from you. But what makes you think the Desired One has come among you?"

"Who else would you be?" Kaltan pointed at Shagonar. "You wear clothing of rich colors that shine in the light. Your hair. Not even Riskers wear their hair that long. And your tent —" He waved a hand. "Soft carpets, cushioned furnishings, gold lampstands. No one lives this well. No one."

Interesting. Damira pressed her twitching lips together. Was this country poor, or were the rulers living well at the expense of the people? Either way, she knew they could exploit the situation for their own gain. She pointed with her chin to a servant. "Kaltan, go with this man. He'll see that you are fed. We'll talk some more later."

She waited until Kaltan left the tent, then turned to Shagonar and Syzyan. "What do you think?"

Shagonar grinned. "I think this is the best news we could have gotten. All you need to do is take on this role as the Desired One and we'll have half the country with us already."

Syzyan pulled up a chair and sat. "Dami, I'm not so sure. We know nothing about this Desired One. If you say you are the fulfillment of a prophecy and they can prove you wrong, then you'll have undermined everything we're trying to do."

"You have a point," Damira said, pursing her lips. "We need to find out everything this man knows about the prophecy to see how we can use it."

"But if you're not the one…"

Use what you're given.

For once, she agreed with the voice in her head. "If I'm not the one," she said, "then I'm not." But she wasn't about to let this opportunity slip through her fingers. She'd find a way to make that prophecy fit her. "Shag, why don't you go have dinner with our guest, and see what you can find out? He might like the Vernian wine."

With a chuckle, Shagonar leaned over and planted a kiss on Damira's cheek. "Your wish is my command. Especially where wine is concerned." He rose and sauntered out of the tent.

"Dami," Syzyan said.

"You're right. We need to find out about this myth. If I don't fit the prophecy, then we find another way."

He nodded, the tension lines around his eyes relaxing. "We don't need it, anyway."

She raised her eyebrows.

"Didn't you notice, Dami? The idea of freedom meant nothing to him. But safety? Did you see that? All we have to do is convince these people their Prime Konamei can't keep them safe and they'll beg us to conquer them. Add to that a promise of a few luxuries in life, and they'll help us overthrow their rulers."

Kill him.

Damira swallowed hard. Every time Syzyan countered her, the voice told her to kill him. Some days, the temptation to remove his opposition seeped through her mind like a forbidden pleasure. Visions of stabbing him would form before her eyes. Maybe one day, the voices would get the better of her and Syzyan would be no more.

No. That wasn't going to happen. Damira ground her teeth together. Syzyan was her brother and she loved him. She and Syzyan, along with Shagonar, would live long happy lives and die serene deaths. She let out a slow breath. Thankfully, today the voice was like an irritating chulu fly she could brush off rather than a menacing sand wolf that made her cower before its rage.

Dragging her attention back to Syzyan, she gave him a small smile. "Perhaps." *Or else convince them that I, as the Desired One, can promise safety.* "As you say, we need to learn more."

"Good. While Shag is charming our guest, I'll go find out if our scouts have anything new to report."

She watched him stride from her tent. They had to conquer these people quickly, before the voices took control of her and she did something she would regret very, very much.

10

Tereka leaned against a birch tree and closed her eyes, letting the summer sun that trickled through the shifting leaves warm her face. She forced herself to listen to the chirping birds instead of the thump of her heartbeat. What was Kaberco up to? Or the Prime Konamei? Almost three weeks had passed since she and her crew had accosted the caravan. And nothing.

Unable to curb her impatience or the restlessness of her band, she decided to try again. This time, they'd go after a caravan closer to Kaberco's home. To that end, they lurked in the trees that lined the Gishin-Trofmose road.

The moments dragged on. She twanged her bowstring, checking its tautness, and fiddled with the bag of amulets tied in her pocket. She glared at the men dozing on the ground. It was a mystery to her how they could remain so calm.

This just had to work. If she succeeded, the Riskers might continue to support her. Otherwise, her rebellion would become a joke to any who knew of it. She would have failed before she got started. And she and her band would be fugitives with no place to go.

A shriek in the sky caught Tereka's attention. One hawk

called to another, then a flock of birds rose into the air. She let out a long breath. Finally. A caravan approached.

Da placed his hand on her arm. "You ready?"

She grinned. "For at least the last hour." She nudged Naco, who was sitting on last year's fallen pine needles, leaning against a tree with his eyes closed. "Get up. There's a caravan asking to be harassed."

Naco opened his tawny eyes and a grin spread across his face. "About time." He jumped to his feet and picked up his bow and quiver.

Around them, Relio, Sebezh, and Alikse were readying their weapons. With a nod, Tereka pushed through the brush and stepped onto the road, followed by all of them except Da. Tereka had been adamant. The risk of him being recognized was too great. He was to stay behind, just in case they needed to spring a surprise on the guards.

The caravan lumbered into sight, the clomping of the horses' hoofs and creaking of the wagon wheels growing ever louder. Tereka, an arrow nocked and ready with two others in her hand, strode toward the sound.

A few heartbeats later, the black-clad guards in the lead jerked their heads up. Tereka assumed they'd seen her, but they didn't call out a warning or wave their swords. They just kept riding.

With a firm tread and head held high, Tereka advanced on the caravan guards. She forced herself to keep her breathing slow and even. About thirty paces from her, the guards halted. The captain pointed his sword at her. "You. They warned us about you. Haven't you had enough?"

"I would ask the same of you." She shouted to make sure they heard her. "Enough lies, enough oppression."

"Who's the oppressor now?" the captain said. "Is your idea of giving people freedom is to get traders taken?"

"No, to liberate them." She frowned. What was he talking about?

"The girl hasn't heard." He snorted and, with a sneer, leaned forward in his saddle. "The ephor of Trofmose didn't take kindly to you slandering the Prime Konamei. Or his syndic. So he did something about it."

Tereka sighed. "He didn't throw Juquila in his dungeon? What a pity."

Several guards laughed. The captain glared at them before continuing. "No, but he did order some traders taken."

Her breath caught in her throat. She swallowed hard. "Oh?"

"Eight, to be exact. Care to know who they were?"

She shrugged. *I need him to tell me. But if I act like it's important, he won't.*

The captain recited eight names, all of them familiar to Tereka. Three especially—Yeroblat, who'd helped her escape Juquila's thugs, Waukomis, a long-time friend of her da's, and his son Kemet, who she once thought she loved. All eight were associated with her da in one way or another.

Her chest tightened and her throat ached from a knot of guilt that made it impossible to swallow. It was her fault they'd been taken.

Naco stirred beside her. "Look to the others." He whispered the words, so the guard couldn't hear.

The other three guards had nocked arrows.

Tereka jutted her chin forward. "Tell the ephor of Trofmose that I don't take kindly to him venting his wrath on innocent traders because I exposed his incompetence and corruption. All that proves is that Kaberco wields his authority only to maintain his power, not safety and fairness. Why you support a man like that escapes me." She locked her gaze on the captain's. "Kaberco will regret this action." She took a step back. "As will you, if your men loose their arrows."

The captain jerked a hand up. All three of his guards let their arrows fly. A muffled grunt told her at least one of her friends had been struck. She raised her bow and shot her three arrows, one after the other. Sebezh and Relio's bowstrings twanged as they loosed their own. Her three arrows hit home, wounding the captain and two others in their shoulders. They wouldn't be able to pull their bowstrings enough to shoot. The fourth had an arrow in his leg, and all had an arrow or two lodged in their leather armor.

A glance told her all of her friends remained on their feet, so whatever the wound, it must not be serious.

With a tip of her head at the captain, Tereka sneered, "We'll be seeing you." She spun around and sprinted back the way they'd come. She plunged into the woods and raced up the narrow trail, the others close behind. When they rounded a clump of pine trees, she stopped. "Who's hurt?" she said between gasps.

"Me." Relio dropped to his knees. An arrow had scraped his cheek and blood trickled down his neck.

"I'll clean him up," Naco said.

Crunching in the underbrush made her snap her head around. A few heartbeats later, Da came into view. "Tereka, are you alright?"

"Yes, yes. But, Da, did you hear?

Da closed his eyes, pressed a hand to his mouth, and nodded. The traders who'd been taken were good friends to both of them.

Alikse frowned. "Why would Kaberco take so many?"

Tereka sucked in a breath through her teeth. "I think he's finally decided what to do about us." She met Da's knowing gaze, wincing at the pain in his eyes.

"Somehow," Da said, "Kaberco knows you were involved in the incident with the other caravan. He must have gotten a good enough description of you to guess the truth. Now he's going after everyone who's had close dealings with either you or me."

An acid taste filled Tereka's mouth as she thought of jovial

Yeroblat or gentle Kemet in the Prime Konamei's copper mines.

"You sure about that?" Relio asked.

Da nodded. "There are fifty or more traders who make Trofmose their home. The traders Kaberco took are the ones I've had the most dealings with."

"We have to do something," Tereka said. Her face heated, and she clenched her hand around her bow. "We can't let them end up the way we did."

"But what can we do?" Sebezh asked. "If we go to Trofmose, we'll surely be arrested." He snorted. "Then there's the small problem of breaking into the ephor's house."

"That's the easy part," Da said. "I've done it myself."

Tereka stared at him. "You broke into the ephor's house?"

"Yes, long ago." He gave her a rueful smile. "I'll tell you about it another time. Breaking in won't be difficult at night. Once you're in, it's simple to find the jail. Getting eight prisoners out without anyone noticing will be the hard part."

"How many of us should go?" Naco asked.

Da rubbed his chin. "No more than four, I should think. You'll have to sneak into the city." He outlined a few ideas for how they would pass through the gates, and how they could get everyone out. "But the question is, who should go?"

"I am." Tereka held up a hand. "Don't even try to stop me, Da. I started this, and I'm responsible."

He regarded her for a moment, then nodded. "Who else?"

"I'm going," Naco said.

Tereka grinned at him. She knew she could trust him. "Who else would like to join us?" She tried to make it sound like she was inviting them to dinner.

Relio snorted. "I'd love to spend a night raiding the ephor's house and creating a jailbreak. But even when you do your trick with your amulet and fix my face, we can't forget my back."

She pressed her lips together. As much as she'd welcome

his help, he was right. The amulets had given him relief from the pain, but the weakness from his old prison injuries lingered. She eyed Alikse, whom she considered a solid ally.

"I was hoping you'd want me," he said, breaking into a wide smile.

That left Sebezh. Tereka studied the man with narrowed eyes.

"What about me?" Sebezh asked. "I'm about to die of boredom, stuck up on that mountain. I'll do anything for a spot of excitement."

"That's what worries me," Tereka said. "Will you be content with a jailbreak and nothing more?" Sebezh was capable of anything, from attempting to kill her, to making an escape. If he was caught and questioned, he was sure to tell all he knew to avoid the worst punishment.

Sebezh's face grew serious. "I'm not such a fool as to cause trouble for you while we all could be caught. I promise."

She traded a glance with Da. He raised his eyebrows, then nodded. She knew what he meant. Take Sebezh, but keep a close eye on him. "Then we're agreed. But there's one more thing. What will we do with eight traders once we've freed them?"

Da whistled. "Good question." He gazed up the trail for a moment. "Tell you what. Relio and I will go talk to your grandparents. See if they have any ideas."

Tereka frowned. Eight more fugitives might snap the Riskers' hospitality like a rotted bowstring. "I hope they do. Now. Explain to me how you got into the ephor's house."

11

J uquila stifled a yawn. Konament meetings could be unbearable. Why were they wasting time fussing about the quality of the wood used to build villagers' houses? Now if Birita the adile was droning on about something useful, like better roads to reduce caravan breakdowns, that would be worthwhile. What difference did it make if the villagers were cold in the winter?

Sweat tickled her forehead under the band of her turban. Couldn't Kaberco get one of his servants to come and fan them? Did they have to be so uncomfortable while conducting the business of Trofmose? Really, if she was in charge...

Kaberco cleared his throat. "If there's nothing else, then we have one more matter to discuss. As you know, a caravan was waylaid a few weeks ago and slanderous lies were told about the Prime Konamei and other officials.

That meant her. Everyone knew it. Why didn't he just come out and say so? Juquila pinned her gaze on Kaberco's face, noting how his olive skin gleamed with sweat. He was feeling the heat, too. And something else was bothering him. He wasn't as focused as he usually was. Her heart beat a little faster, anticipating his next words.

"To prevent any more such events, I've had several traders taken," Kaberco said, shuffling the papers on the table before him. "After they've had a few days to consider what it means to be taken, I'll interrogate them. If they truly had nothing to do with this, they'll be sent to the mines as a warning to others to not associate with criminals. If they are guilty or refuse to cooperate, they'll be executed."

"If you please, are you saying you took some of my traders, not even knowing if they are guilty or not?" Juquila clenched a fist under the table and straightened her spine. "And you didn't have the courtesy to tell me in advance?"

"If you please."

The sarcastic timbre in his voice made Juquila want to scream curses at him. She compressed her lips and allowed him to continue, contenting herself with infusing ice into her glower.

Using the supercilious tone she hated, Kaberco went on. "I had to act while the ones under suspicion were in Trofmose. You know how traders come and go. I wanted to round them all up while I could. When you hear the names, you'll understand."

She tipped her head to the side. "Do tell."

Kaberco read the list. Birita and Kulooq the ludi were silent. Juquila gathered they didn't comprehend the significance of the names. Yavaros, the questor, dropped his head and stared at his hands. He knew.

As did she. The taken were all close associates of her brother-in-law. She stifled a grin. She'd wanted Kaberco to castigate Tarkio for years. Thanks to Tereka and her antics, he'd done just that. But now, how to play this?

"And?" she asked. "It's immaterial who you have on your list. You have no right to take people on mere suspicions. You need more proof than that. Otherwise, you are undermining one of the principles of our fair society." She turned to the questor. "Isn't that correct?"

Yavaros raised his head. "Such an extreme action is unusual. It hasn't been done for decades. Not that I'm aware of."

Birita frowned. "Couldn't you have waited for more evidence?"

Kulooq pulled his bushy eyebrows together. "Or simply interrogated them?"

Kaberco's face darkened.

Juquila held herself still. What a wonderful moment this was, to watch the other konameis turn on him. "Besides," she said. "It was ill-thought out and poorly timed. Have you heard that trade from the south has been interrupted?"

She scrutinized Kaberco's face as she spoke. Did his jaw tighten when she mentioned the south? *Perhaps he knows something he hasn't shared.* "We need more traders on the road, not fewer," she said. "If this state of affairs continues, the entire north will suffer." She leaned back and raised her eyebrows, keeping her eyes on Kaberco.

"And that," he replied, "is precisely the point. Because of the trade situation, I had to take decisive action. The last thing we need is unrest in the north, while the south is in turmoil. Surely you can see the logic in that?"

By now, Birita was nodding. Of course she would. She rarely countered Kaberco in anything. Juquila would have to work on Kulooq a bit more to make sure she had his support when she needed it.

Kulooq, it seemed, didn't need any prompting. "If you please," he said, his high-pitched voice an anxious whine, "what is going on in the south?"

Despite herself, Juquila leaned forward. This was precisely what she wanted to know.

Kaberco crossed his arms. "We are still waiting for birds from the Prime Konamei. I've also sent birds to the ephor of Litavye and surrounding towns. We'll know more soon."

Something about the way he wouldn't look any of them in

the eye made Juquila suspect he knew more than he was telling. She slid her hands off the table and gripped them together. The way his nostrils flared was a clear sign that he found the trouble in the south unsettling.

With an effort, Juquila kept her lips from twitching into a smile. At long last, she might have discovered how to penetrate Kaberco's defenses. Could she convince the Prime Konamei that Kaberco had something to do with the southern unrest? Or that he was exploiting it to break laws for his own pleasure, creating unsafe conditions in the north? It all depended on what was happening in Litavye. She had to find out.

"I also believed it was best to be aggressive," Kaberco said to the questor, "just in case any of these traders had anything to do with the trouble in the south. Many of them have been further south than the capital, so they could have been enlisted in whatever this disturbance is." He lowered his chin and looked down his nose at Juquila. "We already know they are close associates with known criminals. Or at least the family members of criminals."

So, that's how he wants to play. Juquila knew she had to be careful, lest he bring up her relationship with Tarkio and Tereka. Her next move needed to cause the most trouble for Kaberco and the least for herself. She could bring Tereka up by name. Or send a bird to the Prime Konamei, complaining that Kaberco had taken extraordinary action without consulting his konament. The questor and ludi might support her, and that might be enough to get him deposed.

The north needed to stay calm, just as Kaberco had said. Perhaps she could convince the Prime Konamei that the ephor was taking risks and undermining safety, and that she was the one to ensure the peace. That might do it. But how to be sure she'd muster support from at least two of the others?

"What's the real reason for your actions?" she asked. "Is it because they say this girl is none other than Tereka Sabidur, who was taken and seemingly came back from wherever it is the taken go?"

She took a slow, gentle breath, keeping her expression bland. It wasn't easy, with the other three gasping and muttering. Her words were rewarded by the delightful sight of Kaberco's bulging eyes and the vein throbbing in his temple. She stifled a triumphant grin. She'd gotten under his skin.

Juquila spoke as sweetly as she could. "I thought you were supposed to track her down last fall. Why did you fail?"

More murmurs and mutters. Kaberco's fingers curled into fists. He leaned forward. "That's enough, if you please." He looked at the adile and ludi. "You were not informed of the escape of the prisoner, Tereka Sabidur, because it was considered a minor matter. The last we knew, she'd been captured by pirates, so we assumed that was the end of her, that she was no longer a danger to safety and fairness." He paused. "That seems to have been incorrect."

Yavaros held up a hand. "No one should fault you for overestimating the bloodthirstiness of pirates."

The adile chuckled, then held a hand over her mouth as if ashamed. Her pale skin flushed. Juquila shot a glare at her before turning back to Kaberco.

"I mean no harm." She shrugged. "I only brought it up to caution you. Tereka may try to rescue the taken while you are transporting them. Be warned."

She sat back and folded her hands in her lap. Blast the man for having an answer for everything. At least her next moves were clear. First, private conversations with the ludi and the questor. Followed by a bird to the Prime Konamei. Then she needed to find out why her spies in the south had gone silent.

12

ereka cursed the sudden rain shower. After two protracted days of walking, she and Alikse were less than three miles from the gates of Trofmose. And now they were caught in a downpour. Their plan was risky enough without the complication of a storm.

The strap of the bag Tereka had slung over her shoulder chafed her neck, its weight seeming to grow with every step. Cold rain dampened her face.

She trudged after Alikse, who bore four cut logs about the length of his thigh tied together. With a smooth motion, he swung the bundle to the top of his head and steadied it with one hand.

Envious, Tereka let out a huff. He could use his burden as a shield from the rain. She was barely strong enough to lug her own.

At last, the wooden wall of Trofmose loomed ahead, its corners softened by the mist. She shuddered. The last time she'd been in the city, she'd been a prisoner. She hoped that wasn't how this day would end.

As they approached the east gate, her heart beat faster. They joined the crowd of bedraggled villagers pushing to enter the city. Everyone's gray clothing had darkened to dull slate as the rain soaked through, with the bands that circled each left shoulder offering the only touch of color. These bands announced the wearer's profession. Hers was green for farming, while Alikse's was blue for builders.

Her villager's shapeless dress clung to her damp leggings. Rain dripped from her hair as if she'd dumped a basin of water over her scalp. She pursed her lips. Her hair had grown out over the winter, dark and thicker than it had been before her head was shaved during her stint in prison. It had nearly reached the legal length and was chopped off at the chin with straight bangs across her forehead. In her bedraggled state, no one would question her looks.

Of greater concern was Alikse's beard. Village men were required to shave twice a week. But Alikse's beard had grown thick and full since he'd shaved before they left their mountain hideout. It was as long as most men's after a week. Trimming the dark blond hair with a knife only made it look shaggy, not like a typical villager concerned with looking the same as everyone else. At least the rain gave him an excuse to pull the neck of his tunic up to his chin.

How she wished she had her bow. But Da had insisted on taking their bows and swords with him, as no villager would be armed. All she and Alikse carried were small daggers hidden in their clothing. If things went wrong, they wouldn't be enough.

She wondered if Naco and Sebezh had reached their destination, the south gate of the city. Most likely, they'd have an easier time getting through the smaller entrance. Disguised as laborers with brown bands on their shoulders, no guard would question their scruffy appearance or the wooden logs they bore.

And no one would think it odd that Alikse, marked with the blue builder's band, was hauling logs. As a farm worker, she was a different story. With a little luck, no zealous guardsman would peek into her bag. She didn't have a good reason for why she was carrying the wood.

Too late for those concerns now. She told herself they'd slip into the city unnoticed in the throng. Her words did nothing to calm her twitchy nerves.

Just outside the gate, the crowd bunched up. Muttering and murmuring intensified. Tereka bit her lip. What was the delay?

People around her were complaining. "Why so many guards? Why are they checking what everyone's bringing in?"

The crowd edged forward as the guardsmen admitted people into the city, one by one. The crowd's restlessness grew as the wind blew the rain in sheets over the swam, and more people voiced their impatience.

"Hey! We've got families to feed."

"The inns have started serving. Don't make us miss our supper."

"My kids will be worried."

"I've a sick old auntie at home. Let me in."

The complaints grew louder. Tereka looked around at the nervous and angry faces. Would the crowd's anxiety make it easier for her to get into the city, or harder?

Slowly, they inched their way to the gate. Soon it was Alikse's turn.

"What's the wood for?" the guard asked.

"Repairs, if you please."

Tereka nearly laughed. She'd never heard Alikse speak in such a subservient tone.

It seemed to satisfy the guard, though he frowned at Alikse with narrowed eyes. When a gust of wind threw a torrent of rain over the man, he coughed and sputtered. "Get a shave, before I fine you." He waved Alikse through, then beckoned Tereka to approach.

Her heart thumped in her chest, and she swallowed hard.

Sky-god, do you see me? A warmth tingled next to her ribs near the bag containing her amulets.

Shouts from the crowd seized the guard's attention. People behind her were jostling each other. The guard shoved past Tereka toward the disturbance, waving his stick.

"What'cha waiting for?" A woman poked Tereka in the back. "Go."

With silent thanks to the sky-god, Tereka didn't hesitate. She darted through the gate and rejoined Alikse several yards away.

"Now where?" he asked.

She led the way to the market and ducked into an alley. "You go, get what we need. I'll stay here." He nodded, not needing an explanation. They couldn't risk Tereka being recognized. Alikse dropped his bundle of logs at her feet and strode off.

The wait was excruciating. She paced, wrung her hands, and pleaded with the sky-god, but none of that made it any easier. A shrill blast of a horn announced a caravan, most likely an arrival this late in the day. Where was Alikse?

The moments stretched to nearly half an hour before he returned. "Sorry. It seems everyone wanted pasties." He held one out to her and took a bite of his own. "No meat left," he said. "Just cabbage. I got some with berries, too."

Her mouth stuffed with pastie, she nodded her thanks, then swallowed. "I hope Naco and Sebezh are in," she said before taking another bite.

"We'll soon find out. They'll either help us with the rescue or need a rescue themselves."

Tereka paused mid-chew. "I hadn't thought of that. At least they won't suffer too long in jail."

They finished eating, then stood silently, listening to the slowing patter of the rain. It seemed to Tereka that the light would never dim. They should have waited longer to enter the city. This far north, summer days were long-lived, the sun strolling across the sky in no hurry to set.

At last, the sun sank behind the walls of the city. Dusk's gray shadows obscured the few people still on the streets. "Ready?" she asked.

Alikse grunted as he picked up his bundle. "Lead on, girly."

She smirked at his use of Relio's name for her and stepped to the end of the alley. Few people traveled the stony, wet streets, so they made their way quickly, avoiding the inns where traders and others lingered over their ale.

Ducking into another alley, Tereka trod carefully to avoid slipping on the refuse. The stench of urine, rotting eggs, and horse manure assaulted her nose. Alikse sneezed, the rough sound echoing.

The alley led to the river near the center of the city, just east of the ephor's house. The only three-story structure in the city, the building stood on the riverbank, the river's brown water lapping against its wall. Tereka gulped, remembering the last time she'd been inside. Then she'd been a prisoner.

They stood in the shadows of the alley, watching the parapet atop the house. After half an hour, she touched Alikse's elbow. "Only four guards, right?"

"Right. Slow ones, too."

The guards shuffled along the eastern side of the roof, hunched over against the rain. When they turned the corner, Tereka made her move. She trotted to the wall of the house, running as lightly as she could, trying to ignore how the strap of her bundle dug into her shoulder.

Once under the shadow of the walls, she crept toward the river. She felt rather than heard Alikse behind her. She hoped Da's memory proved to be correct.

She stepped into the water next to the house and smiled when her foot settled on a stone ledge. The water came just over her knees. She inched along the ledge, holding her breath. Falling into the water would be disastrous. The guards wouldn't mistake a large splash for the plopping sound of raindrops on the river.

Trying not to let the heavy bag disturb her balance, Tereka clutched at protuberances in the rock wall. How Alikse was managing his much heavier load, she didn't know.

Halfway along the wall, she located the door Da had told her about—the door with no handle, its opening about three feet above the water. She felt along the beam that formed the left side of the door, standing on her tiptoes as she reached up. There was no latch.

Alikse put a hand on her shoulder, then reached over her. He easily found the release and pushed the door inward. Tereka winced as it creaked. Then it stuck, refusing to open more than halfway.

With a low grunt, Alikse lifted his bundle of wood through the opening and shoved it in. He tossed Tereka's sack after it, offered her a hand, and boosted her up. She clambered inside and dragged the wood away from the door.

By this time, Alikse had lifted himself inside. "What next?" he said.

In answer, she groped for her bundle in the gloom, sat on it, and took off her boots, dumping the water on the floor. Alikse sat down on the logs he'd carried. From the splashing sounds, she assumed he was emptying his own boots. "Now," she said, "we wait."

13

A gust of wind blew through the open door. Tereka shivered, her damp clothing adding to the chill in the dim, dank passage. This was the hard part. Waiting for the others.

The south gate was farther from the ephor's house than the one she and Alikse had used, so Naco and Sebezh would need more time to make their way through the city. Tereka closed her eyes and leaned against the wall. She wanted to stick her head out and look, but knew that would be foolish. All that would do would be to give a guard the chance to notice them. She counted Alikse's even breathing. Ten, fifty, one hundred. Still no Naco and Sebezh.

Maybe Sebezh had knocked Naco out and fled. Tereka shook herself to clear her mind of this silly thought. Sebezh had no place to go. If he was captured, he'd be executed. They all had a price on their heads, and no guardsman would hesitate to claim it.

She gave up counting breaths and numbered the slapping noises of the river's waves against the wall. *Whoever thought jailbreaks were exciting? Only that fool Sebezh.* She'd gotten nearly to one thousand when the sound changed from a slap to a splash. She jumped to her feet.

Alikse was already at the door. He peeked out, then waved a hand at Tereka. Then he leaned forward, his head and shoulders disappearing out the door. He reappeared a moment later, bearing a bundle of logs. He tossed it aside and extended a hand. With a grunt, he hauled up Naco, then reached down for Sebezh's bundle. Within a few heartbeats, Sebezh was dripping on the stone floor. Alikse shoved the door nearly shut, leaving just a tiny crack to let in the fresh night air.

Tereka rubbed Naco's arm, a grin spreading across her face. "Any trouble?" she whispered.

"Nope. You?"

"None for us. Dump your boots and let's get going."

While Naco and Sebezh emptied the water from their boots, Tereka and Alikse groped in the near darkness for the bundles of logs. They untied them and lined the logs up along the wall.

When all was ready, Tereka placed her hand on the wall and moved forward cautiously, the others following close behind. She counted the stones until she reached seventeen, then felt for a hidden latch and opened the door. She pushed it ajar but didn't enter.

"What's that for, girly?" Sebezh asked.

"Extra escape route. Da thought it might be a good idea." They followed the downward slope of the corridor until it ended at a metal door. Tereka ran her fingers along the side until she found the hidden latch. She murmured her thanks to whoever had designed these secret tunnels and had used the same latches on all the doors.

Her stomach fluttered. One more step and there'd be no going back. Thrusting her chin in the air, she pulled a knife from her belt and pushed the door open. She wrinkled her nose at the smell of dampness and sweat and fear. She pushed aside a curtain that hung over the doorway and stepped into what appeared to be a storeroom for broken furniture, casks without lids, and piles of leather armor.

From what she remembered of her night in Kaberco's jail, there was only one guard on duty at a time. Hopefully, nothing had changed. She and the others crept through the storeroom and along a narrow hallway, a flickering light in front of her showing the way.

When she came to a corner, she peeked around it. A single guard was dozing, barely visible in the light of a solitary torch on the wall.

Alikse pushed past her. He grabbed the man and squeezed his throat until he slumped in his arms, then laid him gently on the floor. "Hurry," Alikse said.

Tereka grabbed the ring of keys from the guard's belt and darted for the cells. She unlocked the first. A fat man jerked upright, his chins wobbling. "What?"

"Shh. Yeroblat. We're breaking you out."

Yeroblat's eyes widened. "Tereka?"

"Yes. Shh. Hurry."

The other three traders in the cell staggered to their feet. "Follow him." She pointed at Alikse, who nodded and led them back the way they'd come.

She relocked Yeroblat's cell and unlocked the second. Red-haired Waukomis and two traders darted out. Waukomis paused to grip Tereka's arm. "Thank you. Our execution was scheduled for the morning."

A sour taste filled Tereka's mouth. "It was the least I could do. Go."

Kemet was the last to leave the cell. He grabbed her hand. "Is it really you?"

The tension in her jaw eased. She'd found Kemet and the other traders but this was no time for a reunion. "Yes. Shh. Now go."

"We'll talk later," he whispered, then ran after the others.

Tereka locked the cell and placed the keys in the uncon-
scious guard's hand. "Sebezh, go with them. Don't wait for us,
just leave. We'll catch up."

Sebezh nodded. "As you say, girly."

Tapping Naco on the arm, she pointed at the guard with
her chin. "How long before he wakes up?"

"Not long." Naco sucked in a breath. "If we're going to do
this, we need to be fast."

She didn't give herself a heartbeat to think, but dashed out
the door, Naco on her heels. She swung it shut, careful to not
allow the metal to clang. The soft click of the latch falling into
place brought a smile to her face.

It took only a few heartbeats for her eyes to adjust to the
darkness. She retraced their steps, counting the stones in the
walls. At twenty-three, she opened another door with a similar
hidden latch. She bounded up the stairs, counting as she went.
At ninety-seven, she stopped. She ran her hand over the wall
until her fingers encountered wood.

"This is it," she muttered.

Naco snorted. "You don't want to run all the way to the
roof?"

With a snicker, she pushed on the left side of the wood
panel. It slid open. She blinked in the sudden light; grateful it
was dim and diffuse. What was the source of the light? She
brushed her fingers over the barrier in front of her. The rough
fabric and scattered knots told her it was the back of a
tapestry. Glimmers of light peeked around the edges like the
sun shining past the sides of a dark cloud.

Da had said this stairway would lead to the ephor's private
workroom, which was next to his bedchamber. Surely
Kaberco wouldn't be working this late.

She reached up and put a hand on Naco's mouth. He
nodded. She crouched to the floor and peered under the
bottom of the tapestry. A writing table stood in the middle of

a thick carpet. She could only see underneath the table, where a pair of black-clad legs wearing black leather boots was barely visible. Kaberco, it seemed, wasn't one to retire early.

The light flickered as if a rush of air disturbed the flame of a candle. Tereka closed her eyes. *I did that by moving the tapestry. Would Kaberco smell the dank odor of the passage?*

All she and Naco could do was wait. She held her breath. Kaberco shifted his feet. *By all that's safe, he needs to go to bed.* She bit her lower lip. They didn't have much time—what if the guard woke up? Sweat beaded her forehead. Kaberco wouldn't be forgiving if he caught them.

A knock on the door made her gasp. She clasped a hand over her mouth.

Kaberco, it seemed, hadn't noticed the sound she'd made. "Come in," he said, his voice tense and irritated.

A guardsman rushed in. "If you please, there's a problem with the prisoners."

Tereka's heart sank. She reached for Naco and gripped his shoulder.

"Problem? Like what? They want hot tea? Or softer beds?"

"No, if you please. They're gone."

"They're what?" Kaberco growled the words. Tereka shivered at the implied menace.

"Gone. Not there."

"What do the *durak* guards have to say?" Kaberco didn't wait for an answer. Instead, he shoved back his chair and strode from the room. The guard scuttled behind him.

Tereka let out a slow breath. "Should we?"

Naco breathed into her ear. "May as well. We're here. But fast."

If Kaberco returned, it would be the end of her life. She clenched her jaw. The time for half measures was over.

She slid out from behind the tapestry and dashed to the

writing desk. She picked up Kaberco's quill and scrawled a
few words on the document he'd been working on. Then she
replaced the quill in the inkwell.

Her glance fell on another document, this one bearing the
seal of the Prime Konamei, a pine tree flanked by sheaves of
rye. After ordinary greetings about peace and safety, the tone
turned serious.

*The situation in Litavye is desperate. The invading army has
surrounded the city. We expect it cannot endure the siege much longer if it
has not already surrendered. From what we know, these invaders intend to
conquer the whole country...*

An invading army. Dread pooled in Tereka's stomach.
Could that be why Kaberco had ignored her at first, then
responded so harshly by taking eight traders?

A second thought jostled the first. An invader could bring
a new order. Which would mean...

"Tereka! Let's go!"

She met Naco's frantic gaze. He was right. She could think
about the invaders later. Bolting for the tapestry, she ducked
under it. In two heartbeats, she replaced the panel.

They tore down the steps, Naco in the lead. As Naco
neared the bottom, he slowed. They peered into the corridor.
No shadowy forms appeared in the darkness. She heard no
breath but their own jagged panting. Once in the corridor, she
pulled the door shut behind them and sped for the exit.

To her relief, the others were gone. Good. At least they got
away before the guard awoke.

Groping until she found the two logs leaning against the
wall near the exit, Tereka seized one and thrust the other into
Naco's arms. He pushed the door open. Neither moon was
shining. The only light was the twinkling reflection of the
starlight on the rippling river.

She brushed her hand on the door and frowned. "There's
no handle on the outside. How do we get it shut?"

"Don't worry about it," Naco said. "Let Kaberco figure it out." He sat on the threshold and slid into the water. A heartbeat later, she did the same, gasping as the cold water chilled her to the core. Clinging to the log, she let the current push her downstream and away from the ephor's house.

14

Juquila clenched her teeth to keep her lips from breaking into a grin. She fixed her gaze on the sweating man standing in front of her worktable, one of Kaberco's clerks she paid to spy for her. She uttered her next words softly. "Go on."

"By the time the ephor arrived, all the prisoners were gone. Kaberco questioned the guard, but he remembered nothing except being grabbed around the neck before he passed out. He has the bruises to show for it."

"What did Kaberco do?"

"He ordered a search of the house and interrogated the guards, the ones at the doors and on the roof. No one had seen anything. Kaberco raged at them, but there was no explanation. Every door was locked. Even the cells. The keys were in the guard's hand when he woke up."

How Juquila wished she could have been there to witness Kaberco's frustration. She scrutinized the clerk's leathery, dark face. His mahogany eyes met hers, his thick lips didn't tremble. Most likely, he was telling the truth. "That's so very strange," she said.

"It was. It was like they vanished into the air. Then the oddest thing happened."

She raised her eyebrows.

"Kaberco returned to his rooms. Suddenly, he was shouting and cursing. A few guards went running, thinking he'd been attacked."

"Oh, how exciting." She kept her voice calm and even, adding just enough interest to keep the man talking. "Had he been?" What a stroke of luck that would be.

"No. But whoever had freed the prisoners left him a note."

Juquila blinked. "In his rooms?" This was more than a simple jailbreak; she was sure of it. She was beginning to suspect who was behind it.

"On his writing table."

She leaned forward to stare into the man's eyes. "What did it say?"

"I don't know. Kaberco said he'd find the criminal who'd sprung the prisoners or die trying. That's when he announced his decree."

To keep the man from noticing her surprise, Juquila dropped her gaze to the documents on her table. A decree issued without the consent of the konament could only mean one thing. Kaberco was desperate.

"He ordered all his guardsmen to look for the girl. The one who stops caravans," the clerk said, shifting his weight from one foot to the other. "Kaberco described her—tall, dark hair, tan skin, blue eyes. Good archer. A hooligan with no regard for safety."

A warm rush of triumph spread through Juquila. She'd been right. Tereka was the culprit. "What are the guardsmen supposed to do when they apprehend her?"

"Kill her, of course." He shuffled his feet against the wood floor. "They say he sent birds to every ephor in Tlefas informing them of the decree, and of the eight escaped traders. They are also to be killed on sight."

Interesting. And infuriating. She asked the man a few more questions, but he knew little else. By way of dismissing him, she dropped a handful of copper coins into his hand.

As she watched him leave, she tapped her fingers on the table. Poor Kaberco, wondering how Tereka got into his residence. She could enlighten him if she wanted to.

When she was the previous ephor's wife, she learned the secret ways in and out of that house. Knowledge she kept from Kaberco when he moved in.

Years earlier, as the new bride of the ephor, she'd shown her sister and brother-in-law the hidden passages. The three of them had thought it a great game. But only Tarkio had ever used them, coming to her bedchamber one night eighteen years ago to beg for mercy for a friend.

Tarkio must be involved, but this reckless caper didn't seem like him. No, most likely that brat of his, Tereka, did the actual deed. And she had the nerve to leave a note for Kaberco.

Juquila smiled. What she wouldn't give to have seen Kaberco's face at that moment. And even more to learn what the note said. Whatever Tereka wrote, it was enough for Kaberco to know the same girl who'd stopped the caravans had raided his jail.

Twisting in her chair, Juquila examined the map of Tlefas pinned to the wall behind her. The first caravan Tereka stopped was on the road to North Rivash, and the second, on the Gishin Road. Both times in areas close to the mountains. That meant Tereka was hiding with the Riskers. Tarkio, with his license to trade with the savages, would have been the one to take her there.

Waves of heat licked Juquila's face, and she clenched her fists. Tarkio. Always causing trouble, with his insistence on honesty. Had he been corruptible, she'd have been able to get rid of him years ago. With his reputation, it would be hard to get anyone to believe charges against him, even if she falsified documents to do it. No, Yavaros might pretend to accept her claims, maybe even fine Tarkio. But the questor would protect the man if he thought she was using her position to damage him.

But Yavaros wouldn't be able to ignore a charge of harboring a fugitive, especially one that fomented rebellion against the Prime Konamei. Juquila rubbed her hands together. Once Tarkio was gone, that would solve another problem. The head of the trade guild would no longer have Tarkio to stiffen his spine. He'd become her puppet.

Then there would be few left to oppose her. The questor's health was failing. The adile and the ludi were persuadable.

Arching her back like a cat stretching in the sun, Juquila thought about how she'd persuaded Kulooq to support her, which had been more pleasant than anticipated. Words hadn't been necessary when she could use her tongue in other ways.

In any case, she needed to have conversations with the konameis, expressing her concern about Kaberco's ability to keep them all safe, especially after this spectacular failure. And she'd remind them he'd been advised that taking all those traders was a bad idea.

Her children would help. The oldest daughter was one of Yavaros's clerks, and the younger worked for Kulooq. Her oldest son was a guardsman, and the younger twin boys were apprenticed to the adile. They were loyal spies for her. They needed to do some more digging to find out where the konameis' weak spots lay. Everyone had some, it was just a matter of finding out what and where they were. And then she could exploit them mercilessly.

She shook herself. That was the future. What to do now? She couldn't tell Kaberco how she knew Tarkio was involved. That would mean sharing her knowledge of the secret entrances with him. He'd be angry she hadn't told him, and she'd never be able to use them again for her own benefit. Curse Tarkio for doing just that and risking that Kaberco would learn some of the secrets of his house.

The hidden passages weren't the only secrets she kept from Kaberco when he assumed his position after her husband died. She'd promised Valday to give Kaberco all the information he needed, but it was an empty vow she made to a dying man who was no longer useful to her.

No. At the moment, the better play was to capture Tarkio. He'd know where to find Tereka and she'd be able to either turn the girl in as a fugitive, or use her for her own ends. That could be delicious, allying with Tereka to bring Kaberco down. Then she'd destroy the girl at her leisure.

From what she'd heard, no one had seen Tarkio in Trofmose lately. Juquila drummed her fingers on the table. Had he gone on a long trading run? Or was he hiding with the Riskers? She chewed her lower lip. The best person to send looking for him was her clerk, Tarkio's son Tirk. Sending anyone else would put Tarkio on his guard. Surely Tarkio would be so touched by his son's devotion that he wouldn't question his actions.

What Tarkio didn't know was that Tirk was loyal to her, not him. She could count on Tirk to find his father and convince him to return to Trofmose. Then she'd have him and finish him off.

Which left the problem of how to get eliminate Kaberco. Should she send a bird to the Prime Konamei? It would be her duty to inform him that Kaberco couldn't prevent intruders from entering his house, or prisoners from fleeing his jail. He clearly wasn't able to keep Trofmose—let alone the northern region—safe.

She knitted her eyebrows together. The Prime Konamei hadn't responded to her last two birds. A man of action, he was not.

If only the country was ruled by someone bolder, who

wasn't afraid to wield power. That would be the kind of person who would appreciate Juquila's abilities.

Ah, well. No sense wishing for something that would never be. She sighed and pulled her inkwell over. Somehow, she'd have to come up with the right words to spur the Prime Konamei into action.

15

Tereka took a final glance up and down the dusty road. It was empty but for her companions. She wiped the sweat from her face and stepped onto the path that led into the forest. Once under the shelter of the trees, she'd be safe from pursuit. Except for bandits or warboars. Armed as they were with only knives, fighting either could be difficult.

She took a deep breath and brushed off that thought. The shade cooled her sweating face, the scent of pine calmed her spirits. With measured steps, she hiked up the steep slope, seeking a clearing where they could rest. They'd certainly earned it. Since their escape from Kaberco's house, they'd passed four tension-filled days slinking through the wilderness at night and cowering under what cover they could find by day, always alert for sounds of pursuit.

On horseback, the trip would have taken a day and a half. Had she and Naco been alone, they could have hiked it in just over two long days.

But with the eight rescued traders, they had to travel slower than a laden wagon with a lame horse. Every hour or so, Yeroblat would collapse to the ground, splayed in the dirt like a sack of grain tossed from a cart. Once, Tereka suggested sending the younger traders ahead with Alikse, just to make the group smaller. They greeted her offer with snorts and sneers. No one wanted to split up. Not when bandits, warboars, and Riskers roamed the mountain slopes.

As they'd plodded along, she wondered. How had it been so easy to get away? Maybe Kaberco had put all his efforts into searching the city, assuming no one would do anything so unsafe as to float across the river. *So much for the obsession with safety above all else.* It just made Trofmose more vulnerable.

The slope leveled, and the trees thinned. The shade of the forest lightened, and along with it, Tereka's mood. They were getting close. She took a few steps into the clearing and paused, allowing her shoulders to sag.

Naco bumped into her. "Why'd you stop?"

"I think we need a rest, don't you?" She sank onto the dried pine needles covering the ground, inhaling their tranquilizing scent.

He sat next to her. "Sure will be good to be home. Have a few days of regular meals and all that."

"Don't you know it." All they'd eaten during their time on the run was what they could pilfer from the fields. She flexed her fingers. "And I miss my bow."

The rescued traders staggered into the clearing and, one by one, dropped to the ground. Sweat dripped from both of Yeroblat's chins and his face flushed a dusky purple. Two of the older traders lay flat on their backs, their chests heaving.

Waukomis gave her a grin. "Is this our new home? I don't think it will be too warm in winter."

Tereka laughed. "No, just a spot to rest."

Kemet sat beside her. "Would you like me to search for something to eat? Or water?"

Ever since Tereka had rescued Kemet, he'd dogged her, constantly seeking her out, offering assistance and conversation. As annoying as she found it, she understood he was trying hard to make up for what had passed between them. She couldn't help but fall back into the easy friendship they'd once shared. A smile pulled at the corners of her lips when she thought about the days when all she had to worry about was making a fair trade. Her throat thickened. She'd never have that simple, safe life again.

Her lot was with the outcasts and fugitives. Which, if she was honest with herself, wasn't all bad. It was a more authentic life—a braver, more robust existence. And her companions, the former prisoners, had all become friends. Or at least allies, as unlikely as that had seemed when she first met them.

She shivered at the memory of her initial terrifying encounter with Relio and Sebezh. And warmed at the growing friendship between her and Alikse, Savinnia, and Naco.

For a while, she'd thought Naco felt more than friendship, but now he didn't seem to care. He even backed away when Kemet was around, as if giving him room to pursue her.

Maybe she'd mistaken Naco's kindness for something else. Throughout the long winter, he'd never tried to kiss her. So perhaps she'd been wrong about him. She swallowed the lump in her throat and wrenched her thoughts back to the present. "Thank you, Kemet, but no. We're just a few hours from the Risker camp. They'll help us."

His eyes narrowed at the mention of Riskers, making her press her lips together. Disappointing, that he couldn't give up the old prejudices.

To hide her reaction, she looked around the clearing, noticing that Naco had moved away from her and was staring down the trail. A quick count told her they were missing two men. Alikse and Sebezh.

Scrambling to her feet, she darted to Naco's side. "Do you see them?"

He shook his head. "Listen."

She closed her eyes and concentrated. The underbrush crackled, rhythmic crunches that spoke of a man striding rather than an alloe rat scurrying. More crunches. Then a shout.

Her eyes flew open. Had bandits ambushed Alikse and Sebezh?

Naco was already sprinting down the trail. She flew after him. The shouts grew louder, but from the deep rumble of one voice, she knew Alikse was doing the yelling.

A few more footsteps and they rounded a bend. The muscles of Alikse's massive shoulders bulged as he held a slender, dark-haired man by the throat while Sebezh looked on, scowling.

Tereka pushed past Naco. "Alikse, who have you caught?"

The captive jerked his head up and stared at her with wide, startled eyes.

Her jaw dropped. It was her brother Tirk. She hadn't seen him since the day he lied about her in court, and they sentenced her to the Prime Konamei's mines. "What are you doing here?"

"Looking for you." His voice was rough and strained. He squirmed in Alikse's grasp, as helpless to free himself as a mouse in an eagle's talons.

"Alikse, you can let him go. He's my brother."

Alikse released Tirk. He raised his eyebrows and shot a quizzical look at Tereka.

She thought quickly. Alikse and the others knew Tirk wasn't really her brother. But had Da told Tirk himself the truth? She didn't want to risk blurting that secret out quite yet. "Tarkio is his father." Maybe that would be enough explanation for now.

To her relief, no one questioned her.

"Tereka, please, I need to talk to you." Tirk rubbed his bruised neck.

"I'm not sure I want to listen."

"But you must."

"Why? So you'll think up more lies to tell about me?"

A bead of sweat ran down his nut-brown face. "Tereka, please. I am so sorry. Aunt Juquila told me nothing bad would happen to you…"

"You believed her?" She snorted.

Tirk winced. "Call me what you will, fool, *durak*…"

"*Yanshy*r?" asked Alikse.

"Stupid as an egg?" Naco suggested.

"No, stupider," said Sebezh.

"Yes, I suppose I deserve all that. And more." Tirk fixed a beseeching gaze on Tereka's face. "But you have to listen."

"Maybe later. Come with us." Without waiting for a reply, she turned and stalked up the hill. The sounds of laughter drifted through the trees. Now what? She quickened her stride until she reached the clearing.

Two newcomers were laughing with Waukomis. The first was her uncle Lilio, dressed in dark green trousers and a bright red shirt. The other, tall with the same nut-brown skin as Tirk, was Da.

She flung herself into his arms. "How did you find us?"

He pulled her in tightly. "The Riskers of Mikkeliad have been watching for you. When their guards saw you on the road, they sent word to me. Lilio and I were ready to come meet you."

Holding her at arm's length, he scanned her up and down. "No one was hurt?"

"No one. Except the guard we had to knock out. But he should be fine by now."

"Hello, Da."

With a jerk of his head, Da looked over Tereka's shoulder. "Tirk?" His eyes widened. "Why are you here?"

"I tried to tell Tereka. But she won't listen to me."

Da patted Tirk's cheek. "Do you blame her?" He turned to Tereka. "Lilio and I have news for you, and it seems your brother does as well. It's best we tell you all at once."

From Da's tone, Tereka didn't think his tidings were good. She raised her voice. "Everyone, if you please, listen."

Several moments passed before the rescued traders quieted enough for her to speak. "So. We've made it this far. You all know my da, Tarkio. This is his friend, Lilio."

A few traders muttered about barbarians. One shouted, "Are you taking us to the Riskers?"

Tereka hadn't told them that part of the plan, thinking it was better to get to safety first. "No, not exactly."

"Then where?"

She took a deep breath. "Well, you may have noticed that Kaberco is upset with you."

There were a few chuckles and nods, and some scattered curses.

"We are inviting you to live with us." She jerked her chin towards Naco, Alikse, and Sebezh. "And a few others."

"With outlaws?"

"That's as bad as living with lice-infested Risker savages."

"Live with you? In a cave?"

"Do I need to remind you that you are outlaws, too? And the Riskers aren't savages. They took us in last fall." Tereka pointed up the mountain. "Near the summit is a ruined guard tower. We've made it livable. There's room for all of you."

"Walk all the way up there?" Yeroblat sounded as if he'd rather go back to Kaberco's jail.

"It's not so bad once you get to the top," Naco said.

"That's right," said Alikse. "We hunt and fish. Grow and gather. The Riskers help."

Tereka crossed her arms and let the traders voice their objections. Some fretted about the uncertainty of living off the land and some worried that Kaberco would capture them. All had concerns about relying on savages to survive.

How would Tereka find the words to convince them? She

was tired, so tired. Thankfully, Naco and Alikse countered many of the arguments, explaining how they'd made the ruined tower more than just habitable. At times, Kemet spoke up, saying it didn't sound that bad to him.

"Easy for you to say," said Yeroblat. "I've a wife and five daughters. Will I ever see them again? What will happen to them now?"

Others joined him, their complaints about their families forming a raucous chorus.

When the shouting died down, Da stepped forward. "I don't think you understand. You can't go back. You were taken."

He looked around at the frowning traders. "A few days ago, Tirk sent a bird to me, in care of the Riskers of Zafrad, the next camp over. After you escaped from Trofmose, Kaberco issued a public decree to have Tereka killed on sight."

Tereka's throat tightened and her hands trembled. Had Kaberco found her in his rooms, he would have slayed her with his bare hands.

Da was still talking. "Tirk also informed me that Kaberco issued private orders stating if any of you are apprehended, you will be killed, as well. No taking. No trial. Just executed. Any guardsman could do the deed."

"So, there's no going back," murmured Yeroblat. "We'll have to stay here, perched up on the mountain like a flock of terrified birds."

Lilio and Da exchanged a glance that Tereka couldn't interpret. "Well, that's the thing," Da said.

"You can't all stay," Lilio added.

"What?" Tereka's stomach plummeted like a bird shot from the sky.

"Osip, uh, that's my father-in-law, for those of you who don't know," Lilio continued. "Osip consulted the elders of the nearest three camps. They're all in agreement. We consented to eight people staying in the ruin. And that was over many objections. We will not violate the treaty more than we already have. Only eight can stay. And only if you go up to the tower and stay there. No more jaunts to caravans or rescue missions."

A rumble of angry muttering broke out. Sebezh stepped forward. "Haven't you heard? That *balasy* Kaberco put a price on girly's head. Kill on sight. The same for all those we sprung. None of them can go anywhere. Unless they want to end up dead." He crossed his arms. "And neither can we."

16

Tereka leaned against a tree to steady herself, her heart a rock in her stomach. Death at the hand of guardsmen or bandits seemed to be her most likely fate.

Lilio sighed and turned his hands up. "There's nothing I can do to reverse the decision. The best I can offer is to help eight of you find another place to live. Far away from here."

"We understand," Tereka said. She swallowed the sour taste of disappointment. "You've done more than you should have. Do you have any idea where we could go?"

"There's a rumor of more ruins further north," Da said.

"Nothing where the weather is warmer?" Waukomis asked.

"Some ruins lie to the south, yes," Lilio said. "But living closer to Risker camps would put my people in danger. You'll just have to be uncomfortable if you want to live."

"Might be better to take our chances with the bandits," Sebezh growled.

"Or return to the pirates," Naco offered. "They seemed to like you, Sebezh."

Mutters soon turned to shouts. Tereka let them yell. To the

freed traders, Riskers were as bad as bandits and pirates. None of their options held any appeal.

When their argument waned, she appealed to Da. "What do you think?"

He ran a hand through his hair and met her gaze, sadness in his eyes. "Going north is your best choice. Take some of them with you. The rest can stay here."

She looked from Naco to Alikse to Sebezh. The latter scowled. "Oh, no, girly, I'm not going nowhere. I worked too hard all winter to let someone else prance in and enjoy it. Take someone else with you."

Da rubbed his chin. "You'll have to decide that later. I'll try to work something out with the traders with Risker licenses to see about helping with supplies."

"Please, Da. You can't," Tirk said, his voice tense and insistent.

Tereka pulled her eyebrows together. "Why not?"

"That's why I'm here." Her brother stepped closer. "Aunt Juquila sent me to look for Da. She ordered me to bring him back."

Tereka's heart rose to her throat. Tirk's mission could only mean Juquila had something in mind for Da. Whatever it was, it wasn't likely to be good.

She surveyed the group. Some of the freed traders were older. They wouldn't survive long in the wild. Yeroblat could hardly be expected to haul his bulk over mountain trails. He'd barely made it this far.

And Sebezh had a point. They'd toiled all winter. She couldn't imagine Relio giving up their home for others. She didn't want to ask it of any of them. Forcing them to abandon the tower would destroy any of the fragile spirit of cooperation she'd managed to establish.

Only one possibility remained. Da, she knew, would hate it. But the others? She chewed her lip. She'd have to persuade at least seven of them. Taking a deep breath, she said, "There is one other alternative."

All eyes turned to her. She stuck her chin in the air, knowing her proposal wouldn't be well-received. "Most of you know that when we freed our friends, Naco and I went to Kaberco's workroom."

Da's eyes widened. "You didn't."

"I did," Tereka said, trying to ignore her father's pained expression. "I wrote him a note. Then I noticed a missive from the Prime Konamei."

"Oh, joy," Sebezh said. "He knows about us?"

"No. Well, I'm not sure. In his letter, he informed Kaberco that an invading army was about to conquer Litavye." She folded her hands and waited.

A moment of silence, then her listeners all started shouting at once.

"How can this be? Everyone on the other side of the mountains died centuries ago."

"Invaders? Who will defend us?"

"Why hasn't the Prime Konamei fought back?"

Da, she noticed, didn't seem surprised at the idea of people still alive over the mountains. She wondered at that, but decided to question him later. It was more important to deal with the agitated men, all yelling and waving their hands in the air.

Naco whistled, the shrill sound halting the argument. In the ensuing calm, he pointed at Tereka and asked, "Did the Prime Konamei say anything else?"

"Not much. Just that Kaberco needed to keep the north quiet and to be ready. The Prime Konamei promised to fight off the enemy army."

"What does that have to do with us?" Waukomis asked.

"It means," Alikse said, "that now is a good time to make a move against Kaberco. While he's distracted."

"Um, I had a different thought," Tereka said, struggling to

keep her voice steady. "We could go to the invaders and offer our help in bringing down the Prime Konamei."

In the silence that followed, she noted Kemet's wide, shocked eyes, Naco's thoughtful gaze, and Da, shaking his head and mouthing the word "no."

Sebezh was the first to speak. "You can't be serious, girly."

"Why not?" She shrugged. "From what I gather, the invading army wants to unseat our rulers. So do we. Why not work together?"

"I can think of several of reasons," Lilio said. "Starting with, we don't know what these invaders' plans for Tlefas are once they've toppled the Prime Konamei."

Da shook his head. "Just because you have similar aims doesn't mean your intentions are the same. What you plan for good, they could intend for evil." His face was grave.

"How else will we find out if we don't ask?" Tereka said.

"Girly's got a point." Sebezh stepped close to her, pointed a finger in her face, then spoke low so no one could overhear. "I think you want to know if this invader is the Desired One, so it doesn't have to be you."

"And what's wrong with that?" she shot back. She moved away from him and raised her voice. "Here's the thing. Only eight can stay. If I leave, that means only seven have to go somewhere else."

"But if you go to the invaders, will you be able to leave if you want to?" Naco asked.

A sudden chill shot through Tereka's veins as she remembered what it was like being a helpless prisoner. She shook it off and studied Naco's tanned face and wrinkled brow. "I don't know. But I've been able to escape prison and pirates, and now Kaberco."

With a glance at the still-arguing traders, Lilio pulled her to the side. "Don't presume the amulets will save you from deliberate folly."

Naco, Sebezh, and Alikse drifted over. Tereka felt bad for

poor Da, left to deal with a pack of angry, frightened traders. She turned to Lilio with a huff. "I'm not presuming anything. I'm saying we need to make sure the Desired One isn't among the invaders before we oppose them. And if the Desired One is, we should work with that person. Right?"

"What's the Desired One?" Tirk asked, as he and Da gave up on pacifying the bickering traders.

"I'll explain later," Da said.

"Know this," Lilio said with a grimace. "The elders were clear. Anyone who leaves here cannot come back or even seek shelter in any Risker camp unless Kaberco rescinds his decree. We can't take the chance that a passing trader would see you and either kill you or turn us all in. Hide here or go far away."

His shoulders slumped and the corners of his mouth drooped. He looked around at the assembled group. "Osip tried. But they reminded him that last fall when you showed up, they only wanted to allow Tereka to stay. He talked them into allowing all eight on the promise of no more. Now they refuse to budge on the number. They don't care who stays, just so it's not more than eight."

"I think that's fair," said Naco. "And I'll go with you, Tereka."

Tereka jerked her head to stare at him. "What?"

"We've talked about this over and over. We can't stay on the mountain forever. It's time to do something. Seems to me, finding out if we want to ally with these invaders is a good way to start."

Reveling in the warmth of his eyes, Tereka smiled at him.

"I'm sure Savinnia will come as well," he added.

She glanced at Sebezh and Alikse.

Alikse nodded. Sebezh frowned, then spoke. "I'll go with you. Like he says. I'd rather do something than freeze up on that mountain."

"That's five," Tereka said. "Do you think we can count on Relio?"

"That *yanshyr* wouldn't miss this for anything," Sebezh said. "Neither would Hinat."

With a skip in her step, she rejoined Da and Tirk, who'd walked back to the now-calm traders. "I have good news," she said. "Seven of us will be leaving."

"To go where?" Da narrowed his eyes.

Tereka winced. "To find out if the invader is a worthy ally."

His mouth twisted into a scowl. "Tereka——"

"Can we talk about this later? The main thing is, we just need one more to leave."

By now, the others were listening intently.

Da rubbed his chin. "Are you thinking of Poales?"

She let out a long breath. "He's still frail from the fever he had last week." She chewed on her lower lip. "I think he'd want to come, but he can't even climb the stairs. If he doesn't go, then…" Tereka eyed the rescued traders. They all began talking at once, all explaining why they shouldn't be the one to go.

"You'll just have to draw lots," Lilio said.

As the rescued traders pointed at each other, Tereka assessed them. Yeroblat shouldn't go. She'd refuse him if he volunteered. Three of the older ones were slumped over, arms folded, eyes down. They didn't have the strength or the courage to build a home in the wilderness.

Two others were arguing with Da. "Why bother to rescue us if we are to be fed to the warboars?" one roared. "We might have been able to prove our innocence and regain our freedom."

Tereka almost laughed. By having them all taken, Kaberco had made a statement and would never admit it had been a mistake.

"I'll go."

Kemet had stepped forward. Waukomis' face crumpled. He vigorously shook his head.

"I'll go with you. Let the others stay here." Kemet looked at Tereka. "If you'll have me."

She didn't want him to come. She wanted him to be safe in the quieter life he'd always wanted. At least in the hideout, he'd be out of danger. She tapped her fingers on her lips. Could she count on him if things turned dangerous?

On top of that, he complicated matters. She wasn't sure she wanted to discover what his feelings were for her. Or hers for him. And she didn't want to deal with how Naco felt—or didn't feel—about it.

But, of course, she couldn't refuse. He was the youngest of the rescued traders, the most likely to survive the trip, and a superb archer. Only the sky-god knew what waited for them, but having another person who could fight had to be a good idea. Ignoring Naco's frown, she looked at Kemet. "Thank you." She faced the others. "And thank all of you." She laid a hand on Lilio's arm. "How long do we have to get ready?"

17

"Do you see anything?" Tereka tipped her head back to peer through the thick branches of the pine tree. Naco had been forced to climb high. Here in the middle part of the country, the oaks, ash and beech trees grew tall and their foliage was dark green and lush. Summer had asserted itself long before it had in the north, the air warming quickly as the sun rose.

Naco's voice floated down to her. A few pine needles fell on her head and a branch cracked. Several heartbeats later, Naco jumped to the ground.

"Well?"

"I saw them. An enormous camp, hundreds of tents, it looked like. On the plain south and west of Anbodu."

She answered Naco's grin with one of her own. After fifteen days of trekking through the mountains, they'd found the invading army. She silently thanked Da and Osip for the rough map they'd sketched, and for their advice to stick to the mountains until they were south of Anbodu, then to move west. Their wisdom was now proven. Tereka and her band had reached the lowlands in the territory controlled by the invaders, free of immediate danger from agents of Kaberco and the Prime Konamei.

Their travels had started well. As expected, Relio, Hinat, and Savinnia were eager to ally with the invaders and poke a stick in the Prime Konamei's eye, as Relio had put it. Poales had offered, but in the end, they decided he'd be the best one to stay behind. He could show the others what needed to be done to survive in the ruined tower and be the liaison between the traders and the Riskers.

The surprise had been Tirk's insistence on coming with them. He said he owed his sister whatever help he could give her. Juquila could think he'd gotten lost searching for Da or eaten by warboars. He didn't care.

He also didn't put much credence in Tereka's thoughts that the Desire One could be among the invaders. "Sounds like a bunch of fairy tales to me," he'd said. "Although, if the Prime Konamei outlawed any mention of the myth, maybe there is something to it."

That flash of insight from her brother made Tereka rub the back of her head and tug on her hair. She and Da had agreed not to tell Tirk about her true father and the possibility that the prophecy was about her. But would it be worse if he figured it out on his own?

Tereka wasn't sure she should have let Tirk come along at all. No matter what Da said, she didn't think she could trust him, the one she'd believed for so long to be her twin, who'd been her ally during the many years of abuse at the hands of the woman she called mother. With just a little prompting from Juquila, he'd turned on her. After that shocking betrayal, it would take a lot for him to regain her trust.

Da had tried to talk Tirk out of it, but her brother was adamant. In the end, she'd conceded. At least if Tirk was with her, he couldn't report anything to Juquila.

The problem, she realized, was that Tirk was not the only

one she didn't trust. If things went awry, who could she count on? Naco, Savinnia, and perhaps Relio or Alikse. Certainly not Sebezh.

And now, finally, they were about to approach the invaders. Her stomach fluttered and she rubbed her hands together. At long last, she'd meet the Desired One. And be free of this burden she felt so inadequate to bear.

But what if this newcomer wasn't the Desired One? Ice coursed through her veins and she froze as if cornered by a warboar. She didn't want to think about that.

Naco put a hand on her shoulder. "Tereka."

She looked into his face, his tawny eyes tight and concerned.

Scuffling on the path caused her to jerk her head to the side, muscles tensed for a fight. She let herself relax when she saw Tirk and Kemet approaching, Kemet in the lead.

He strode to Tereka. "What news?" As always, he ignored Naco's presence.

"Naco saw the camp," she said. "We're just about there." She glanced at the sky, the rose and lavender streaks of dawn fast disappearing under the rising summer sun. "Could you two tell the others? And get everyone packed up?"

"Sure," said Tirk with a grin. "Can't wait to see what Sebezh does when he finds the sand I put in his boots."

Kemet snickered, then gave Tereka a long look before following Tirk down the path. Tereka rolled her eyes. Tirk and Kemet seemed to think this journey was some great adventure, a chance to be free from the oppressive rules that taught them to fear everything, regulations that instructed them to cower from any danger, allowing someone else be bold and brave. They didn't realize their companions were getting tenser the closer they got to the invaders, and for a very good reason. These strangers could easily decide to not believe them and execute them as spies.

Tereka toyed with sending Tirk back but decided against it. He did have his uses, she had to admit. He'd been a good buffer between Kemet and Naco. Since he had no idea what was going on between the three of them, he was all the more effective.

Truth be told, she had no idea what was going on, either. She frowned as she followed Naco back to where they'd camped. Naco still kept his distance but glowered whenever Kemet came near her, while Kemet went out of his way to defer to whatever Tereka said. She snickered to herself, remembering Sebezh's comments about Kemet's slavish devotion. But she wasn't sure what Kemet felt about her. Was it guilt? Or did he want to resume things with her?

So far, he hadn't tried to talk with her, for which she was grateful. She wasn't sure how she could tell him she was no longer the girl she was before the Prime Konamei's copper mines. That girl was gone. Kemet needed someone unscarred by the corruption in the land. Someone who didn't wake up in the middle of the night panting and sweating, terrified that she was back in a prison camp.

Her pulse quickened. They'd now reached the final stage of their journey. On the way, they'd camped near Riskers who gave them fresh bread and snippets of news. The invaders had taken control of the south. As long as people went about their business and didn't cause trouble, the invaders left them alone. No one had been taken into slavery or pressed into service in the army. And most surprising of all, the invaders actually paid for the food they took. A small price, to be sure, but better than commandeering goods. All of which gave her hope that whoever led the invaders would at least listen to them.

When they reached the flat land, her breath came faster. They'd only been attacked by warboars once, bandits twice, and survived a lightning strike that torched the tree they huddled under to escape the rain. That, she knew, was the easy part. Now they had to convince these invaders that they wanted to help, that they weren't spies or saboteurs. If the news they'd heard was true, maybe the invaders' leader had benign intentions. Which made it more likely the Desired One had come.

They walked to the northwest and skirted a hill. A group of riders on horseback were galloping toward them. Tereka shaded her eyes and squinted. Surely, they weren't some of the Prime Konamei's guards. They had to be part of the invading army. The blood whooshed in her ears, driven by her quickening heart.

She pulled her bow from her shoulder and strung it, then took three arrows from the quiver at her hip. Several of the others did the same. Naco, Relio, Alikse, and Tirk drew swords. She wiped her sweating palms on her tunic and continued to stride toward the riders, her head held high.

As they drew near, she let out a breath. These weren't the Prime Konamei's guards. These riders wore long tunics the color of sand tied with brightly colored sashes, some green, some yellow. They all wore hats so closely fitted they looked molded to their skulls. The leader's hat had a spike with a knot on top.

"I think we've found our new friends," Relio said.

"Sure hope they think that about us," Naco said.

Tereka ignored them and the sour churning in her stomach, and kept walking until she was ten paces from the leader's chestnut horse. He stopped, his nine riders moving in a circle around her group. She tilted her head to look up at the man. "Peace and safety."

The man frowned. "Why are you trespassing on Emperor Shagonar's lands?"

She tipped her head to the side. To her surprise, she'd been able to easily understand his speech despite his odd accent. So Emperor Shagonar was the ruler of the invaders. "We mean no harm, if you please." She tried to keep her tone smooth and calming. "We came to offer our services." She hoped the man didn't catch the quaver in her voice that betrayed her fear.

"Services?" The man's thick black eyebrows raised. A few of the riders snickered.

Their mockery made her stiffen her spine and speak with more confidence. "Yes. We're tired of the Prime Konamei's rule. We believe the Emperor may be our best hope for freedom."

"So you say." The man's frown deepened. "Then why are you standing before me, with arrows nocked and swords drawn?"

"If you please, we're fugitives from one of the Prime Konamei's ephors. When we spotted you, we didn't know if you were his guardsmen or not." She gave him what she hoped was a disarming smile and shrugged. "In dangerous times, it's prudent to be careful, no?"

"Hmm." He raked his eyes over Tereka, then scowled at her friends. "Surrender your weapons, and we won't kill you. We'll see if His Loftiness is interested in your"—he snorted— "services."

Tereka exchanged looks with Relio and Naco. The latter shrugged and sheathed his sword. "Not much we can do against riders."

She nodded, replaced her arrows in her quiver, unstrung her bow, and placed the bow and quiver on the ground. Then she stepped back.

When all had placed their weapons in a pile, the leader pointed at them. "I see swords, bows and quivers. Do you have any knives?"

With a smirk, Sebezh added a pair of long knives to the pile. The rest of them did the same.

"Are you sure that's all?" the man asked. "Because we will search you."

A few more knives landed on the mound.

"Good." He ordered three of his men to search Tereka and her group, and three others to collect the weapons. "Carefully, now. Just in case His Loftiness wants them returned to their owners. But just to be sure, hand over your packs."

Tereka slung her pack to the ground and stared into the distance as one of the riders felt her up and down, relieved when he finished. He'd been quick and businesslike. Not like the leering and groping guards in the prison who let their hands linger where they pleased. To her relief, he hadn't found her amulets. They had a way of concealing themselves when they didn't want to be found, and apparently, this was one of those times. She was still marveling over this ability when the leader motioned for Tereka and her group to walk toward the war camp.

An hour later, they were seated in a round tent with white felt walls and a matted floor, which the soldiers called a yurt. A brazier stood in the center, a hole in the roof open to the sky. Cushions dotted the floor. They were told that food would be brought to them, and they weren't to leave the yurt for any reason. Or they'd be killed on the spot.

The hours dragged as day turned to night and still, they hadn't been summoned. Tereka spent the time pacing around the yurt and wringing her hands. Had she made a terrible mistake? Did the delay mean the Emperor didn't take them seriously and would have them killed when he got around to it? Or was he occupied with weightier matters?

When the yurt was nearly dark, a soldier entered, bearing a large jug. He lit the fire in the brazier. He poured water from the jug into a teapot and set it over the flames. A second soldier came in carrying a tray. When he set it on the floor, Tereka saw it held a collection of mugs, a loaf of bread, and cheese. The bread and cheese were already sliced, giving them no excuse to ask for a knife.

Once they'd eaten, the only light in the yurt was from the tiny flames in the brazier. When they wearied of speculating when they'd see the Emperor, they unrolled the mats piled by the door and settled down to sleep.

Laying on her back, Tereka stared at the moonlight that spilled through the hole in the roof. Somehow, she thought joining the invasion would be easier.

18

A fter two days of pacing around the yurt, Tereka considered its felt walls to be as hard as a prison cell carved into rock. She and her friends argued endlessly about what they should do, while she wondered if she'd led them all to their deaths.

Late in the afternoon of the third day, a soldier appeared and announced that the Emperor was waiting to see them. Tereka's heart skipped a beat. She jumped to her feet and straightened her wrinkled tunic, glancing at her companions. They were bedraggled and dirty, having worn the same clothing for days, since the last time they'd been able to wash them in a mountain stream. That seemed like ages ago. None of them resembled warriors or sages or someone whose help an emperor would welcome.

She put her hand on her side, fingering the small bag tied into her pocket, the pouch that held her five dragonfly amulets. The amulets were still, not vibrating as if danger was near. She stood a little straighter. Surely coming here was the right move. She hoped.

Her friends' jaws were tight, their mouths pressed shut. She was sure she looked the same, tormented by the same thought—this summons could mean the start of an alliance or the end of their lives.

Lifting her chin, Tereka followed the soldier from the yurt. No one spoke. Naco walked on one side of her, Relio on the other. Some of the weight she carried felt lighter. Whatever was going to happen, she wouldn't face it alone. Overwhelming gratitude washed through her for everyone who'd insisted on coming with her on this dangerous mission. They could have found a place in the mountains to wait out the war. Yet they chose to go straight into the heart of it with her.

Four others accompanied the soldier who'd summoned them, all bearing short, curved swords. Tereka shook her head. Did they really think she and her companions would attempt to escape in the middle of a camp of armed men?

Their escort marched them through the camp, through neat lines of identical white yurts, past soldiers cleaning weapons or sharpening swords. She scrutinized the men. Many were tall, with olive skin and black hair, like their escort. Others were even taller, with dark brown skin and flaming red hair. Still others were short and stocky, with pasty white faces under black hair. Then a few blond men with golden-tan faces strode by. All wore black leather armor over red tunics and sand-colored leggings, along with determined looks on their faces. The Prime Konamei's guards could no more best these warriors than they could capture the moon with a fishing net.

After muttering to himself, Relio elbowed Tereka. "What do you think, girly? If you took these people and bred them together, what would you get?"

She thought for a heartbeat, then stared at him. "What we have in Tlefas. A mix of everything. Only a handful who are very dark or very pale." She glanced at the soldiers once more. "If I doubted before, now I know. Our ancestors fled from them."

Relio snorted. "Let's hope they're not so bloodthirsty as we've been told."

They walked down several rows of yurts to the center of the camp. Here the white structures were bigger and stood upon wooden platforms. Some had painted doorways, the blues, reds, and yellows adding an odd note of cheer.

Their guide led them to the largest yurt, tall and wide, towering over the others. A red banner flapped in the breeze overhead. The banner bore a black scorpion, its claws outstretched to the flag's corners. The yurt's red door had a golden handle and was studded with black stones that glinted in the sunlight, arranged in a mosaic that formed twin scorpions. Thin gold lines in intricate patterns were woven into the felt that bordered the door.

Tereka shivered. This Emperor Shagonar must be very wealthy if he could afford to make even his door handles of gold.

The soldier herded them into the yurt. Tereka's eyes widened. The inside was bigger than her grandparents' house. Tall poles supported the roof. Carpets woven in bright shades of red, green, and yellow covered the floor. A red screen blocked the back half from view. A man she assumed to be a scribe sat behind a writing table piled with documents.

Near the middle, next to a brazier were two large chairs with carved arms, both made of black, glistening stone. Red gems studded the chairs' legs.

Two richly dressed people occupied the chairs. The man, Tereka thought, must be Emperor Shagonar. He looked to be about ten years older than her da and had smile lines around his eyes and mouth. His eyes were tawny, his olive skin unlined, and he lounged on his chair as if he were completely at ease with the world. She pulled her eyebrows together. The Emperor's casual pose wasn't what she expected from the Desired One.

A woman occupied the chair next to him. She had long dark hair and skin the same olive color as the Emperor. Like him, she wore a tunic that extended to her knees, tied at the waist with a sash. Her tunic was scarlet, with gold and silver embroidery forming intricate patterns. Leggings of the same shade covered her lower limbs, and her feet were encased in red slippers with upturned toes. Her hands were hidden in her wide sleeves. A black rabbit dozed on her lap.

Unlike Emperor Shagonar, the woman sat stiff and straight, as if her spine were the shaft of an arrow. In contrast to the Emperor's warm, tawny eyes, hers were cold and dark gray. Tereka at first thought the woman to be the Emperor's age, or perhaps a little younger. Then she winced as if in great pain, the skin around her eyes wrinkling and her mouth tensing. At that moment, she seemed older than anyone Tereka had ever met.

The man at the writing table spoke, his tone like someone used to being obeyed. "Who are you, and why are you here?"

Tereka's mouth went dry. She swallowed hard and licked her lips. "If you please, we are seeking Emperor Shagonar."

The guard behind her punched her in the back. "Your Loftiness," he growled.

She struggled to regain her breath. "My apologies, Your Loftiness."

"Well, you've found him," said the man on the throne, raising an eyebrow. "Who are you?"

So she'd guessed correctly. "Your Loftiness, my name is Tereka Sabidur, and I am from Trofmose in the north. My friends and I are fugitives from the ephor of Trofmose. We came to offer you our help."

Deep wrinkles appeared between the woman's eyes. "Help us do what?"

Her heart hammering, Tereka struggled to speak. "If you please, to depose the Prime Konamei." Now she'd done it. Committed herself. And all the others.

The Emperor smiled. "Why would you want to do that?"

Tereka took a deep breath. *To learn if you are the Desired One.* She swallowed those words before they could burst from her mouth. She and her companions had discussed this over and over during their trip and had argued about it while they'd been confined to the yurt waiting to appear before the Emperor. Now she'd find out if the answer they'd prepared would be sufficient. Or doom them from the start.

She explained how she'd been taken on false charges and sent to a prison camp to mine copper, where she'd met most of the others. She told of their escape and how they'd hidden in the mountains. As Da and Osip had instructed, she didn't say the Riskers had helped them. Nor did she mention prophecies or amulets.

The woman sat back and frowned. "That doesn't make sense to me."

"Why not?" the Emperor asked.

Fixing her cold eyes on Tereka, the woman said, "If you had a safe place to hide, why leave it? Why risk everything to come to us?"

Without understanding why, Tereka had the sense this woman could see deep into her soul. The dragonfly amulets grew cold, chilling Tereka's side through the cloth of her tunic. They'd never done that before. "Well, Your Loftiness, it's because of what we did a few weeks ago." She shot a nervous glance at Naco and Relio. "We stopped a few caravans and told the traders the Prime Konamei has been lying to them."

Motionless except for the blinking of her eyes, the woman stared at Tereka, who took her silence as a sign of interest and continued. "After the second one, the ephor of Trofmose rounded up eight traders. Our friends. So we, um, we broke into his jail and freed them."

The Emperor laughed. The woman frowned at him. "Where are they now?" Her voice was harsh and suspicious.

"We left them in our hiding place, where we'd spent the winter. Most of them are older and in poor health." She hoped the woman didn't see through that half-truth. Something about the woman's icy demeanor told her lying wouldn't be tolerated. "If we all stayed there, we probably wouldn't make it through the coming winter."

"Why didn't you seek help from the Riskers?" The woman's question was pointed, almost like an accusation.

Tereka held her breath. These people knew about the Riskers? What else did they know? "They weren't able to help us."

"Or didn't want to." The woman held Tereka's gaze captive for several heartbeats, then exchanged a long glance with the Emperor.

Fearful about the outcome, Tereka pressed her lips together. Was this woman the Emperor's wife? She seemed more than a consort, almost as if she wielded power in her own right.

The longer the silence dragged on, the harder Tereka found it to control her shaking knees. Sweat formed on the back of her neck, dampness under her arms. Part of her wanted to tell them about her amulets and the power they held, in the hope that the Emperor would be more willing to welcome them.

But she'd promised Osip, Lilio, and Da over and over to keep that knowledge to herself until she was convinced beyond doubt it would be to her advantage. Like an arrow once released, she'd never be able to recall the words once spoken. She worried her lip between her teeth and concentrated on staying still, on keeping her chin up.

At last, the woman spoke, addressing the Emperor. "I see no reason to trust them. Or to think they'd be of any use to us in battle. Perhaps we can use them for archery practice. Let them run a bit, see who can hit them."

A few of Tereka's companions gasped. Relio mumbled something that sounded like a curse. Whatever he said, Tereka agreed.

Emperor Shagonar shook his head. "I'm not so sure, Dami. Let's ask Syz." He turned his head to the side.

The man at the writing table rose and approached. "Let's think a moment," he said. "Perhaps we could find a use for them. They could tell us all they know about this ephor of Trofmose, this Kaberco who doesn't seem ready to accept your rule. They might have valuable information. Even if, as you point out, they wouldn't be much help in battle."

The woman frowned, vertical lines forming in the center of her forehead. She raised a hand, keeping it hidden in her sleeve, and rubbed her temple. Then she addressed Tereka. "You heard him. Will you tell my brother, the Supreme Jianjun of our armies, all you know about this ephor, how things work in your country, and anything else you can think of that will help us depose the Prime Konamei?"

Tereka's knees wobbled, and she pressed a hand to her heart. So this Dami, whoever she was, would give them a chance and not kill them immediately. She nodded. "Of course."

"Good. Syzyan, I leave them in your hands." The woman's penetrating gaze did not leave Tereka, a gaze that felt like a shard of ice piercing her heart. "Just make sure you're useful. We won't feed anyone who isn't."

The one named Syzyan told them to follow him. Tereka was relieved to escape the woman's scrutiny, her cold, hard eyes. A chill crawled up Tereka's spine, and she shivered. Something about the woman called Dami made her very nervous indeed.

19

Tereka and her companions followed Syzyan out of the yurt. He summoned a soldier, a burly man with dark bushy eyebrows, and ordered the man to take them back to their quarters. "I'll speak with you all in the morning," he said. "Go easy and well."

A breathless, sweating soldier ran up to Syzyan. He stood straight and touched the first two fingers of his right hand to his temple, lowered the arm to hold it horizontally across his chest, and bowed his head.

"Yes?" Syzyan said.

The man raised his head and held a scroll out to Syzyan. "A dispatch from Noyan-u Darga Orlok, Loftiness."

Syzyan took the scroll, nodded, and disappeared into the Emperor's yurt.

Stumbling after the bushy-eyebrowed soldier, Tereka was barely conscious of Naco's hand gripping her arm, holding her upright. Her amulets were lumps of ice against her side, chilling the blood that surged through her veins. Her heart raced even faster than when she was quivering under that woman's piercing stare.

When they arrived at their yurt, the soldier pointed for them to enter. "Food will be brought."

Tereka stepped inside. Naco helped her sit on a mat. She released a long breath and let her shoulders slump.

"Are you alright?" he asked.

She held up a trembling hand. "Guess that was harder than I expected."

Relio dropped next to her. "Yeah, especially the part about target practice."

"Why did we come here?" Sebezh asked.

"Because you volunteered," Relio snarled.

Sebezh curled his lip. "I didn't come to be a prisoner. That could have been arranged without all that walking."

He had a point. "Listen," Tereka said. "Once they learn to trust us, things should get better."

Tirk and Kemet sat across from her, their eyes wide. "This doesn't feel safe to me," said Kemet.

Alikse and Hinat nodded their agreement. Alikse lowered his bulky frame to the ground. "That woman scared me. She could teach that *yanshyr* of a prison commandant a thing or two about keeping order."

Savinnia sat down next to Tereka. "You look pale."

"So do you." Sweating as if she'd sprinted up a mountain, Tereka wondered how she could be so cold and so hot at the same time. She put a hand on her side and fingered the amulets. They'd lost that icy cold feeling that had unnerved her. Slowly, she took a few deep breaths. "I'll be fine once we eat."

Kemet moved to kneel in front of her. "Are you sure?"

"Yes, yes." She had to smile at his concern. Naco pushed a tin mug of water into her hand. She grasped it and gulped the contents down. She hadn't realized how thirsty she'd been.

The scraping sound of the door opening startled her. Evening sunshine spilled into the dim yurt, which had previously only been lit by the fire in the brazier. Her stomach grumbled. She hoped whoever had come was bringing the promised food.

Her eyes swung to the door. A servant—or so Tereka guessed from the plain brown tunic and leggings she wore— entered the yurt carrying a large urn. She was followed by another bearing a covered tray, and a third with two large baskets. They were all followed by a young man dressed in a cobalt-blue tunic and black trousers made of a fabric that shimmered in the light. He stood back, arms folded, watching the servants light six tall candles, set out covered platters, plates, and spoons, and place a pot of water over the flames of the brazier. One picked up the full waste bucket and replaced it with an empty one. Then the servants filed out of the yurt.

Tereka raised her chin and studied the blue-clad youth, who, so far, hadn't uttered a single word. He was dressed in the same style as Shagonar, although his clothing was plainer, more like Syzyan's rather than the opulence of the Emperor's. She wondered why he was there and if she should address him.

Finally, he spoke. "Why do you not eat? The food was brought for you."

Relio laughed. "In that case, I don't know what we're waiting for." He sat at the low table, grabbed a plate, and removed the cover from one of the platters. The aroma of spiced meat made Tereka's mouth water.

The others crowded around the table. Tereka struggled to her feet, a few black spots dancing in front of her. Naco appeared at her side and helped her to move to a cushion on the floor. An instant later, Kemet set a full plate in front of her, shooting a glare at Naco. Tereka dropped her eyes to avoid laughing. This was ridiculous.

She took a bite, savoring the warmth in her mouth. Strength rushed down her arms and legs, and her lightheadedness vanished. She turned the young man. "If you please, we don't know who you are."

He moved to sit across from her. "I am Farnaz." He paused. "I think you met my relatives."

"Emperor Shagonar is your father?" Naco asked.

Farnaz smiled. "No. My uncle. The Supreme Jianjun Syzyan is my father."

"What's a Supreme Jianjun?" Relio asked.

"The general commanding all the Emperor's armies, over all the other jianjuns."

Tereka considered that. Armies. The Emperor had more than one. "And the woman with Emperor Shagonar?"

"Damira, my father's sister."

It took her a moment to work out the family relationships. Her tongue was heavy in her mouth and she couldn't think of anything to say. She groped through her mind for words as if searching for something in the dark. "Thank you for bringing the food, Your Loftiness. You didn't have to do it yourself."

He tipped his head and smiled. "You're right, I didn't. And I'm not lofty." He lifted one shoulder in half a shrug. "Just Farnaz will do. I came because I was curious about you."

"As we told your—"

Farnaz held up a hand. "I know what you told my uncle. That's not what I'm interested in."

Naco picked up a round of flatbread and tore off a piece. "What are you interested in?"

With a little smile as if embarrassed, Farnaz turned to Savinnia, who was seated next to him. He gestured at her dress. "Well, for one thing, why do all the villagers wear gray clothes?" He pointed. "Most of you wear the same color, except for those stripes on your shoulders. What does that mean?"

Relio chuckled. "It's how they keep track of everyone. We all wear gray. The colors say what your job is." He pointed at Alikse. "That blue means he's a builder. Or should be."

"Should be?" Farnaz tipped his head to the side.

Alikse spit an olive pit into his hand. "If you heard our

story, you know we're fugitives. These clothes, well, we borrowed them."

"She's a trader," Relio pointed at Tereka, "or was one. So she should be wearing brown. Like him." He jerked his chin toward Kemet. "Those are the rules. The Prime Konamei's guards wear black, traders, brown, gray for everyone else."

Savinnia leaned forward. "Is it not the same where you're from?"

"Oh, not at all. The different regions have different fashions, but the colors and cloth are anyone's choice."

"I like these people," Savinnia said.

Tirk piled rice onto a plate. "We choose to dress the same, to make sure everything is fair."

Farnaz raised an eyebrow. "Really? How does that work?"

While they ate, Tirk talked about the safety and fairness the Prime Konamei had promised to all. Tereka watched Farnaz closely throughout. He didn't say much, just encouraged Tirk with innocent-sounding questions.

She exchanged a glance with Naco, who shrugged. Relio pressed his lips together and slowly nodded. She agreed. Better to let Tirk babble on about the Prime Konamei's rules. After all, they wanted to help Shagonar overturn the old regime. How much harm could it do to tell Farnaz about taxes and trade routes? Still, she felt his visit wasn't as innocent as he pretended.

When they'd eaten all the stew, rice, and vegetables, and had drunk three pots of tea, Farnaz stepped to the door of the yurt. Servants entered, took away the plates and platters, and brought more water for tea plus loaves of round bread about the size of large apples.

Naco held one up. "What is this?" He frowned at his hand. "It's sticky."

"Red bean buns." Farnaz took one in his own fingers. "They're Uzhasovian."

"What's that?" Tereka asked.

"Uzhasovia? You don't know of it?"

She shook her head.

"Vernia? Otrechia? Razdelia?"

"No, we've never heard of them."

"Do you know anything of the lands over the mountains?" Farnaz asked, taking a seat on the floor near her.

"Not much." she confessed. "We know that centuries ago, to escape a civil war that never ended, people from the lands across the mountains fled here and established the nation of Tlefas. For all we knew, everyone there was dead."

He smiled. "We call your country the Abandoned Lands." He poured himself a cup of tea. "Well. Yes, there was a war. It lasted so long that all the men from your part of the world were drafted into it and died. The remaining people moved east. Hence, the land here was abandoned. The war dragged on for several centuries. We called it the Endless War. It didn't end because the warlords didn't want it to. Then my father, aunt, and uncle decided to do something about it. They found a way to end it. My uncle has ruled Razdelia ever since."

"Why are you here?" Tereka asked. She studied his face. Was his uncle the Desired One? When Farnaz wrinkled his brow, Tereka hurried to explain. "Not here in the yurt, here in Tlefas."

Something flickered in Farnaz's blue eyes. "Once we liberated our own country, we thought we were done. But we heard your people are oppressed and we want to help them, too."

"But won't starting a war be worse than leaving us how we are?" asked Relio.

"Perhaps," said Farnaz. "But that doesn't change the fact that you are not free people."

Tereka couldn't argue with him on that point. She chewed on a bean bun, nearly moaning at the sweetness, allowing the others to debate just how oppressed the people of Tlefas were.

Even taciturn Hinat jumped in to denounce the questor who had ordered him taken and sent to the mines.

When the conversation lagged, she asked, "Can you tell us more about Razdelia?"

"Oh, yes." Farnaz sat up straight. He described the four countries and their cultures. Tereka had a hard time following what he was saying.

"So let me get this straight," Alikse said. "Uzhasovians are tall, brown-skinned, and red-haired, love to quote proverbs and fight in wars, and think they are better than everyone else."

The corners of Farnaz's mouth twitched. "True, but I wouldn't tell them that."

"Izolliyans are short, have white skin and black hair, live in a land of volcanoes and ice, use frozen rivers as roads in the winter, and want to be left alone," Kemet said.

"Vernians are tall, blond, love symmetry and poetry, and allow women to rule," Savinnia said. "Sounds like a place I'd like to go."

"Otrechians are olive-skinned with different colored eyes and love their horses like members of their own families," put in Naco.

"Of course," Farnaz said. "Our horses are our life. They are what makes us free."

"And Otrechians believe Vernians are barbarians," said Sebezh.

Farnaz gave them a wry smile. "Well, some. Not all."

"Really?" Tereka said. "We have something similar, with the villagers convinced the Riskers are savages. How did you get beyond that?"

"Well, it started when my aunt and uncle defeated the warlord trying to take over the country. Once their rule as Emperor and Empress began, they vowed to treat all equally, not just their own Otrechian people. Then her brother married a Vernian. And had me."

Tereka looked him over. That explained it. Farnaz had Jianjun Syzyan's thin upper lip, strong, stubborn chin, and broad shoulders, but his skin was golden rather than olive and his eyes blue instead of gray.

Before she could come up with another question, Farnaz asked one of his own. "Who are these Riskers?"

Now she knew she'd been right to be a nervous about Farnaz and his questions. This was approaching dangerous ground.

Naco jumped in to answer. "They are descendants of people who didn't want to trade their freedom for safety and all the Prime Konamei's rules. We have a treaty with them. They contain the bandits and wild beasts that roam the mountains. The Prime Konamei leaves them alone and allows limited trade."

Out of the corner of her eye, Tereka studied Farnaz. His hands were clasped tightly together, not relaxed like when they'd been discussing the fashions of Razdelia and the literature of the four races that occupied it. He was truly interested in Riskers. *Why?*

Farnaz sipped his tea. "I wondered who they were."

Before she could respond, Tirk did. "Our da, mine and Tereka's, had a license to trade with the Riskers. He could tell you all about them."

"Is that so?" Farnaz asked. "Did he ever take you there with him?"

Tereka's pulse drummed in her ears. Now she thoroughly regretted having brought Tirk.

"No," he said. "Da never took me." His face twisted, then he turned to Tereka. "Did he ever take you there?"

Her throat constricted. What could she say? "Oh, once or twice." She shrugged. "It wasn't very interesting." *Sky-god, forgive me.*

"We've heard all kinds of odd stories about them." Farnaz

ran a finger around the rim of his tea cup. "Like they have magic charms, maybe amulets."

"We've heard that, too," Sebezh said.

It was all Tereka could do to not fling her tea in his face.

"Yeah, that we have." Relio snickered. "But who can believe tales like that? It's like believing in Marka the Talking Duck."

"It's a Singing Goose, you *durak*," Sebezh said.

Farnaz laughed. "Whichever it is, it sounds like a child's fable, like the one we have about a magic being that will grant your wishes if you rub the side of an oil lamp." He sipped more tea, then offered to pour for Savinnia. He filled her cup, then offered her a second bean bun. "There was another story we heard. Some myth about a Desired One destined to bring a new order to the land. Have you heard it?"

The muscles in Tereka's neck tightened. He was slick, this Farnaz. Pretending to fuss over Savinnia, to make sure she had tea and sweet buns. All the while getting them relaxed and talking. She forced a laugh. "Desired One? Desired for what?" She looked at Naco, then Relio. "You know anything about that?"

"Not me, girly." Relio chortled. "Maybe you should send some soldiers to an inn and listen to what people say after they've had some ale. You might hear all kinds of tall tales."

"Especially now the weather's turning," said Naco. "Chilly, long nights bring out all the wild stories."

The tension in Tereka's neck eased. *I'll have to thank them later.* The conversation shifted to the weather in central Tlefas during the autumn months.

The door opened, and the servants returned. Tereka's eyes widened at the sight of the bundles they carried. She'd thought she'd never see her pack again.

Farnaz stood up. "Now that you have your possessions, tomorrow you can go to the bathhouse. Then, I believe, my father will want to talk with you." He stepped to the door and paused. "I hope you'll be comfortable here. You will be, as long as you're useful."

20

Damira drained her tea and set the empty cup down on the table before her, careful to not break the delicate porcelain. Her blackened, shriveled fingers were clumsy and could barely sense the warmth the tea imparted to the cup. She rubbed her aching head, straining to listen to the reports Syzyan was reading aloud.

"What does it mean, Syz?" she asked.

Syzyan lowered the scroll. "It means, Dami, that the southerners are coming around to accepting our rule. We've given them a bit of freedom in exchange for not fighting us. So far, that seems to be working."

"At least the south is cooperating." She rested her hand on the warm soot-colored fur of her rabbit, caressing the slumbering animal.

A map lay spread in front of them. Syzyan pointed to a thick line. "We've also been able to intercept several caravans with grain and vegetables from the central regions."

"Good," put in Shagonar. "I'd hate to go without fresh bread."

"More to the point," Damira said, "it might help starve

the northern region into submission. Who does this Kaberco think he is?"

"He seems to be the only ephor willing to risk his own safety to protect his people." Syzyan shrugged. "For that, I have to admire him."

Damira scowled. Kaberco was in their way. She needed to conquer the land, and quickly. Then and only then could she put the amulets aside and give her aching head a rest. And maybe, just maybe, she'd get some of the normal feeling back in her fingers and toes, and a respite from the stinging pain.

Shagonar plucked a candied nut from a plate and crunched it between his teeth. "Syz, what do you think of those fugitives? The ones who say they are fleeing Kaberco?"

"That's a good question."

"They're spies," Damira said.

"How do you know?" Syzyan asked.

"I just know." She didn't want to admit that her amulets were uneasy. Syzyan never liked hearing her talk about them that way, as if some sentience was behind the power they gave her.

"She could be right, Syz." Shagonar tossed a nut in the air and caught it in his mouth. "I had the sense they were holding something back."

"See? I'm not the only one." Damira flashed Shagonar a broad smile. He reached for her hand and massaged her fingers.

"They could be spies," Syzyan said. "But, if I were them, I don't think I'd tell everything I knew. I'd want to hang onto a few tidbits." He smiled. "Just to make sure the people in power continued to think I was useful." He looked Damira in the eye. "I still remember what it was like to be a fugitive, seeking refuge anywhere I could find it, unsure whom to trust and whom to fear."

Damira leaned back and let out a breath. She hadn't forgotten, either. Those horrible weeks spent crossing the desert after an Izolliyan war band massacred their families. When they were robbed by bandits, turned away by Riskers, and threatened with prison by the guards who served the Prime Konamei.

Heat climbed up her neck, and she narrowed her eyes. No, she'd never forget. "Maybe we should kill them. Just to be sure. And to warn anyone else who wants to send spies."

Her brother stiffened and Shagonar's fingers stilled. After a moment, he continued his gentle rubbing. "Well," he said, "we don't have to decide today. Let's keep an eye on them and find out what they know. They could be telling the truth."

She let out a huff. As much as she hated to admit it, Tereka and her band looked like fugitives. The part about the Riskers refusing to help rang true. Just to please her brother and husband, Damira was willing to wait, to learn more about the strangers. Perhaps she was overreacting to assume they were spies.

"I agree," said Syzyan. "There's a lot we don't know about how this government works and who holds the power."

Syzyan could be right. He was, occasionally. But her amulets were jittery. And when they were jittery, her feet and hands stung, and her head ached. She rubbed the rabbit's silky fur, finding little relief in its warm softness.

"They could also tell us about Kaberco as a person," her brother continued. "That's information we can use."

The air before Damira's eyes rippled, signaling the onset of a ferocious headache. "If they tell us the truth."

"We'll question them separately, and over several days," Syzyan said. "Soon we'll know who is lying and who isn't."

Kill them. Kill them.

Damira took a few deep breaths, fighting to suppress the fiendish voices in her head. Her amulets had never been so agitated. She didn't like it. Her thoughts tossed and swirled like dry sand in a howling desert wind. Letting Syzyan interrogate the fugitives would please both him and Shagonar. But the pain was stinging and stabbing its way up her legs. Killing the strangers might be the way to ease the agony. Whenever she thought of executing them, her pain lessened and the amulets seemed to calm. The amulets were telling her to dispose of the spies.

But Syzyan and Shagonar made good points. They could use more information about the people they were about to conquer and rule. Gleaning it from these fugitives would save them the trouble of sending spies.

Syzyan tapped his fingers against his chin. "We also might be able to use them in another way. Perhaps as envoys."

"What do you mean?" asked Shagonar. Damira was glad he'd asked the question. Her jaw was aching too much for her to even attempt speech.

"I mean, one way to end this would be to get Kaberco to surrender. We could use the fugitives to deliver a message to him, to convince him he cannot win against us. That would save a lot of bloodshed and resolve things sooner."

Sooner. Damira liked the sound of that. She nodded. "But if they have nothing to tell us, we kill them. Right?" She was rewarded by a sudden cessation of the stinging pain in her legs and feet.

Frowning, Syzyan studied her face for a few moments. Damira glared back. Why did he have to be so difficult?

After a pause, he nodded. "Give me some time, all right? I want to dig deep, and that isn't the work of a few days."

The stinging in her toes intensified. Her amulets didn't want her to wait. If she insisted on killing the fugitives now, would she get lasting relief from the pain? But then she'd have to deal with these two, who wouldn't be pleased. She rolled her shoulders. Pressing her lips together, she pushed back against her amulets, ignoring the voice in her head with its haunting chant of, *"Kill them."* Better to make the amulets wait for now. She could handle them. She'd always been able to.

"Fine." She shifted to rest her head on Shagonar's shoulder. "I'd like to sleep now."

Syzyan stood. "Go easy and well."

The moment he left the yurt, Damira sagged in her chair.

Shagonar stroked the top of her head. "I'll get you more tea."

She watched him pour another cup, the steam wafting the scent of jasmine into the air. Syzyan could have a few days, a week if he wanted it. In the meantime, she was going to find out why her amulets were upset. Once she knew who was responsible, they wouldn't draw a single breath more.

21

Heat flushed through Kaberco's body and a vein on his head pulsed. He stared at the message he'd received earlier that morning. For weeks he waited for the Prime Konamei to respond to his last four birds, and this was all he got?

Scuffling in the outer office caused him to raise his head. Someone was demanding to see him. Well, fine. If his clerk sent them away, he'd be grateful. If not, he wasn't in a mood to accommodate anyone. Not today.

The door opened slowly, and his clerk sidled in. "If you please, the syndic would like a word."

He released an exasperated sigh. He'd rather wrangle with a warboar than Juquila. Kaberco clenched his teeth and pulled his lips into a grimace. "Certainly. Send her in."

Shoving the message under a stack of documents, he rested his elbows on his writing table. A few heartbeats later, Juquila sauntered into the room, the bronze chain draped over her shoulders clanking softly as she moved. He shifted his own shoulders, feeling the weight of the gold chain that marked him as ephor, the highest official in the region. *Would she rather wear gold instead of bronze?*

"Peace and safety, Kaberco." She crooned the words as if she was trying to soothe a hissing cat.

If he had claws, he'd scratch her. "Peace and safety," he responded, his tone cool like a late autumn rain. He pointed to a chair. "What can I do for you?"

She settled herself in the wooden chair, straightening her bronze chain and smoothing her gray skirt. Her dark eyes looked enormous under the slate-colored turban that covered her hair. She fixed those luminous eyes on Kaberco.

"If you please," she said. "I just wondered if you had any news of the criminal who halted my caravans and terrorized my traders."

"Terrorized" wasn't the word Kaberco would have chosen to describe Tereka's actions, but he wasn't about to argue. "Sadly, there is none. Only a hodgepodge of rumors. Perhaps the warboars ate her." A fate Tereka might not deserve, but Juquila certainly did.

Her eyes flickered. "You don't believe that, do you now?"

He shook his head. "No."

"And the traders who escaped from your jail?"

Was she sneering at him? He stared at her for five heartbeats, imagining what it would feel like to strangle her with that bronze chain. Then he hit on a better idea. He'd take the battle to her. "Who knows?" he said, attempting to sound unconcerned. "You lived in this house for fifteen years. You wouldn't have any notion of how someone could get in and out without being seen, would you?"

Juquila fluttered her long, dark eyelashes and smirked. "If I did, I would have told you. That would have been useful to know."

It would have indeed. And what was even more useful to know—she was lying. The batting eyelashes gave her away. Flirtation was her favorite way to distract from her falsehoods. She knew about the door to the river and the hidden tunnels and staircases. He'd stake his life on it.

How Tereka had learned of them was another question. But not as important as understanding why Juquila hadn't told him, and why she was prevaricating now. "Pity. I would have thought you'd have been better informed."

A muscle twitched in her jaw, telling him his insult hit a nerve. He repressed a grin. "So, Juquila, where do you suppose your niece is now?"

"I think the Riskers are hiding her, as well as the others. You should raid the nearest camp. You'll find them, I'm certain."

Kaberco turned that over in his mind, searching her suggestion for hidden traps like a miner sifts ore for impurities. Perhaps the Riskers would be willing to hide one girl, but not eight traders, especially not on top of the criminals who'd escaped with Tereka last fall. "Are you speculating, or do you have evidence of this?"

He met her gaze directly, challenging her to reply. She had no proof. On his orders, the ephor of Gishin visited the two nearest Risker camps, Zafrad and Mikkeliad. The elders were more than cooperative, allowing a full search of their camps. Kaberco was certain no fugitives had taken refuge with them.

She rolled her eyes and waved dismissively. "I don't have any witnesses, if that's what you're asking. But there's no other place they could be."

Her face was relaxed, which made him think she believed what she was saying. She didn't seem aware of the rumor that Tereka had fled to the invader, to join forces with him. And that she didn't go alone. It made sense that the traders she'd rescued would switch to the other side. They had nothing more to lose. "Oh? I heard she allied with the invading army."

Juquila snorted. "That's just idle scuttlebutt. What would a man with an army want with a trader? That girl has nothing that would help him."

True, but in war, every ally you had was one less enemy. Kaberco rubbed his chin. "You could be right," he said. "But invading a Risker camp violates the Treaty. I can't do that unless I've appealed first to their elders, and then to the Prime Konamei."

"Surely the Prime Konamei would support you."

The intensity in her voice made him look more closely at her face. Her eyes blazed and her lips were tight and tense. What was her game? The last thing he needed was to get snared by one of her traps. Not now.

"He's got other matters to think about." Maybe a direct approach would confuse this slithering snake. "Juquila, what do you want?"

"What do you mean?" She jerked her chin up.

"You obviously want something from me. Save us both some time and just tell me. What are you after?"

She laughed. "Oh, Kaberco, you do like to make things difficult. All I want is a safe, fair, and prosperous society. And to ensure anyone who works to undermine it is removed so they are of no danger to anyone else." She shrugged. "I heard you had a bird this morning and wondered if it was news that you'd share." She gave him a sad look. "Perhaps not."

Sitting up straighter, Kaberco looked her in the eye. *I can play just as well as you, Juquila.* "The bird was from the ephor of Paamiat, informing me of a pirate ship sighting in Zaliv Bay." He waited for her to nod, then continued. "If you please, if you have no other pressing business with me, I have some that demands my attention."

Juquila got to her feet in one smooth motion. "Thank you for your time." Her tone was anything but grateful. "Peace and safety, Kaberco."

With irritating slowness, she strolled from the room. Her idea of raiding the Riskers was intended to set him up for something. That snake had turned into a spider, weaving a web of iron bars to trap him. He rubbed his sweaty hands on his trousers. He couldn't afford to underestimate her wiles. Even tiny spiders could have venomous bites.

Kaberco waited until the door closed fully behind Juquila before cursing her soundly. By all that kept them safe, could she be more annoying? Not to mention, her games hid some dark motive.

Grinning to himself, he dug through his documents to find the message he'd received earlier. Maybe Juquila believed it was all about pirates. He hoped so. At least she wasn't sure if he'd heard from the Prime Konamei.

He smoothed the message out, studying the uneven penmanship. The Prime Konamei's scribe hadn't even bothered to write with a pretty script. This told of a man who was rattled and rushed.

The message itself was bland.

We have the invading army of the self-styled Emperor Shagonar contained and the situation well in hand.

Right. Only if you call being besieged in your own capital well in hand.

We count on you to keep our people in the north safe.

Kaberco cursed. That was his sworn duty, and all he'd tried to do over the past nineteen years, ever since he became ephor of Gishin and then moved to Trofmose to oversee the entire region. Why can't that fool give me some actual news? Should I expect food shortages? Or is this Shagonar preparing to move north?

Now that trade from the south would be interrupted, they needed traders more than ever. Thanks to Tereka, eight were now out of his reach, including two with licenses to trade with the Riskers. He would have to inform his adile Birita about this, so she could look to their food stores.

What else? Would they be overrun with refugees? Or worse, by an invading army? He shivered, not wanting to even think about trying to defend Trofmose from an army. The worst they'd ever had to contend with was the occasional bandit attack. And those outlaws never came near the city.

He shoved his chair back and stalked to a cabinet. He

removed a flask and a tumbler. Returning to his seat, he poured a glass of lavender liquid. Porrimian brandy. Just what he needed right now.

The spirits burned their way to his stomach, banishing his chill. First things first. The enemy at home.

What was Juquila up to? She'd been rather chummy with Kulooq lately. Is she just getting lonely at night, or is she planning something? He drummed his fingers on the table. Yavaros had never liked Juquila, but he seemed a bit warmer to her. If Juquila formed an alliance with Yavaros, then they could easily persuade Kulooq to petition the Prime Konamei to have Kaberco removed.

And I can't let that happen. Because then they'll have me taken. Leaving my people helpless in the face of this invader, this cursed Shagonar.

But even if he remained ephor, how could he stop an army? Shagonar had an immense force. Kaberco snorted. All he had were a few squads of guardsmen, most of whom thought fighting bandits was the height of bravery.

He leaned over the map spread on his table, tracing a finger from Trofmose south to Anbodu to the surrounding country where the enemy army had camped. Then he tapped his finger on the Orkhana River. That would be the best place to fight them off.

Pouring himself more brandy, he considered that the order to "keep my people safe" was open to interpretation. *I think it means to do whatever is necessary.* Which meant raising an army.

Kaberco drained his glass and refilled it. Mustering an army wasn't going to be easy. For generations, they'd taught the people that weapons were unsafe and should only be handled by the Prime Konamei's guards. Half the guards were useless, scared of the shadows cast by their own swords, good only for keeping an already cowed population in line.

What fools they had been. Of course, weapons were dangerous, especially for those who didn't know how to use them. He pressed his lips together. In the Trofmose region, he had about five hundred guardsmen. Would he be able to train them for battle? He could teach archery and swordplay. Courage would be a different matter.

Some traders had illegally learned to handle a bow. He ran through the list of those he suspected—Tarkio, Tereka, Waukomis, Kemet. A few of the others who'd escaped his jail. The bravest ones who could help in a fight. He gripped his empty glass. With an effort, he set it on the table and released it with a grunt. No good would come from hurling it against the wall.

Somehow, he'd have to find people with backbones. People who would fight and were willing to learn. He'd start with his guardsmen. Then he'd work on traders and laborers and anyone else he could identify. He bit down on his lip to distract himself from feeling overwhelmed by the daunting task. But he would not permit any invaders take over without opposition.

How to find recruits for his fledgling army? A slow grin stretched across his face. Yavaros was just the man to help. He'd love the extra power and wouldn't have time for Juquila and her games. Unless she was playing a different, more deadly game altogether.

22

The rabbit purred contentedly as Damira stroked its black fur. She savored the softness under the fingers of her right hand. The warmth of the small animal soothed the stinging pain, especially the smallest finger, now shriveled and blackened down to where it joined to her palm.

Damira didn't understand what all the fuss was about. Shagonar and Syzyan were pacing around the yurt like caged sand wolves, snarling at everyone who got in their way. All they were doing was wasting time. The solution was obvious.

Giving the rabbit one last stroke behind its ear, she let her hand fall still. "Are you quite finished yet?"

Shagonar stalked over to sit beside her. "This is not good news, Dami."

"Not good news for whom?" She gave him a slow smile.

Syzyan paused his pacing and frowned. "What do you mean?"

She waved at the parchment lying on the writing table in front of her. "What do we care if the impotent Prime Konamei kills a few of our spies and threatens us if we don't leave? Does he really believe we're going to comply after his southern territories rolled over and let us take them? That we've come all this way only to pack up and depart at the first sign of resistance?"

Her brother rubbed his chin. "I'd say not surrendering was the first sign of resistance."

Damira scoffed. "Fine." Syzyan always had to be so precise. "The first sign of serious resistance. But this plays right into our hands."

The two men exchanged a glance. She narrowed her eyes. They knew what she would suggest. They'd better not oppose her.

"What do you have in mind?" Syzyan asked, his dark eyebrows pulled together and his jaw taut.

Burying her fingers in the rabbit's fur again, Damira forced a smile. She spoke sweetly, trying to cover her irritation. "I think we should take a stroll to the gates of Anbodu. Let the Prime Konamei understand our opinion of his edict. And give him a demonstration of our power."

Syzyan mumbled something about diplomacy being more effective than force, that words were more powerful weapons than swords. She wasn't listening. Her amulets were warming up, pleased with her idea. The ripples in the air disappeared and her head ceased its throbbing.

She picked up the rabbit and placed it in its cushioned basket, then stood up. "Shall we?" With effort, she minimized her limp and made her way to the door. She didn't bother to wait for Syzyan and Shagonar to agree, or to look over her shoulder to see if they'd follow her. She knew they would.

Less than an hour later, she was riding toward the gates of Anbodu with Shagonar, Syzyan, and two full arbatus of ten men apiece. They made a good showing, her archers sitting tall in their saddles, their Otrechian horses bred for speed and stamina, far better than any of the horses she'd seen in Tlefas. The autumn sun glinted on the metal trim of their leather armor. A cool breeze breathed fresh air on Damira's face.

The city of Anbodu sat on a low hill close to the mountains that formed the eastern border of Tlefas. It was, Damira thought, a defensible location. Too bad for the residents, the high stone walls and iron gates wouldn't be enough.

They neared the gates and stopped just out of arrow range. The ramparts bristled with guards, many holding bows with nocked arrows. More sentries stood ready on top of the stone towers that flanked the gates.

"His Loftiness Emperor Shagonar and Her Loftiness Empress Damira demand an audience with your Prime Konamei," the herald shouted. "If he desires peace and safety, he will speak with them now."

The guards atop the walls ran back and forth, their shouts barely audible. Damira smiled. At least that got their attention.

As they waited, more guards lined the parapet atop the walls, standing shoulder to shoulder across the entire south side of the city as far as she could see. "Syz, how many sentries do you think they have?"

"That's a good question." He ordered two men to ride around the city, to count the guards and note their positions.

As the two rode off, the guards let their arrows fly. None hit their targets, falling several yards short.

Shagonar laughed. "They shoot worse than our children."

Then a shriek cut the air. An arrow had found its mark in one of the scouts they'd sent out. A lucky shot had pierced his neck. He slumped forward, then slid from his horse.

Heat surged in Damira's face. "Tell them they shouldn't have done that."

While the herald shouted the message, Syzyan put a hand on Damira's arm. "We need to tread lightly."

She shook him off. Her amulets were telling her to kill them all. She wasn't about to do that. Nor would she let this go unanswered. No, she was going to end this standoff quickly. She would bring peace to both realms. If she had to profess she was the Desired One to succeed, so be it. No one else had shown up to claim the title.

"Tell them this is their best chance for a true and lasting peace. Their best opportunity to be free of oppression. We come to liberate, not enslave. The Prime Konamei cannot stand against the fulfillment of prophecy, even if he calls it a myth."

A stinging pain across her head made her wince. She meant every word, although the amulets didn't approve. It didn't matter. She could still bend them to her will.

The guards answered with another volley of arrows, most aimed at her other scout, who was attempting to drape the body of his fallen comrade over his horse's saddle. One arrow scraped the horse's neck. The mare screamed and bucked, kept from bolting only by quick action by her rider.

"Tell them they have angered us," Damira said. "And this is how we will repay them."

"Dami—"

"No, Syz. We need to show them our power." She waited for the herald to shout her message. Then she reached for her amulets and clutched them in her fingers. She raised her gloved hand over her head, the sun glinting on the red and black gemstones. Taking a deep breath, she pulled at the power. Then she pushed.

The tower on the left side of the gate blew up, sending stones into the air. Thrashing guards soared high above the city and crashed to the ground, their screams ending when their bodies thudded onto the rubble.

The pain in her head dissipated like the dust from the ruined tower, blown away by the autumn breeze. She flexed her stinging fingers, smiling as the agony faded. For the first time in weeks, her pounding headache and the burning in her hands and feet ceased.

She waited for the breeze to blow the dust away, relaxing on her mare. Maybe Shagonar would accompany her on a ride later. She raised her voice to get the attention of the herald. "Inform them we prefer to be benevolent. We don't want to destroy their city or kill its residents. If they surrender in three days, we'll be happy to discuss terms. No one will be killed, and we'll even allow the Prime Konamei to rule as an under-lord in our realm. We intend to be magnanimous. If they try our patience, well, then they'll see. Tell them we await their response."

Damira turned her horse and rode away, the smell of dust and cries of the wounded filling the air. A whiff of air blew her hair from her face and she smiled. Using the power made her feel ten years younger. She could get used to this.

23

A week had passed since they arrived in the Emperor's camp, and Tereka had yet to see her weapons. Farnaz insisted they'd get them back, in time. He seemed sincere in his assurances, which did nothing to ease the prickling on the nape of Tereka's neck.

Nor did the regular visits from several of the Jianjun's officers, who questioned them endlessly about Kaberco, the Prime Konamei, and Tlefas' military preparedness. Sometimes they'd interrogate them as a group. At other times, they'd take one person to another yurt. That she and her friends had little to say about the Prime Konamei's plans and less about his armed forces didn't seem to bother the officers. They simply returned the next day to pose the same questions.

Every night, Farnaz visited their yurt, flirting with Savinnia and asking naïve-sounding questions about all aspects of life in Tlefas, peppered with a few about children's stories and myths and the Riskers. So far, no one had dropped even a hint that they knew more about the Desired One than they were letting on. But Tereka recognized it was just a matter of time before someone slipped. Or Sebezh decided spilling what he knew might convince the Emperor he was useful.

Today Farnaz, along with twelve armed guards, had escorted them to one of the many practice ranges set up on the outskirts of the camp. Fifteen round targets the size of a shield were propped against bales of hay near the bluff overlooking the river. Tereka counted ten groups of what looked like ten soldiers readying their bows.

Tereka filled her lungs with the cool fall air. She'd always loved this season, when the weather turned crisp and invigorating after the heat of summer. This far south, the autumn was mild, with barely a hint of winter. Not like Trofmose or their mountain hideout, where snow might already be falling.

She watched the nearest group loose their arrows, three shots each within the span of two heartbeats, nearly all hitting the center. Farnaz had explained that his father wanted him to assess their abilities. Tereka wasn't certain if that was the real reason for bringing them to the range, or if it was to show off the impressive skill of his archers. She eyed Farnaz's escorts, who had locked their gazes on her and her friends. She assumed the guards were there to ensure neither she nor her companions attacked Farnaz.

Her talents must remain hidden, she knew. If the Emperor heard the Desired One was prophesied to be a skilled archer, he might associate the prophecy with her. Tereka wasn't ready for that to happen, not quite yet.

Farnaz divided them into groups of three, saying one group would shoot at a time. He pointed at Tereka, Naco, and Sebezh. "You three shoot first." He motioned for the others to sit on the ground ten paces to the side.

Tereka took a position in front of the target, Sebezh on one side of her, Naco on the other. She pursed her lips. At that distance, the center red spot was as big as an alloe rat's eye. Even with the unfamiliar bow, she'd have no problem hitting it if she tried. Wiser to aim for the yellow, blue, or green rings that circled the red spot, or better yet, the white outermost ring.

Sebezh nocked an arrow and released it. With a resounding thwack, it hit the green ring near the bottom of the target.

Naco huffed and raised his bow. His arrow barely grazed the target's edge. He muttered a curse and reached for a second arrow.

"Good thing some of us spent the winter learning to shoot instead of playing with fish," Sebezh said as he nocked another arrow.

A muscle in Naco's jaw twitched, but he remained silent.

Naco's right, Tereka thought, admiring the firm line of his jaw along with his self-control. Better to not let Sebezh provoke us. She nocked an arrow, then let it fly. It lodged in the yellow ring, just below the center.

"Off your game, girly?" Sebezh asked. "I've never seen you miss before."

"Really?" asked Farnaz.

Tirk chimed in. "Da always said Tereka was one of the best archers he knew."

Tereka pressed her lips together. Tirk had to compliment her now, just when she didn't want him to. She glared at Sebezh and gave him a small shake of the head, then nocked another arrow and released it.

It hit the yellow ring just above the red circle. "Oh, great shot," said Kemet.

First Tirk, now Kemet. She wished they'd all keep quiet. Even when she tried to downplay her skills, they had to comment on her talent. She released another arrow. This one splintered the last one she'd shot. Blast. She needed to pay attention if she was going to convince Farnaz she was only a passable archer.

"Nice shooting," Farnaz said. "Are many as good as you?"

"Our da is," put in Tirk. "He's the one who taught us."

"He's a trader, right?" Farnaz asked.

"Yes," Tirk said.

Farnaz asked a few questions about trade and the condition of the roads in the north. Tereka pretended to give Naco a few pointers so Farnaz wouldn't think she was listening.

"Oh, but he likes trading with the Riskers," Tirk said.

Tereka's breath caught. How had they got on that topic?

"Why?" asked Farnaz. "I thought they're barbarians."

"The Riskers," Tirk said, "sell honey, beeswax candles, and white bread. Those are quite profitable, as only konament members can buy them. The prices are high to ensure the traders don't tell anyone, or try to sell them illegally."

"So your da has spent much time with Riskers." Farnaz eyed Tereka and her brother.

Don't say it, Tereka silently pleaded. Don't let him ask what else Da knows about Riskers. Or why Tirk and I look nothing alike.

Naco handed her a waterskin. She thanked him and took a drink. *Maybe I should dump it over Tirk's head.* She glanced at Naco, then flicked her gaze at Tirk, wordlessly begging Naco to do something, anything, to get Tirk to stop talking.

"Did we ever tell you how we fought pirates to escape from prison?" Naco asked.

Farnaz looked up. "That's right. You were in prison."

"Well, all of us except Tirk and Kemet," Tereka said.

"They missed all the fun," said Relio. "Girly here was determined to get free. When they told us they'd let us go if we fought pirates for them, she insisted on trying. We went with her. Couldn't let her do it alone."

That wasn't exactly how Tereka remembered it, but no matter. Farnaz's eyebrows were raised, betraying his interest. Tirk, she was glad to observe, had shut his mouth and hung his head, no doubt remembering just why Tereka had been imprisoned.

Relio chuckled. "So we start fighting, and the guards who

were supposed to help us remained on the side, placing bets on who would die first. We ran to a tower and stood on the roof. Threw rocks at anyone who came near until all the pirates were dead."

Tereka nodded. Relio's version was close enough to the truth. Farnaz didn't need to know how she found the second dragonfly amulet that led her to a hidden cache of weapons.

"That's when they let you go?" Farnaz asked.

"Nope." Sebezh let out a curse. "That's when those *yanshyri* sentenced us to the salt mines."

"What's so bad about that? You were already in the copper mines," Farnaz replied.

"What's so bad about that?" Relio rolled his eyes. "I'll tell you. The copper mines were above ground. Sure, we toiled in a pit. But we could see the sun. Breathe fresh air. The salt mines are underground. Once they send you down, you never come up."

Farnaz's eyes were wide. "How did you escape?"

"Good question." Relio's eyes crinkled. "Girly and Savinnia distracted the guards, Alikse cracked a few necks, and Sebezh finished the rest with a sword." He guffawed. "We'll have to tell you the long version some other time."

"Is it true?" Tirk asked Tereka. "They were going to send you to the salt mines?" His voice cracked on the last words.

"Yes. But we didn't end up there." She smiled gently. "That's the important thing."

"Want to try a few more?" Naco handed her three arrows.

As she took the arrows, her fingers brushed against his. Tingling warmth spread from her hand to her toes. She bent her head, pretending to tighten her bowstring.

Naco moved a little closer. Had he felt it too? When she looked up, he was staring at her as if she was some wondrous sight.

Her breath came a little faster. She stared into Naco's eyes, unable to pull her gaze away.

"Hey, girly," said Sebezh. "Are you going to shoot today or next week?"

Startled, she stepped back. She glanced at Sebezh, then at Farnaz. The latter was deep in conversation with Relio, Alikse, and Hinat, questioning them about their escape from prison.

Taking a breath, she nocked and released an arrow. It struck the middle ring, slightly above the center. Naco released an arrow, this time hitting the outermost ring.

"Good," she said. "That's better."

"It's not the best I can do."

His words sounded like he meant archery. But his smooth, caressing tone seemed to imply something different. Unless she was hearing a meaning he didn't intend.

"I'm sure it's not," she said, giving him a playful smile. When he grinned, she jerked her chin to his bow. "Let your breath out before you release," she told him. "Like this." She nocked an arrow and breathed in as she pulled the string back. She let the air out of her lungs and released the arrow. It lodged precisely in the center of the target.

"Beautiful shooting, Tereka," shouted Tirk.

He's an idiot. Why can't he shut up? And I'm a bigger idiot. What am I doing, letting Naco distract me like that?

Farnaz appeared at her side. "You must have made your father proud. Does your brother shoot as well?"

Sebezh's snort answered the question for her.

"Oh, but there are many equally good, if not better." She gave Farnaz an embarrassed shrug, hoping he believed her.

"I've not seen any. If you're this skilled, what must the Desired One of legend be like?"

She stiffened, ice seeping through her veins. "Oh, much better, I'm sure."

He narrowed his eyes. "I wonder if you've heard about the gates of Anbodu."

"The gates? What of them?"

"Yesterday, we received a message from the Prime

Konamei, telling us to leave his lands. My uncle, aunt, and father rode to the gates of the city. They told the Prime Konamei he needed to make peace now, that he can't stand against the fulfillment of prophecy."

Tereka stopped breathing for a heartbeat. A smile tugged at the corners of her mouth. Did that mean Emperor Shagonar was the Desired One? "What did the Prime Konamei say?"

"I don't know. Before his answer came back, his guards shot one of our soldiers. My aunt was most displeased. So she gave them a reason to surrender."

By this time, her friends had gathered around. "Which was?" Tereka asked.

"My aunt used her amulets to destroy one of the towers next to the gates. Then she told the Prime Konamei that if he surrenders within three days, she'll discuss terms. If he makes her wait and prolongs the siege, she'll be less benevolent."

"Your aunt?" asked Relio. "Isn't Emperor Shagonar the one with the power?"

"Oh, he has some amulets, lesser ones. My aunt bears the three Amulets of Power."

The earth seemed to tilt under Tereka's feet. How could this be? She carried two dragonfly Amulets of Power, those with three stones in the tail. She thought there was only one remaining. Could there possibly be three more?

That the Empress, not the Emperor, carried the amulets didn't surprise Tereka. She'd sensed something threatening about the woman, a menace she'd never felt before.

What did surprise her was the use of amulets to destroy and kill. The sky-god normally didn't permit the power to be used in that way. But then, if the idea was to end the oppression of the Prime Konamei without a prolonged siege or a bloody battle, maybe faster would be better.

At any rate, the prophecy didn't state whether the new order brought by the Desired One would be an improvement.

Tereka's skin crawled. She didn't want to ally with someone who would be a harsh tyrant.

She shook off the thought. No, the Desired One couldn't possibly be evil. Otherwise, why would this person be desired at all?

Perhaps the Empress was like Tereka, trying to make sense of scraps of prophecies. And perhaps she made a bit of a mistake. Or were the amulets she wielded channels of an evil power?

If they were, Tereka knew she'd have to leave. She swallowed the lump in her throat. Leaving might not be so easy. Perhaps it would be better to stick around to figure out how to defeat the empress.

And then I'll have to be the Desired One. Her throat tightened. *No. I can't be.*

Naco attempted to catch her eye, but she ignored him. She didn't want to talk to anyone.

Tereka handed her bow to Hinat. "It's your turn. I'm done." She walked away, unable to shake the feeling that she'd made a horrible mistake in coming to the Emperor's camp.

24

That evening, Tereka sat alone, as far from the light of the brazier as she could, her knees pulled up to her chin, her arms wrapped around her shins. Kemet had tried to get her to eat but gave up after she snarled at him. Naco had simply left a cup of tea on the floor next to her.

Farnaz stopped by, ostensibly to bring them a special tea he'd told Savinnia about. He claimed it calmed and soothed through its light floral flavor. Tereka stared at the cup on the floor next to her. For some reason, she didn't want to even taste it.

Most of the others gathered near the brazier, where Farnaz was teaching them a game he called Ya Pei. Three teams of two players matched tiles painted with flowers, mythical beasts, and Uzhasovian heroes.

As they played, Sebezh, Alikse, and Relio lounged on cushions off to the side, betting on the outcome. Tirk and Naco outmatched Hinat and Kemet, but Savinnia and Farnaz won nearly every round.

Groans and cheers greeted the end of another game. Savinnia laughed and thanked Farnaz for their eighth win.

"Oh, it wasn't just me. You're quite clever, you know."

Savinnia flushed and dropped her gaze.

Tereka frowned. By her best guess, Farnaz was at least three years younger than Savinnia. Surely, she wouldn't be interested in him. Or would she? Thoughtful, cultured Farnaz was nothing like bullying Sebezh or coarse Relio. Tereka winced at the thought of gentle Savinnia hurt by the charming Farnaz. She didn't like the idea at all.

Apparently, Naco was thinking along the same lines. "Maybe we should change partners," he said, "and see who's really good."

"Right. You and Savinnia should take on Tirk and Hinat. Kemet and Farnaz can play together," Relio said. "That should be fair."

They all debated who should play with whom, with Relio and Naco united in suggesting Savinnia pair with anyone but Farnaz.

Farnaz, judging by his smirk, seemed quite aware of what they were doing. "What do you think, Savinnia? Who would you like to play with?" He posed the question in a smooth tone, but Tereka couldn't help wondering if another meaning lay behind it.

"She's tired of you," Naco said.

Tereka smiled. Naco was so protective of Savinnia. Like Tirk had once been of her. Then her heart sank because Naco never spoke that way to Kemet to get him to leave her alone. Maybe she'd misread him. His flirting on the archery range might have meant nothing more than a desire for a little fun.

"Perhaps the time for games is coming to an end," Farnaz said, stretching out his arms in a yawn.

Jerking her head up, Tereka watched him closely. She wasn't so sure he was talking only about games of chance. She picked up her tea, stood, and walked toward the brazier. "Have you grown weary of winning?"

He gestured for her to sit near him. "My aunt asked me to

tell her about my afternoon and what I observed on the archery range."

"Oh?" Tereka's mouth went dry, and she took a sip of her now-chilly tea. She lowered herself onto a cushion, dreading Farnaz's next words.

"She was most interested to learn that a girl whose father trades with Riskers was the best archer on the range, surpassing even our own men."

"My da taught me to shoot so I could defend myself."

"We've seen the Prime Konamei's men shoot. None come close to your level of skill."

Her shooting at the range hadn't been that impressive. She shook her head. Surely Farnaz didn't know she'd missed a few shots on purpose.

"What of it?" Tirk asked. "She's a great archer."

"There's the minor matter of a prophecy," Farnaz said.

Tereka tensed. Did the Empress suspect her?

"Prophecy?" Tirk sneered. "You mean the myth of the Desired One? She can't be. She's my sister."

"I see you believe that," Farnaz said. "Perhaps you don't know that in the south of your country, in the regions we have liberated, many welcome the idea of the Desired One who will bring a new order. This myth, as you call it, was outlawed by your Prime Konamei generations ago. Now, the idea that my aunt fits the prophecy has caught fire and is spreading toward the north."

"Is she the Desired One?" Tereka asked.

"She could be the one to bring a new order," replied Farnaz. "She wants nothing more than a guaranteed peace. No war." He gazed at Tereka. "She's willing to pay any price to obtain the peace. And she's not afraid to use her amulets."

Tirk snorted. "She has magic amulets? There's no such thing."

Relio smacked him on the shoulder. "How do you think she destroyed the gates of Anbodu?"

"Magic amulets? That's impossible." Tirk scooted to sit closer to Kemet and further from Relio.

Tereka grabbed the hair on the back of her head and tugged on it. Something bothered her about all this, and she couldn't quite figure it out.

She thought back to all Cillia had told her about amulets. Destroying things was never mentioned as one of the powers. Although, Cillia admitted she knew little about the Amulets of Power.

The three Amulets of Power. Tereka carried two. What three did Empress Damira wield? And how to ask without arousing suspicion? She wrinkled her face, trying to look puzzled. "Are there really magic amulets?" she asked. "How would they work? Do they make sounds, like thunder?"

"Oh, no," Farnaz replied. "Light flashes."

"White light? Like the moons and stars?" Tereka's heart beat a little faster. "Or yellow, like the sun?"

"Or perhaps green?" asked Sebezh.

While she could have hit him, she controlled herself and pulled her lips into a small smile. She raised her eyebrows, her attention on Farnaz.

"Green?" Farnaz narrowed his eyes. "No, my aunt's amulets flash with red light."

Feigning confusion, Tereka nodded slightly. Her dragonflies flashed purple and green. "I can't picture them. What do the amulets look like? Are they pretty?"

"You don't know?" Farnaz seemed puzzled. "They're shaped like scorpions about the length of a finger, made of black stone embedded with red gems. The Amulets of Power have three red stones forming the tail."

Tereka stared at him, struggling to keep her jaw from dropping. Scorpions. Not dragonflies. Red and black, not green and purple. She swallowed hard and attempted to speak casually. "I bet they're beautiful."

"Some people think so," Farnaz said.

"Are there magic amulets made of different colored stones?" Sebezh asked. "Or a different shape. I've heard of some such things."

"Like what?" Farnaz asked.

Don't say it, Tereka begged silently. At least the others had the sense to keep their mouths shut.

"Oh, some kind of insect, maybe a dragonfly," Sebezh said. "Green and purple stones, from what I hear."

"Where did you hear that?" Tirk asked. "That sounds like some kind of traders' tale."

Good. Tirk's ignorance of all things amulets might make Farnaz believe she also knew little about dragonfly amulets.

Farnaz eyed him, his lips twitching as if he wasn't sure whether to mock or pity her brother. "My friend, the dragonfly amulets are real. The Riskers have them. They use them to heal, among other things. But the Riskers are not the original makers."

With an effort, Tereka kept from jumping. Maybe Farnaz could tell her something Cillia didn't know. "You don't say." She kept her tone quiet, as if she wasn't vitally interested in his reply. "Then who did?"

He stared into the flames of the brazier for a heartbeat. "My mother's people, the Vernians."

Tereka racked her brain. Who were the Vernians? Oh, yes, the blond people from the east. The ones the Otrechians thought were barbarians.

"My father is Otrechian," Farnaz said, "brought up to despise the Vernians, partly because of their worship of the sky-god."

That fit what Tereka knew about the sky-god being the power behind the dragonfly amulets.

Tirk laughed. "That's another myth, the sky-god. Funny how all our myths came from people over the mountains."

Relio rolled his eyes. To Tereka's relief, he remained silent and let Farnaz continue.

"In any case," Farnaz said, "the makers of the scorpions hated the dragonfly wielders. So much that they swore to kill any of them."

Tereka's hands went cold. She resisted the urge to touch the bag in her pocket that held the four dragonflies she carried. What would the Empress do to her if she learned about them?

Farnaz looked up with a smile. "My grandfather bore a dragonfly that he used for healing. He's one of the few captured by Uzhasovians who managed to avoid being killed for possessing it."

Letting her gaze travel over his face, Tereka judged Farnaz to be sincere, as if he believed what he was saying. But why was he telling them this? It could be part of a larger game, even though he'd said the time for games was over. She darted a look at Savinnia, whose attention was fixed on Farnaz. Was he using Savinnia as an excuse to hang around them? Or did he have feelings for her that prompted him to warn them of potential danger?

"But why," Relio asked, "would your aunt care if anyone has dragonfly amulets? She's got her own set, and rather powerful ones, from the sound of it."

"Because she has sworn to destroy any user of the dragon-flies." Farnaz grimaced, but continued. "Wielders of the drag-onflies are enemies of users of the scorpions. It's been that way for centuries. She wouldn't hesitate to kill any of them."

The room had gone still. Tereka kept her eyes on the fire, trying very hard not to meet anyone's gaze. She worked her mouth so she could speak around the dryness. With a toss of her head, she shrugged. "A great leader like Empress Damira with all her loyal generals and massive army has nothing to fear from a few pretty trinkets that are used for healing."

"You could be right." Farnaz tilted his head, frowning. "Still, if I owned dragonfly amulets, I'd make it my business to get as far away from here as I could." He turned to Savinnia. "What do you say? Shall we try another round?"

The conversation switched back to the game. Tereka watched in silence, noting that Farnaz let himself be defeated no matter who was his partner. Her heart thumped with each click of the tiles. Was he trying to send her a message? Or was all this talk a clever trap to force her into revealing herself and her amulets?

25

A cool wind stirred the air, carrying the shouts of officers drilling their men, the whinnies of horses, and the tramping of feet. Tereka followed Farnaz as he led them to the edge of an open field. The warm afternoon sun took some of the chill from her limbs, a chill that lingered after Farnaz's cryptic warning from the night before.

She'd refused to speak to anyone after that, retreating into her thoughts. Was Farnaz telling the truth that Damira would kill her if she learned about the dragonfly amulets? Or was he mistaken? He seemed sure of what he was saying.

If only she knew more about the scorpion amulets. Or any of the Amulets of Power. Farnaz, so far, seemed to be her best source of information. The question was how to extract more from him without him suspecting why she wanted to know.

Farnaz strode past the sparring foot soldiers to a field where riders were training. Tereka watched in awe as a group of ten riders, which Farnaz called an arbatu, galloped in a line toward a row of targets. When they drew near, they veered to the left to ride alongside the targets. Then they shot without slowing their horses. From the thuds of the arrows, Tereka knew all ten had hit the mark. Her eyes widened. Not only did ten arrows bristle in the targets, but they all protruded from the center rings.

This was a well-trained fighting force. The Prime Konamei had nothing like it. His guardsmen were only capable of dealing with drunks, thieves, and bandit attacks on caravans. And they weren't very good at the last. Tlefas could not fight off this invasion.

Relio nudged her. "What do you think, girly? Know any guardsmen who can do that?"

Tereka winced. "We could never defeat them."

But maybe they weren't meant to. If Damira was the Desired One, then perhaps her victory would bring the new order predicted in the prophecy. Tereka let out a heavy sigh. While she still clung to that hope, everything she learned about Damira made her doubt that idea more and more.

A horn sounded and all the arbatus stopped what they were doing and jostled into formation. The foot soldiers lined up in columns of ten, the riders in their own columns. All stood with heads high and backs straight, like a precisely laid-out pine forest.

Farnaz touched her elbow. "My aunt and uncle are coming to review the troops."

In the distance, two riders approached, followed by several others. As they drew near, Shagonar's opulent clothing and Damira's red tunic glinted in the sunshine, the gold and silver threads sparkling like sunlight on the ocean.

They rode up to Tereka and her friends. Farnaz stepped forward. "Aunt, Uncle, I greet you."

His aunt nodded. "So you're showing our guests what our troops can do?" She looked at Tereka's group. "What do you think?"

Tereka's mouth went dry. Her mind was a void, empty of any intelligent thought.

Relio cleared his throat. "Your Loftiness, I, uh, think they're quite impressive."

"Impressive?" Sebezh snorted. "Invincible, I'd say. Your Loftiness, the Prime Konamei has nothing that can compare. Unless he has a hidden army somewhere that no one knows about."

The Empress smiled all the way to her eyes. "Does he have any magic at his disposal?"

"Oh, no," said Tereka. Had she spoken too quickly? "If you please, Your Loftiness, magic, even the very mention of it is outlawed."

"If you talk about it, you get taken. Never to be seen again," put in Naco.

As the Empress studied their faces, Tereka's amulets turned icy. Why did this woman's presence have that effect on them?

"So you say." The Empress Damira's cold eyes didn't waver. "I hope you speak the truth. If you are lying, I will know."

Forcing her face to remain bland, Tereka focused on the Empress's horse.

"You, girl, what's your name again?" the Empress asked.

Tereka started. "Me, Loftiness?" Why was the Empress singling her out?

"Yes, you."

"I'm Tereka, if you please." Dampness formed on the back of her neck and under her arms.

"So, Tereka, tell me. Why are you the leader of your group? Don't say you're not. I've seen how they all look to you. And I've heard they follow your orders."

The dampness turned to full-on sweat. Tereka frantically tried to come up with a reason that had nothing to do with Riskers, amulets, or the fulfillment of prophecy.

"I suppose it's—"

Relio cut her off. "It's because we couldn't agree on anyone else. This was the only way to have peace."

The Emperor laughed. "That's one way to get power."

His wife pursed her lips. "So, Tereka—who is the leader because no one else was acceptable to all—how do you keep discipline among your followers? What power do you have to get them to obey?"

This question was even harder. Tereka resisted the impulse to rub her sweaty palms together.

Alikse spoke up. His bass voice rumbled through the air. "She threatened to cut our balls off."

For a heartbeat, the Emperor stared at him, then burst into deep gales of laughter. He leaned over his mare's withers, a hand on his stomach. At one point, his guffaws shook him so violently that Tereka thought he'd slide off his horse. The guards behind him were grinning, but the Empress remained impassive.

When the Emperor recovered his composure, he sat up straight and asked, "You believed her?" His lips twitched as if his snigger would erupt into a laugh.

"We did," said Naco. "You should have seen what she did to the man who groped her when we were in prison."

Tereka didn't dare look at Sebezh, the man in question. He surely didn't want to be reminded of that incident, and she didn't want to provoke him. Not with the Empress studying her with narrowed, suspicious eyes.

"So that's how you do it?" The Empress gestured with her head. "Let me show you how I keep order."

Four soldiers dragged two others in front of the two sovereigns. Tereka flinched, seeing the bruises on the men's faces.

"You see," the Empress said. "These are deserters. They seemed to think they could simply walk away and go home." She shook her head. "Why they thought they could do this, I have no idea."

Farnaz's breathing sounded ragged. Tereka's heartbeat sped up as she wondered why he seemed so edgy.

The Empress leaned forward in her saddle. "What do you have to say for yourselves?"

Both men shuffled their feet and looked down.

"You don't know our ways." Empress Damira turned back to Tereka. "Deserting is a deep offense against honor. In less enlightened times, we burned deserters alive or locked them in a cage and abandoned them in the desert as food for the scorpions. I prefer a different approach."

Tereka gripped her shaking hands together.

"No. Please." One man dropped to his knees.

A cunning sneer crawled across the Empress's face. "You would prefer more pain than less?" She spoke kindly, as if she were offering the man a choice of figs or dates. She held out her hand, a hand covered by a black glove. Something she grasped in it sparkled with red stones.

The kneeling man shrieked and fell over, writhing on the ground.

Staring at him with her mouth open, Tereka folded her arms over her stomach. This couldn't be happening. Cold spread through her side, its source the bag in her pocket, the pouch that held her dragonfly amulets.

The Empress tipped her head to the side. "You see, every now and then we have to make an example. Just to keep order in the ranks." She lifted her hand, and the man screamed.

The smell of burnt flesh stung Tereka's nostrils. Heat flooded her face, and she ground her teeth. How could the Empress torture this man? Someone had to stop this. Why didn't the Emperor do something?

"And if everyone else who plots desertion or any other disloyal act knows what faces them, we don't have problems." Empress Damira smiled. She turned to the other man. "What should I do with you?"

"Be quick. I beg you." The man's voice trailed off in a whine.

"Oh, too bad. I don't think I will." She let the sunlight glisten on the thing in her hand.

Tereka's eyes burned, stung by hot tears. The jeweled

object in the Empress' hand must be one of the scorpions. Tereka could barely stand to look at it. No wonder her amulets were as frigid as stones under a snowdrift.

Blood trickled down the second man's face. He let out a cry and clutched his ruined eye.

The man's whimper cut to Tereka's soul. This was pure evil. She had to stop this. She took a step forward.

Naco seized her tunic and pulled her back. "No." He growled the word into her ear.

She shook her shoulders in an attempt to release herself from his grasp. Out of the corner of her eye, she spotted Farnaz, his eyes wide, shaking his head at her.

With a deep breath, she retreated a step. Naco and Farnaz were right. Anything she said to oppose the Empress would make her, and her friends, the next targets of this horrifying power. Nothing she had or knew could combat the power the Empress wielded, this power to wound with a thought channeled through an amulet.

"You." Empress Damira glanced at the man on the ground, "you've gone quiet on me." She lifted her hand and there was a loud crack. The man's leg bent at an unnatural angle. His bellow of pain filled the air.

"Dami," Emperor Shagonar said. "I think you made your point."

"So soon? But as you say." She held up her hand and narrowed her eyes. In a heartbeat, the two men were nothing but red mist that floated in the air under the gentle autumn sun. The mist settled on the ground, leaving a damp spot in the dust.

Tereka clamped a hand over her mouth, swallowing the bile that threatened to burst from her throat. She would not throw up. That would bring the Empress's attention to her, attention she did not want.

Savinnia moaned. Others gasped. Emperor Shagonar's and Farnaz's faces were set like granite, showing no expression at all. Did they agree with what the Empress had done? The Emperor, at least, seemed to want to cut it short.

The soldiers in their lines stood so still they seemed like they weren't breathing. Tereka's own breath caught in her throat and her ribs tightened when the Empress gave her a smile, a smile that did not reach to her dark gray eyes.

"And that, my friend," she said, "is how to keep discipline. Or deal with those who would deceive you. You'll do well to remember." She pulled on the reins of her horse and turned it to the right, Emperor Shagonar doing the same.

As they rode away, Relio cursed. Tereka could only stare at the damp spots on the ground. Her amulets were lumps of ice against her ribs, freezing past her skin and bone to her very core.

One thing was clear. They had to flee before the Empress learned of the dragonfly amulets she carried. Or they'd be nothing more than spatters of red dew on the grass.

26

Willing her writhing stomach to settle, Tereka tore her gaze from the damp spots on the ground. Two men stood there mere moments ago. Now they were nothing but red mist vanishing under the midday sun.

Vaguely, she heard muttering around her. How could anyone even think after what they'd just witnessed? She could barely breathe after that display of Empress Damira's brutal love for causing pain. What a fool, a *durak* she was to have thought Damira could be the Desired One.

Her mouth tasted like she'd rubbed a dusty camel's hide on her tongue. Acrid bile surged in her throat and she forced it back down.

She brought her friends here. She was to blame. Her ribs tightened, and she struggled to draw a breath. Tirk, Naco, Savinnia, they'd all die. All because she refused to face the truth. She carried two Amulets of Power that had found her when she needed them most. That should have been enough to convince her.

But how could she oppose the Empress? Her feeble efforts

to unseat Juquila had been futile. What good would she be against this woman who had powerful amulets—and an army —at her disposal?

Tereka's head spun. She wasn't worthy of being the Desired One. So far, all she'd done was to lead her followers into danger.

Uncertain where she was going, she stumbled from the practice range. She had to flee the place Damira had misted the men. And to avoid her friends. Surely they'd blame her for bringing them there. They'd be right.

The war camp was so large that Tereka wandered for hours, conscious of a guard who trailed her every step. All around her, soldiers wearing scarlet tunics and black trousers sharpened swords and fletched arrows. Others groomed horses and carried away the muck.

Camp followers garbed in shades of clover green or sky blue or goldenrod yellow boiled soup and stirred meat sizzling in pans over open fires. From time to time, they left their work to dart into the dimness of a yurt with a soldier. Tereka didn't want to imagine what they were doing. It brought back memories of what Savinnia had been forced to do while they were in prison, and what had nearly happened to her. Tereka shoved the frightful recollections from her mind.

All of these people were going on with their lives as if nothing had happened. Perhaps they didn't know. Or maybe they'd seen someone misted before and were accustomed to it. The scent of frying meat brought back a memory of the tortured deserters. Her stomach churned, forcing her to swallow hard to keep from spewing her mid-day meal on the ground.

She arrived at the edge of the camp and stared off to the north, the guard who'd shadowed her all day standing twenty feet away. Somehow, she and her friends had to escape before the Empress decided to search for the dragonflies. Of course, the dragonflies had a way of hiding when they wanted to, but

Tereka suspected the scorpions could sense when they were around. Perhaps the dragonflies had gone icy to warn her. Or perhaps going cold prevented the scorpions from knowing where the dragonflies were.

Either way, Tereka didn't want to test the power of her amulets. No, she and her friends had to leave. Then they could figure out what to do to stop Damira.

Idly, she watched an eagle soar overhead. The faint clinks of sword against sword from the practice field sounded like an unskilled harpist plucking the strings, unable to find a melody.

The ache in her chest grew sharper. What could eight do against an army? Even if they convinced all the Riskers to fight with them, they had no chance against Damira and her scorpions.

A touch on her shoulder made her jump. She spun, fists clenched, expecting to see a soldier charged with hauling her to the Empress.

"It's just me," Naco said.

She sighed, letting her hands relax. In the setting sun, his tawny eyes turned gold and his firm jaw was sharply outlined. "Oh, Naco. What are we going to do?"

He ran his hand down her arm and squeezed her fingers. "We do what we're good at doing."

"What's that?"

"Escaping."

Tereka snorted and elbowed him. "I hope we can pull off one more." Her shoulders sagged as she stared at her feet. "But I don't know how."

"Makes you want to be captured by pirates again, doesn't it?"

"At least we had a chance against them. Even if we figured out how to escape from here, what then? If that Empress caught us, called us deserters…" She shuddered.

"Being misted would be the best part of it," Naco finished.

With a gulp, Tereka imagined Damira torturing Savinnia, Naco, and the others. Even Sebezh didn't deserve that fate.

And their suffering would be all her fault. Guilt twisted her stomach. She wrapped her arms around herself. "Naco, I can't deny it anymore. That woman, Damira—" Tereka winced as she said the name. "She can't be the Desired One."

"No, she can't."

Ash-colored clouds hovered over the hills in the distance. Tereka gazed at them, grateful that Naco wasn't pushing her. But acceptance did not come easy. Admitting something to herself was one thing. Saying it out loud was like jumping into a river. Once she took that leap, there was no going back. And the truth, like the current, could drown her.

"Which means—" Tereka shuffled from side to side. She couldn't make herself utter the words.

"Yes?" Naco prompted, his voice gentle.

"I must be the Desired One."

She didn't know what she'd been expecting. The sun continued to warm her face, the breeze still puffed at her hair.

And Naco grinned. "Now you see it."

"You knew?" She frowned at him.

"Most of us did."

"Why didn't you say something sooner?"

"We did, more than once." He shrugged. "I got the idea that you stopped listening to what anyone had to say on the matter."

For a few heartbeats, Tereka held his eyes. "You're right," she said. "Nothing you could have told me would have made me feel like the Desired One. I still don't."

"What's a Desired One supposed to feel like?"

She glared at him. "I don't know. Confident? Capable? Worthy?" She scoffed. "Anything but me."

"Just because you don't *feel* capable or worthy, that doesn't mean you aren't. Besides, I've seen you lead. You're good at it.

If I didn't know better, I'd never suspect you doubted yourself."

Tereka stared up at the half moon in the sky.

"Maybe coming here was a mistake," he said. "But we all knew that you'd have to accept your destiny on your own. Too bad we had to come face to face with a monster, but here we are."

Overwhelmed by a searing wave of shame, Tereka fixed her eyes on the ground. Her stubborn refusal to accept who she was hadn't just endangered herself, but all the others. Maybe Juquila's insults about her being worthless spawn weren't so far off the mark. Her face burned. "I'm so sorry for dragging you all here."

Naco shook his head. "We had no place else to go. Besides, we understood why you found it so hard to deny you were the fulfillment of a centuries-old prophecy. You thought the Desired One would be larger than life."

"But instead it's me." A nameless orphan. "Headstrong, helpless, with no idea what to do."

"Don't forget resourceful, brave, loyal, and committed to helping others. I think that's a good start."

Some of the cramping shame in her stomach eased. "Thank you. But coming here was a failure."

"I don't think so."

"You don't?"

"No. You wanted to learn if the Emperor was the Desired One. We know that he and his wife are not. You've accepted that you are."

"I should have figured that out without risking all our lives." She rubbed her tight throat.

"Well, that's true. But we've also learned a lot about what we're up against."

She had to admit he was right on that point. "I still don't know what to do."

"Why do you think you need to have all the answers?"

Tereka laughed bitterly. "Isn't that what it means to be the Desired One?"

"Really?" Naco cocked his head. "I thought it had something to do with bringing a new order."

"And I know how to do that even less than how to get us out of here."

"Have you considered asking the sky-god? That's worked before."

The sky-god. Of course. The sky-god had saved them from being massacred by pirates. And now she realized that was what Cillia had been trying to tell her months ago, that she should try to sense where the sky-god wanted to lead her. She told Naco about her conversation with her grandmother. "I am fifty kinds of a *durak* and thirty kinds of a dolt," she added. "How could I have forgotten that?"

"You've been a little busy, I'd imagine."

"All this time, I've been looking for someone else to be the Desired One, because I felt unworthy. Unable." She gave him a wry smile. "I thought the Emperor, and later the Empress, with all their power, were worthy to fulfill the prophecy. That only someone who knew how to lead could be worthy." She smacked her palm against her forehead. "Instead, I missed the obvious. The sky-god, the source of the prophecy, will guide me."

She pressed her hands to her lips. After a moment's thought, she reached into the hidden pocket of her tunic and gripped the bag that held her amulets. "Could it really be this simple? All I have to do is ask?" She closed her eyes. "Sky-god, please. What do I do?"

The blood whooshed in her ears as she waited, eyes shut. After a few heartbeats, she clenched her fist and let her hand drop to her side.

"Well?"

Opening her eyes, she looked at Naco. "I'm not sure. But I

did get a clear sense we should leave. I think we should get out of here and trust the sky-god to guide us."

Naco nodded. "We're going to need all the help we can get."

Tereka shivered. "You know how this will end if we're caught."

He touched her cheek with one finger. "You and I will be clouds of red mist that merge together in the wind."

27

D amira spurred her horse to gallop through the camp. She ignored the cries of the people who scattered seconds before she trampled them. All she wanted was to flee to the solitude of her yurt.

When she arrived, she brought her mare to a stop and vaulted from the saddle, cursing at her pain and at the groom who tried to steady her on her feet.

She rushed into the yurt. "Out. All of you," she said to her servants. She dropped into a chair and put her head into her shaking hands. What had just happened?

Those deserters deserved death; there was no question about that. Every commander in Razdelia would have ordered their executions. But what caused her to torment them?

It had been many years since she'd tortured a man. The last had been an Izolliyan warlord who bragged about sending his warbands to rape and rob isolated Otrechian clans. Easy pickings, he called them.

A surge of rage had welled within her when she overheard his boasting. He and all his kin had deserved every wound she inflicted on them. Once he was no more than broken pieces scattered for the sand wolves and buzzards, she'd promised Syzyan and Shagonar never to torture again.

Since then, she'd been able to control the urge to use the power to destroy, to fight the voices that commanded her. Why had she failed today? And worse, why had she enjoyed inflicting pain?

Damira rubbed her stinging hands together. Those refugees. Something about them agitated her amulets, that amplified the voices in her head to a thundering crescendo nearly impossible to withstand.

A single dragonfly wouldn't cause so much anger. Her amulets had tolerated the one Syzyan's father-in-law used for healing. They'd warmed and buzzed a little, but that was nothing more than the growling of a watchdog. When those refugees were near, her amulets were hot, like they'd been in a fire. They sent pulses of power into her hands, making them sting.

No, her amulets sensed multiple dragonflies. Most likely, powerful ones.

Kill them all.

She gripped her hands together, not wanting to give into the voices. That's when she did horrible things. And Shagonar and Syzyan looked at her as if she were tainted and evil.

The worst thing was that she enjoyed torturing people, at least while she was doing it. The headaches and sting of the power disappeared. She could breathe freely and felt like a weight had been lifted, as if she'd received the strength and vitality of a woman fifteen years younger who'd never known anything but perfect health. And the emptiness inside faded when she caused pain.

What had happened to the girl she used to be, the girl who took risks to provide food for her family and sang her younger siblings to sleep? The girl whose greatest joy was riding on the steppe with Syzyan and Shagonar? How could she enjoy inflicting pain on another person?

What's not to enjoy about using power?

Where did that thought come from? From her, or the amulets? She stifled a sob and rubbed her eyes. What kind of monster had she become? Is this what happened to Wei Fang?

The door opened. Shagonar entered the yurt and stood a few feet away from her. "How are you feeling?"

"Oh, Shag."

Syzyan followed Shagonar inside. "Dami, what did you just do?" His tone wasn't angry as she'd expected. Sorrow and disappointment softened his accusing words.

She stiffened her spine. "What I had to do."

"Yes, yes, they were deserters." Syzyan let out a long breath. "But to make them suffer? Wasn't killing them enough?"

He's attacking you. Kill him.

Damira shook herself, dismissing the thought. "How dare you question me? I did what I deemed was necessary." Part of her wanted to confess, to allow Shagonar and Syzyan to tell her what to do. Maybe Shagonar could use his amulets to counter hers, just a little. Or at least assure her that he still loved her and didn't think she was horrible.

One thing was evident, however—Syzyan could not witness her doubts. His answer would be to put the amulets away and never use them again. She'd do that once Tlefas was subdued and fully under her control. Then she wouldn't need the scorpions anymore.

Her head throbbed, as if the amulets didn't like the direction her thoughts had taken. Maybe she should listen to them. They'd never led her astray when it came to gaining power. Even when she did dreadful, loathsome things.

Every time she let them lead her, she took another step closer to her goal. One more adversary eliminated, one fewer obstacle between her and her lifelong dream—guaranteed peace in the entire land. A peace that would last. A peace without raiding war bands or scheming warlords or corrupt rulers. She'd force them all to live without fighting. Then she could rest.

She scowled at Syzyan, unsure how to get him to back down.

Kill him.

Never. She would not turn on her brother.

Syzyan crossed his arms. "Dami, did the amulets push you to do that?"

"No." She glared at him. "They wouldn't do that. But they are warning me."

"About what?"

"The strangers. I think one of them bears dragonflies."

"Are you sure?"

"Yes. My amulets are agitated when I am around them."

"Are you certain the refugees are causing it?" He shook his head. "I'm not convinced you have the amulets under control."

Deep down, she wanted to scream that he was right. That he had to help her. But she knew his first proposal would be to get rid of her amulets. And that she could not do. "Syz, you don't know what you're talking about."

"Dami, we can't torture the men," Shagonar said.

"I agree," said Syzyan.

"Fine." She spat the word out. "Then you handle discipline. See if you do any better."

Syzyan nodded. "Yes, that's a good idea. I'll go talk with our Noyan-u Dargas." He spun on his heel and left the yurt, hurrying as if he feared she'd change her mind.

Kill him.

The stinging in her hands intensified. She looked at Shagonar. He studied her face. "Dami, please. No more of this. We can win this war another way."

Kill him.

Kill Shagonar? She shuddered. Never. That would make her as evil as Wei Fang. She'd die first. The coppery taste of blood made her realize she'd chewed on the side of her mouth. No, she'd never be like Wei Fang. She had to convince Shagonar that allowing the amulets to lead was the best way to win.

28

Tereka's thoughts swirled in her head like a flock of startled birds as she plodded beside Naco. She was the Desired One. She supposed she'd always known it, ever since her uncle Tikul told her of the prophecy. All the same, she didn't want to be a mythical figure. That someone who'd been so abused and downtrodden would save the country didn't make sense to her.

But then, Naco's behavior made little sense either. He vacillated from avoiding her, to glaring at Kemet, to waxing poetic about being mist together forever, as if that was a fate he looked forward to. She let out a huff. Should she just ask him what he felt for her? If she'd read what she wanted to see into his behavior, then things could get awkward.

Her face and neck grew hot, and she dipped her chin toward her chest to hide her blush. No, that question would have to wait. She needed his help with the conversation she was about to have with the others. As uncertain as she was about Naco's feelings for her, she was clear about his opinion on her role as the Desired One. Now was not the time to risk shaking his support.

The sun set and Dabney rose, its orb nearly three-quarters

full. The first stars appeared before they reached their yurt. Tereka paused outside the door. She didn't hear the usual laughter. No doubt everyone was as sobered by the day's events as she had been.

Naco pushed open the door. He stood back and motioned for her to enter. She stepped into the yurt, eyes blinking in the light. The brazier's flames jumped in the draft from the open door. The candles flickered.

"There you are, girly." Relio pointed at a cushion. "We've been waiting for you."

She sat down and glanced at the low table. "Is there any tea? I suppose you've eaten all the food."

Savinnia stood up. "I'll get you and Naco some. If you even want to eat."

Tereka grimaced. "No. Tea will be enough for me." She looked at Relio, eyebrows raised. "You want to talk about something?"

He met her gaze, his gray eyes stern, their usual weariness more pronounced than during their worst days in the prison. "What's your opinion about Damira now?"

"Meaning, do I still think she's the Desired One?" She shook her head. "No. That much is obvious."

"And you came to that conclusion because?" Sebezh asked.

"The Desired One will bring a new order. This new order must be a change for the good. Otherwise, why would anyone desire the one who brings it?"

Alikse nodded. "That's what I thought."

A deep stillness fell on the room, like the heaviness in the air before a storm. The only sound was the crackling of the flames in the brazier. Tereka glanced around. Everyone was staring at her. "I suppose, well, I must be the Desired One."

"Now, you tell us," Relio said. "After we're trapped in the camp of an evil sorceress."

"I always knew it was you," Kemet said.

She shot him a look. *Really?*

Tirk rolled his eyes. "You're the Desired One? My sister?"

Tereka gulped. She knew Da hadn't told Tirk the complete story, but this wasn't how she wanted to break the news to him. "Well, Tirk, I'm not your sister."

He shrugged. "I know. Half-sister."

"Oh, he doesn't know. This is going to be good." Relio leaned back with a grin.

"Four sheaves, he makes her cry," Sebezh said.

"No," Alikse said. "Six says she doesn't cry, but he does."

"Seven says he wets himself," put in Hinat.

"What are they talking about?" Tirk scowled and crossed his arms.

Glancing at the door of the yurt, Tereka wished she could take him outside. But they'd been told not to leave their yurt after dark. "Well, Tirk, it's like this. I'm not your sister, not even a half."

He let out a harsh shout of laughter. "Who are you trying to fool?"

She sat next to him so she could whisper. "Tirk, listen to me. You know I'm not Groa's daughter. But I'm not Da's, either."

Tirk frowned. "But—"

"Didn't you ever wonder why we look nothing alike? I'm the daughter of a village girl from Gishin and a Risker. Da traded with the Risker family and knew them well. After my parents married, they fled to the south. Kaberco pursued them relentlessly. A few months after I was born, he killed my father and took my mother captive."

His eyes narrowed, Tirk's stare froze into an icy glare.

"Tereka fits the prophecy," Naco said. "The father wouldn't live to see his child's first steps. The mother wouldn't hear the first words."

"Da knew my parents were in trouble and went after them. That's why he wasn't home when you were born. Your real twin sister died soon after Da brought me back. So he and Groa raised me as their own."

"Why didn't I know about this?" Tirk's voice shook and his cheeks darkened.

"Because Da would have been taken if anyone discovered who my real parents were. I would have been killed. They might have taken Groa as well, leaving you to grow up in the ludi's home. Would you have liked that?"

Tirk scowled at her, then shook his head. "You, the Desired One? Impossible." He waved his hand at the others. "Everyone except me, it seems, knew all about it. You didn't see fit to tell me."

She reached to touch his arm, then let her hand fall. "I would have told you, but—"

"But you didn't trust me."

I didn't. And I was right not to.

He snorted. "That was before. Once we came here, couldn't you have said something? Anything?"

She looked at the young man she'd once thought of as her twin, her ally, her confidant. She still wasn't sure she could trust him to the end. "You're right. I should have told you sooner."

How could she penetrate his anger and get him to see reason? Convince him that she'd kept her secrets to avoid getting them all killed. "That was then. I'm telling you now. You saw Damira, what she did. If she knew I was the Desired One, I'd be dead in a heartbeat."

"If you truly are this mythical leader, what are we going to do now?" Tirk asked. "How are you going to defeat someone who has magic amulets?"

"With some of her own," Relio said.

Tirk jumped up and backed away from Tereka. "You have amulets? Risker magic?"

"Keep your voice down," Tereka said. Why couldn't he take things more calmly? "Yes, I do. Four dragonflies. Two belonged to my parents. The other two belong to the Desired One."

Once he'd moved away as far as he could within the confining walls of the yurt, Tirk paced back and forth, muttering.

"If your family quarrel is over," Relio said, "he does ask a good question. What do we do now? I don't suppose we want to ally with Damira anymore."

"That's the truth," said Tereka with a shudder. "Our best move now is to get away from here as soon as we can."

Sebezh snorted. "Clever. Then we'll get caught as deserters and tortured. Or misted. Great end to the story."

"He's right," Hinat said. "We're stuck here."

"I don't see a way for us to leave unnoticed," Kemet said.

"No?" Naco replied. "Escaping is our specialty."

Tereka could have kissed him for that. She flashed him a smile.

"Naco's right," Savinnia said. "We may only be passable copper miners and indifferent farmers, but we do know how to get away."

"We barely evaded a handful of prison guards," Sebezh countered. "I think we're better off allying with the one who's going to win. She has a power like no one else, and that includes you, girly. Your amulets are no match for hers."

"Tereka and her amulets got us out of tight spots before," Alikse said.

Sebezh spat out a curse. "We nearly died in the process."

"We should trust Tereka," Naco said.

"Trust her?" Sebezh cursed again. "She lied to her own brother. What makes you so sure she won't lie to us?"

If Sebezh felt that way, Tereka wondered if it would be better to leave him behind. No. She couldn't do that to him. Damira would most likely torture him to find out their plans.

"Well," drawled Relio. "The boy did betray her first."

She shot a look at Tirk, who was still pacing and muttering. At least he didn't seem to have heard Relio's words. She didn't want to upset Tirk any more than he already was. And now he probably yearned to return home. Naco, she knew, wanted to go, as did Savinnia. Relio and Alikse most likely were ready to leave. Kemet hunched into himself. She guessed he wanted to flee but feared to risk it. Hinat would go along with Sebezh.

The situation demanded she play this very carefully. "Well, as far as I'm concerned, no one is going anywhere. Sebezh raises a good point. Damira isn't going to allow us to stroll out of here. We'll just have to make the best of it."

She exchanged looks with Naco, who nodded, and Relio, who winked. At least they understood her meaning.

Sebezh let out a huff. "That's the first thing you've said that makes sense."

Ignoring him, Tereka went to sit next to Tirk. He curled his lip. "Don't talk to me. I don't think I ever knew you." He stood up and stalked away.

29

T ereka fought back a retort as she watched Tirk tromp to the other side of the yurt. He dropped to the floor and put his face in his hands. She was wondering whether she should approach him when the door flung open. Two guards stalked in.

One pointed at Tereka. "Emperor Shagonar commands your presence. And that of your brother."

She swallowed hard. Now what? The others all wore the same startled, wary expression, eyelids flared wide, jaws slightly slack. Naco stepped toward her.

The guard raised a hand. "Only them."

With a shrug, Tereka walked toward the door. "Then let's go. We shouldn't keep His Loftiness waiting."

Out in the cool twilight air, she welcomed the light Dabney's nearly full orb shed, making it easier to hold her head up as she walked. Tirk kept his eyes on the ground as he plodded beside her. She would have liked to have an ally accompany her to this summons, but that was not to be. Silently, she trailed after the guards, Tirk keeping pace with her.

They skirted Shagonar's yurt, passing through the camp to

the far side. A few yurts stood apart from the others, surrounded by sentries. Tereka narrowed her eyes and the hair on the back of her neck stood up. It was an odd place for a meeting.

Pointing to the last yurt, the guard barked for her to enter. Tereka pushed the door open and walked in, Tirk on her heels.

This yurt was brightly lit, with several braziers blazing in its center and masses of tall candles on small tables off to the sides. Damira, Shagonar, and Syzyan sat on plain wooden chairs between the tables. The three were dressed in their usual ornate tunics and leggings, the gold and silver threads glinting in the flickering light, the red and black fabric of their clothing shimmering faintly.

The scene reminded Tereka of being on trial, when Kaberco and Juquila were her judges and sentenced her to be taken. She shuddered. That was not an experience she wanted to repeat.

The two guards followed her into the yurt, one pulling the door shut behind him. The other poked Tereka in the back, forcing her to approach the seated rulers.

Emperor Shagonar occupied the middle seat. He tipped his head. "Thank you for coming."

Tereka nodded in return. "Our pleasure, Your Loftiness. If you please, why are we here?"

The Emperor studied her face. "We want to liberate Tlefas as quickly and bloodlessly as we can. As you know, we freed the south in a matter of weeks with little bloodshed. The center of the country is coming around. But there is opposition in the north."

Kaberco. As much as Tereka despised the man, she was thrilled he was standing up to these invaders. She ground her teeth to contain her grin. "What do you want us to do?"

Jianjun Syzyan leaned forward. "We are seeking allies. People who can help persuade the citizens of the north they'd be better off with new rulers. But before we place our trust in someone, we need to know them. We must be sure they will work for us, not against us."

The Empress shifted and frowned. Her brother swiveled toward her, but when she didn't say anything, he continued. "The two of you could be of great help. To that end, we need to know more about you."

"Well, we're from Trofmose," Tereka said as she tried to catch Tirk's eye. "We've told you we're twins. Our da is a trader, mam a vendor."

"Yes, your parents." Emperor Shagonar tapped his fingers on the arm of his chair. "Tell us about them."

Tereka forced herself to breathe slowly. Better let Tirk answer that one. He'd at least believe what he was saying.

"There's not much to tell," Tirk said. "Da was gone a lot. Mam took care of us. We have a younger brother who's nearly four."

"Where did your father go?" Jianjun Syzyan asked.

"He traveled all over the north," Tereka said. "Often to Shinroo and Gishin, sometimes as far south as Anbodu. Or west to Utoro and Paamiat." She shrugged. "I was his apprentice, so I've been to all those places. If you'd like to know about them, I can tell you." She didn't think that information would help them much.

"Don't forget the Riskers," Tirk said.

Her heart lurched. Just the people she did not want to bring up.

"Yes, the Riskers," the Emperor said. "What can you tell us about them?"

"Not much," Tirk said. "It's forbidden to interact with Riskers. They're superstitious barbarians—savages—and are unsafe. Other than traders with special licenses, no one has anything to do with them."

Maybe he was trying to help, Tereka thought. But bringing up the Riskers wasn't especially wise.

"Do you have anything to add?" the Jianjun asked Tereka.

"No, Tirk is doing fine." *Please don't ask me anything. Please.*

"That's surprising," the Jianjun responded. "I thought your da had a license to trade with Riskers. Didn't you ever go there with him?"

The blood surged in Tereka's ears and her heart raced. "He felt I shouldn't go there until I had finished my apprenticeship and was a trader in my own right. You know, taking a girl to savages was a bit risky."

"Is that true?" Jianjun Syzyan turned back to Tirk. "Did you ever hear of your sister going to the Riskers?"

"Well…"

Tereka cut him off. "Da brought me along once. Tirk doesn't know anything about it. That was just before I was taken and Tirk and I hadn't seen each other for months."

Empress Damira sneered and rubbed her hands together. "Enough of these lies." She extended her hand. "He's holding something back. He will tell me."

Tereka recoiled at the sight of the woman's blackened and shriveled fingers. Something in Empress Damira's hand glowed an angry red. She held her hand up and red light flashed at Tirk.

He yelped and clutched his arm. A burned streak ran down his forearm onto his hand. Tereka's throat clenched. Gasps from the Emperor and the Jianjun tore her attention from Tirk to them. Both had slack jaws. Emperor Shagonar was shaking his head.

"Are you sure you're telling the truth?" The Empress growled the words.

"Yes." Tirk's voice came out with a whimper. "She's my twin. Why would I lie about her?"

His words stabbed Tereka in the gut. He'd lied about her before. Was he about to betray her again?

Empress Damira waved her hand. Tirk dropped to his knees and clutched his head.

"You look nothing alike," Damira said. "Are you sure you're twins?"

Tirk lay on the floor, moaning. "I've told you," he gasped. "Everything."

Tereka's mouth went dry. Her hands were sweating. *That should be me on the floor. No matter what he's done in the past, he doesn't deserve this.* "If you please," she said. "Often twins of different sexes look nothing alike."

By now, Tirk had gone limp and silent. Tereka's breath caught in her throat and she lunged for him. "Tirk?" She placed a hand on his chest and focused, fighting her rising panic. Finally, she felt it, the faint throb of his heart. She sagged over him. He was still alive.

"What about you?" Empress Damira asked. "Do you have anything else to say?"

Slowly, Tereka got to her feet. Should she lie? Or tell the truth and hope her amulets could protect her?

"Dami." Emperor Shagonar said. "Stop."

"But—"

The Emperor pointed to Tirk. "He knows nothing. There's no point in questioning him further."

"But what about her?" The Empress raised her hand, the red stones of her amulet twinkling in the candlelight.

Jianjun Syzyan let out a sigh. "She knows the towns of the north. She could be of use. We could have her tell her story of abuse at the hands of the Prime Konamei and his ephor in Trofmose. That could sway the north away from them and toward us."

Empress Damira narrowed her eyes. "We can't use her if we don't trust her."

Tereka attempted to look young, innocent, and malleable. Wide eyes, chin down. Maybe that would do it.

"She came here offering her support. I think we should try to use her." Jianjun Syzyan spoke softly, as if trying to calm an angry cat.

"I don't know." The Empress lowered her hand, but only slightly. "There's something odd about her."

Emperor Shagonar leaned over to her. "You say that about any girl who can shoot as well as you. Besides, if we don't treat her well, she won't want to cooperate with us and we won't gain any advantage from her at all." He raised an eyebrow at Tereka. "Am I right?"

The Jianjun waved a hand. "You don't have to answer that. Please understand, we must be certain of our allies. In our long years of rule, we've been betrayed by many. My sister just wants to be sure of you." He motioned to the guards. "Take them back to their yurt. And send them a healer."

With her steely eyes locked on Tereka, the Empress said, "I'm still not convinced. You'll have to prove yourself to me. But know this. My amulets are uneasy. They sense the presence of the evil dragonfly amulets. When they find the bearer, that person won't spend one more heartbeat without pain. And their death will be neither pleasant nor quick."

30

Syzyan burst from the yurt, tears pricking his eyes. What happened to the sister he loved so much? She'd turned into someone—something—he didn't recognize.

He shuddered, thinking of the smirk that had twisted her lips when she burned the boy Tirk. Even worse was that glimmer in her eyes when she'd invaded the prisoner's mind. This was not the girl he'd grown up with.

Tipping his face to look at the sky, Syzyan yearned for his wife. *Oh, Anzali. How I need you now.* A lump formed in his throat. He longed to have someone to share his agony, but he was the Supreme Jianjun, general over all the armies. He had to maintain an appearance of strength.

The guards outside his yurt stood ramrod straight. He nodded to them. "I'm going to walk. Two of you follow, the other four stay here." He turned and plodded down the row between the yurts. Creaking leather told him his guards had obeyed.

As he strode through the camp, Syzyan's stomach quivered at the scent of cooked game. Soldiers' laughter floated from the yurts, audible but muffled by their felt walls. How could they sound so carefree?

The answer came quickly. Because they didn't allow their sisters to become monsters.

Stones and bones, I have to stop this. But how?

His strides slowed as he left the camp behind. A figure paced near the river, backlit by the risen moons.

Syzyan squinted, then relaxed. "Farnaz, why are you here? I thought you'd be with the refugees."

His son continued to stare at the flowing water. "I, I didn't..."

In the dim light, it was hard to tell, but Syzyan believed he read many of his own emotions in his son's face. Doubt. Fear. Horror. He sighed. For now, he needed to answer Farnaz's questions.

"My son, I feel the need for a walk. Will you join me?"

Farnaz's head jerked up, and he frowned. "Am I in trouble?"

A smile tugged at Syzyan's lips. "No. I just want some company." He turned to his guards. "Wait here for us."

He walked fifty paces to the west, knowing his guards wouldn't object as long as he remained in plain sight. The double moons gave enough light that they cast shadows, so it was unlikely anyone could come upon them unawares.

Syzyan stopped about ten paces from the riverbank. "See the reflection of the moons in the water?" Dabney, the larger moon, had waxed to nearly three-quarters full, while little Zlu was a sliver of a crescent. Their reflections seemed to dance with each other, moving forward and back with the rippling current. "It brings to mind how we used to fish in the Yinga River."

"And you'd pretend to need my help to bring our catch to land." Farnaz smiled. "Somehow, I knew you could easily do it by yourself, but I felt so grown up to work with you." He stepped closer to his father. "Do you think we'll ever fish there again?"

Despite his grim mood, Syzyan laughed. His boy always

brought such joy to his heart, but the feeling was soon replaced by the grip of an icy hand. He beseeched whatever gods were out there to protect his only son.

Because Syzyan knew he wouldn't be able to do it. He let out a slow breath. "I'm not sure." His pulse throbbed over one eye. He feared to bring up the subject he knew was troubling his son, to confess his own part in the evil that now faced them. But he could wait no longer. He spoke quietly, hoping the sound of the water would keep his guards from overhearing. "There were some events today that perhaps were disturbing…"

Farnaz took a step closer. "More than disturbing." His voice shook. Whether it was disgust or fear, Syzyan couldn't tell.

"It's my fault."

"What my aunt did?"

"You know our story. How the three of us, your aunt, uncle, and I learned to use the scorpion amulets."

"And you quit."

"I did. I hated that stinging sensation in my fingers and toes and the fleeting sense that some malevolent mind was trying to infiltrate my own."

"You never told me that part." Farnaz moved back, his wide eyes gleaming in the moonlight.

"Listen, and you'll understand why." Syzyan pressed his lips together. "Using the amulets comes with a price, and Shag and Dami never seemed bothered by that. They gladly worked to master the amulets. Then Dami became Second Wielder. She defeated Wei Fang and took control of Razdelia."

"That's one thing I never understood," Farnaz said. "If my aunt controlled all three Amulets of Power, why did my uncle become the Emperor?"

"Because Otrechia would never accept a woman ruler. I had another reason for encouraging that arrangement. I was concerned that the amulets were starting to control my sister.

Naming Shagonar the Emperor, the acknowledged ruler, would mean he'd be the one making policy, not her."

Syzyan listened to the splash of the water against the river's banks. Eighteen years had passed since those days. They'd brought peace and stability to the country. "Crowning Shag emperor turned out to be a good move. The people like him and respect him. Once the country was at peace, Dami rarely used her amulets. I let myself believe that she'd freed herself of the hold they had over her."

"But what happened?"

"You happened. Your mother and I married shortly after Wei Fang was defeated, and you arrived the following year. Dami and Shag waited to marry until they controlled Uzhasovia and Otrechia, then they had an enormous state wedding. But in the years that followed, no children."

Farnaz shuffled his feet. "What did the doctors say?"

"None of them had an explanation. Dami had several miscarriages and a few stillbirths. No child survived. After one delivery, she fell sick with a fever for weeks. She kept saying the death of her children was the price."

"The price of using the amulets?"

"Perhaps. Or some debt the amulets expected her to pay. I always wondered how she was able to defeat Wei Fang. Maybe the amulets made a bargain with her." He closed his eyes. *What a* durak *I was not to question her then.*

After a few moments, Syzyan continued. "Anyway, when you were about ten, your mother and Damira both became pregnant. Dami was terrified she'd lose another child. Your mother offered to use the healing power of her dragonfly amulets. Dami reacted as if Anzali had proposed poisoning her. I decided my family's health required a trip to Otrechia, and we departed."

"So, that's why we lived on the steppe for a few months."

"Yes. Shag agreed with me that you needed to learn how to ride and hunt like an Otrechian. And I think he knew I feared for my wife's life." Syzyan sighed. "Word came that Dami delivered a healthy girl who was expected to live. I thought it was safe to return, but a few weeks later, the child sickened. Dami was frantic. It didn't help that your mother's health seemed to improve with every day of her pregnancy, and the child within her was active." He swallowed the lump in his throat.

"That would have been—"

"Your sister." Syzyan blinked the tears from his eyes. The pain of losing his daughter still stung, worse than using the amulets ever had. "Dami's child wasted away and died. She became like a crazed sand wolf, seeking something to destroy. The next thing I knew, your mother suddenly died, and our child as well."

"Why?"

"No one knew. The doctors said it was a fever. There was plague in the city, so that made sense." He hung his head. "Over time, though, I began to wonder. And now, seeing what she's capable of, I think it may have been Dami's doing." He rubbed a hand over his mouth. He'd never told that to anyone. Whether the writhing shame he felt came from suspecting his sister or failing his wife, he didn't know.

"She killed my mother, and you did nothing?" Farnaz's tone rose to a shout. He clenched his fist and punched Syzyan's shoulder.

The guards raced toward them, swords held aloft.

"Go ahead," Farnaz spit out the words. "Let them kill me. I'd rather die than belong to you."

31

The full weight of Syzyan's failures cascaded on him like a collapsing tunnel in a mine. He'd thought losing his wife was the worst that could happen. He'd been wrong. And now his own folly trapped him in a pit with no way out.

"Loftiness, stand back," a guard shouted.

Syzyan held up a hand. "It's fine, go back. We're fine."

He waited until the guards had retreated before addressing Farnaz. "I can't blame you for how you feel. Some days, I don't want to know myself." *And now, through my stupidity and cowardice, I've lost my son.*

"Then why didn't you do something?"

"Because at the time, I didn't know. Dami had been so overjoyed at your birth, I couldn't believe she'd deprive me of a second child. It was too monstrous to imagine."

"But you sent me away."

"Yes." Syzyan wanted to hug his son but didn't dare. "Dami was crazed with grief. She took it out on one of the servant's daughters. I hushed that up with a title and a land grant. But I was so afraid for you and what Dami could do in her madness." He gripped Farnaz's forearms. "I know it must have been horrible to lose your mother and then be packed off to live with your grandfather. But I couldn't let anything happen to you."

"Why did you bring me back?"

"Because Shag and Dami named you their heir. I thought that meant Dami had accepted she'd never have a child."

"I didn't want to return, you know."

Syzyan nodded. "You made that very clear." He slid his gaze to meet Farzan's. "But now?"

"I was angry with you. Those first few months without my ana, without you, were agony. For a long time, I believed I was to blame for Ana's death, and that was the reason you exiled me to Vernia. Now I understand why." He frowned. "But you continue to allow your sister to rule even if you suspect she killed my mother?"

"I'm not sure how to stop her at this point." Syzyan let out a slow breath. "And I'm still not entirely certain she did kill your mother. What I did know was that Dami needed to curb the use of her amulets for her own protection—and to protect the people who'd put their trust in us. Shagonar and I labored long to ease her grief and bring her back to reason. We never imagined she'd turn into a tyrant."

"She didn't."

"No, not for many years. After her daughter died, Dami changed. She became convinced that enemies lurked on all sides. For a while, she thought the cooks were poisoning her food and her maid would drown her in her bath." Syzyan smacked his hand against his forehead. "Telling you this makes me wonder if we all hadn't gone mad. Dami from grief, and Shag and me because we didn't take her amulets away."

"Why didn't you?"

"Because her frenzied delusions went away when her amulets were near. Over time, she grew calmer. Shag and I hoped for the best." He shook his head. "But you're right. We should have tried harder. Maybe convinced her to use only the lesser amulets." He paused, searching Farnaz's face. "You're not as angry as I thought you'd be."

"I want to stab you with a thousand daggers." Farnaz turned and faced the river. "But I can't, because I've been having the same argument with myself. I watched my aunt mist two men. How can she have such horrific power? I don't want to believe she enjoys using it. But I can't deny what I saw with my own eyes."

The boulder that had crushed Syzyan's soul lifted. His son had declared he'd rather die than belong to their family, but what he'd just said showed he understood, at least somewhat. "So, here we are."

"Yes, here we are, father, and I don't understand why. The refugees tell me they didn't even know we existed."

Syzyan's stomach rolled over and sourness filled his mouth. "Over time, your aunt became convinced that an invasion was imminent. If she wasn't pointing a finger at the Izolliyans or railing against the pirates that plagued our southern shores, she was looking west, here to the Abandoned Lands. She sent numerous spies who returned saying the inhabitants were preparing to attack. She showed their reports to Shag and me."

"I saw them, too. I believed her."

"As did I. As did your uncle. We couldn't dismiss those reports as delusions. So, we mustered our army and marched over the mountains. And what did we find? A fearful people unable to fight off a roving war band, let alone an army." He couldn't keep the bitterness from his voice.

"What are you saying?"

Forcing himself to breathe deeply, Syzyan considered on his next words and a suspicion he barely admitted to himself. "I believe those reports were lies. Somehow, those cursed amulets gained control over your Aunt Damira. I was a fool to think she would succeed at what many others had failed to do —master the power behind the amulets. Instead, she's ended up like so many others who dared wield the Amulets of Power. Manipulated into committing acts of great evil."

He gazed out at the river. "This is my doing. Shag and I had planned to take her amulets from her after we felt secure in our rule and believed the peace we'd established would hold. I let Dami convince me otherwise. She was so good at controlling the scorpions, I grew complacent and trusted her word." He shook his head and cursed. "A greater fool never lived."

"Father, please. No use thinking that way. It can't be undone."

"That, my son, is true. A thousand sages could think for a thousand years and not devise a way out of this." Syzyan's throat constricted. "This is my fault. I am Dami's older brother. I was head of the household and I failed to protect her from this evil." He balled his hands into fists and rubbed them into his eyes.

Farnaz slid an arm around Syzyan's waist. "You did the best you could, Father."

Syzyan snorted. "I'm glad you think so."

An owl swooped low over the river. It had no trouble hunting alone, Syzyan thought. *But I need an ally.*

Would Farnaz be the right one? With all his being, Syzyan wanted to protect his son, to send him away from the carnage he was certain Damira would unleash if she wasn't stopped.

"You once wanted to work with me to reel in a fish," he said. "I need your assistance now. Will you help me?"

"What do you want me to do?"

"Help me make things right. You've spent time with our guests. Could any of them be the Desired One?"

Farnaz shook his head. "None of them have claimed the title. They say it's only a myth."

"How can that be?" Syzyan said. "Half the people in the south are already hailing my sister as the Desired One. They seem to know all about it."

"Who knows?" Farnaz shrugged. "Perhaps the story is more widely told in the south. But I suspect these refugees know more than they're letting on. One of them is definitely skeptical of the myth. The others? Well, I'm not so sure."

Syzyan let out a breath. "Damira thinks one of them carries dragonfly amulets."

The whites of Farnaz's eyes gleamed in the moonlight as he realized what that meant. "Unless they can prove they don't—"

"They need to flee," Syzyan finished. "I'm not sure I can convince her to let them live much longer."

"Turning people into mist is evil." Farnaz shuddered.

"I agree. No one should have that power."

"Can't my uncle help?"

"I'm still thinking about that." Syzyan thought about the look on Shagonar's face as Damira tortured the deserters. "I think he wants to free Dami from the amulets, but if she learned he was conspiring with us, she'd never trust him again. We need at least one person she'll listen to. It's best I wait to talk with your uncle."

"What are you going to do now?"

"Have you warned the refugees that if they have dragon-flies, they need to leave?"

"Yes, just last night."

"Good. After today, they'll be even more eager to go. If they get away, they can spread the truth about the force that's invaded their land. If one of them is the Desired One, they'd be free to act."

"Does the Desired One even exist, Father?"

Syzyan let out a long sigh. "I wish I knew. An old Vernian prophecy describes how the Desired One of the west will conquer the evil from the east. I hope we can count on the truth in those words."

Farnaz sucked in a breath. "If they're true, then we're on the side of evil. And we'll lose this war."

"Would defeat in battle be worse than supporting an evil power that threatens to destroy us all? The Desired One, who carries three dragonfly Amulets of Power, could be the only one powerful enough to overwhelm the scorpions." Syzyan swallowed hard against the tightness in his throat. "For your mother, your sister, the men who were misted today, and all the other victims of this madness, I must act. Even if I don't survive the attempt."

He waited for a somber Farnaz to nod. "I'm glad you agree. Now, all we have to do is figure out a way to help the refugees escape that won't get them killed."

"Or us."

Syzyan let out a wry chuckle. "If only we could count on that. Spend as much time with them as you can. Find out everything they know about the north, everywhere they've been, everything they've ever done. Something you learn will give us the answer." Syzyan gently pulled Farnaz into his arms and whispered into his ear. "I know I can depend on you. If this ends badly for either of us, know that I am profoundly sorry I didn't stop it sooner. And I will be proud of you to the end."

32

D amira flexed the stinging fingers of her right hand. Was the fiery pain intensifying? She placed her hand back in the bowl of water infused with herbs, water that had been cool and soothing but had warmed so that it barely offset the prickling heat.

The only sound was her own ragged breathing. She wished Shagonar would return. He'd stalked out after she'd interrogated Tirk, not even glancing in her direction, leaving her to rely on a guard to help her hobble back to her yurt.

The horror she'd seen in Shagonar's eyes when she'd burned Tirk disturbed her. Did he not see that she needed to find the bearer of the dragonflies? And that coddling these refugees—if that's what they really were—wasn't getting them anywhere?

Straining to keep from sobbing, Damira took slow, deep breaths. If only she could end all this. They could return to the way things were when they were happy. When Shag looked at her with love and not with the wariness of a gazelle that had scented a venomous snake.

Her husband didn't understand. The amulets hurt her, pushed her, demanded that she kill the bearer of the dragonflies. She couldn't kill everyone until she found that vile person. If she could identify her enemy only by inflicting pain, then so be it. Except Syzyan would never forgive her. And Shagonar would stop loving her. Why couldn't they understand? She wasn't an evil, bloodthirsty killer. She was no rabid sand wolf.

A servant entered the yurt and bowed. "Your Loftiness, one of the refugees requests an audience."

She raised her eyebrows. "Which one?"

"He says his name is Sebezh Einkorn."

Damira frowned. Who was that? "Send him in." She pulled her hands from the water and concealed them in the flowing sleeves of her silk tunic.

The man entered the yurt, moving with just the right combination of confidence and deference. *Interesting.* He stopped several paces from her. She studied his face. Thick, sensual lips perched over a jutting jaw covered with a scruffy red beard. Sloping shoulders topped his large frame. He looked like a mix of tanned Vernians and brown-skinned Uzhasovians.

"What do you want?" she said.

"If you please, Your Loftiness, I think you should know something."

"What is this something you think is so important that you interrupt me this late at night?"

He flinched at her imperious tone, or at least she thought he did. It was difficult to tell in the candlelight.

"It's about Tereka Sabidur. I don't think she's told you the whole truth about herself."

Damira suppressed the smile that twitched the corners of her mouth. She knew there was more to be learned about that girl. "Go on."

"Some of her relatives are Riskers."

Gripping her hands together, Damira forced herself to remain impassive. "How do you know?"

"When we escaped from prison, she led us to the Riskers. Turned out her father was one of them. His family gave us a place to live and helped us get through the winter."

"Her father wasn't there?"

"No. From what I heard, he was killed when she was just a few months old."

The blood thrummed in Damira's ears. *The father won't live to see his child's first steps.* That's what the prophecy said. "What about her mother? Was she a Risker?"

"No, a villager. Rumor has it she was taken. We heard she might have been held in the same prison we were in. But we left before Tereka found out for sure."

Damira nodded, trying to feign indifference. "When was her mother taken?"

"Oh, right after her Risker husband was killed."

The mother won't hear her child's first words. Another part of the prophecy. Damira's heart fluttered. "So, this Risker. What did he look like?"

"I don't know. I'm told Tereka favors him, except she has blue eyes like most of his family. His eyes were green."

A green-eyed man who was a skilled archer, who passed his skills to his child. Farnaz said she shot well. The last piece. Tereka must be the Desired One.

Kill her. Kill her. Destroy her.

The voices of her amulets buzzed in her head. "Do you have anything else to say?" Her tone was sharper than she'd intended, but it was hard to be bland with the stinging pain shooting through her limbs.

Sebezh winced as if she'd struck him. She sucked in a breath. The power was escaping from her when she didn't want it to. She tipped her head to the side and sent a tendril of power into his mind, seeking to calm him. "Please, speak. Tell me everything."

"If you please, she has amulets. She uses them to heal people."

Damira stifled the screaming voices in her mind. "What kind of amulets?" She wasn't able to keep the growling menace from her voice.

"Dragonflies, if you please." Sebezh's knees were visibly shaking.

The voices grew shrill, piercing her brain as if a buzzard had shrieked in her ears.

"What do they look like?" Her words jumped from her mouth in an angry snarl.

"I've never had a good look at them." Sebezh scratched his face. "Purple and green stones."

Useless. This *durak* was useless.

Kill him.

"How many stones are in the tail?"

"One, maybe two. Or three."

She stood up, her eyes wide and staring, a scowl twisting her mouth. Why didn't this idiot know? Pressure built in her head and she nearly gasped. There was only one way to ease the pain. Tereka would have to die.

A glance at Sebezh halted her in her tracks. His mouth was hanging open, and he was cowering away from her, cringing like a whipped dog. His eyes weren't just wide and fearful. The loathing in them caught her breath. Exactly like Shag and Syz when I misted the deserters.

Ice crawled through her veins, spreading a nauseating chill through her body as if carried by a swarm of locusts. Her knees wobbled, and she sank into her seat. She released her breath slowly, as if controlling the air while it left her lungs could restrain the impulse to destroy. She would have to be careful. What would be the point of defeating her enemies if she lost Shagonar and Syzyan? She rubbed her burning fingers against her legs.

Kill her. Destroy her.

Yes, that would have to happen. But perhaps she didn't have to be the one to do it. She rested her aching head against the backrest of her chair. "Thank you for telling me. This is valuable information." She narrowed her eyes slightly. "I presume you expect a reward?"

"I, I just want to be your loyal servant."

Oh, this one was clever. He knew better than to ask for riches or power. "Loyal servants are vital to any ruler. But they must prove themselves." She knotted her stinging fingers together.

Kill her. Destroy her.

"I'll do anything," Sebezh said.

"Good. This is what I need you to do for me. One small favor, and I'll know you're on my side. And be assured, I lavishly reward those who demonstrate their loyalty." She raised her eyebrows. When he nodded, she continued. "All you have to do is kill Tereka and bring me her amulets."

His eyes flickered, but he nodded. "As you say."

She smiled. His reply was no surprise. Some people were no more than tools, willing to do anything to get close to power. The voices ebbed, the pain subsided. *Excellent. I can eliminate that threat without Shag or Syz getting upset with me.* She jerked her chin toward the door to dismiss him. "Think about how you'll kill the girl. It can't look like someone hired you to do it. Find an opportunity and do the job."

He nodded.

"And"—she stared at him until his knees resumed their trembling—"do not tell anyone about our conversation or ever repeat the things you've told me. If I learn you have, your death will be the most painful one my amulets can inflict."

33

Juquila stormed up the steps of the ephor's house. Blast Kaberco. What was so important that he sent one of his clerks to tell her he required her presence immediately? He'd become imperious in the days since the invasion of Tlefas, testier and less willing to listen to anything she had to say. That needed to end.

The clerk had run ahead of her, clearly under orders to report to Kaberco. She'd show him. With a smirk, she slowed her pace, sauntering down the corridors of the house. How she loved living there when she was married to Valday. Not that she enjoyed him, that old flabby man. But the three-story residence with the luxurious carpets, exquisite glassware, plush furniture, and servants to wait on her certainly had its charms. She missed the maid who'd brushed her hair. The pretty girl had been amiable, even smiling when Juquila joked no one could ever know about her long hair hidden under her turban. One benefit of being married to a konamei. No mandatory haircuts for her. *Safety and fairness for all. What a farce.*

A guard at the foot of the stairs that led to the ephor's private quarters saluted her. She ignored him and ascended with deliberate steps, taking her time. She didn't want to arrive out of breath. And irritating Kaberco by making him wait amused her. She smiled, thinking about how she could use this crisis, whatever it was, to provoke him further.

She ambled down the long corridor to the konament's meeting room. Thick carpets muffled her footsteps. The only illumination was the sunlight streaming through the window at the end of the hallway.

One of Kaberco's servants stood outside the door. The girl inclined her head and wordlessly opened it. Juquila swept past her.

Only the other four konament members were there, but the room seemed crowded. Perhaps because they were all shouting. Whatever the reason Kaberco had summoned them, it was causing quite a stir.

As she stepped into the chamber, Juquila controlled her expression, showing only mild interest. The others didn't seem to notice her presence. Birita, the adile, was red-faced, her turban askew. Her lips trembled as if she was about to cry. Kulooq, the ludi, was pounding on the table with a clenched fist. Yavaros, the questor, was bellowing at Kaberco, demanding he do something.

Juquila fingered the bronze chain that hung over her shoulders. How long should she wait before interrupting?

"At last." Kaberco scowled at her. He jerked his hand, pointing at her usual seat. "I'm so glad you were able to make it. I hope I didn't tear you from anything important."

His sarcastic words sailed past Juquila as if they were dust motes floating on a breeze. With a few light steps, she glided to her chair and gracefully sat down. "I was rather busy. Can you tell me what the fuss is about?"

Kulooq stared at her. "You don't know?"

"About?"

Kaberco shoved a rolled-up document toward her. "You haven't seen these?"

With a shrug, Juquila reached for the paper and spread it out.

Residents of the north,

Why do you allow yourselves to be oppressed by those who care nothing for your safety? They force you into labor so they can live comfortable lives, while you who toil gain no reward.

She kept her eyes on the writing. Whoever wrote this had written the truth. She couldn't deny that. But who had revealed the secret?

Our siege of Anbodu has your Prime Konamei trapped. His attention is on his own survival and well-being, not yours.

He has also failed to tell you the Riskers tire of their lives in the mountains and no longer care to honor the treaty. They are massing for an attack.

Juquila pursed her lips. It was unlikely the Riskers would break the treaty, although the threat of an attack by the barbarians was a fear stoked by the Prime Konamei to keep the villagers in line. The writer of this screed was clever to use it to stir up anxiety.

Your ephor, Kaberco Gougin, is helpless to save you. He and his konameis can do nothing for you.

Ordinarily, she'd welcome any criticism of Kaberco. But this slur included her. That was insufferable.

We hear that the Riskers have recruited bandits and pirates to their cause. They have united in exploiting the weakness of your Prime Konamei and his minions to plunder your land.

I, Shagonar Ortan the Peacemaker, Emperor of Razdelia, will send my army to save you. To rescue you from the Riskers, bandits, pirates, and any others who have threatened you. And from the Prime Konamei and his servants who have oppressed you. Join me and you will learn what a truly peaceful, safe, and fair life can be.

So that's who was behind this. The Emperor had probably questioned some of the southern konameis, learned the actual state of affairs in Tlefas, and was using that information to his advantage.

Juquila looked up at Kaberco. "It seems this Shagonar doesn't have a high opinion of you."

He curled his lip. "You don't want to know what I think of him." He cursed and gestured at the paper in front of her. "He sent birds carrying bundles of these papers. They were dropped all over town. I'm surprised you heard nothing of it."

She rubbed her chin. She'd ordered her clerks not to disturb her while she reviewed the tax revenues for the month. There had been some extra noise in the outer office, but she'd ignored it. "What about the other towns in the region?"

Kaberco huffed. "I sent birds to the ephors. So far, only Shinroo has responded. They got the same message. I'm guessing all the others have as well."

A bead of sweat rolled down the questor's brown cheek. He glared at Kaberco. "What are you going to do about it?"

"For one thing," Kaberco said, "I don't believe the pirates and bandits are trying to unseat the Prime Konamei."

"How would you know that?" asked the adile. "Do they consult you?"

The ephor's olive face flushed. Juquila had never seen Birita attack him like that. Could she persuade the woman to help her oppose him? "Yes, do tell us how you know their plans," she said.

Nostrils flaring, Kaberco glared at her. "Think about it. Pirates and bandits are businessmen first and foremost. You, of all people, should understand this."

Juquila narrowed her eyes.

He pulled in a long breath, forcing himself to calm down. He was sure he'd regret using that patronizing tone with her.

Kaberco exhaled deliberately, then spoke slowly, as if explaining complicated matters to a child. "They rely on others to produce food and goods, so there is something for them to steal. If the country falls apart, no one will produce much of anything. If a stronger ruler takes over, it will be harder for them to operate." He shook his head. "No, they have no incentive to do anything. And it's inconceivable that they'd ally with the Riskers."

Finding it hard to keep her expression mild, Juquila ground her teeth together. Kaberco just loved to lord it over her, act like he knew everything and she knew nothing. What made it more annoying was the fact that he did have a point about the pirates and bandits. And he was most likely right about the Riskers. From all she'd heard from her traders, they were content with the terms of the treaty.

Which meant the Emperor was lying in an attempt to convince them to surrender. Did that mean he didn't think he could defeat Kaberco, or was he playing a game of diplomacy?

The others argued. Kaberco and surprisingly, Kulooq, thought they should resist, while Birita wanted to capitulate. Yavaros crossed his arms and added little to the discussion. Juquila waited for a lull before asking her question. "If you please, what progress have you made raising your army?" She twitched one side of her mouth up in a mocking sneer.

"Not much, if you must know. Very few, other than traders, are willing to even consider learning to fight." Kaberco matched her sneer with one of his own. "Perhaps if you hadn't been so adamant against allowing traders, herds-men, and farmers to arm themselves, we'd have more people who would make effective soldiers."

"Oh, I'm not the only one," Juquila said. "You know as well as I do the Prime Konamei fiercely opposed arming the population."

"This is pointless." The questor crumbled the Emperor's message into a ball. "What's done is done. We need to decide how to answer this propaganda. The people will demand to know what we are doing to keep them safe."

Yavaros was right, Juquila thought. What are we going to do? Not about the people; they were of little consequence. But what about ourselves?

Kaberco's voice rose until he was shouting. "We tell them this is a pack of lies from someone who wants to intimidate us. That more than ever, we need them to help defend our villages. We will not give in to this invader." As he spoke, he fastened his gaze on each of his konameis in turn. The ludi nodded and smiled. The adile looked away, while the questor's face was impassive.

How much support does he have? Juquila knew it didn't really matter. Kaberco could not defeat the invaders.

When he came to her, she met his gaze head-on. "I'm not so sure I agree." When his expression hardened, she added, "If you please."

"Why not?" He hurled the words out like knives aimed at her chest.

"Training an army is a fool's dream," she said. "You will never have a force ready to oppose the Emperor's thousands. From what I hear, life in the south is peaceful and orderly. Nothing much has changed. So why not surrender? It would be better to ally with these people than to make them our enemies."

After studying her face for a moment, Kaberco turned away. "What do the rest of you think?"

The adile spoke up quickly. "I agree with the syndic. If we submit, we won't suffer the death and destruction of war. We won't have to rebuild. We'll be able to live as before."

The ludi shook his head. "We have no reason to believe that this emperor will allow us to be free. We only have the word of someone who wants control. What will he do when he gets it?"

Juquila stared at the man. Now, he develops a backbone? Now, he starts thinking for himself? She stifled a huff of irritation.

The questor ran a hand through his iron-gray hair. "I think we gain nothing by yielding. We're better off waiting, perhaps trying to negotiate terms to buy ourselves some time, and to try to discern just how sincere the Emperor is."

"That makes three in favor of not surrendering," Kaberco said.

"That's your decision?" Juquila sneered. "You're all fools. I've half a mind to send a bird in response, offering my help."

Kaberco stood up. "Know this. If you do, I'll have you imprisoned. The konament has duly voted and you have no right to oppose our decision."

She stared back at him. He could do that. But she was sure he'd chosen the losing side. For now, she needed to retain her position, so she could use it to gain favor with Emperor Shagonar. If Kaberco learned of her plan, she'd be taken. If she was successful, she'd have found a way to finally oust Kaberco. It was a gamble she was willing to take.

Tipping her head to the side, Juquila lowered her eyes. Using her sultriest voice, she said, "Of course. And I apologize. The threat of an invasion has us all on edge. You know I will always back you up, Kaberco."

He pressed his lips together and nodded. "Good. Now, let's prepare our response."

The others debated wording and tone and offered suggestions. Juquila cooperated just enough for Kaberco to believe she was sincere in her loyalty pledge. Just enough for him to keep his focus on the threat from the south and overlook the one from within.

34

The silence in the yurt pressed on Damira like the heavy air before a thunderstorm. She shifted in her chair and winced at the stinging pain that shot up her legs. For the past three days, her only company had been her pet rabbit and the servants who brought her meals and massaged her aching limbs and head.

The thickness in her throat threatened to choke her. She hadn't seen Shagonar since she'd interrogated Tirk. At least her husband had kept up appearances that all was well. One of her maids mentioned that he'd been living in Syzyan's yurt, telling everyone he didn't want to disturb Damira because she was ill.

His words were truer than he knew. She didn't have to pretend that her entire body hurt. But the stinging agony caused by the overuse of the amulets or defying their will was not her only pain. She also felt the ache of longing, of rejection, and the fear that Shagonar's love was lost to her forever.

She crumpled in her seat, holding her rabbit to her chest, nuzzling its obsidian fur with her lips. *Oh, Shag. Will I ever see you again?* She closed her eyes and rocked from side to side, willing the black despair to recede.

The door to the yurt opened. "I'm not hungry," she said to whoever had invaded her lonely suffering.

Slow, heavy footsteps approached her. "I'm sorry to hear that."

Her eyes flew open. Shagonar was standing in front of her, his face drawn. For a moment, she couldn't believe what she was seeing. She gasped and held a hand out to him. "Shag."

He grasped it and sat beside her. "How are you feeling?"

"Better, now that you're here." A sob forced its way out of her throat. "I've been so alone…"

His tawny eyes roamed over her face. "I'm sorry. I just, I don't know. Maybe I was wrong. But, snake's teeth, Dami. I'd thought you'd promised not to torture anyone ever again. And the other night, it appeared—"

"I don't enjoy it, if that's what you think." Damira met his gaze head-on. *May he never know that's partly a lie.*

"I'm glad to hear that." He tipped his head to the side, massaging her fingers and giving her the half smile that never failed to make her knees weak. "Do you mind if I eat? You should have something, too."

"Yes, Shag, whatever you want." Food held no appeal for her. But if choking down a few bites would keep him next to her, she'd swallow slugs if he asked her to.

She leaned against the high back of her chair, content to watch him summon the servants who carried in steaming platters of fried rice, sautéed chicken and vegetables, and mounds of dates and figs. One woman lingered to brew tea, then scurried out at Shagonar's command.

He piled food on a plate and placed it on the low table next to her. "Do you need help?"

"I can manage." She couldn't let him see how just the act of holding a spoon made her blackened fingers ache. It had been years since she'd been able to use the thin eating sticks the Uzhasovians favored. She bit into a date, savoring its sticky sweetness. "Have we heard from Anbodu?"

Shagonar rolled his eyes. "Not a word. They've been sending birds north and have received quite a few back. No doubt they're asking about the leaflets we dropped on five towns in the north." He reached for a flagon of wine and poured the crimson liquid into a glass.

It was too early for wine, but Damira didn't want to say anything to make her husband's dimples fade. "That was clever to incite the northern towns to doubt the Prime Konamei."

His grin made her catch her breath. For the first time in years, he looked like the easygoing boy she'd fallen in love with.

"Yes, it was," he said. "Syz wasn't sure it would work. The lack of response from Anbodu suggests that it did."

"So you were right all along."

He bit into a fig. "These are good. Not mushy, like dates." He chewed and swallowed. "We'll see. Now we're having another debate." He launched into a detailed explanation of his scheme for attacking Anbodu, compared to Syzyan's more cautious plans.

Damira paid little attention. She nodded, made encouraging noises, and offered support for his views. Anything to keep him talking with her, close enough for her to touch. If she didn't have him, she'd lose her will to fight to control the amulets. Then all this pain would have been for nothing.

She was sipping her third cup of tea when Syzyan strode in. He paused near the entrance, his eyes narrowing as he examined her face.

"Join us, Syz," Shagonar said. "You'll be happy to know your sister agrees we should wait before moving against Anbodu."

Syzyan removed his round hat with the golden spike and sat on a cushion near Damira. "I'm glad to hear it. Why?"

"Because, as you have said, we want them to trust us and believe that we will keep our promises." She set her teacup down. "We gave them three days to surrender under the terms that the Prime Konamei could retain some of his authority. It's been seven days. So, he wants to keep all his power. Fine. We make sure the people know he's willing to risk a long siege and destruction of the city. Maybe they'll pressure him to surrender. If not, we move."

"You're right." Syzyan poured himself a cup of tea. "It would be better to have them capitulate." He sipped. "Not just the people of Anbodu. The more people we convince to believe we will keep our promises, the easier it will be to secure the peace."

Damira leaned forward. "Do you have anything in mind?"

"Well, yes. I've been thinking. The ephors in the south tell me that everyone loathed the practice of taking those who had offended the regime in some way. Whether they were lawbreakers or simply asked the wrong questions, offenders were taken and never seen again."

Which isn't a bad way to keep order, Damira thought. Fear is a powerful motivation to obey. "I can see why people with no power wouldn't like that."

"So we've abolished the practice in the south. Once we did that, most of the opposition to our reign died out." Syzyan reached for a fig. "Which got me to thinking. What happens to the taken?"

Shagonar poured another glass of wine. "Well, the refugees say they were put to work in the Prime Konamei's copper mines."

"Right." Syzyan nodded. "What if we liberate the prisoners? We could offer them a place in our army or they could return home. Either way, we will have gained favor from them and their families."

"That's brilliant," Shagonar said. "We wouldn't have to send many men. Two, maybe three arbatus?"

"At least." Syzyan bit his lip. "We don't know what resistance the guards will put up. And we'll need to send a big enough force to keep the prisoners from turning on whoever liberates them." He turned to Damira. "What do you think?"

Her amulets buzzing, she considered her answer. Something about this plan didn't sit well with her scorpions. "Freeing the prisoners is a good idea, but I don't think they'll be in any condition to fight, even if they want to."

"That's a good point, Dami," Shagonar said. "Why would they even believe us? They might suspect they're being freed just to be slaughtered."

"That's the flaw," Syzyan said. "We need to gain their trust."

"Perhaps bring them wine and new clothes?" Shagonar asked.

Syzyan nodded. "That could be a good start. But maybe send a messenger they would believe. One of their own. Like one of the refugees."

Offering a sliver of carrot to her rabbit, Damira kept her eyes on the feeding animal. Her amulets were hot and the voices in her head were murmuring.

"I like it," Shagonar said. "Which one? The girl that leads them?"

"She would be a fine choice," Syzyan said. "She's well-spoken. But maybe some of the others, too? Like that big growly one. Relio, I think his name is?"

"Yes," Shagonar said. "And the blond one with the massive hands. They say he can crack a man's neck with a single twist. If they ran into trouble with the prisoners, he'd be a valuable one to have."

Should I go along with this or not? Damira stroked her rabbit as she considered. Letting Tereka out of her sight was risky. But if she could send Sebezh on the mission, he'd have an excellent chance of killing her.

She swallowed hard, trying to suppress the stinging in her feet.

Kill her. Kill her. Kill her.

The amulets were screaming, filling her aching head with stabbing pain.

"What do you think, Dami?" Syzyan asked.

Damira sank her fingers into the rabbit's soft fur. To agree would be a gamble. If Tereka wielded dragonfly amulets, Sebezh might not be able to kill her.

Perhaps, if she agreed, she could get something in return. She wondered how badly Syzyan wanted to send the fugitives away. Was this really just a means to win over the population? "I'm not so sure. The mines aren't that close. Liberating all the prisoners could take weeks."

"True." Syzyan pursed his lips. "But it will be worth it. We'll establish ourselves as benevolent and fair, far superior to the Prime Konamei." He ran a finger over the map. "Besides, we're in no hurry. We control all the food coming from the south. Anbodu will run out of provisions, eventually. In the meantime, we can send a few arbatus to protect the southern and western caravans. If that drives the bandits north, all the better. We'll give Kaberco one more problem to deal with."

Stabbing pain lanced through Damira's head. Maybe Syzyan was in no hurry, but she needed action, or the pain from her amulets would kill her. "What you say makes sense, Syz. But we should give the Prime Konamei a reason to think twice about waiting us out.

Syzyan frowned. "How?"

"We demonstrate our power to the Riskers."

"What will that do?" Shagonar asked.

"Two things. On the one hand," she said, "we show the Riskers our power, which might convince them it's futile to oppose us and compel them to surrender to us."

"Perhaps." Syzyan drummed his fingers on the table. "It would be best to secure the cooperation of the Riskers. That way, we could prevent them from aiding the Prime Konamei and anyone else who resists us. Everything we hear of the Riskers indicates they want to be left in peace. We can offer to leave them be if they help us, or at least deny help to our enemies. But I'm not sure attacking them is the best way to communicate that."

"And your second reason to attack the Riskers, Dami?" Shagonar asked.

"Well, there are a lot more villagers than Riskers, so I think it's important to subdue the villagers first. We know they fear the Riskers. Any attack on them would make the villagers more likely to favor us."

Syzyan grinned. "Dami, I didn't know you studied ancient Uzhasovian war strategies. Advance by a hidden route while repairing the road in the open. Very clever of you."

Damira lifted her rabbit and buried her face in its fur. It wouldn't do for Syzyan to witness her glee that he was going along with her scheme. Or allow him to suspect she had another goal in mind. She nuzzled the rabbit, then lowered it to her lap.

"So, we're agreed." Shagonar gulped the remains of his wine. "When should we visit the Riskers?"

"Oh, the sooner, the better, don't you think?" Damira appealed to her brother. She needed to appease her amulets if she didn't kill Tereka immediately, as they were demanding. Otherwise, the pain would make her lose control.

Shagonar rolled his shoulders. "Why not tomorrow?"

"We only need to impress them, Dami," Syzyan said. "No need to kill anyone."

"Of course, Syz. I promise."

Kill them.

That's what her amulets wanted. She wasn't sure what she wanted.

"And," Syzyan said, "I think we should still try to free the Prime Konamei's prisoners."

Damira ran a hand over her lips. So, Syzyan wasn't going to let that idea go.

Reaching for a flagon, Shagonar poured the remainder of

its contents into his glass. He frowned when there was only enough to fill it halfway. "I agree. The more people we can persuade to our side, the better."

"The question is, how many of the refugees should go?" Syzyan counted on his fingers. "There are nine of them. Maybe send four or five?"

Whatever happened, Damira thought, both Sebezh and Tereka needed to go. "I think we should ask the fugitives if they want to be part of the liberation, to test whether their support is sincere." She smiled. "And if they all ask to go, we keep one behind. Just to make sure the others come back."

Syzyan gave her a piercing look. "That's fine with me. I'll send them off tomorrow."

Returning her brother's stare, Damira wondered why he was in such a rush to send the fugitives away.

His face stilled and she couldn't read the expression in his gray eyes. He was plotting something, that much she was certain. She'd have to make sure he didn't interfere with her plans. Or her amulets might force her to take action against him that she'd later regret.

35

A burst of wind shook the felt walls of Syzyan's yurt, making the flames in the brazier shudder. Damira shivered in the icy draft. She drew her cloak tightly around her shoulders and buried her stinging fingers in its plush fabric.

Her brother pulled a candelabra closer to himself. He and Shagonar sat at a low table, reviewing reports from their aides, missives from the ephors of the southern regions, and a plea for negotiation from an ephor in the center of the country.

She let their words float past her. All night, she'd wrestled with the problem of how to arrange for both Sebezh and Tereka to be in the party sent to liberate the prison camps. Syzyan had a suspicious look in his eye anytime she made a suggestion. She didn't want him to conclude she had hidden motives.

"Anything from the north?" Shagonar asked.

Syzyan wrinkled his forehead. "Nothing. I would have thought at least one ephor would want to talk. Not a one."

"That Kaberco has things firmly in hand." Shagonar dropped the document and reached for the teapot.

"That's what puzzles me," Syzyan said. "The south and

part of the center gave up without a fight. As if they were too afraid to even resist. Why is their reaction different from the north?"

Damira pressed her lips together to contain a smirk. "You pose a good question. But why are you asking us?"

"What do you mean?" Syzyan asked.

"When those fugitives arrived, I wanted to kill them. You both thought they'd be useful. Now you want to commission them on a potentially useless errand. Wouldn't it make sense to ask them these questions before you send them away?"

Shagonar smiled and offered Damira a cup of tea. "What would we do without you?"

Warmth spread through her, melting the icy fear that made her dread she was losing him. She accepted the tea and smiled back. "Find someone else to do your thinking for you, perhaps?" She waved at the servant. "Go fetch the fugitives." She turned to Shagonar and Syzyan. "Let's see what they have to say." She shrugged and sipped her tea as if this conversation was of scant interest to her.

Her brother and husband nodded and resumed their discussion of how best to occupy the troops during the siege of Anbodu. Damira let her shoulders relax. *Good.* She'd have one last chance to discern whether Tereka had dragonflies. She'd thought long about searching the girl but abandoned the idea. Legends claimed the amulets had a way of hiding if they didn't want to be found. Frisking Tereka would only put the girl on her guard. If the amulets weren't found when the fugitives were searched when they first showed up, they wouldn't be discovered now.

It was of no consequence. Soon, Tereka and Sebezh would be on their way to the prison camps. If he killed her, she'd be free of Tereka and whatever amulets she possessed. That potential claimant for the title of the Desired One would be eliminated.

If Sebezh failed, no matter. He was a snake, that one,

ready to slither to the winning side. Loyalty was just a word to him. She'd find another way to dispose of Tereka.

CHIN UP, back straight, Tereka entered the yurt. Damira had to admire her courage, or at least her display of it. Did that confidence come from bearing powerful amulets? Her own amulets warmed the moment Tereka stepped over the threshold.

Tereka's friends filed in after her. Tirk remained near the back of the group, his eyes wide and he shuffled his feet from side to side. Damira smiled to herself. At least she had one person out of that bunch properly cowed.

Syzyan looked up. "Oh, you're here." He pointed to the brightly colored cushions scattered on the mat-covered floor on the other side of the low table. The cushions' scarlet, topaz, cobalt, and emerald squares were stitched with gold and silver threads that gleamed in the yurt's dim light. "Please, sit. Would you like some tea?"

Glancing from Syzyan to Damira, Tereka wrinkled her forehead before sitting on a cobalt cushion. "Yes, Your Loftiness, if you please." Her companions settled onto cushions. They kept their eyes fixed on Syzyan, their movements slow and wary, like a rabbit that sensed a predator.

Damira eyed them, careful to keep her expression bland. The one with coppery skin and tawny eyes that reminded her of Shagonar's sat behind Tereka, the girl he claimed was his sister by his side. The brash one who seemed like he wanted to lead sat next to Tereka, the blond one they said could break a man's neck with a twist of his hands on her other side.

Her eyes slid over Sebezh and the other two before returning to Tereka. Did the girl have amulets or not?

A servant filled teacups and placed them on the table.

Tereka reached for one, but pulled her shaking hand back and didn't take it.

So, she's not so brave as she wants us to think. Damira suppressed a smile. She cast her power toward Tereka, sending just a flimsy, seeking tendril.

Other than the familiar sting of the power in her fingers and toes, she sensed nothing. Either Tereka didn't have amulets or she was hiding them well. Damira twisted her hands together and sent her power around the other fugitives. No hint of a dragonfly.

She pressed her lips together. That girl had to be the bearer of the dragonflies. Why else were Damira's scorpions warm and vibrating? There must be some way to rattle Tereka, to get her to drop whatever protection she had around her amulets that obscured their presence.

Syzyan leaned forward, unrolling a map of Tlefas. "We have a question for you." He pointed at Litavye. "When we first arrived, the ephor of the southern region immediately embraced us as liberators. We had no problem in the south convincing people they would be better off under our rule."

"Yes, that's what we heard," Tereka said. She picked up a teacup and cradled it in her hands.

"Here in the center," Syzyan pointed to Anbodu. "It's been a little more difficult, which we anticipated. The Prime Konamei doesn't want to give up his power and the people appear to be loyal. But they haven't put up much resistance."

Shagonar snorted. "All they've done is retreat behind their city walls, leaving the villages to fend for themselves. Had we wanted to destroy them all, we could have."

With her lips pursed, Tereka nodded. Damira noted her acknowledgment of that truth.

"But here, in the north," Syzyan tapped Trofmose, "we have Kaberco Gougin, who refuses to submit. Why do you think that is?"

Tereka sipped her tea and managed to set the cup down

without clinking it. Damira observed the girl's spine was no longer as stiff as a spear and the muscles around her eyes had relaxed. Syzyan was doing what he does so well, making people trust him.

"Kaberco is relentless in his pursuit of power and wealth, all in the name of safety and fairness," Tereka said. "He'll stop at nothing to achieve them. He must think your rule won't be safe or fair."

"Where did he get that idea?" Damira asked. She spoke softly, trying to put Tereka at her ease. That would make the blow fall harder when she did attack the girl.

"Well, you did invade our country." Tereka shrank a little and softened her tone. "If you please, Your Loftiness."

"True, we did," answered Damira. "But it was necessary. We had received word that your Prime Konamei was about to attack us."

36

T ereka's jaw dropped. A few curses and mutters from her friends told her they were equally stunned by the news. She rubbed her eyes and blinked. "That's not possible."

The Empress gave her a stony stare. "We can show you the reports from our spies. Once we got the word, we knew we could not allow Tlefas to invade."

Swallowing hard, Tereka scoured her memory. This just couldn't be true. "I, I never heard of even a rumor of that."

Shagonar laughed. "I don't suppose the Prime Konamei consulted you on matters of policy."

"No, he didn't. But this is impossible. They always told us no one had survived the Endless War. No one knew about you until your army marched over the mountains."

"Your rulers have never lied to you about anything?" Jianjun Syzyan asked.

"They lie all the time." Tereka let her head droop.

"And then some," put in Relio.

"You see, then," Damira said. "They assured you that you were safe because no one lived on the other side of the mountains. They insisted that everyone had to dress, eat, and live the same. Yet they lived in unimaginable luxury. They claimed you were working toward prosperity, while in reality, it was never to be realized for everybody. They promised peace but couldn't even control roving bandits."

"All that is true," Tereka said slowly. The Empress's words were swords that cut through the deception that was Tlefas. Even though Tereka agreed with everything the Empress said, it felt like her world had shattered.

Damira went on. "Your rulers made their treaty with savage Riskers, who had no intention of doing anything for anyone that didn't enrich themselves. In fact, they were plotting to invade your villages themselves."

Tereka stiffened and stifled her reply. That, she knew, wasn't true. Why would the Empress lie now?

When the Empress locked her narrowed eyes on Tereka's face, a chill ran down her spine. *She suspects I know she's lying. But why would that be important to her?*

"We are attempting to end the siege of Anbodu and liberate Tlefas as soon as we can," Syzyan said. "We hope you will help us."

"I've wanted to bring down the Prime Konamei for months," Tereka said. "But I need to be sure that whatever new order comes in is better than what we had."

"I can reassure you on that point." Damira leaned forward. "Eighteen years ago, an Izolliyan war band wiped out our camp. They killed our families, and we three," she gestured to the Jianjun and the Emperor, "survived only through luck. We attempted to flee to Tlefas, but were robbed by bandits and no one, not villagers or Riskers, would take us in. With no place to go, we returned to our homeland and gave ourselves in service to a warlord. When his army was destroyed, we were refugees again."

Her voice shook as she spoke. Tereka heard rage and anguish in her tone. The Empress had suffered great loss and hardship.

Emperor Shagonar laid a hand on his wife's arm. "We saw much death and destruction," he said. "The warlords were content for the war to drag on. It was almost like a game to them, to see who could win this year, who the next. What people, livestock, or crops were destroyed in the process was of no significance. They could always raid someone else."

His face twisted. Tereka could feel his sadness over the death and destruction he'd witnessed.

"So we vowed we would stop it," the Empress said, fixing her eyes on Tereka once again. "We met a warlord who trained us in using magic amulets. When I took possession of the three Amulets of Power, I defeated the wickedest of the warlords. Then we united Razdelia into one country. And yes, at times, we had to be harsh. But finally, at long last, we ended the Endless War."

Syzyan ran a finger down the side of the map where the mountains lay. "We toiled for eighteen years to restore the country. Now our people truly have peace and prosperity. No one wants to return to the old ways of continual war. When we were threatened from the west, we knew our duty to protect our people. And resolved to unite with whoever lived in this place we called the Abandoned Lands, so everyone could enjoy a lasting peace."

Even though the Empress's face was bent over the map, Tereka had the sense the woman was studying her from under her eyelashes, seeking a reaction.

But what was she to think? The Emperor and the Jianjun sounded sincere, and the pain in their voices seemed genuine. Tereka tipped her head in a slight nod. "It seems you've done well by your people. Ending a war is a noble pursuit."

"I'm glad you see that," Damira said. "But we didn't ask you here to tell you our history. What I want to know is this— why is this Kaberco so brave among a nation of cowards?"

Tereka jerked her chin up. "Not everyone is a coward." She let out a huff. "But many are. I think it's because they've made safety their god. Which makes them fear any possible risk. Even the tiniest thing becomes a threat."

"But what about you?" Syzyan asked. "You don't seem to be that way."

She grasped the hair on the back of her head and tugged it. "I think, perhaps, because I'm a trader. We have to face danger on the road. Some of us were willing to fight when bandits attacked, not content to allow the Prime Konamei's guards to do the work."

"Would you say the Prime Konamei's guards are courageous?" Shagonar asked.

"Most of them? No." She snorted. "They'd just as soon let bandits slaughter an entire caravan of traders rather than risk their own lives."

Jianjun Syzyan cast his eyes over the other fugitives. "Your companions. They weren't all traders, were they?"

"Oh, no. Only one of them. Most of the rest were prisoners with me."

"Is that why you opposed the Prime Konamei?" he continued.

All of them nodded, and a few answered, "Yes."

"Of course," Tereka chimed in. "None of us had anything else to lose."

"What about the other prisoners?" Syzyan asked. "Would they fight against the Prime Konamei?"

"I suppose so." Tereka shrugged. "None of them want to work the mines. I'm sure they'd rather go home. As long as the Prime Konamei is in power, they can't."

"Then we should liberate the miners," Shagonar said.

Tereka sat up straighter. Whoever these people were, that was a plan she could get behind.

"And make them our allies," Syzyan said, "before Kaberco or anyone else gets the same idea. What do you think, send one arbatu for each camp? Or perhaps two?"

"It's one thing to free them, but another to rally them to

our cause," Shagonar said. "Why would they believe soldiers from an invading army? These are a suspicious and fearful people. They'd probably only believe one of their own."

The Jianjun nodded. "Tereka, would you go with some of our men to free the miners? And convince them to fight for us?"

Needing a moment to comprehend what she'd heard, Tereka crossed her arms. "If you please, Your Loftiness—"

"We'd be happy to, Loftiness," Relio said. "Anything to get vengeance on those *yanshyri* guards."

"Good," Syzyan said. "As for the rest of you, who among you will go with Tereka?"

All of Tereka's companions volunteered. She wasn't surprised. *Of course, they'd welcome a chance to leave.*

"You all want to go?" Syzyan said. "But forgive me. How do we know you'll come back?"

Empress Damira laughed. "That's easy. Have her brother stay behind. He'll be unharmed, as long as she returns." She smiled at Tereka. "That's only fair, right?"

Tereka's breath caught. She shook her head. "I can't leave my brother."

Tirk's brown face had turned dusky gray and sweat beaded his forehead.

"If you please, Your Loftiness." Tereka leaned toward Emperor Shagonar. "My brother has recently been injured—"

"Then he's not fit to travel," the Empress said.

"Don't worry. He won't be a hostage," explained the Jianjun. "If you're worried for his safety, I'll have my son Farnaz move into the yurt with him, with his personal guard. No one will be permitted near without my permission." He drummed his fingers on the table. "Besides, I have a task for your brother. He can write messages to Kaberco and the other ephors who resist us. Maybe he'll persuade them to see reason."

As Tereka hesitated, Naco leaned over to her and put his

mouth against her ear. He faintly breathed five words: "Remember what the sky-god said."

The sky-god had told her to leave. She knew that was right. Somehow, she had to get away, to fan the fires of resistance. It was the only hope of saving them all. But to go without Tirk felt like a horrible betrayal. Dirty. Evil.

Was that how Damira started? Had she been a girl who wanted to end a war, before she was consumed by the love of her own power and importance? And ended up doing dreadful things to achieve her aims until she grew to relish causing pain and ruling by fear.

Tereka bit hard on her lip. She'd never be like Damira. Maybe she'd have to make difficult choices, but she'd die rather than become a force for evil.

With a long breath, she met the Empress's gaze. "Yes." Tereka faltered as she said the word, reluctant to commit herself to a course of action that would leave Tirk alone and defenseless, even though Jianjun Syzyan had promised his safety.

"Then we're agreed." The Empress gave Tereka a broad smile. "You'd best get ready to depart. There's no time to waste."

37

D amira opened her eyes. The dimly lit yurt was silent except for the crackle of the flames in the brazier and Shagonar's even breathing. She had slept well for the first time since the fugitives had arrived. Tereka and her band had left the day before, the officers in charge of the arbatus accompanying them under strict orders. They were to cooperate with Tereka in liberating the mines, but not hesitate to kill her or any of her companions if they tried to escape or turn the freed prisoners against them.

She grinned, thinking of Shagonar's speech to them just before they left. Of his promise to reward them richly for their loyalty and support. He believed what he was saying, but if all went well, not all of them would return. Sebezh had winked at her with a smirk that made her sure of it.

Savoring the absence of the stinging pain, Damira stretched. Her amulets had calmed. The tormenting buzz in her head had disappeared.

So, she was right. Tereka bore the amulets. Now, if only that *durak* Sebezh could kill the girl and make it look like an accident. He had to. Otherwise, the scorpion amulets would be enraged. She shuddered, remembering the stinging, burning pain of their wrath.

The arbatus' officers had been told to thoroughly cremate anyone who perished on this mission. Under no circumstances were they to leave bodies for wild animals to devour. Or leave amulets for someone to find and use. Not that she told the officers that part.

But what if Tereka used her amulets against Shagonar's men? She could kill them all. Damira tapped her finger against her lips. No. Tereka wouldn't do that. She'd come back for her brother.

Then what? Would Tereka wield her dragonfly amulets to oppose the scorpions? Or would she first attempt to rally the Riskers?

Kill them.

Yes, the Riskers should die. Supposedly, they all carried dragonfly amulets. That the Riskers used the Vernian perversion of the scorpion amulets didn't surprise her. It was just one more reason to count them as enemies.

Kill them.

A band of steel tightened around her head. *No. Don't listen to the voices.* She couldn't kill them all.

She stretched, rose slowly, and set her stiff feet on the floor. She hobbled to the door of the yurt and peeked out. Her retinue had left their main camp the day before and traveled to a spot just south of Anbodu. The mountains loomed in front of them, the faded green of the pines breaking up the muddy brown and ash gray of trees bereft of their leaves. A short walk up the slope would bring them to the closest Risker camp, Duarbiad.

Days ago, they'd sent envoys to all the Risker camps, asking for their allegiance. Replies came swiftly from Duarbiad and its nearest neighbor. From the tone of their refusals, Damira didn't expect any different from the others. Now she was going to teach the insolent barbarians of Duarbiad a lesson.

Kill them all.

No. Not that. Syzyan and Shagonar wouldn't like it. She clenched her teeth and shoved the voices to the back of her mind. The familiar headache settled into place. She had to endure a little longer. They'd subdue the Riskers, then the Prime Konamei. When that happened, Kaberco would have to capitulate. They'd unite the land and make war impossible. Then they could go home, secure. And she could put the amulets away.

Or could she? Every time she'd tried in the past, her fingers stung as if she'd grasped nettles. Her feet would be so wracked with burning pain she could barely walk.

Her chest tightened. Using the amulets brought stinging pain. Not using them made it worse. Her eyes grew wet and her limbs weakened. She shook herself, vowing to find a way to control the pain and manage the amulets. Once they were secure.

She shuffled back to the bed and sat next to Shagonar's sleeping form. Gently, she pushed his black hair from his coppery tan face. She kissed his cheek, brushing her lips over the dark stubble that covered the place where his dimple formed. "Hey. Are you going to sleep all day? We have a Risker camp to visit."

The dimple dented his cheek, and he snaked an arm around her.

Damira melted into his arms. It had been so long since he'd held her like this. If only this moment could last forever.

Two hours later, she was riding behind Shagonar and Syzyan, surrounded by three arbatus of their best archers. They rode up a mountain path, alert for warboars and other dangers.

The weak sunshine of late autumn seeped through the bare trees, making strips of light and dark on the pathway ahead. Damira inhaled the cool air in deep breaths, savoring its freshness that both soothed and invigorated.

They had nearly reached the top when a man stepped into the path, a bow raised with an arrow nocked. "Who are you, and where are you going?"

Shagonar pressed forward, passing the guard who'd led the way. "I am Emperor Shagonar Ortan. The response your elder gave to my last message was unsatisfactory. So, I have come in person to give him another opportunity to offer a more satisfactory reply."

The man shook his head. "He doesn't want to speak with you. His answer was clear."

With a frown, Shagonar turned to Damira. "Be kind."

She smiled and nudged her horse forward. When she was no more than twenty paces from the Risker, she summoned the power of her amulets and entered the man's mind. Gently, she pushed on his emotions to make him agreeable. "But he'll want to see us now," she said.

Kill him.

If she wasn't careful, entering the man's mind could destroy him, so she pulled the power back. Not that this man was important, but Shagonar would be displeased.

"Well, yes." The man's face twisted, and he shook his head. "Why don't you come with me?"

Damira rode after him, with Shagonar, Syzyan, and the guards following. It was inconvenient that her brother and her husband opposed using her power to its fullest. They didn't even want her to play on the man's emotions. It took hours of debate to convince them this was the best way to make their point. *If they'd stop arguing with me, everything would be so much easier.*

Half an hour later, they filed through a pass and entered a valley. They were met by fifty Riskers, men and women, all wearing brightly colored tunics, trousers, or dresses. The apple reds, goldenrod yellows, and pine greens were bright against the faded tan of fields harvested months ago.

They lined up about thirty paces from the pass. Every one of them held bows with nocked arrows. Each face was set as if molded of granite—stern frowns and hard eyes silently warning Damira and her companions to leave.

A brave front. Too bad it's futile.

Shagonar stopped his mare about twenty paces from the group. Damira and Syzyan halted their mounts on either side of him.

A gray-haired man with heavy eyebrows set over angular cheekbones and a broad nose stepped forward. "We told you that Duarbiad declines your offer. We have every right to decide our own fate. Now leave."

Kill him.

For half a moment, Damira wished she'd never heard of magic amulets. She sucked in a breath. What evil thought was that?

Kill him.

She swallowed hard. The voices were becoming merciless and insistent.

"You forfeited your rights a long time ago," Syzyan said.

The man snorted. "And why is that?"

"Eighteen years ago, my friend, my sister, and I fled Razdelia. We sought sanctuary in your camp. But we were turned away twice and threatened."

Damira shuddered. Syzyan had left out their fear of being imprisoned, their aching hunger, and their desolation when they realized they'd have to return to Razdelia and the horrors of the Endless War.

Syzyan drew a deep breath and sat taller on his mare. "Now we have returned. This time, not as homeless vagabonds, but as conquering sovereigns. If you submit to our rule, we will be more merciful to you than you were to us."

Glancing at the people on either side of him, the man's eyes widened, then his face reddened. "We have a story from long ago that strangers arrived, trying to gain entrance. But we assumed they were villagers causing trouble. And we all believed that the Endless War had killed everyone east of the mountains." He lowered his bow. "If we were mistaken, I am sorry we didn't help you." He lifted his chin. "But we will not surrender."

"I'm sorry about that," Shagonar said. "Perhaps we can persuade you."

Her three amulets held tightly in her fist, Damira raised her hand. She looked at the nearest house and summoned her power, shooting a flame of light at the dwelling. Within a heartbeat, it exploded and burst into flames.

Almost as one, the Riskers released their arrows. With a flicker of a finger, Damira stopped their flight, sending them crashing to the ground. She did the same for the second wave of arrows, and the third.

Kill them. Destroy them.

She didn't want to do that. Why couldn't they be reasonable? "You cannot stand against us," she said.

The elder tilted his chin up and squared his shoulders. "That power you wield comes from scorpions and is spawned by an ancient evil. We will never submit to you."

"Then you have made your choice." She looked at Syzyan, who pressed his lips together and nodded.

Preparing her power, Damira concentrated on another house. The voices shrieked in her head, begging her to destroy. Demanding that she torture, maim, and annihilate.

No. She'd promised Shagonar and Syzyan she wouldn't hurt anyone. They'd agreed to her burning a house or two or throwing a cow into the air. Perhaps she was wrong to kill people.

Her amulets howled, their fury echoing in her head. She sucked in a breath. There were dragonflies nearby. This was why she was doubting herself and her amulets were so enraged. The dragonflies and their evil users had to be destroyed. The scorpions demanded it. Finally, she was going to exact vengeance on these selfish, cowardly people who refused to help them years ago.

The pounding in her head increased. *No killing. Just show them the power and teach them a lesson.* That's all Syzyan and Shagonar had agreed to.

The stabbing pain increased, as if someone had plunged a knife into her head. Where were these weak thoughts coming from? Was that the influence of the dragonfly amulets? Her breath came in gasps and black spots spun before her eyes. She clutched her horse's mane to keep herself from falling. If the pain got worse, she'd die. There was only one way to stop it.

She released the power, letting it enter the people in front of her and every living soul in the camp. She sensed two more off in the fields. Let them live to tell the other Riskers the folly of defiance. The amulets screamed for release. She pushed more of the power free, letting it enter the houses and the barns and the animals.

Then she let go.

Red light flashed, illuminating everything as if it were drenched in blood. The Riskers, their livestock, their houses and barns, turned to red mist. For a few moments, it hung over the ruined camp, then floated away in the autumn air that had turned as cold as a winter's night.

Her soldiers gasped.

Syzyan's mouth hung open. "Dami…"

Damira tried to not let the disgust on his face and the horror on Shagonar's detract from her moment of victory. As she turned her horse to head down the mountain trail, she spoke to her archers.

"Do you see why we told you not to fear, for we could never be defeated?"

38

Tereka arched her spine, trying to ease the strain on her shoulders. Seventeen days of travel, most of them spent on horseback, had left her with a stiff back and sore thighs. She shifted in the saddle, seeking a more comfortable position, knowing it was futile. No matter how she sat, nagging unease still quivered in her stomach.

She thought over the past few weeks as her horse plodded through the dust stirred up by Alikse's mount. They'd left the day after Emperor Shagonar tasked them with liberating the prisoners. He'd sworn to reward them for their loyalty. Was he sincere, or were those empty promises? Tereka still wasn't sure.

At any rate, she didn't much care about promised rewards. The pledge to keep Tirk safe was far more important. She hunched her shoulders. She deserved her aching muscles and her chafed-raw skin. What a coward she'd been to leave her brother behind.

That thought had tormented her for the past seventeen days, even though Tirk had talked with her long into the night, insisting that she had to go. Who else, he argued, would get word to Da and the Riskers? She had to warn them about Empress Damira's evil power.

When Tirk had failed to convince her, Naco pulled her aside and repeated the words he'd whispered to her when Jianjun Syzyan first made them the offer. The sky-god had directed her to leave as soon as she could. As much as she hated to admit it, he was right. The best she could do was extract a promise from Farnaz that he'd keep her brother safe.

Then they'd begun their trek southwest, accompanied by sixteen full arbatus of soldiers. Some were archers, some swordsmen. One hundred sixty men marched with them, counting the leader of each arbatu, the sixteen Arban-u Dargas. Leading them was the higher-ranked Jagun-u Darga, named Berlok, whose leathery, wrinkled skin told of many years spent under a hot sun. He seemed to be on surprisingly familiar terms with the Emperor and his Jianjun.

The first days of riding were agony for Tereka and her friends. Few of them except Hinat—who'd been a rancher before he was taken—had ever ridden a horse before. Her own experience on horseback had been limited to the time she and Da had fled on horseback from Trofmose and the threat of Juquila's thugs.

Relio and Sebezh seemed to suffer the worst. At least, Tereka thought so, based on the number of inventive curses they spewed with nearly every step. She couldn't help feeling a nasty glee whenever Sebezh complained.

Tereka channeled her anxiety for Tirk into practice with her amulets. Now that she was away from the Empress, she had no fear that the woman would find her and her dragon-flies. As she rode, she'd slide her hand into her pocket and grasp them. Then she'd focus her mind on the sky-god.

At first, she sensed very little. As time went on, a presence —an intelligence and a love more immense than the sky— started to make itself known. She still didn't know how to use her dragonflies against the scorpions, but somehow, she believed the presence would tell her at the right moment.

After twelve days, they'd reached the first of the prison

camps. To no one's surprise, all the prisoners agreed to fight against the Prime Konamei. Even most of the prison guards were avid to join Emperor Shagonar's forces. Berlok left three arbatus of men to patch up the sick and injured, pack up all the camp's food and weapons, and escort the newly freed prisoners to the Emperor's war camp.

Over the subsequent five days, Berlok led them to two more prison camps. The guards and prisoners at those camps reacted the same as they had at the first, putting up barely more than token resistance.

Now, they approached the fourth and final prison camp, the one Tereka was most eager to liberate and the one she dreaded the most.

"What do you think, girly?" Relio rode up on her left side. "Will that *yanshyr* commander welcome us back?"

Tereka snorted. "Somehow, I doubt it. He's probably never forgiven us for defeating his pirate friends."

She surveyed the landscape in front of her. They were riding down a dusty road, the sere, sandy terrain as barren as she remembered. In the distance, the silhouette of the tall wooden fence of the camp broke the horizon. As they approached, the iron gates became visible. The metal spikes that topped the wall glinted in the afternoon sunlight shining through scattered clouds that resembled twisting wisps of smoke. Surrounding the wall was a deep and wide ditch filled with sharpened stakes. No one would survive a fall into that.

How many months had it been? Tereka remembered they'd fled the prison in Rozhal, sweltering in the final days of summer. Now it was Camalu, the tail end of the autumn. Over twelve months had passed since they escaped.

Which meant more than a year since she'd had any word of her mother. Iskra could have died since then. Or the commander could have killed her out of spite, angry that Tereka and her friends had absconded. If he had, she'd make him regret that decision.

Creaking leather to her right snagged her attention. Her jaw tightened. Surely, it wasn't Sebezh again. Why couldn't he leave her alone? He'd stuck to her like old honey during the entire trip. A curse formed in her mouth. She choked it back when she caught a glimpse of Naco's dazzling smile.

The breeze tossed his dark hair back from his face as he leaned toward her. "Berlok says his men will subdue the camp. While they're doing that, we can go for the commander."

Relio guffawed. "Berlok knows just what we want. I've been wanting to get a few swings in that *yanshyr* commander for a long time."

"Don't kill him," Tereka said. "I need to talk to him first."

"Whatever you say, girly. But when you're done, get out of my way."

The vanguard came to a halt outside the iron gates. One of the Arban-u Dargas rode up to it and beat on it with his sword. The clanging sound startled the ravens perched on the spikes. They took flight, their squawking cutting the chilly fall air.

Two guards sauntered to the gates. "Who are you?" the taller asked.

Tereka squinted at him. He didn't look familiar.

Berlok spoke up. "We are from the army of His Loftiness, Shagonar the Peacebringer, Emperor of Razdelia, come to liberate you from the oppression of the Prime Konamei."

The shorter guard gawked at them. "That can't be."

"Why not? Do we look like the Prime Konamei's effete guardsmen?" Berlok waved a hand at the seventy armed men behind him. "We are from Razdelia, across the mountains to the east. We heard how the Prime Konamei oppresses you. We will set you free. Inform your commander we will speak with him."

The two guards looked at each other with wide eyes. After a heartbeat, they turned and fled.

"Well, we have a few moments before they return," Berlok said. He motioned to his men.

Four burly soldiers bearing hammers with heads as big as Tereka's and handles as long as her arm stumped to the gate. They proceeded to beat the metal with rhythmic, clanging strokes. By the time Tereka and her friends had dismounted and staked their horses, the men had broken the bars and bent them enough that a man could easily walk through.

As they had done with the previous three camps, Berlok timed their arrival for late in the day, after the prisoners were in their barracks. He explained to Tereka that the prisoners would be weary from the day's labor and would put up less of a fight, and that it would be easier to find all the guards when they were patrolling the barracks rather than the expanse of the mine.

By this time, guards bearing drawn swords were sprinting toward the gates. "Step lively, the party's coming," Berlok said.

Two by two, the soldiers slid through the opening in the gates, each of the seven arbatus posting a pair of men to watch the horses.

Tereka wiped her sweaty palms on her trousers. This fight would be almost equal in numbers. The prison camps had about seventy guards. After leaving men at each of the three liberated encampments, Berlok was down to seventy, plus Tereka and her friends. Which added five swordsmen, Tereka and Kemet with their bows, and Savinnia with her throwing knives. Tereka's heart pounded. The other camps hadn't put up much resistance. Perhaps they'd been cowed by the overwhelming size of Berlok's forces. That wouldn't be the case today.

Once Berlok's soldiers had entered the compound, Tereka slid her bow from her shoulder, grabbed three arrows, and stepped through the gates. She ran a few steps and scanned the prison yard. The commander's office stood near the back of the yard, with the kitchens and guards' quarters behind it.

The prisoners' barracks stood in rows of five on either side of the yard. A few guards were running from barracks to barracks, locking the convicts inside. Her mouth went dry. Were they planning to fight, or did they simply want to keep the prisoners contained?

The door to the low, gray building that housed the commander's office burst open. The commander—a tall, muscular man—charged out, a long sword gripped in his huge hand. "Where is the *yanshyr* who broke my gates?" he roared.

Berlok advanced, flanked by ten soldiers, their spears and shields in position. "I have come on behalf of His Loftiness Emperor Shagonar—"

"Yes, I heard the message," the commander said. "You can tell that *balasy kassil* Shagonar to slink back to whatever rock he's crawled out from under. If you live that long." With a yell, he charged at Berlok.

The commander was brave, Tereka had to admit. Too bad he never expected trained soldiers would come to liberate the prisoners. Had he thought this through, he'd have readied his archers.

Guards poured from around the sides of the building, shouting and swinging their swords. Berlok's archers, who were positioned on either side of the prison yard, let arrows fly at the advancing men.

Tereka grabbed Kemet's arm. "Let's help."

She trotted off, Kemet on her heels. He followed her to a position near one set of archers. She nocked an arrow and took careful aim. Her target fell, an arrow in his knee.

After a few moments, the guards and Berlok's soldiers had merged. Tereka shoved her arrows back into her quiver. Kemet pulled his sword and charged into the fray.

Squinting to survey the chaotic scene, Tereka saw Relio and Hinat both hacking at one man. From Relio's shouted curses, Tereka guessed that was a guard that had delighted in humiliating the prisoners.

Naco was fighting behind Berlok, with Sebezh nearby. Where was Savinnia?

Her breath caught when she spotted the girl, helping a bleeding Alikse limp out of the battle. Tereka dashed toward them.

A guard knocked Savinnia over and kicked Alikse in the back. Tereka drew a knife from her belt and threw it. The blade skimmed the man's chin. He looked up and raised his sword. Holding it before him, he charged at Tereka.

She drew a second knife and waited for the guard to take one, two, three steps toward her. She raised her arm to throw, her eyes fixed on her target.

A body collided with hers. The impact knocked her to the ground. Her face banged into the dusty soil. She gasped as a blade penetrated her side. Shoving against her assailant, she rolled away.

Before she got to her feet, the guard she'd been aiming for sprinted near her. He readied his weapon, honing in on Tereka. She scrambled frantically, trying to gather her feet under her so she could stand. The stabbing pain from her wound made each movement an agony. The approaching guard was close enough that she could see his yellowed teeth and the beads of sweat on his face. Two more steps and he'd reach her.

Hinat surged forward and swung at the guard, slicing off his arm. Sebezh stumbled into Hinat and they both tumbled in a heap. Hinat let out a yell.

Blood gushed from the stump of the guard's arm. He gasped as large hands seized his neck from behind. With one twist and a loud crack, Alikse ended his life, then dropped his lifeless body to the ground.

Tereka scrambled back. Who had knocked her over? She hadn't been able to see his face, and he'd lost himself in the melee of fighters. All she'd noticed was he wasn't wearing the black clothing of the guards. The nearest person was Sebezh, who was lying on the ground, gasping for air, bleeding from a deep gouge in his side. Hinat lay next to him, lifeless. Naco stood over Sebezh, holding a sword to his throat.

Staggering to her feet, Tereka winced as she put weight on her right foot. "What are you doing?"

"He tried to kill you," Naco snarled. "Then, when Hinat saved you from the guard, Sebezh killed him."

"No, not true," muttered Sebezh.

"He might have," said Alikse. "Or he might have tripped. Hard to say."

The noise of clanging swords faded. Tereka spun to assess the battle. Only one pocket of resistance remained. The rest of the guards sat on the ground, their swords piled in front of them.

She pressed a hand to her side. Her tunic was damp and sticky. She didn't think the knife had penetrated past her ribs, but she didn't want to find out. She could not allow wounds or pain or blood to slow her down.

Gripping the bag with her amulets, she asked for the healing power. Warmth flowed into her side and the sharp pain ceased. Then she stumbled to Hinat's side and dropped to her knees. A lump formed in her throat. Quiet Hinat was dead. Gently, she closed his staring, lifeless eyes. Stifling a sob, she staggered to her feet. She had to make sure Hinat's death wasn't in vain.

Berlok was still sparring with the commander. Blood dripped down the commander's face from a slice on his forehead. Berlok's sword flashed in the rays of the setting sun. The commander's sword flew out of his hand. Tereka let out a long breath. They'd won.

"Sit." Berlok pointed his sword at the commander.

Slowly, the man sank to the ground.

"Do you surrender your camp?"

The commander nodded, a muscle twitching in his jaw.

"Our offer stands. Anyone who wishes to join the Emperor's army is welcome. The rest can return to their homes. Any who oppose us will remain here, under guard." Berlok looked down at the commander. "Know that no one in the other three camps opposed us. Most of them, prisoners and guards alike, are now on their way to the Emperor's war camp." With a wave of his hand, he gestured to Tereka and her companions to approach.

They strode up in silence, then stood in front of the commander. Sweat broke out on Tereka's hands as she remembered how this man had offered them freedom to fight pirates, all the while counting on the pirates to kill them. How he'd sentenced them to the salt mines to spend the rest of their lives underground, never to see the sun again.

The commander scowled at them, then his eyes widened. "What are you doing here?"

Relio cursed and spat on the ground at the commander's feet. "I thought you'd be happy to see us. Your runaway children have come home."

"You." The commander curled his lip and raked his gaze over them. "Relio. Sebezh. Tereka. Savinnia. Naco. Alikse. You should have been eaten by desert cats." His eyes flickered over Kemet, confusion dimming his expression.

No, he wouldn't recognize Kemet. Tereka wasn't about to introduce them. Her insides quivered and her mouth went dry. This was the moment she'd been waiting for. She would interrogate the commander and discover if her mother still lived or had perished long ago.

39

Tereka rubbed her sweaty palms on her tunic. She eyed the commander, studying his coppery hair and pale, freckled skin. His bulbous nose and protruding chin dominated his thin lips. Those lips were pulled back in the cold, cruel sneer that used to send waves of fear to her core.

Relio barked a laugh. "I know you've got something to say, girly. Talk all you want. If I recall, this *yanshyr* has some excellent brandy." He headed for the commander's office, Alikse on his heels.

Berlok kept his eyes on the commander. "Tereka, you wish to speak with this man?"

She stepped forward, her heart pounding in her throat. Her mouth was as parched as the dusty prison yard. She wasn't sure she'd be able to get the words out.

The commander curled his lip. "What do you want? An apology?"

His rudeness unlocked her frozen tongue. "When I was here, you made an offer of freedom."

"Yes. But you squandered it."

"I wanted freedom for another." The blood whooshed in her ears. "Where is she?"

He pressed his lips into a thin line and lowered his flat gray eyes. "Dead."

Ice trickled through Tereka's veins.

"Or alive. I don't know." The commander bared his teeth in a feral grin. "Who cares about *zhalapus* and whores?" He spat at the ground near Tereka's feet. "Especially that one, who was trouble from the day she arrived here."

With a howl, Tereka lunged for the man. Naco grabbed her arm and yanked her back. "Why waste time with this *durak*?" He leaned to whisper in her ear. "She was on the never-to-be-released list. Of course, he knows. He's toying with you."

Tereka froze in place, unable for a moment to even draw a breath. She nodded. "Will you come with me?"

"Certainly. Let's bring a few soldiers, too."

She nodded and strode to the outbuildings in the rear of the yard. Dimly, she was aware of Naco and Savinnia walking on either side of her and the soft creak of a few soldiers' leather armor behind her.

Her face burned, and she clenched her fists. Iskra had to be here. During Tereka's imprisonment, she heard a rumor that a woman who'd married a Risker lived in the camp. The commander verified it, just before sentencing Tereka to the salt mines. Tereka ground her teeth. If her mother wasn't alive, the commander would find out what it felt like to be toyed with.

Their first destination was the kitchen. Inside, a group of ten women with shaved heads huddled together, shaking and crying. One screamed when Tereka and Savinnia entered.

To show them she wasn't going to hurt them, Tereka held up her hands. With a few quick words, she informed them about the Emperor. She told them his soldiers had defeated the prison guards, and the captives were now free. "No one will harm you," she added. "Stay here, go about your work. We'll leave in a day or so. We can take you to the Emperor's war camp or the nearest town. Your choice."

Silence met her words. The tear-streaked faces gazed at her with flat, unfeeling eyes. "Did you not hear what I said?" she asked.

The oldest of the women got to her feet, pulling herself up by the edge of the table. Deep lines crossed her face. "How do we know what you say is true?"

"You'll just have to believe me." She pointed to Naco and Savinnia. "We were prisoners in this camp last year. The commander sentenced us to the salt mines, but we escaped. Did you hear anything about that?"

One of the women giggled, a girlish sound that seemed out of place in such a big-boned woman. "Of course, we did. It was hard to know what the commander was most angry about, the escaped prisoners or the stolen horses. The dead guards? He didn't care much about them."

The old woman gave Tereka an appraising look with her piercing hazel eyes. "Let's say we believe you." She motioned with her head to the yard. Shouts and laughter filled the previously silent area. The news must have spread among the convicts. "Who's keeping that lot in line?"

Tereka motioned to the soldiers who'd accompanied them. "These men will guard you." She hoped Berlok would make good on her guarantee. "If you leave the building, I can't make you any promises. I don't know what the other prisoners will do with their freedom. Staying with the Emperor's soldiers is the safer course."

"Then we should prepare supplies for the journey," the old woman said.

Surprised that the woman was taking the sudden change in her circumstances with seeming unconcern, Tereka blinked. But the woman hadn't had much control over her life for years. She must think any change was bound to be for the better. "Very good," Tereka said. "But first, hold out your arms."

The woman stared at her. "I don't understand."

Thrusting out her arm, Tereka bared her wrist. "Show me your wrists, if you please." Riskers tattooed the name of their beloved on their wrists. Iskra's tattoo would read "Xico," and would prove her identity.

One by one, the women complied. Tereka took a quick look, then stepped back. None of them bore any tattoos. "Are there any other women here?"

"Just them in the brothel," the old woman said.

Tereka shuddered and pressed a shaking hand to her face. Slaving in a kitchen for eighteen years would have been bad enough. What horrors had her mother endured in the brothel all this time?

Thanking the woman, Tereka turned and left. She asked a trio of the soldiers to guard the door and the others to accompany her. She led Naco and Savinnia to the back of the kitchen area, past the laundry to a low building with small windows covered by thick iron bars.

Her breath coming in ragged gasps, Tereka tried to ignore the thumping of her heart. She sped up until she was nearly running. Iskra wasn't in any of the other camps. The commander didn't know if she was dead or alive. Tereka had to face the possibility that she wouldn't find her mother. What she couldn't bear was the not knowing.

Still, Tereka held on to hope. She imagined what it would be like to feel her mother's embrace, to hear why she loved Xico enough to run away from her home. And to get to know the woman who'd sacrificed herself for her infant daughter.

Ever since she'd heard the rumor that her mother still lived, Tereka had envisioned the scene in her mind many times. Iskra would wrap Tereka in her arms. Tereka could finally look into her eyes. Finally, she'd know a mother's love. Her mother would reveal the name she had chosen for her.

She placed her hand on the doorknob of the brothel and went in.

In the dim light, Tereka had to blink several times before she could see. The room had a bench along one wall and reeked from the piss bucket that stood in one corner.

A middle-aged woman with black eyes and short auburn hair lounged on a mat on the floor. She jumped up when Tereka entered. "Didn't expect to see someone like you here." There was a watchfulness in her eyes, the wariness of a person who expects the worst.

"Summon all the women, if you please," Tereka responded. When the woman hesitated, Tereka asked, "What is your name?"

For a few moments, Tereka thought she would refuse to answer. "Arabani," she reluctantly said. "Who wants to know? I haven't seen you around." She stood up and lit a lamp. "Did the commander send you here to work?" She frowned, looking at Savinnia, then past her to Naco and the soldiers crowded in the doorway. "You and the other girl will do. But them? Are they here for entertainment?"

"Them? What? No——" Tereka sputtered, too embarrassed and flustered to speak.

Naco interrupted. "The commander is no longer in charge. Get the others, if you please, and we'll explain."

Arabani scurried off, calling out names. "Zeefa, Marzool, Fanjeel, look sharp. There's men waiting." She ran down the corridor, knocking on doors. She returned more slowly, taking the time to peek in all the rooms to make sure the occupants were responding. "They all had a late night," she said. "And it's a little early for them to start work."

"I can wait." Tereka leaned against the wall. The blood whooshed in her ears and she pressed her lips together. *Don't get your hopes up.*

One by one, the women gathered. These were cleaner than the kitchen help, with short hair rather than shaved heads, their gray clothing unstained. When all seven had gathered, Tereka shared her news once again. They besieged her with questions. All wanted to be assured of their safety. All wanted to return to their homes. "And you're certain, you promise, that the men with you won't want to use us?" they kept asking.

"Yes," said Tereka. "I can promise you that. I think you've been used enough." Somehow, she'd have to ensure that Berlok honored her words. She repeated her warning to stay inside, then asked to look at their wrists.

"As long as that's all you want to see, blue eyes," said a girl with golden hair and a knowing smirk.

Not knowing how to respond to that, Tereka concentrated on the women's bared wrists. None had tattoos. Other than Arabani, the others were too young to be Iskra. Mechanically, she asked, "Are there any more of you?"

"Oh," said Arabani, "there is one. She's a bit old, and slow."

"An old woman works here?"

"She did when they first brought her in. That was long before I arrived. When she got aged and ugly, they had her stay as kind of a servant for the rest of us. Here she comes now."

A woman with matted, ash-colored hair shuffled down the corridor, barely able to pick up her feet. Tattered and filthy gray rags hung from her skeletal frame. Vacant eyes the color of smoke stared at the women, the soldiers, then settled on Tereka. Fear rose in her eyes, and she wrinkled her face like she was about to cry.

By all that's fair, thought Tereka, how long has this old hag been here? Forty years?

Arabani moved slowly toward her and reached out her hand. "Show the girl your wrists."

"No!" The woman thrust her hands behind her back.

"Nothing to see! Nothing there!" she shrieked. The scent of urine filled the air, and a pool formed at the old woman's feet.

Tereka clamped a hand over her mouth. There was no point in tormenting this woman. She wasn't Iskra.

"Now, now, dearie," Arabani persisted, "not to worry. We've all shown her, and nothing bad has happened." Gently, she pulled her arms to the front. A tear dripped out of the old woman's eye.

When Tereka reached for her right hand, the woman jumped as if the touch had burned her. Not a mark on her grimy forearm. Tereka dropped it and reached for the other. The woman resisted, but eventually showed her wrist.

Peeking out from a mass of scars was what only could be a tattoo of a capital letter X. Tereka stared, unable to even blink.

40

The world tilted and whirled. Afraid she would collapse, Tereka searched for something to steady herself. Her stomach knotted and her head spun. This crone with a broken mind couldn't be her mother. Shaking her head, she staggered a step back, uncertain of her wobbly knees. It was impossible. But an X tattoo marked the woman's wrist. "Iskra?" she whispered. "Are you Iskra?" Tereka inched forward, dreading the answer.

The woman cackled. "Iskra? That's me."

Tereka gulped. How could that be? Iskra would only be about thirty-five, not well into her sixties, not a withered woman who looked older than Tereka's grandmother. Frost numbed Tereka's hands. "Are you sure?"

"Yes. Yes. Iskra."

To stifle a sob, Tereka pressed her hand to her mouth. Her chest ached and her knees threatened to buckle under her. Maybe this was the wrong Iskra. Even though she knew she was clinging to false hopes, she asked, "Where are you from, Iskra?"

"Here."

"And before you came here?"

"There." A faint smile crossed her face. "Everything fell. Water from clouds. Leaves from trees. White flakes from the sky."

That must mean the north, thought Tereka, her hopes sinking like a stone hurled into the river. "How long have you been here?" she asked.

The woman shuddered. "Long time. Bad place." She clenched her eyes shut. Hunching her shoulders, she raised her hand as if to ward off a blow.

Tereka traced the letter X on Iskra's wrist, gently stroking her filthy scars. "Is this for Xico?"

Iskra jerked her arm from Tereka's grasp, pressed her fists to her eyes, and howled, "Xico's dead!" She hung her head and moaned his name, her agonized keening cutting Tereka's heart like an arrow piercing flesh.

"Is she always like this?" Tereka looked helplessly at Arabani.

"Some days, yes. Sometimes, worse. On bad days, she's violent, biting and scratching everyone who comes near, screaming that she won't go with Udbash, whoever that is."

Udbash. The man Kaberco tried to force Iskra to marry. Tereka closed her eyes, steeling herself for Arabani's next words.

"From what I heard, she had a bad time of it even before they brought her in. Tortured and raped and who knows what else. For the first few years, she was kept for the guards' pleasure. Some of those beasts were brutal." She pressed her lips together, shaking her head. "After six or eight years, Iskra started to lose her mind. The men had no more use for her, so she was sent to the kitchens. They couldn't handle her, so she came back to us. We take care of our own." She shrugged. "She's not the first to end up this way and won't be the last. Poor thing. They must have done horrible things to her. She's terrified of men now."

Tereka stumbled to a stool and sat down. Her mind was as

blank as a cloudy night sky, with no light to illuminate the way forward. What was she to do with her mother?

Iskra leaned against the wall, her face in her hands, her body trembling like a birch tree in a windstorm. From time to time, a sob burst from her lips.

The neckline of Tereka's tunic felt tight enough to choke her. She tugged at it. "Arabani, will you help me?"

She looked at Tereka, her hazel eyes wary. "Do what?"

"Wash her up, get her into some clean clothing." She pointed at Savinnia with her chin. "Savinnia and I will help you."

"What do I get out of it?"

"I'll pay you well. I'm sure you don't have much money. A few coins will help you get home once the war is over."

"Humph. If we live that long." Arabani raked her gaze over Tereka's face and folded her arms across her skinny frame. "Who is she to you, that you would do anything for her?"

"I think," said Tereka, then paused, barely able to get the words out—as if saying them would confirm a truth she didn't want to admit. "She's my mother."

"Then you must be the baby she cries for at night," Arabani said.

Tereka swallowed hard. "Does the baby have a name?"

"Not that I ever heard. She just weeps for Baby when she's not wailing for Xico."

Blinking the wetness from her eyes, Tereka let out a breath and pointed to her mother's wrist. "Why all the scars?"

"It's a savage Risker custom to tattoo the name of their beloved on their wrists. I heard the commander burned her tattoo off with acid. She stole ink from the commander's office and used a nail to recreate her tattoo. So they burned it again. This happened more than once. As her mind came and went, she couldn't always remember her Risker's name. So she cut it into her arm."

Arabani pulled Iskra's ragged sleeve up. Her left forearm was covered with scars, many shaped like an X, others the ragged letters that spelled Tereka's father's name.

Tears gathered in Tereka's eyes. Her heart grew heavy, as if it had taken the weight of Iskra's agony into itself. What had her mother suffered all these years? Her stomach writhed and a sour taste filled her mouth. She stepped to Iskra, who cringed. "Iskra," she whispered. "We're going to take care of you."

Iskra's eyes widened, and she shook her head, cowering against the wall. "No. No. No hurt."

Sidling up to Iskra, Arabani took her by the arm. "There, there. I'll be right here with you." She cast a glance at Tereka. "See that you make this worth my while. It will take you and me and your friend, and maybe a few others, to get her to take a bath." She thrust her chin out and hardened her voice. "That's why we don't try very often. You understand."

"I do," said Tereka. While they hadn't done much, they'd at least kept her mother fed and clothed, such as it was. She reached into her pocket and pulled out a gold coin. "I will give you two of these if you can get her clean and dressed for a journey."

"You'll pay me two scales?" Arabani stared at the coin. "I'll do the best I can."

Tereka looked at Savinnia. "Will you help?"

Savinnia brushed a tear from her eye. "Of course."

"I'm grateful," Tereka said, "but can you get started without me? I need a heartbeat or two." Without waiting for an answer, she pushed past Naco and the soldiers and burst out of the brothel. She slumped against the wall of the building. Her stomach heaved, and she spewed the bread and stew she'd eaten earlier onto the muck of the prison yard. Her face sweated and tears stung her eyes. She wiped her mouth on her sleeve and spat. Resting her hands on her knees, she let the sobs escape her throat.

Strong arms grasped her shoulders and pulled her upright. She slumped into Naco's embrace, burying her face in his shoulder. When her breathing calmed, she stepped away from him, wiping her damp face. "They broke her."

"They did." His voice hitched. "I'm so sorry."

The compassion in his voice brought a fresh rush of tears. "This isn't what I expected. I was prepared to find her dead. But this? This is worse."

"Worse that she's alive?"

"Is she really living?" She sniffed and wiped her nose on her sleeve. "She sacrificed herself for me. She paid for it every day. And now she's ruined forever."

"Are you sure about that?"

She stared at him. "What can be done for her?"

"Well, if I had magic amulets that could heal people, I'd try using them before I decided all was lost."

Of course. Tereka clasped her hands together. "You're right." She stepped to the entrance of the brothel. "What if it doesn't work?"

He shrugged. "Then it doesn't work. She won't be any worse off than she is now." With his chin, he pointed to the door. "Go ahead. I'll talk to Berlok about protecting these women."

With a nod, Tereka ducked back inside. Iskra's screams filled the air. Tereka followed them to the brothel's kitchen, where Iskra sat on a chair, held down by Savinnia and one of the other women. They'd gotten Iskra's grimy clothing off her and draped her in a sheet.

Arabani held up a pair of scissors. "Do you want me to cut her hair?"

Tereka looked at the matted tangles on Iskra's head. She thought she saw insects crawling in the mats. "Yes, if you please. But first, could I have a moment alone with her and Savinnia?"

"If you must." Arabani patted Iskra's hand. "I'll be right back, dearie. You stay here, yes?"

Iskra was humming a droning tune and didn't respond. Tereka swallowed the lump in her throat while she waited for Arabani and her helper to leave. Then she pulled out her amulets.

"Oh, good idea," Savinnia said.

"Naco suggested it. We'll see what happens." She held the four amulets in front of Iskra. "Sky-god, please."

The amulets warmed her hand and flickered with green and purple light. Iskra slumped a little in the chair and stopped humming. Then she blinked a few times.

Holding her breath, Tereka waited. What would her mother's next words be?

"Pretty. Pretty." Iskra tapped an amulet with one finger and giggled.

Letting her hand fall to her side, Tereka screwed up her face to fight back more tears. "It didn't work."

Savinnia touched her shoulder. "It might take a while. But look, she seems calmer. That's something."

Tereka studied her mother. Savinnia was right. The terror had left Iskra's eyes, and she'd stopped squirming in the chair.

"What am I going to do with her?" Tereka rubbed her face and the back of her head. She tugged on her hair. All this time she'd hoped for a joyous reunion with a mother who would love her, not a broken woman who cowered at every sudden noise.

"She needs somewhere safe."

"The best place I can think of is with my grandparents," Tereka said. "Maybe my grandmother can heal her. Or at least help her." She shoved the amulets into their bag and rubbed her hands together. "That means we need to go north."

"Pretty." Iskra stood up, letting the sheet fall to the floor. She patted Savinnia's face. "Pretty."

"Thank you. You are too." Savinnia smiled, retrieved the linen, and draped it over Iskra. Tereka shuddered to see the twisted scars and red welts of fresh insect bites that covered Iskra's emaciated frame.

Tereka bit her lip. She didn't know what the Desired One was supposed to do, but hiding in a Risker camp was probably not it. And given Iskra's confused state, she couldn't leave her with unfamiliar people.

"Savinnia, if we manage to get my mother to the Riskers, would you stay with her? Iskra seems to like you, and maybe a familiar person would help."

"I'll be glad to. I'm not much help in a fight and I have no desire to go back to that emperor's camp." Savinnia dropped her tone to nearly whisper. "This could have been you or me, had we been in prison longer."

"It almost was." Tereka shuddered and her mouth went dry. "Thank you for helping."

She opened the door to admit Arabani. "We're ready for you."

Arabani gave Iskra an appraising glance. "She's calmer. That's a mercy. You two hold her down and talk to her while I cut."

The two women took positions on either side of Iskra, who sat docilely, humming a wistful tune. With a few quick snips, Arabani reduced Iskra's hair to a gray stubble.

"Now for the bath, shall we?" Arabani said. She pursed her lips and looked at Tereka. "Since she's quiet now, we can manage without you. I'd rather you go to whoever is in charge and make sure he'll keep us safe."

Tereka opened her mouth to protest, thought better of it, and nodded. "Naco's already gone to Berlok. I'll find out what he decided."

She lurched outside. Twilight had fallen, the final rays of the sun painting the sky a faint purple. Tereka looked at it as if in a daze, unable to make sense of what was happening.

What torture had her mother endured? How could the commander have allowed such brutality? How could the Prime Konamei think such a system was fair and just?

Her grief heated into anger and she ground her teeth. Someone needed to pay, to suffer the same torment Iskra and every other captive had endured. Her muscles quivered. That commander deserved to be hung. No, castrated first. Then cut limb from limb. Then hung. Or flung into the salt mines to let the prisoners there deal with him. They would not be merciful.

She pounded the outside wall of the brothel. If only she had amulets that could be used as weapons. She'd turn that commander into red mist. She'd destroy the whole camp.

And why stop there? Juquila and her thugs, Kaberco, and the Prime Konamei who ruled over the whole corrupt system would be next. All of them nothing more than red mist.

Rage bursting from her in a shout, Tereka's breath came in ragged sobs. If she wasn't careful, she'd be as evil as that Empress. If Damira had suffered even a piece of what Iskra had, no wonder she was so quick to use her power, so prone to remove any threat.

Tereka gulped down her sympathy for Empress Damira. She gritted her teeth. *I'm nothing like her. There's no excuse for repaying evil with more evil. I won't become her.* She rested her aching head against the wall and closed her eyes.

A cough drew her attention to a man standing a few feet away. "What do you want?" she asked without looking up.

"To see if you've finished making arrangements for your mother," Naco said.

Had he overheard her outburst? Her face heated. "I, um…"

"Have had a very trying and disappointing day." He gave her a sympathetic smile. "Berlok has promised guards for these women. He would also like to hear your testimony about the commander. That will help him decide if he'll take him back to the Emperor as a prisoner or execute him here." He chuckled. "Relio and Alikse already volunteered to do the job. I told Berlok you might want to be the one."

Did she? Did she want to kill the man who'd allowed her mother to be tortured and abused? It would give her a sense of release to know that evil man was dead. But still…

After a few moments of thought, she shook her head. "No. I'll give Berlok my opinion, but it's his decision to make, and his sentence to execute."

"That's how I felt." Naco took her arm and led her away from the brothel. "Now that you found your mother, what do you want to do?"

"Take her to my grandparents. Then we do as Tirk asked. We warn the Riskers and Kaberco about the Empress and her amulets."

"Sounds good to me. I'm ready to be away from these Razdelians already. But how will we do that? Berlok won't let us leave because we want to. Not if the Empress ordered him to bring us back."

"No, he'd have us shot as deserters first." Ice scuttled down her spine. "Or have the Empress turn us into mist."

41

Tereka shifted in the hard chair, seated in what used to be the commander's office. Her cheeks burned every time she thought of what atrocities her mother suffered under that man's command. She shoved her hands into the pockets of her tunic, willing herself to wait, to not use her broken and filthy nails as weapons to gouge out the commander's eyes.

The room was as stark as it always had been, the floors rough wood, the walls covered with a sloppy coat of whitewash. Dark stains on the floor testified to the harsh punishment the commander enjoyed doling out to his prisoners. He believed making an example of a few would keep the rest in line.

But instead of using the office to intimidate like the prison commander, Berlok had welcomed Tereka and her friends as honored guests. A steaming platter of meat pasties sat on the table, their aroma filling the air. Alikse and Kemet were happily devouring them, while Relio and Sebezh helped themselves to the commander's supply of Porrimian brandy.

With a chuckle, Berlok waved to his aide, who promptly removed the brandy bottle. Tereka studied Berlok's face. He seemed to be a man used to command, a fair man, even compassionate. He'd accepted Tereka's explanation that Savinnia was caring for Iskra and excused her absence.

He was a soldier first, though, and clearly loyal to the Emperor. How would she convince him to disobey orders and let her band go?

"Do I understand correctly?" Berlok asked. "You lost only one man?"

"Yes," replied Tereka. "Hinat."

"I am sorry. I have a few injured, but no casualties. I've ordered my men to cremate the dead guards. I'll have them keep your friend's body separate, and to wait for you if you'd like to have a few words spoken over him before the cremation."

She nodded her thanks, while peering out of the side of her eye at Sebezh. He didn't seem to be disturbed at all by Hinat's death. Was Naco right that Sebezh had tried to kill her, and that he killed Hinat to prevent him from saving her?

She didn't have a chance to ponder that question, as Berlok asked to hear of their time as prisoners. He patiently listened to Tereka's account of how the commander had sentenced both her and Savinnia to a men's brigade, and how Savinnia had become Relio's toy just to survive. Just telling the story made Tereka's skin twitch, as if an army of lice crawled up her spine and over her head.

Flicking his gaze from Tereka to Relio and back, Berlok said, "Yet when you escaped, you stayed with this man."

How could she explain her complicated relationship with Relio? The man had kept Savinnia as a sex slave but stoutly fought with Tereka against the pirates and guards who planned to slaughter them all. More than any of the others, Relio understood Tereka's challenges in leading their little band of rebels. "He was a formidable ally against our common enemies."

"The commander." Berlok narrowed his eyes.

"And the Prime Konamei," Relio put in. "Don't forget that *yanshyr.*" He swilled the lavender liquid in his glass and belched. "He's the worst of the lot."

For a heartbeat, Berlok rested his gaze on Relio's face, then looked at Tereka. "The commander must have been evil indeed, if you would ally with this man."

"Evil, indeed." She recounted what she'd learned about what he'd done to her mother over the last eighteen years. With every sentence, her anger at the injustice and cruelty grew. By the end of her recitation, she was shouting. "His abuse drove all reason from her mind! She's a battered husk, with little sense of who she is! And you still question how to decide his fate?"

Other than a quiver of the muscle in his jaw, she had no idea what Berlok thought of her outburst. Would he take it as a challenge to his authority?

"Thank you." His face was as impassive as a stone wall after a windstorm. "You've given me much to consider. If I decide to execute him, I'll inform you. I'm certain you'll all want to witness it."

Though Tereka tried to divine his intention, his slate-gray eyes were unreadable.

"Is your mother able to travel?" Berlok asked, leaning back in his chair.

"I don't know." Tereka took a deep breath and shook her head. "One moment she's calm, and a heartbeat later, in hysterics." She sighed. "The woman in the brothel told me that sometimes she knows the people around her. Other times, she thinks they're all enemies, and bites and scratches and hits, trying to fight them off." She held her hands toward Berlok. "I think it would be cruel to take her to a soldiers' camp. She's terrified of men as it is. I'm not sure what she'd do surrounded by thousands."

Berlok frowned. "You want to stay here with her?"

"No," Tereka said. "I've been thinking. Perhaps it would be best if I took her to my grandparents."

"The Emperor is expecting your return."

"Oh, of course. But His Loftiness has other things to worry about. Bigger problems than my poor mother who was tortured into losing her mind. I think the only thing to do is get her somewhere she can be looked after in safety."

"But your family is in the north, is it not?" He shook his head. "I could perhaps allow you to take her south…"

"We don't know anyone in the south." Tereka balled her shaking hands into fists until her fingernails dug into her palms. What could she say to persuade this man to agree? "Savinnia has offered to stay with her, so I would be free to help liberate Tlefas from the Prime Konamei." Would Berlok interpret that as wanting to assist the Emperor? She rubbed her sweating hands on her thighs.

Berlok shook his head. "I'm afraid you'll all have to come back with me."

42

Tereka's breath caught. Going back to the Emperor's camp would mean sure death.

"You wouldn't have to go all the way to Zafrad," Kemet said.

Startled by his sudden entry into the conversation, Tereka jerked her head to look at him. "I wouldn't?"

"No," he answered. "All we need to do is escort Savinnia and your mother to the nearest large town, maybe Tyov. They can join a caravan and go on by themselves. That leaves the rest of us free to return to the Emperor."

Kemet was right. He'd come up with the perfect solution. She gazed at him, keeping the elation from her face. She drummed her fingers on her knee.

"They'd need someone to travel with them for protection, and in case Savinnia needs help with Iskra," Naco said. "Maybe you should go, Kemet. You know the traders the best."

Tereka nodded. Judging by the dark circles under his eyes and hunched shoulders, the strain of their perilous situation ate at Kemet more than the others. He should be the one to escort Iskra and Savinnia.

"Not a good idea," he said. "To get to the Riskers, we'd have to travel through Trofmose, and my face is known there. I think Alikse should go. He's from the south. No one would know him. He'd be the best protector for Savinnia and your mother."

His intent gaze made Tereka look away. Kemet clearly was trying to rekindle the feelings they'd once shared, even if it meant sacrificing himself. He didn't understand why they could never resume their old relationship. She'd seen the horror in his eyes when she and the others talked of their days in prison or with the pirates. They'd endured a brutal ordeal, and Kemet would never fathom the depth of their scars. Just like Tereka could never comprehend the wounds that had left her mother such a shattered wreck.

She appealed to Berlok. "What do you say? I think we could get to Tyov in less than a week. Savinnia and my mother could easily join a caravan there. The rest of us could travel back more quickly and rejoin the Emperor four or five days later."

"So even though I was ordered to return with all of you, I am to allow two of you to leave?" Berlok frowned.

"Only Savinnia and one other. Perhaps Kemet. It wouldn't be hard to disguise him. He's a trader and would be able to help her find a caravan." Tereka took a breath. "He'd also be a good person to tell the traders about conditions in the south, and how the Emperor has freed the prisoners. That might persuade Kaberco to surrender." Probably not, she thought, but Berlok doesn't need to know that.

"Suppose I allow this. The question is, can I trust the rest of you to return?"

By force of will, Tereka hid her dismay. How astute of Berlok to ask the question. The answer was plain in her mind —she couldn't go back. Empress Damira already suspected her.

"Well, my brother Tirk is still with the Emperor. I won't abandon him. And Sebezh is wounded and not fit for hard riding. You can keep him if you think Tirk isn't enough reason for me to go back."

Sebezh chortled and spat. "Nice try, girly. He knows there's no love lost between you and me."

She scowled at him. "That's true. But I wouldn't want you to die on my account."

"Really? Then why are you dragging us all over the country, stirring up a rebellion? If any of us die, it's on your head."

"Someone shut this *durak* up," said Relio. "We're all here because we want to bring down the Prime Konamei. If we die in the attempt, so be it. It will be a death we chose. Far better than wasting away in that *yanshyr's* copper mine."

Kemet flinched. Naco and Alikse nodded.

Berlok looked from one to another. After a pause, which to Tereka seemed like an hour, he fixed his eyes on her. "If I permit you to take your mother as far as Tyov, and allow Savinnia and one other to escort her to your grandparents, will you give me your word that the rest of you will return?"

Tereka met his gaze. "We will return." Maybe not right away, and not as an ally. "You can count on it."

"She's lying." Sebezh let the words out in a snarl.

Naco and Relio cursed. Tereka bit the inside of her mouth to keep from showing her irritation.

"How can you say that?" Kemet asked. Tereka hadn't had time to fill him in on the details of Ilinat's death, and what she and Naco suspected about Sebezh.

"Kemet, you *durak*." Sebezh curled his lip. "You've been hoodwinked by this girly and don't even know it."

Berlok leaned forward. "So, Tereka promises to return. Four of her supporters believe her. Only one does not. Can you tell me, Sebezh, why you think she's lying?"

Here it comes, Tereka thought. He's going to spill everything he knows about the Desired One and amulets. Her strength ebbed and her shoulders sagged. *Berlok will never let me go.*

Sebezh opened his mouth, then closed it. His face darkened. "I just know."

Tereka blinked. *What made him stop?*

"You just know?" Berlok said. "That's not enough. Still, I would be careless if I didn't take measures to ensure you keep your promises." He surveyed Tereka's group. "Sebezh will return with us."

"Send me with her," Sebezh protested. "I'll make sure she comes back."

Her stomach clenching, Tereka fought the urge to slap the man. She did not want Sebezh with them, getting in the way of her plans. And she most definitely did not want to kill him if he did.

Berlok looked at him coolly. "Since I'm not sure if you're lying about Tereka, I'm already suspicious of you. And, as she pointed out, you are wounded and not fit for hard riding. No, you come back with us."

Sebezh scowled. Tereka held her breath, waiting for Berlok's next words.

"But," Berlok continued, "you do raise an important issue. So, Tereka, I will allow Savinnia and Alikse to escort your mother to your grandparents. You and two of the others may accompany them as far as Tyov. That should be enough protection from bandits and whatever dangers you meet in the desert. Which one of the other three will stay behind?"

Oh no. Tereka gulped. She didn't want to leave any of them. Kemet? That wouldn't be fair. He had no idea what he was getting into when he offered to go to the war camp with her. This brutal world he'd been thrust into was destroying him.

Naco? She couldn't lose him. Not now. Not when there was so much left unsaid between them. And she was daring to hope that the feelings she had for him could turn into so much more.

And Relio? She never would have expected it, but more and more, she relied on his dauntless insolence to keep her spirits up. Not to mention, he was a fearless fighter. Her eyes moved from one to the other.

"You're just going to let them go? What will you tell the Emperor?" Sebezh asked. "And the Empress?"

Tereka clamped her lips shut. She wanted to hit Sebezh over the head, hard. Something about the way he bounced his knee and blinked as if he had dust in his eye convinced her he had his own schemes. If Sebezh was working with the Empress, he must have already told her Tereka was the Desired One. Her life would be short if Damira decided to believe him. Tereka held her breath, willing Berlok to not be swayed by Sebezh's words.

Berlok snorted. "I can explain to them." He pointed to the map spread on the table in front of him. "I've taken under consideration your pleas for the men in the salt mines. I'm going to send a full arbatu to free them. From what you tell me, it's more than half a day's journey. I estimate it will take three days to liberate the miners, salvage anything of value from the mine, and escort those who are willing back here."

He fixed stern eyes on Tereka. "If you leave in the morning, that gives you three extra days to get to Tyov and return." He pointed at a spot on the Orkhana River a few hours west of the Emperor's war camp. "I expect to see you here in ten days. Look for us at the place we camped the first night after we left the Emperor. If you're not there or waiting for us in the Emperor's camp, I'll report you as deserters."

They might just have a chance. But ten days? That would barely get them to Trofmose, let alone give them time to convince Kaberco of the danger he faced. He was the only one left who'd even try to resist the Emperor's forces. But he'd never know how much peril he was in if he killed them on sight.

Then there was the Empress. Once she realized Tereka wasn't coming back, Tirk and whoever returned with Sebezh wouldn't have much time. Then what atrocities would the Empress commit?

Relio shook his head, his heavy eyebrows pulled tightly together. "I don't know. Why would you risk the wrath of the Emperor for girly's mother?"

"Because I've known His Loftiness since he ruled over nothing more than the mare under his saddle. He trusts me."

Tereka studied Berlok's coppery face. Now she noticed the determined chin, gray eyes, and thick black hair, features that were very similar to those of the Emperor and Empress. Were they related in some way?

"So, who's staying behind?" Berlok asked.

Who should she pick? Tereka swallowed hard.

Naco leaned forward. "If you please, I will."

Berlok laughed. "I'm not sure why you volunteered, but I accept. I've seen enough of you two together to know she'll be back for you."

Looking hard at Naco, Tereka wondered if she should protest. Should she refuse to let him endanger himself for her? Iskra had sacrificed for her and ended up a broken shell.

Steady as ever, Naco met her gaze. "I trust you to fulfill your obligations. I know you'll come for us."

She stared into his eyes, shoving down the thought that she was about to sentence him to death. The weight of her calling as the Desired One pulled on her, as if dragging her into a pit, darker and deeper than any mine.

His gaze hardened. "You know what you have to do. This is the only way."

Her throat tightened. Leaving him behind felt wrong, like the coward's way out. She gripped her hands together to keep herself from throwing her arms around him and begging him to let her choose one of the others.

But he was right. It was the only way to get her mother to safety and to warn the Riskers. And whatever resistance Kaberco still commanded. Plus, the sky-god had told her to leave. She had to obey.

Feeling like she'd roasted her heart over the open flame of a brazier, Tereka nodded.

43

D amira could hardly believe what she was hearing. She stared at Berlok as if her gaze could burn a hole through his skull. "Tell me that again."

"We freed the prisoners—"

"Not that part. The bit about the refugees. Where are they?" Her voice rose as she spit out the words.

"Dami," Shagonar said softly.

She shot a glare in his direction. Neither he nor Syzyan seemed suitably disturbed that Berlok hadn't brought all the fugitives back.

"Well, one died liberating the last prison camp. Another was wounded about the same time. He's here."

"And his name is?"

"Sebezh. If we can believe anything that comes hissing out of his mouth."

Sebezh. He failed her.

Kill him.

Stinging pain shot through her hands and she gripped them together. Oh, Sebezh would pay for his failure.

"The dead man? Who was he?" Syzyan asked.

"Hinat."

So, Sebezh was wounded, and his ally was dead. "Were any of the other refugees injured?" Damira asked.

"Just minor things, mostly. Tereka was stabbed, but it seems to have been a trivial wound."

"Why didn't you bring her back with you?" She kept her tone low but allowed a hint of menace to creep into it, like a scorpion crawling toward its prey.

"I told you. She wanted to take her mother——"

Damira waved a hand as if striking an unseen enemy. "Yes, yes. But I commanded you to make sure she returned."

"I didn't forget. That's why I insisted that one more of her followers come back immediately. I thought between her brother, Sebezh, and this other, she'd have reason enough to return."

"Who is this other, and why him?"

"His name is Naco, and he volunteered," Berlok said. "I accepted him because I saw how stricken Tereka was when he spoke up. It confirmed what I'd suspected, that this one is important to her. More than the others."

So, Berlok wasn't a complete *durak*. And he'd given her interesting information. The question was how to use it.

Her amulets had been calmer ever since Tereka left. Either she, or one of her party, carried dragonflies. And if Sebezh was to be believed, it was her.

With the unsettling news that Tereka was on her way north, Damira's amulets had sprung to life, stinging her limbs and making her wince. The voices in her head demanded death. "Bring Sebezh and this Naco here."

Berlok spun on his heel and left the yurt.

"What do you want with them, Dami?" Shagonar asked.

"We need to know if Tereka is—or thinks she is—the Desired One. If she's fled to mount opposition to us, or really does intend to return." She ignored the strained look on her husband's face. He'd been that way for weeks, tense and somber. He was getting too much like Syzyan.

She curled her lip and turned her gaze toward her brother. He was studying his hands as if he could read the secrets of the universe in the lines on his palms.

If only he'd stop challenging her about the amulets. Then they could quickly wrap up their conquest of Tlefas, establish control the way they had in Razdelia, and be done with all the wars and fighting. The three of them could go back to the close camaraderie they'd shared in their days hunting on the open steppe.

Her amulets were urging her to get rid of Syzyan, but she would never kill her brother. The pain in her fingers and head increased. *I will not give in to it.* She would master the power. Sweat beaded on her forehead. The stinging pain crawled up her legs, making it difficult to breathe.

The door to the yurt opened and Berlok strode in, followed by Sebezh and Naco. Damira smiled and motioned for them to approach her. "Thank you, Berlok. You obeyed promptly." Her voice hardened. "That's what I expect. Obedience. Every time."

He stared at her, an incredulous look on his face.

Damira returned his gaze with an icy stare of her own. This *durak* presumed too much based on their long relationship. He needed to be reminded of his proper station.

A stinging wave of pain shot through her. Her head pounded and dark spots twirled in front of her eyes. She couldn't fight the voices any longer. She focused her gaze on Berlok. "This is what happens when people don't obey."

Berlok stiffened.

She didn't give him time to react further. She used her power to enter his mind. His coppery face turned gray. She pushed the power. In a heartbeat, Berlok was red mist dissipating in the yurt's dim light.

Sebezh moaned, his face as pale as bones bleached by the desert sun. Naco's eyes went wide, the tawny centers looking like tiny spots in white rings. He gripped his hands together, but not before Damira saw them trembling. Good. They got the message.

Surprisingly, Shagonar and Syzyan were silent and still as fallen trees. Perhaps, for once, they recognized the wisdom of her actions.

"Now, tell me about Tereka. Sebezh, you claim she carries dragonfly amulets." She paused to savor the twist of anger on Naco's face. That one knew as much as, if not more, than Sebezh. "How many does she carry?"

"Four, if you please."

Damira hurled a bolt of burning light at Sebezh. He clutched his chest and fell to his knees. "Liar."

"No, it's the truth."

"Then why didn't you tell me this before?"

He cowered, pulling his shoulders up as if to hide between them. "Because I didn't know. But while we were gone, I searched her things when she was bathing. I found her amulets. Two are small, with only one stone in the tail. The other two—" He gasped, drawing a ragged breath. "The other two have three stones."

Damira set her expression like the rocky face of a cliff. Two Amulets of Power. Tereka might not be the Desired One. Or she hadn't found the third. Or Sebezh was lying. "What do you say, Naco?"

The man's face was red and his fists were clenched as he glared at Sebezh. Clearly, he didn't like the idea of Sebezh spilling Tereka's secrets. He must have feelings for the girl.

Naco met Damira's piercing stare and answered evenly. "Sebezh is telling the truth."

"Is Tereka the Desired One?" Damira leaned forward.

"She doesn't seem to think so."

"That's not an answer." She shot her burning light at him, knocking him to the floor. He lay on the hardwood, writhing and gasping.

Kill him. Destroy him. Mist him.

A touch on her arm turned her attention from Naco. "Dami, we don't need to do this." Shagonar spoke softly, but his tone was insistent.

"Why not?"

Syzyan leaned over. "We don't want to break our tools before we finish using them." Wisps of anger laced his words like tendrils of smoke from a brazier scented the air in a yurt.

She bit her lower lip, thinking. Before she could respond, Shagonar spoke up. "Take them away, put them with Tirk. Guard them well." As the guards did his bidding, he patted Damira's hand. "They're our hostages, right?"

Fine. She'd talk with Naco later to find out all he knew about Tereka when Shagonar and Syzyan weren't around to interfere. As Sebezh turned to go, she caught his eye. She wasn't finished with him yet.

"We need to keep them alive if we're going to lure Tereka back here," Shagonar continued.

"And we still want to use Tirk to negotiate with Kaberco," Syzyan chimed in. "If we kill them all, what good will they be?"

Her husband and her brother made perfect sense. Except they didn't hear what she heard, over and over.

Kill them.

But she'd try to ignore the voices. She didn't like the wariness in Shagonar's eyes. Or Syzyan's grim demeanor. She stared down her nose at her brother. "They haven't done much good so far."

"I don't know," Shagonar said slowly, his voice taut. "They've told us some things. We might be able to use them in other ways." He gave her a little smile, the one that made her heart flip over. He seldom showed it to her anymore.

She offered him a whisper of a smile in return. "All right. We wait. But if she's gone north, she could try to ally with Kaberco."

"I doubt it," Syzyan said. "Remember what Tirk told us?

About all the evil Kaberco did to her? And how he's vowed to hunt her down?" He shook his head. "It's more likely he'd kill her."

Shagonar nodded. "True."

"Not if they both want us gone. They could decide they are better off as allies." Damira crossed her arms, frowning. "We need to get her back before that happens."

"It will take something big." Shagonar rubbed his chin. "We could have Tirk send another letter to Kaberco."

Damira scoffed. "For what? He hasn't answered the other three we sent."

"Well," said Syzyan, "it's possible he's still considering his response. Or he's working with the Prime Konamei and the other ephors of the north." He shrugged. "Perhaps he didn't receive the birds. We assumed the ephors in the south told us the truth about which birds would fly where."

Leaning back, Damira listened to Syzyan and Shagonar speculate on Kaberco's plans and their possible countermoves. None of what they said promised to ease the pain the amulets were causing her. She knew the only thing that would placate them was the death of her enemies.

When Syzyan and Shagonar paused, she offered her own idea. "Well, perhaps we should try another move."

They both looked at her.

"We could invade Anbodu."

"Isn't that what we're trying to avoid by negotiating with them?" Syzyan said.

"Yes, but that hasn't worked. I grow weary of it. This has dragged on long enough." She pointed an accusing finger at her brother, its shriveled blackness appearing like the end of a charred spear. "You two insisted that a negotiated settlement would make it easier for us to assume control. But we're no closer to a treaty now than when we started."

She gripped her withered, aching fingers together. "Because of it, we look weak. The Prime Konamei seems to be growing a spine and is mounting opposition. Our soldiers are bored and restless. You've said it yourself—there are only so many trenches we can make them dig, only so many drills we can set for them and only so many caravans for them to guard. It's time they had a battle."

"For what purpose?" asked Syzyan.

"For one, if we kill the Prime Konamei, he'll be gone. We set Shag up in his place. Kaberco and Tereka will have lost their ally in the center, and it will only be a matter of time before they are forced to surrender."

Her amulets must have approved because the pain ebbed. She stifled a sigh of relief. Syzyan was studying her face, his brows drawn together and his expression tight. He still wasn't convinced.

"In any case," she continued, "toppling Anbodu will force Kaberco to come south. Winter will arrive soon in the north, so he'll need to fight us here. He can't afford to let us consolidate our rule while the snow flies."

Damira looked from Syzyan to Shagonar. "And to make sure of it, we'll send Kaberco an ultimatum. This time we'll use the Prime Konamei's own birds."

Her jaw tightened. What was wrong with them that they didn't admit she was right? "Don't you see? If we defeat Kaberco, Tlefas will be ours. Then we'll just have to take care of the few Risker holdouts and a bandit or two."

Syzyan and Shagonar exchanged looks. "Is that really what you think we should do?" Syzyan asked.

"Yes. I'm certain of it."

"Well," said Syzyan, "I'll have to talk with the generals. Let's send the Prime Konamei a final message. Surrender in five days, or we invade the city. While we wait, we can stage drills in sight of the city, so they can see what they're up against." He stood up. "Dami, I'm worried about you—"

"I'm fine." The words came out curtly, more so than she intended. "Thank you, Syz. Now go plan your battle." She

smiled at him. He answered with a curt nod and marched out
of the yurt.

Shagonar was already ordering food and wine. Good. The
more he drank, the less he noticed her pain. There was a time
when that would have bothered her. But not now. She didn't
need him fussing at her to use the amulets less.

She had to conquer Tlefas. Then she'd win Shagonar
back, and they'd enjoy their reign for the rest of their lives.

44

L ater that afternoon, Syzyan slouched at his writing table. He had a map sprawled in front of him, but he couldn't focus his eyes enough to read it. *Stones and bones, Dami, what have you become?* He shivered, bile surging into his mouth. How could she have misted Berlok?

"Father?" Farnaz's tentative question cut into his thoughts. "You were saying?"

Syzyan jerked his head up. "Yes." He blinked and resumed poring over the map. He traced a small river that ran from the mountains to Anbodu and curved around the capital. The water formed a natural defense that would be hard to breach. "Make a note to inventory our exploding arrows. We'll need them to break through the city walls." He tapped his fingers on the table. "If we have less than four hundred, set them to making more."

Before Farnaz could answer, the door to the yurt opened and Shagonar ambled in, bringing with him the sour smell of wine.

"Do you have any red, Syz? I'm all out," he said loudly enough to be heard five yurts away.

"Don't you think it's a little early?"

"You work too hard, you know that?" Shagonar pointed at an unopened bottle standing on a low side table. "Farnaz, would you pour for all of us?" He dropped heavily onto the cushions near the table. Farnaz knelt as he poured three glasses of the ruby-colored wine.

Shagonar took one, held it up, and said, "To the open steppe." He drained the glass and set it down. "Please." He gestured with his chin to the wine bottle. Farnaz refilled his glass.

"What brought this on?" Syzyan asked. "I miss the steppe, too, but we've not been to Otrechia in years."

Tossing his wine back with a gulp and a belch, Shagonar didn't seem to hear the question. "Listen," he said. "I think we should review the troops."

What a peculiar mood, Syzyan thought. Shagonar had always been a bit flighty, but this shift was more abrupt than usual. "Are you looking for anything in particular?"

"I'm concerned about the brigade of Izolliyans on the western flank." He put his glass down with a thump.

Syzyan pursed his lips. The last he knew, all the Izolliyans were located on the southern flank. Shagonar clearly had something more than a surprise troop inspection in mind. "We should take a look, then." He glanced at Farnaz. "While we're gone, you can check on the explosives."

"We should bring him with us, Syz. It's time he learned how to assess a military position."

This was getting odder and odder. They'd been using Farnaz to inspect troops for months. Syzyan nodded. "We'll all go."

They strolled across the camp, a handful of guards in tow. Shagonar kept up a steady stream of comments, only pausing when the pounding of the blacksmith's hammer drowned him out. His observations on each Arban-u Darga's horses, troops, and weapons were incisive and insightful. Syzyan was pleasantly surprised. He'd thought

Shagonar had ceased paying attention to such details long ago.

Shagonar didn't stop walking until they left the laughter of soldiers, shouts of orders and neighing of horses behind. He only halted when he reached the bank of the Orkhana River. He stood staring at the rushing water, the only sound the hiss of the current.

"Did you bring me here to meditate on the rapids," Syzyan said, "or do you have something to say?"

Shuffling back a step, Shagonar motioned to the guards, directing them to move out of earshot. Once they obeyed, he released a long breath. "Syz, there's something wrong with Dami."

"You just noticed?"

"I kept telling myself it was nothing. Or the cruelty was necessary until we made peace. But I can't ignore it any longer. What she did to Berlok—" He pressed a hand to his mouth. "I nearly vomited on my shoes."

Syzyan rubbed his stinging eyes. "I know." His shoulders sagged as if bent under a massive weight.

"I keep thinking back to that day when our camp was massacred," Shagonar said, his face a crumpled mess. "You and Berlok and I returned from the hunt and discovered—" His voice broke.

"Nearly all of them dead. Your mother and my baba, raped and dying. Dami more terrified than if had she been cornered by sand wolves."

"And she was the one who found Berlok's son, miraculously alive among the dead."

"Those two were all that was left of our clan." Syzyan's throat tightened, and his stomach felt heavy. "How could she mist him?" He let the tears trickle over his cheeks.

"Father?" Farnaz's voice quavered. "Are you saying my aunt misted Berlok?"

Syzyan let out a deep, jagged breath. His belly cramped

and a sour taste returned to his mouth. Sweat broke out on his forehead. He couldn't bring himself to answer.

"This is my fault." Shagonar moaned and gripped his face in his hands as he paced along the river. "I let her convince me that the miscarriages had nothing to do with the amulets. I told myself she was right." He snorted. "I repeated the lie so many times I believed it as truth." His voice cracked. "Syz, I know I told you Dami recovered after our daughter died, but it wasn't true. She was different, somehow. Brittle. Unstable." He turned and stumbled back toward Syzyan and Farnaz. "I don't know her anymore." He staggered and sank to the ground.

Dropping to his knees, Syzyan clung to Shagonar. "I don't either." He held his friend until they both stopped shaking. With a sigh, he released Shagonar and sat on the damp soil.

Farnaz slowly lowered himself next to Syzyan. "Father?"

Barely able to meet his son's wide and frightened eyes, Syzyan put a hand on Farnaz's knee. "Yes. Your aunt misted Berlok." *Damira has turned into a monster. And I allowed this to happen.*

Shagonar twisted his fingers together. "She never was like this. But now she takes pleasure in causing pain. It's as though she enjoys devouring people like a glutton gulps down cakes."

His friend was right, Syzyan realized. He swallowed hard. His beloved sister had become an evil to be feared. With an effort, he pushed out words. "I agree. But, Shag, it's not all your fault. I should have known. She proved how far she'd go to win when she used me as bait to trap Wei Fang. She resolved to prevail, even if it cost me my life. My best chance to stop her was right after she defeated Wei Fang, and I squandered it."

"What about me? Snake's teeth, I was so taken with being emperor, I didn't notice what was happening to my own wife." Shagonar grabbed the neck of his tunic and tugged, ripping the silk. "I'm a spineless coward. A *durak* for not stopping her years ago."

"If you're a spineless *durak*, so am I. When this is over, we can punish each other. If we live that long." Syzyan bit his lip. "Shag, did you notice? She no longer speaks of bringing freedom or peace. Now she says that Tlefas will be ours. It's the power, the control she wants."

"It's those cursed amulets. She can't master them anymore."

Syzyan read sorrow in Shagonar's eyes, mixed with the horror he felt himself. "That's what I think. The amulets are pushing her to kill anyone who opposes her."

Shagonar sucked in a breath. "If she could mist Berlok, how long before she comes after one of us?"

Gritting his teeth, Syzyan willed the little food he'd eaten to stay in his churning stomach. "I've been wondering that myself. We have to stop this."

"We should have prevented it long ago." Shagonar hung his head and dug in the dirt with his finger. "You were right, Syz. We never should have had anything to do with those blighted amulets."

"I've yearned to hear you say that for a long time," Syzyan said with a sad smile. "And now, I'm very sorry this day has come. I should have done more to stop you both."

"You were up against a rather determined woman."

"Who is now a woman obsessed."

"Or maybe possessed."

Farnaz gasped. The three of them sat wordlessly, staring at the water until the quacking of ducks broke the silence.

Shagonar pulled a stone from the hard ground. "But what can be done? With those scorpions, she's invincible."

"Well," said Syzyan, "from what I remember from our studies, if an Amulet of Power is destroyed, its Wielder will die."

"You're not saying—"

"No. I don't want that to happen. The scrolls also said that if a Wielder first gave up an amulet, and then it was destroyed, the Wielder would survive. Maybe in pain, maybe a cripple, but still alive. And free of the amulet's power."

"But how do we do that?" Shagonar rubbed his face. "Even if she was willing to give up all three, how can they be destroyed?" He shook his head. "And don't ask me to try. I can barely stand to hold a two-stoned amulet anymore. I use the smaller ones to help me with things that are growing too hard."

"What do you mean?" Syzyan fought a rising panic. He didn't want to lose Shagonar, who'd been his friend since before he could walk.

"I'm not sure how to explain. It's like the amulets have drained my strength, made me old before my time." He shrugged. "Look at me. I'm barely a year older than you. But you look ten years younger."

Syzyan studied Shagonar's face. The strong lines of his chin and jaw were still there. But his high cheekbones were more pronounced than they had been in his youth. The laugh lines around his eyes and mouth were joined by a network of wrinkles that crossed his cheeks. With a pang, he realized his friend did look like a much older man.

"More than that," Shagonar said. "I've seen you swing into the saddle as easily as when you were sixteen. Now, without the amulet, I need a groom's help. And I'm not about to ask for it."

In their younger days, Syzyan remembered, his friend had been so brave, always willing to take a risk. Now, he had to admit, Shagonar walked stiffly like an old man, on feet that plainly hurt.

Shagonar glanced over his shoulder. "Those scorpions are eating her alive. Have you noticed? Not only are her fingers shriveled—nearly all of her right hand has turned black." He sighed. "Dami's getting more anxious by the day. Yesterday she accused Izumi of trying to poison her."

"Izumi has been her maid for over ten years."

"I know. It made me wonder," Shagonar said. "After what happened with Berlok, I'm convinced. It won't be long before she comes after you. Or me."

"But is it possible to act without alerting the amulets?" Syzyan rubbed his chin. "They seem to keep Dami informed of any plot against her." He scrunched up his face. "And if we destroy her amulets, will we end up killing her?"

"I hope not." Shagonar looked at the river.

"Can we do anything against magic amulets?" asked Farnaz.

Syzyan drew a deep breath. "I think there's only one person who can help us." He looked at Shagonar and Farnaz's blank faces and nearly laughed. "Tereka. The girl who carries dragonflies."

"I don't know, Syz." Shagonar shook his head. "Do those amulets even have any power?"

"My wife thought so. And you've seen them heal."

"As if healing properties will do any good against amulets that can turn a man to mist in a heartbeat." Farnaz's voice was shrill.

With a glance over his shoulder, Syzyan saw the guards standing in a semi-circle many yards away, all facing the camp. He laid a hand on Farnaz's arm. "Softly, my son. Listen. Tereka was here for weeks. I think she had the dragonfly amulets with her. Dami sensed their presence but somehow wasn't able to find them. That makes me suspect the dragon-flies have a power we don't understand."

He bit his lip. "Paveh, your grandfather, always said that in a fight, the sky-god would make sure the dragonflies defeated the scorpions. He said the wielder of the dragonflies could ask the sky-god for the power to destroy the scorpions, and it would be granted. If Paveh was right, then Tereka can defeat the scorpion amulets."

"What do you propose?" Shagonar leaned forward.

"Dami is about to send Kaberco an ultimatum. I suggest we get Tirk to write letters to both Kaberco and his sister. Dami might agree that an appeal from a brother might work better than demands from an invader."

"How will that help us?"

"In two ways. Tirk could be coached in what to write, to phrase it in a way designed to arouse his sister's suspicions. Or perhaps he could be convinced to send a second, private message to Tereka, telling her our hopes."

Shagonar raised an eyebrow. "That assumes that Tereka and Kaberco have allied."

"Isn't that what you would do? Ally with the only other person who's opposing your common foe? Even if they are your sworn enemy?"

"I suppose." Shagonar juggled the stone in his hand. "But doesn't Kaberco think all the amulets are evil?"

Syzyan bit his lip. "Probably. But if he's desperate enough, he'll be willing to give them a try. And if he thinks Tereka has a power that can help him, he'll be less likely to kill her."

"Suppose that's true," Shagonar said. "Tirk is no fool. If Dami were to find out about his second message, he'd be dead. Why would he help us?"

"That's where Farnaz comes in."

"Me?" Farnaz's eyebrows lurched together.

"Tirk, as Shag says, is no fool. He'll never agree to anything that comes from either of us," Syzyan explained. "But perhaps a little encouragement from you, in the name of protecting Savinnia—"

"How did you know about that?" asked Farnaz.

"The servants I assigned to the refugees are my spies."

Farnaz stared at his father for a moment. "So, I tell Tirk to ask his sister to destroy my aunt's amulets? And that the drag-onflies will give her the power to do it?"

"Yes, that's about it." Syzyan lowered his eyes. "I hate that it's come to this. But we have to stop Dami." He swallowed the lump in his throat, the lump that threatened to choke him. "For now, all we can do is play along with her, as if we support her in the use of her amulets. While trying to prevent her from misting anyone else."

"If Dami catches Tirk, you know she'll torture him to find out who else knew about his private letter," Shagonar said. "Not to mention what she might do to us."

"That's where we need you." Syzyan looked earnestly at his lifelong friend. "Do whatever it takes to keep her happy and content while we wait for our assault on Anbodu. Do whatever it takes to keep her from asking questions."

"You're asking me to—" Shagonar shuddered.

"You are her husband."

"But she's not the girl I married." Shagonar hurled the rock in his hand into the river. "I'll have to drink a bottle or two of wine to get the thought of her misting Berlok out of my mind first." He winced. "It will feel like bedding a snake. What if all my efforts at distracting her don't work?"

"Then I will confess that I put Tirk up to it. You and Farnaz will know nothing about it. I'll count on you two to find another way to destroy the scorpions."

Farnaz's eyes widened. His olive skin paled and his mouth hung slack.

Shagonar's coppery-tan face had taken on a greenish tinge. "I wish I could argue, but you're right. We let this go on too long. More shame to us. We have to do whatever it takes to stop it. Even if we all end up as red mist.

45

Tereka paced around three massive oak trees, letting the pale autumn sun warm her face whenever she crossed out of the shade. She stared across a barren field, the cut stalks of harvested rye now drooped over the damp ground, yellowed and brown. In the distance stood the wooden walls and stone turrets of Tyov. She chewed the inside of her cheek, anxious about events within the city.

They'd traveled for six arduous days. As they plodded north and east, the sand and gravel of the desert gave way to plains and pastures, then fertile farmland. Just after mid-day, they trudged up a stony rise and onto the Great Road that cut through the center of Tlefas, running from Attu in the north to Litavye in the south. To Tereka's delight, they stumbled upon the road just south of Tyov, the regional center of the central province, precisely where they wanted to be.

The rough terrain hadn't been the toughest part of the trip. Iskra was the problem. They couldn't trust her to sit astride a horse alone. She'd jump off on a whim. Also, since she shrieked every time one of the men touched her, Tereka and Savinnia took turns holding her in front of them, an hour at a time. Whenever they switched, they made sure Iskra relieved herself. They'd made that mistake too many times.

Every night Iskra jolted from sleep, screaming. Tereka and Savinnia did their best to calm her. For some odd reason, Iskra would sometimes respond to Alikse's soothing deep voice when she cowered from Tereka or Savinnia.

After every frenzied nightmare, Tereka called on the sky-god to calm her mother. Usually, that sufficed to get her to sleep for a few hours. Then the entire ordeal would repeat. Fatigue ground Tereka like a millstone, crushing her will to carry on.

At the moment, Iskra sat on the ground near their staked and hobbled horses, for once seemingly content. Thankfully, Savinnia and Alikse were getting better at managing Iskra's terrors. They just might be able to get her to Cillia without attracting too much attention.

Tereka let out a huff and gazed at the city, wishing she could see through its wooden walls. She and her companions had debated the details of their plan for days. In the end, she'd seen things their way. Because Kaberco had placed a price on all their heads, it was risky for any of them to enter the city. But Tereka was the Desired One. She had to get to the north, even if the others didn't. She was the best choice to stay outside the walls with Iskra.

Reluctantly, she'd allowed her friends to venture into Tyov, hoping that whatever sketches of their faces appeared on wanted posters weren't accurate. Sky-god willing, they'd be able to conduct their business and get out of the city without arousing any interest.

Kemet's charge was to sell two of the horses. That way, they'd have enough money to pay for Savinnia, Alikse, and Iskra to ride a caravan north through Attu, Trofmose, and all the way to Gishin. Relio was to find out when the next caravan was leaving for Attu, the nearest large town, and to negotiate a price for three passengers. Alikse's task was to scour the market for sedative herbs, just in case they'd need them to contain Iskra. And Savinnia sought clothing to replace Iskra's soiled garments. All of them would buy food for the journey.

Once Iskra and her escorts were safely on the caravan, the rest of them would ride hard, swinging to the west of Attu, then around to the north to return to their mountain hideout. From there, they'd try to convince the Riskers—with their amulets—to join Tereka's fight against the Empress.

Rubbing the back of her head, Tereka tugged on her hair harder than usual. Would the Riskers be willing to fight? Would the threat of an invader who wielded scorpion amulets be enough? Probably. She doubted the Prime Konamei had even thought to ask the Riskers for help.

The sun moved higher in the sky. She gnawed her lip. Surely Relio, at least, should be back. It shouldn't have taken him long to inquire about a caravan and buy some pasties. Savinnia's errand wasn't a difficult one, either.

She pulled her cloak tightly around herself, shivering in the chill autumn wind. Where were her friends? And for that matter, were Tirk and Naco still alive? She grimaced, tormented by guilt as she wondered about their fate.

At least Iskra was quiet. For the last hour, she'd been humming to herself, seated on the ground, building a pile of dirt. Then she moved closer to one of the ancient oaks. Iskra put a hand on its thick trunk, stroking the rough bark. Had Tereka and Iskra joined hands, they wouldn't have been able to reach around it. And it was the smallest of the three.

This stand of three trees had withstood much, lone sentinels on a hill near neither city nor road nor river. Tereka picked up a brown leaf from the ground and ran it through her fingers, wondering how the tall oak trees survived winter storms and summer droughts. An eagle soared down and perched on one of the tree's barren branches.

Iskra resumed digging in the dirt with a stick.

"Pretty, pretty."

"What's pretty, Mam?"

"Pretty." Iskra scrabbled at the dirt. Her stick broke and her face screwed up. A sob burst from her.

"It's alright," Tereka said. "I'll dig for you." She chose a rock and scratched at the dirt.

Iskra patted her hand. "Dig."

Tereka pressed her lips together. Whoever had tormented her mother into losing her mind deserved to have all his limbs pulled off one by one. As did Kaberco, who'd hunted her relentlessly and murdered her husband before her eyes. Tereka's knuckles whitened as her fingers tightened around the sharp stone.

"Dig. More."

"Yes, yes." Anything was better than nervously waiting for the others or having to soothe a hysterical Iskra. Tereka felt a vibrating warmth in her side near the pouch that held her amulets. She put a hand over them. What did this mean?

Her feet tingled, prompting her to stand. As if following an unseen guide, she walked around the tree to a spot in the center of the space framed by the three oaks. She dropped to her knees and resumed digging.

Tottering over to kneel beside Tereka, Iskra again told her to dig.

If it kept her mother calm, she'd dig a hole big enough to swallow both moons. A few heartbeats later, the rock she was using as a shovel scraped something hard. Probably another stone. She pounded the hard spot. Instead of a click of rock against rock, she heard a clang. She'd hit metal.

Iskra clapped her hands and giggled. "Pretty."

Tereka dug faster. Her heartbeat quickened. She was as excited as her mother to uncover whatever was buried in the dusty soil. In a few moments, she extracted a small metal box from the dry ground.

She brushed the dirt from the lid. The metal was inlaid

with an intricate, symmetric pattern of violet stones the size of her smallest fingernail. With shaking fingers, she opened the catch to find an oiled cloth. She pushed the stiff folds back. Then she nearly dropped the box.

"Pretty." Iskra laughed.

The purple and green stones of a dragonfly amulet glittered like sunlight on the ripples in a pond. Tereka plucked the amulet from its wrapping and held it up. Three stones dangled, forming the tail. It was the third Amulet of Power. She closed her fist around it and sat back in the dirt, tears pricking her eyes.

This was the confirmation she needed. Her lingering doubts fled like morning fog on a hot summer day.

She was the Desired One. Her breath grew ragged. *Well, sky-god, if you chose me, I need your help. Show me what you want me to do.*

Possibilities raced through her mind like fire through a dry field. With three Amulets of Power, surely she'd be able to cure Iskra. She'd have her mother, finally. And she'd be strong enough to oppose the Empress. The sky-god wouldn't let her down. That much she knew. For the first time in weeks, her spirits lifted. They might just come out of this war victorious.

Leaning against the largest oak, she closed her eyes, losing herself in a daydream of living with her mother and grandparents. And somehow, Naco was there as well.

Iskra stirred next to her. Tereka opened one eye. Her mother's head was drooping, and she seemed to be dozing. Good. Tereka jiggled the amulet in her hand. Maybe she could try some healing? The amulet immediately went cold. *Perhaps it's not the time for that right now.* She shoved the amulet into the bag where she kept the others and tied it securely in her pocket. Shutting the box with a click, she tucked it into another pocket.

A distant sound made Tereka glance toward the city. A man ran across the field toward them. She squinted. Red hair shone under the sun. Kemet. Finally. She jumped to her feet and sprinted to meet him.

"Tereka! Run!"

Now she saw them. Six riders approaching from the city. Pounding hoofs from the south told her more came from that direction. She spun and dashed to her mother. Hauling Iskra to her feet, she tried to hurry her to the horses. Iskra let out a wail and stumbled. *Come on, come on.* Tereka pulled her along, trying to reach the horses before the riders overtook them.

Within heartbeats, they were surrounded by twelve of the Prime Konamei's guards wearing black leathers and waving long swords. Iskra sunk to the ground, sobbing.

One of the riders dismounted and stalked toward her. "Tereka Sabidur. It's been a while."

She took in his cold hazel eyes, his barrel chest and broad shoulders that loomed over her. "Kaberco Gougin." She swallowed. "You're a long way from home."

He smirked. "I could say the same for you. But unlike you, I'm here on the Prime Konamei's business. I rode south to find out more about this Emperor Shagonar's military position. And as luck would have it, I was in the stables when another of our old friends showed up. Kemet Okashi. I think you know him."

By this time, one of the guards had dragged Kemet up. Her friend's face was bruised and blood trickled down his neck.

Kaberco laughed. "A loyal fellow, that one. He wouldn't tell me anything. Not how he'd escaped from my jail. Or why he was selling horses that bore the saddles and tack of the invaders. Had I not been there, the stable master might have believed his tale about being a refugee from the war who stole the horses after his village had been burned." He curled his lip. "But I knew better."

Tereka looked at Kemet, who was glaring at Kaberco with defiant eyes. "So you caught us," she said. "Now what?"

"We join your friends, of course.

"Friends? We don't have any," Tereka said.

"The three of you are traveling with five horses?" Kaberco shook his head. "Kemet here was seen entering the south gates with some rather seedy-looking people. I'm sure they've been found by now. So let's go."

"Where?"

"Into the city. The ephor will be pleased to know we've rounded up several dangerous criminals. Even during an invasion, we are working to keep the people safe. I think we'll have a public execution, just so everyone understands that during these challenging times, keeping the rules is the smart thing to do."

Iskra let out a shriek and wrestled out of the arms of the guard holding her. She darted across the field. The guard sped after her. He brought the hilt of his sword down on her head, and she crumbled into the dust.

"No!" Tereka yelled. "How could you do that to a scared old woman? You're a worse monster than the Empress."

Kaberco slapped her face. "You be quiet."

Tereka shuffled back, wincing as a guard tossed Iskra over his shoulder.

Jerking his chin, Kaberco pointed toward the city. "Now move."

She stumbled off, guardsmen clutching her arms on either side. Was this how it was going to end? The amulets were of no help. She'd lost everything. Even the hope of the sky-god. It had all been for nothing.

46

The guard shoved Tereka into a dimly lit cell and dumped Iskra on the stone floor. He slammed the door shut with a clang. The harsh sound echoed in the dank, fetid air.

Dropping to her knees, Tereka touched Iskra's face. Her skin was cold, but she was breathing, little whimpers escaping her lips.

Musty-smelling straw was piled in the corner of the cell. Tereka dragged her mother to the heap and sat on it, trying to ignore the rustling within. Bugs or rats, she didn't care. She needed to calm Iskra and warm her up. Rocking gently, she held Iskra in her arms. Kaberco and his men were beasts to abuse an obviously ill woman.

A noise from the next cell broke into her thoughts. "Tereka?"

She looked up into Savinnia's frightened, tawny eyes. "Yes. Are you alright? Where are the others?"

"I'm fine. They're here, just in their own cells. Except Kemet."

"Yeah, what happened to him?" Relio's voice growled faintly from down the row.

Tereka explained how he'd been caught. "I'm sure they'll bring him along soon." Unless they've already killed him. Her throat tightened at the thought.

The scraping of a metal door drew her attention to the stairs. Several pairs of heavy footsteps descended. As their owners approached, she let out her breath. Kemet was among them. They prodded him to a cell at the end of the corridor and shoved him in.

Two large men stood in front of Tereka's cell. One was Kaberco. The other was a stranger to her, a man with sloping shoulders and stone-gray hair. Like Kaberco, he wore black leather. He also bore the ceremonial gold chain of an ephor draped over his shoulders.

He studied Tereka. "This is Tereka Sabidur? Somehow I thought she'd look more frightening."

She didn't respond to his sarcasm. Let him mock.

Kaberco pointed at the man. "This is Eltolad, ephor of Tyov. We've been discussing what to do with you. A taking wasn't enough to teach you to respect the rules about safety and fairness. So, what shall it be?"

"Whatever you decide, you deserve much worse," Tereka responded. She held her head high and her voice steady.

"Why is that?" Kaberco scoffed. "I've always been loyal to the Prime Konamei. You allied yourself with the enemy. And now you've come here as spies."

Relio snorted. "That's what you know. Sounds like your spies have let you down."

"Can you deny that you went to the invader's war camp four weeks ago?" Kaberco leaned toward the bars.

Tereka got to her feet and took a step closer to him. "No, I don't deny it. After the unfair, no, corrupt trial you inflicted on me a year ago, I decided that the Prime Konamei's reign was neither safe nor fair. And unlikely to result in prosperity for anyone other than those in power. When a new leader arrived, I went to see if he was the Desired One of prophecy."

Kaberco and Eltolad flinched. The older man glared at Tereka. "Just saying those words could have you taken."

"At least I'd know what to expect. I made some good friends among the taken." She wrapped her fingers around the cold bars. "Besides, you may not have heard. We liberated the prison camps and the salt mines. Most of the prisoners are on their way to join the Emperor's army. You can be sure they have no love for the Prime Konamei."

From their startled expressions, she knew the news hadn't reached them. That meant there was little communication between the south under the Emperor and the other regions of the country.

"You did that?" Eltolad's voice shook with anger.

She lifted a shoulder in half a shrug. "It was the least I could do."

"You're right," Eltolad said. "Beheading is too good for her."

"Don't you want to know why we're here?" Tereka tipped her head to the side.

Eltolad sneered. "To spy for our enemies?"

"No, we've left the Emperor."

Relio chimed in. "You could call us deserters if you like. Just add it to our list of crimes."

Kaberco rubbed his chin. "And why would we believe that?"

Tereka pressed her lips together. May as well tell him the truth. *I'm going to die, anyway.* "Because it became obvious that the Emperor is not the Desired One."

"He doesn't claim to be," said Kaberco. "It's his wife."

"Damira." Tereka shook her head. "She's not the Desired One either."

"How do you know that?"

Could she convince them? Eltolad had already decided against her. From Kaberco's glower and crossed arms, she knew he would not be easy to persuade.

"Because she carries three amulets in the shape of scorpions. With them, she controls a destructive power. I've watched her turn people into mist with little more than a thought."

Both men burst into laughter. "You expect us to believe that?" Kaberco said.

"We've seen it too," Alikse said.

"You may not want to believe them," Kemet called from his end of the corridor. "But it's true. You know me, Kaberco. Why would I invent a tale like that?"

Kaberco curled his lip. "I can think of seven reasons without even trying." He turned back to Tereka. "So, you ran away because of a fairy story?"

"No. Because I didn't want to be misted into oblivion."

At that moment, Iskra opened her eyes. She sucked in a ragged breath and shrieked. She clambered to her feet and staggered to the iron bars. "You! Evil!" She spat in Kaberco's face.

He lurched backward with a curse.

Tereka put her arms around Iskra. "Shh. It's alright."

Iskra trembled in her arms, then sagged against Tereka, whimpering. "Don't let him take me. Don't."

"That woman should be flogged for spitting on an ephor," Eltolad said.

Raising her head, Tereka locked her gaze on Kaberco. Blood pounded in her ears, sending surges of heat through her veins. "She spat on him because he deserved it." The words flew from her mouth like eagles diving for their prey. "He claimed to be her friend but tried to marry her to a brute. All because she learned the truth about the Riskers and loved one of them."

"What are you talking about?" Kaberco's voice was thin and pinched. "I don't know this woman."

"You don't recognize your old friend Iskra?" Tereka said. She pulled Iskra toward the bars and showed Kaberco her wrist. "See the scars where they burned the tattoo with acid?

And the marks where she dug the X into her skin so she wouldn't forget his name when her mind was going? You're the one who drove her to madness, even if you weren't the one who brutalized her. And you say you work for a safe and fair society. I asked you once before and I ask you again. Safe and fair for whom?"

Kaberco recoiled as if she'd struck him. Even in the dim light, the paling of his olive skin was noticeable. She glared at him for a few heartbeats, then tightened her arms around Iskra, holding her close.

Eltolad pressed a hand over his mouth. "Is that what happens to those who are taken? Hard labor is one thing, but this…"

"Little Iskra." Kaberco's voice shook. "I'd hoped she died quickly."

Tereka curled her lip. "Oh, yes. Better death than a happy life free of the Prime Konamei's rules. Don't you see why the Emperor's promise of freeing us from an oppressor was appealing to me? And why I had to find out for myself if he was worth following?"

The two ephors stared at each other for a long moment. Then Eltolad spoke. "I think we have to make a choice. Either we execute them all now, as the danger to society that they are, or use them to help us drive out the invader."

"What do you propose?" Kaberco asked.

"It might be easier just to kill them." Eltolad looked from Tereka to Kaberco.

"You and your cowardly guards are going to fight off an army by yourselves?" Relio cursed and spat. "Seems to me you need all the allies you can get."

As repulsive as the idea of working with Kaberco was, it was Tereka's only choice. She swallowed the bitter taste in her throat. "And if you want help from the Riskers, I'm the one to get it."

Kaberco rubbed his chin. "Yes, you and your da."

"Riskers!" Eltolad scowled. "Ally with barbarians?"

"We might need them." Kaberco narrowed his eyes and raked them over Tereka's face. "But can I trust you?" He looked at Eltolad. "What do you say? Should I take them north with me? Or do we end them now?"

47

T he door to the cell swung open with a protesting creak. Tereka blinked in the torchlight and tightened her grip on Iskra's sleeping form. Being awakened at midnight could only mean one thing. They were being taken.

"Come." The guard spoke softly, almost gently.

"Where?"

"Kaberco commands it. Come. If you please."

The politeness startled Tereka. That wasn't how guards addressed the taken. She remembered that horrifying experience all too well.

"I'll need help with my mam," she said. "Can you bring my friend Savinnia?"

The guard silently withdrew. A few heartbeats later, Savinnia knelt by Iskra's side. With a few grunts, Tereka and Savinnia raised Iskra's dead weight and half carried, half dragged her from the cell.

Relio, Alikse, and Kemet stood at the foot of the steps. "Do you know what's going on, girly?" Relio asked.

"If you please, no talking," the guard said. "Follow me."

Alikse gathered Iskra in his arms and carried her up the

stairs. With every step, Tereka felt as if they were approaching their doom. Whether a secret midnight trial or a moonlight execution, she wasn't sure. The hair on the back of her neck prickled. She ran a hand over her amulets. They were neither hot nor cold. Odd. They weren't giving her any notice of danger.

They emerged into the frosty night, the sky clear and star-studded, Dabney's full orb soaring overhead. The guard led them through one courtyard to another.

Kaberco stood by a saddled horse, one of ten horses bridled and ready for riding. Tereka recognized the horses they'd been riding before Kaberco captured them.

"You're all here?" he said. "Then let's go."

"Where?" Tereka, Relio, and Savinnia all asked at the same time.

He swung into his saddle, ignoring their question and Relio's muttered curse. "What are you waiting for?"

A guard led a mare to Tereka. Kaberco might be leading them to their death. Or was he taking them away from Elto-lad, who had seemed eager to execute them? She mounted the horse. Alikse lifted Iskra in front of Tereka and helped settle her in a comfortable position. The rest of them mounted their horses and followed Kaberco into the night.

A few hours later, Kaberco called a halt. His guards efficiently made camp, building a fire and tending to the horses. Much to Tereka's surprise, Kaberco returned the saddlebags that still held their possessions, except for their bows, arrows, and knives. She had to admit she would have confiscated their weapons as well, had she been in his position.

Kaberco gestured for them to sit near him on one side of the fire. "I suppose you want to know why you are here."

"Of course," Relio said. "If you're going to kill us, just say so, instead of hiding your plans like a fox."

With a scowl, Kaberco continued. "After I agreed to allow Eltolad to hold you in his jail, we argued long and hard about what to do with you. His first thought was a public execution. Good for morale, he claimed."

"Certainly not for our morale," Tereka said.

"I convinced him that since you committed crimes in the northern region, it was most appropriate for you to be tried in Trofmose. Then the people whose safety you jeopardized could witness your punishment."

Tereka clenched her jaw. She'd had enough of Kaberco and his trials. Hers certainly had been anything but fair. From the muttering of her companions, she guessed their thoughts mirrored hers. "So, you agreed to execute us in Trofmose?" She didn't understand why he'd go to all that trouble. Most likely, he planned to kill them on the road and be done with them. Her shoulders sagged.

He twisted his lips into a smirk. "I didn't tell him exactly what I planned in the way of justice. If you obey my commands as we travel, I'll think about working with you against the Emperor."

She jerked to attention. "You will?"

"Yes." After a long moment, Kaberco continued. "I will promise you one thing, no matter what. After we arrive in Trofmose, I will see to it that Iskra—" His voice cracked on the name. "Is escorted to whomever you want to care for her."

From what Tereka could see of his face in the firelight, he seemed sincere. "I want her to go to my father's family," she said.

"The Riskers? Why to barbarians?"

"Because those barbarians treated her better than you did, the civilized protector of safety and fairness for all." She infused her words with as much sarcasm as she could.

Relio chuckled. "You tell him, girly."

"And besides, even if you do make mocking jokes about myths and fairy tales, the Riskers have magic amulets that heal. I hope they can repair the damage you caused."

"Anyone," Kaberco said, scowling, "who uses those cursed amulets should be killed."

Despite the chilly night, sweat prickled the back of Tereka's neck. Her heart raced, causing her chest to ache. *What if he learns of my amulets?*

"Still," Kaberco continued, "if that is your wish, I will honor it. But I will not allow you to take her there yourself."

"If you please, would you allow Savinnia and Alikse to accompany her? You've seen for yourself how Iskra fears most men. And Alikse will be protection for them on the road."

Kaberco rubbed his jaw. "Yes. They can go. I will send four guards with them as far as Gishin, to the foot of the Guarded Path that leads to the Risker camp. After that, they are on their own."

That was more than Tereka had hoped for. "Thank you."

"Now that we've agreed," Kaberco said, "I have questions. How many soldiers does this Shagonar have?"

For the next few hours, Kaberco questioned them all, sometimes alone, sometimes as a group. He asked the same questions over and over. How many soldiers in the Emperor's army? How disciplined are they? How skilled? What weapons do they use?

Those queries didn't bother Tereka. She freely told Kaberco all she'd observed. But when he got to the amulets, her heart pounded.

With a curled lip, he asked, "What do these amulets look like?" He sneered at the answer. "And they do what?"

Each time she described a misting, Kaberco bored into her eyes with his own, arms folded across his massive chest. "Anyone who uses such things is clearly evil," he said. "Dangerous. I'd kill them on the spot."

Sweat dampened her palms and her limbs felt weak. She didn't dare tell him she carried not one but five dragonflies, for whatever good they did her. That was a secret she'd have to keep until Iskra had made it to the Riskers.

If she possessed amulets that could mist people, she could use them as a weapon, or at least as a threat. But how to harness the power of the dragonflies, other than for healing, was an enigma to her. Kaberco, on the other hand, wouldn't waver for a heartbeat. If he knew what she carried, his reaction would be swift, decisive, and brutal. She didn't want to be on the receiving end of his wrath.

48

Tereka tightened her arms around Iskra, who slumped limply against her, head bobbing with the motion of the horse. Even the clacking of the horse's shoes against the stone streets of Trofmose didn't rouse her. Which was all for the good. Every time Iskra noticed Kaberco, she screamed as if the sight of him was a knife twisting in her eye.

Pulling on the reins, Tereka guided her bay gelding after Kaberco's stallion to the stables behind his house. The corners of her mouth twitched as she recalled the last time she'd visited, sneaking in through the hidden river entrance and liberating the jailed prisoners.

Naco's confidence had given her the courage for that caper. Her throat tightened. Would she ever see him again?

Her nose twisted from the stench of the butcher's shop, the smell of rotting offal mixing with Iskra's sweat. Trofmose's odors hadn't improved since she'd left the city, never expecting to return.

At least they'd made good time from Tyov, taking only five days for the journey. That meant only it was only one day past the ten days Berlok had allowed her. Her breath hitched as she imagined what the Empress had done when she realized Tereka hadn't kept her promise. Was she torturing Naco and Tirk nightly? Or were they already red mist?

Kaberco tossed the reins of his horse to a groom and jumped from the saddle. He waved at Tereka and her friends. "Follow me and be quick about it." He stalked through the stables to the back entrance of his house. Pausing only to mutter a few words to the guard, he vanished inside.

Alikse vaulted from his mount and rushed to Tereka. He eased the sedated Iskra from Tereka's arms and held her while Tereka and the others dismounted.

Walking as quickly as her stiff muscles allowed, Tereka headed for the door, Alikse behind her, carrying Iskra. Kemet, Relio, and Savinnia followed in their wake.

"Peace and safety," the guard said.

"Peace and safety," Tereka responded mechanically.

The guard pointed to the stairs. "He's waiting for you on the third floor."

Tereka raised an eyebrow. Interesting that Kaberco would have them go to his private quarters. She'd half expected the guard to herd them into the damp and dark basement cells.

As she ascended the winding back stair of Kaberco's house, the ephor's shouts filled the air. "Nivi! Where are you?"

A young woman wearing a plain gray dress and leggings scurried up the stairs, pushing past Tereka.

Kaberco stood at the top of the stairs. "Nivi. We have guests. Three women, three men. Make up rooms and have hot water and clean clothing brought up. And food for all of us. Lots of it."

Nivi turned and fled down the stairs.

After an inscrutable stare at Tereka, Kaberco led the way down a corridor with smooth, white walls hung with bright-colored tapestries. Iron scones held massive candles. Kaberco moved silently over the thick carpet that ran the length of the corridor. He opened a door and pointed for them to enter.

Relio put a hand on Tereka's shoulder. "Me first, girly." He walked into the room and let out a string of curses.

Tereka's heart raced. So far Kaberco had kept his promise to keep them safe, but what was making Relio curse? She followed him into the room.

"No wonder you all cling to your power," Relio said, glaring at Kaberco with his hands on his hips.

Kaberco's olive skin darkened. He should be shamed, Tereka thought. The room was filled with luxuries unheard of to the common people. Thick patterned carpets covered shining wood floors. Tan, cushioned divans held scarlet and blue pillows. A bed with a thick mattress supported by a wooden frame instead of a heap of straw. And Kaberco had at least one servant to draw water and bring food. If they survived this war, she'd make sure those in power could no longer deceive people with their lies about fairness for all.

Kemet's eyes bulged. "I didn't believe Tereka when she told me. But I guess you've lied to us all this time."

With lowered eyes, Kaberco shut the door. "Please, all of you, sit."

One by one, they took seats on the overstuffed divans. Tereka and Savinnia flanked the still-drowsy Iskra.

Standing tall in front of them, Kaberco gestured to their surroundings. "I brought you to my private rooms as a sign of trust. You can see for yourself I've just revealed one of the biggest secrets in Tlefas." He held up a hand in response to the muttering that broke out. "I didn't create the system. And yes, I benefited from it. But that's not important now. We have a common enemy."

"If we don't help you, then what?" Relio asked.

"Tereka has already agreed to rally the Riskers. And I expect you all to fight with my army. If you don't, well, then I'll do as Eltolad advised. I'll send your heads to the Emperor as a warning of what will happen to his entire army."

"Surely, you don't expect Iskra to fight?" Tereka said.

"No." Kaberco shook his head. "This is what I propose. You all rest here for the night. Then in the morning, as I promised, four of my men will escort Iskra, Savinnia, and Alikse to the Riskers."

"Why can't I go?" Tereka asked.

"Because I've placed a hefty price on your head. Dead or alive. Even if I rescind that order, do you want to assume everyone will get the word?"

"But—"

"You're known here, like your friend Kemet. The others have a better chance of getting through without being recognized."

She rubbed the back of her head and tugged her hair. He was right. Even with his guards for protection, her presence would jeopardize Iskra's safety. "But who will talk to the Riskers?"

"Your da."

"Do you even know where he is?"

Kaberco grinned. "I'm assuming he's with the Riskers. No one has seen him for weeks."

"Why would he help you?"

"First, because I've sent Iskra back, clearly well-tended, to which Alikse and Savinnia can attest. Second, you will send letters to him and anyone else to whom you care to write."

Tereka crossed her arms over her chest. "And the rest of us are hostages?"

"Oh, no. You're my emissaries. Kemet to the traders, to convince them to fight. You to the Riskers, through your da. And the three of you will tell my lieutenant every single thing you know about Shagonar, his amulet-wielding wife, and their army."

He fixed his eye on her. She couldn't help but notice his gaze wasn't confident. "Are we agreed?" His words held a pleading tone she'd never heard from him before. He must be growing desperate, to be willing to work with criminals like her.

A glance at the others told her that her friends were skeptical at best. Relio scowled. Alikse pursed his lips.

For over a year, her thoughts had been focused on a single goal: to oust those who wielded their power in a corrupt system. One of her first targets was Kaberco, the man who'd sent her to the prison camp and had her assigned to what should have been certain death in a men's brigade.

When faced with a greater evil in the person of Empress Damira, she'd thought to join forces with Kaberco, the only ephor willing to stand against the invaders. But considering the move was one thing. Acting on it was another. Could she be certain he'd keep Iskra safe until she reached the Riskers?

She balled her hands into fists. He'd hunted both her and Iskra as if they were beasts. He'd gladly accepted the benefits awarded him by a corrupt regime. Her stomach churned at the idea of calling him an ally. And not least of his sins, he collaborated with her odious aunt Juquila. "What will you tell your konameis about us?"

Kaberco stroked his chin. "That Iskra and Savinnia are relatives of some of the konameis of smaller villages around Tyov, fleeing the war. Alikse is their guard. They have relatives in Paamiat, so I've sent them there."

Paamiat. The opposite direction they needed to go.

He must have seen the doubt in her face. "Just in case someone decides to follow them and cause trouble. Don't worry, my guards will make sure they get to Gishin and the Riskers safely."

"And the rest of us?"

"I'll introduce you, once I've convinced them they need to work with you."

Tereka stroked the soft fabric of the divan. His words were plausible, his reasoning sound. If Kaberco planned to kill them, he would have thrown them in his jail. What's more, a few times along the road she'd seen the glint of tears in his eyes when he looked at Iskra. Maybe he truly wanted to atone for what he'd done. Maybe.

Heaviness settled on her shoulders. She let out a long sigh. She didn't like it, but working with Kaberco was their best chance. She'd realized as much back in the Emperor's camp, even if she found it hard to swallow now. Somehow, she'd have to tell Kaberco about her amulets and hope he didn't skewer her on the spot. Bile rose in her throat, and she choked out the words. "We'll help you."

"Good. Nivi will see to you. Ask her for whatever you need, and she'll try to provide it. Just don't expect her to reply." He stood up. "Now, I have business to attend to. Know that my guardsmen have orders to kill you if you attempt to leave your rooms." He walked to the door. "Peace and safety."

49

K aberco escaped into the corridor and pulled the door shut. Fatigue rushed over him like an avalanche. His muscles ached from the long ride, his face was raw from windburn. *I deserve every bit of this pain and more.*

What had happened to him? As a new ephor, he truly believed in building a safe, fair, and prosperous society. Now he saw himself through Tereka's eyes, as one who exploited his position while falsely mouthing platitudes about high ideals. He'd twisted the words for his own gain. That was more despicable than a despot who was at least honest about his intentions.

He stalked to his suite and shucked his clothing off, scattering his cloak, pieces of leather armor, and tunic on the floor. Steam wafted from the tub in his bathing room. He had less than an hour before the real challenge of his day.

The hot water eased his sore limbs. He sank lower, wanting to submerge into its embrace and never emerge. It was a gamble, trusting Tereka and her friends. But Tereka was likely to cooperate, at least until she knew Iskra was safe. Her fear of the Empress who could turn men into mist was real. He was certain of that. Tereka sincerely wanted to be rid of the eastern invaders. Who else she wished to be free of, he wasn't so sure.

Climbing from the bath, he dried and dressed in fresh black leathers. He draped the gold chain of his office over his shoulders, aligning it to hang equally low on his chest and back. While his body felt clean, shame curdled his insides— shame over how he'd sentenced Iskra to a lifetime of misery.

While he was bathing, Nivi had tidied the bedroom and brought bread and cheese, along with a flagon of wine. He'd miss the servants. But he couldn't go along with this farce anymore.

After he ate, he walked to the far end of the corridor, to the chamber where he met with his Konament. With any luck, none of them would have shown up early, and he'd have time to collect his thoughts.

A high-pitched voice from within the room made him curse. The adile. But who was she talking to and why were they already here? He spun on his heel, intending to return to his suite. He could do his thinking there, then go start the meeting. They could wait a heartbeat or two for him.

He'd only taken a few steps when the questor appeared at the top of the stairs, huffing from the exertion. Kaberco stifled a curse, and pulled his lips back in a smile. "Peace and safety, Yavaros."

Yavaros nodded. "Peace and safety. Glad you're back. Were you successful?"

"I suppose that depends on your definition of success." He shrugged. "Come on, I'll tell you all about it." He led the way down the hall and opened the door.

Standing aside to allow Yavaros to enter first, Kaberco listened, hearing three voices now. The high tones of the aging adile, the ludi's reedy tenor, and the sultry, caressing voice of Juquila. He swallowed hard. He desperately needed time to decide just how much to tell his konameis. This could go badly if he wasn't careful. And if it went very badly, he might end up taken.

Kaberco straightened his back and strode into the room. As he'd guessed, the three konameis were in their seats near the fireplace, seated by order of precedence, the ludi furthest from the fire, flanked by the adile and Juquila. Yavaros settled himself into one of the seats nearest the fire, leaving the other for Kaberco.

"Peace and safety," Kaberco said, nodding to them all. He strode to a cabinet and pulled out a map of Tlefas. "Konameis, I know it's cold, but our meeting will be more productive if we sit here." He moved to his seat at the head of the table and unrolled the map.

With a groan, Birita rose from her chair. She made her way to the table, the wooden chain of the adile draped over her shoulders barely visible under her gray shawl. She swaddled a scarf around her throat, twisting it around her neck so that it met the bottom of her turban.

The jingling chains of Yavaros and Juquila heralded their approach—his silver, hers bronze. They took their seats, the questor to Kaberco's right, Juquila on his left. The ludi slid into his space next to Juquila, while the adile sat next to Yavaros.

"As you know," Kaberco began, then waited for them to turn their faces to him before continuing, "I traveled south to discover for myself how far the invader had moved into the central region and to determine if there were any weaknesses." He traced a finger on the map. "Anbodu is besieged. The invaders control everything south of the capital, all the way west to the sea."

"Everything?" Juquila asked.

"Yes. Apparently, the Emperor sent some of his soldiers after bandits and had them executed. Of course, the southern towns were grateful. I've also heard reports that the Emperor has seized control of the copper and salt mines." *And freed the prisoners. But maybe I won't share that.*

"What of the rest of the central region?" Yavaros tapped the map.

"They are terrified, naturally. The ephor of Tyov is wavering. He's reluctant to surrender but doesn't want his city and farmlands to be destroyed. The news from the south, what little there is, is that people aren't suffering. Some even prefer the new rule."

"We could have you taken just for uttering those words," Juquila snapped.

Yavaros nodded. "Sounds like treason to me. And that is a taking offense."

50

"Taken for telling you the truth?" Kaberco forced himself to speak blandly. Now was not the time to rile up Juquila. No sense poking a snake before she rose to strike. "I only repeat what I have heard. For all I know, it's propaganda spun by the Emperor."

"What about the army?" Yavaros asked. "Is it as large as they say?"

"Larger, I'm afraid. And well trained." He spent most of the next quarter hour explaining the placement of Shagonar's troops, the way his mounted archers could hit any target while galloping, and the discipline of the ranks.

"So, you are saying they cannot be defeated?" Juquila said.

"I didn't say that. I explained that we are up against a well-trained, mighty foe." Blast the woman. *Twisting my words to scare the others.*

On the map, Yavaros ran a finger along the River Isoturp to the southern city of Litavye. "Any hope for help from the south?"

Kaberco gave him a wry smile. "What hope I had is quickly disappearing. The last bird I received from their ephor brought word they aren't going to oppose Shagonar. They're not happy to have been conquered, but he's letting them live as they please. He's abolished many of the rules about dress and made Volunteer Day, well, voluntary. So as of now, I would count the south out."

"Suppose we defeat this invader," the adile said slowly. "Will we have to fight the south?"

"Good question." Kaberco raised an eyebrow. She wasn't usually that astute. "I suspect not. It appears they just want peace and are willing to negotiate to get it."

"Why isn't that our stance?" asked Juquila.

"Because we chose the path of caution. A wise choice, as it turns out." He forced himself to keep the gloating out of his voice. She'd pressured him relentlessly to ally with Shagonar. When she learned the truth, that would be one of his most satisfying moments as ephor.

"Why do you say that?" the adile asked, her tone sharp.

Kaberco looked her in the eye. "Because I have eyewitness reports of some atrocities committed by the Emperor's wife, who appears to be the power behind his throne."

"Oh?" Yavaros wrinkled his forehead.

Focusing on the questor, Kaberco tried not to look at Juquila, who, he assumed, was no doubt fascinated by the idea of a woman controlling an Empire. "They say she carries three magic amulets that can turn men into mist."

Yavaros stared at him for a heartbeat, then laughed. "You believe that?"

Juquila chuckled. "Perhaps your travels have overtired you. Now you want us to put credence in fairy tales and myths."

Swallowing the curses that begged to be unleashed, Kaberco forced himself to be calm. "Had the news come from only one source, I would have laughed as well. But too many people told the same tale. I heard the fear in their voices. No, this Damira carries a real power. One that we have no weapon against."

"But amulets?" the adile said. "That can't be."

"No?" said the ludi. "Have you never wondered why even speaking of amulets is enough to get someone taken? If they didn't exist or had no power, why would we have such a law?"

The adile gulped.

Kaberco jumped in. "As our ludi said, there is no doubt that magical amulets exist. If they didn't, then why would amulets—or any mention of them—have been outlawed? Just because their existence was publicly dismissed as a dangerous myth didn't make it so."

The questor sighed. "Our ancestors most likely thought they'd gotten rid of the threat such power holds. Rather short-sighted of them. Having a magical weapon would be useful now."

"Too late to worry about that," Kaberco said. "The question before us is what to do about this invasion."

"The obvious choice is to cooperate with the Empress," Juquila said. "Better to make a bargain with her than wait to be killed." She curled her lip. "Or turned to mist, if you insist on believing that."

The other three began talking at once, offering suggestions for terms of surrender. Kaberco folded his arms on the tabletop and let them talk. They wouldn't listen to anything he had to say until they had voiced their fears and argued their concerns.

When their debate died down, Yavaros turned to Kaberco. "You've been quiet. That means you have another idea."

"I do." Kaberco leaned forward. "Your argument in favor of surrender is that we have no weapons against magic amulets."

"You said that yourself," Juquila said.

"I did. But that doesn't mean no weapon exists."

Four puzzled faces stared at him. Had the situation not been so grave, he would have laughed. He bit his lip. *They aren't going to like this.* "Have you forgotten?" he said softly. "The

Riskers have amulets of their own. Perhaps they would be able to combat this threat."

Almost in unison, four voices answered. "No. Not the Riskers."

Kaberco let his eyelids flutter closed for a heartbeat. Yes, that had been his first response. But Tereka and her friends had convinced him that the Empress had a real, deadly power. As much as he despised the idea, they were going to have to ask the Riskers—and their amulets—to help.

Each of his konameis had an opinion. Kaberco again let them argue among themselves, some shouting, others nearly whimpering.

"We can't join forces with savages."

"It's against the law."

"Only the Prime Konamei can change the treaty."

"We can't trust them."

Kaberco waited for them to quiet down. "Konameis. If you please," he said. "Am I to understand that you all want to ally with this invader? Without even consulting the Prime Konamei?" He stared at each of them in turn, starting with Juquila and ending with Yavaros. "Have we not vowed loyalty to him and our safe, fair, and prosperous realm?" Bile rose in his throat at those last words. *What a sham we've all been living. But right now, that's all we have.*

Yavaros let out a long breath. "Yes, we have sworn. We should send a bird to ask him what we should do."

"We can't just sit here and do nothing," Juquila said. "And it would be folly to rely on barbarians for help."

Kaberco remembered the one time he'd been in a Risker camp, shortly after Iskra had fled. The Risker elder was clean, cultured, and had comforts in his home that rivaled any Kaberco himself enjoyed. *Compared to the Riskers, we are the barbarians.* "Our syndic is correct. We can't sit idle. That's why I have been raising an army."

"But if we can't defeat them—"

He cut Juquila off. "It doesn't matter. What we need is leverage. If they think we'll be hard to defeat, then they'll be more likely to make concessions. Surely you understand that simple principle of trade."

From the steely glare she gave him, he knew he'd over-stepped. Insulting Juquila would not help him, no matter how much she deserved to be put down. He tapped the map. "I've been in touch with the other ephors of the north. They will send what men they can spare. Many of the traders already agreed to help."

"And Tyov?" Yavaros asked.

Pursing his lips, Kaberco weighed his words. He didn't want to reveal his alliance with Eltolad, just in case Tyov was overrun before they could move. "He's considering his options."

"You can't mean he's approaching the Riskers." Juquila could not have sounded more skeptical.

"Of course not. No Riskers live anywhere near his terri-tory. But he concurred with my idea of asking them for assistance." He pointed to the eastern mountains. "If the Riskers have amulets that can at least counter the Empress's, that will give us a chance. I say we don't make any decisions until we have the answer to that question."

Juquila sneered. "No. It's stupid to ally with barbarians because a few people are spooked by a rumor of magic amulets. And only a lunatic would lead a rag-tag band against a battle-hardened army. We need to make the best terms we can, now, before this Empress turns on us."

Kaberco clenched his jaw, willing himself to not respond to her insults. He set his heated face like flint and concentrated on breathing evenly.

The ludi nodded. "The Prime Konamei wouldn't expect us to let ourselves be killed. That would most assuredly be unsafe."

The questor stared at his hands. Sweat trickled down

Kaberco's neck. *If I can't get some support, they might turn on me. At best, I'll end up having to do Juquila's bidding. Yavaros will side with the majority, and Kulooq has long been under Juquila's thumb.*

Turning to the adile, Kaberco said, "Think about it. All we need is a few days. We'll send a messenger to the Riskers and a bird to the Prime Konamei. Two, three, four days at the most. In the meantime, we can come up with the terms of surrender. Our terms."

The adile stared at the map. "What if they strike in the meantime?" Her voice was strained and high-pitched.

"That's a possibility." Kaberco pressed his lips together. "But I don't think they will. They'd have to travel quickly, which is hard for an army of that size. Most likely, they'll ride out the siege of Anbodu. Only after they hold the capital will they look north. So we have some time."

With a sigh, the ludi fingered the wool chain draped over his shoulders. "In that case, let's ask the Riskers and the Prime Konamei. And prepare to be subjects of Damira and Shagonar."

Kaberco's tension eased. The ludi usually sided with Juquila. This meant Kulooq had strong feelings against surrendering. Perhaps Kulooq and Birita would be enough to sway Yavaros. Should he speak or wait? A hasty move could tip Yavaros the wrong way.

The only sound in the room was the crackling of the fire. Then Yavaros shifted in his seat. "In the absence of word from the Prime Konamei, we have no legal grounds to either capitulate or seek help from the Riskers." His pale blue eyes found Kaberco's gaze. "However, preparing terms for surrender and approaching the Riskers is reasonable. That's what I advise."

"Then I'll send the messages today," Kaberco said, his tone grave. He caught a glimpse of Juquila's contorted face as she stalked out. A shudder made his shoulders twitch and the hair prickle on the nape of his neck. An angry Juquila was trouble. He'd better watch his back.

51

J uquila stomped down the steps of Kaberco's house, her breath forming clouds of mist that twisted angrily in the frosty air. Didn't the rest of the Konament understand the best course was to ally with the strongest power? Those fools had just signed their own death warrants.

Kaberco was dreaming if he thought they could win a skirmish with the Emperor's army. His guardsmen possessed the courage of alloe rats and could barely hold off a few bandits. If Empress Damira really could turn people into mist, she was the one to court.

Bah. Something wasn't adding up. Kaberco, of all people, proposing to ally with Riskers. Something had changed to make him entertain such an idea for even a heartbeat. He hated the Riskers with a fiery rage that could melt stone.

A cold wind made her cloak flap and took her breath away. By the calendar, it was Camalu, the last month of autumn. But winter came early in the north, and this year was no exception. She yanked her cloak tighter around herself and strode across the square. Gray-clad villagers scurried to get out of her path.

The market was teeming with vendors. So far, the war in

the south hadn't affected them much, but that could change. At least the central region had already sent grain for the winter. Her clerks informed her that they'd received several loads of dried fruits and pickled vegetables from the south before the invasion. They'd have enough to eat during the winter months, as long as people didn't tire of cabbage and potatoes. Perhaps she should talk with the adile about rationing food, just to be sure.

A shrill horn blew. Whether it was a caravan coming or going, she didn't care. She forced her thoughts to Kaberco. Why the sudden eagerness to join forces with Riskers? Had he received orders from the Prime Konamei? That was unlikely. Kaberco would have shown them the message to ensure their cooperation.

No, he was up to something. Whenever he was irritated by opposition, his nostrils flared. And flare they did, when she suggested making peace with the invader.

Perhaps he planned to sell them out to the invaders and his talk of an army and an alliance with the Riskers was a way to stall. That would be the smart move, to keep anyone else from contacting the Emperor first. She bit the inside of her cheek. She'd mull that idea over later.

A sudden gust of wind shoved her a step backward. Would Kaberco side with the Emperor? No, more likely, he was plotting some kind of resistance with the Riskers. Kaberco was the sort who would die doing what he thought was right. So even if the Riskers let him down and they all were destroyed by Shagonar's army, Kaberco would die thinking he'd been right. To perish in the name of keeping the people safe would be honorable in his eyes. What a fool.

The trouble was, she didn't know if Kaberco had chosen the Riskers or the Emperor. And her next move would depend on that. Operating blind could be fatal. Kaberco would happily have her taken if she was caught breaking the law. And that *durak* Yavaros would gladly help him.

No, she would not end up in prison. Or worse. She was going to make her own plans. And to do that, she needed information. She jiggled the coin purse hanging at her waist. She had plenty of bronze sheaves and silver stones. All she needed was one guardsman who'd be happy to trade information for silver. One who'd been traveling with Kaberco would do quite well. The perfect candidate sprang to her mind. Once she'd spent some time with him, she'd know which way the wind blew.

Damira stood in her stirrups, squinting. The gates of Anbodu were just visible a few miles away. The cold air blew her hair back. She tipped her face up, letting the wind chill the heat from her pulsing headache.

She'd waited a week, and the Prime Konamei hadn't responded to their ultimatum. Now was the time to show him the folly of his decision.

Urging her mare into a canter, she left Syzyan and Shagonar behind. Her lip curled as she thought of their opposition to her plan. What made them think shooting a few exploding arrows at the city walls would be enough? Not so. They needed to make an overwhelming show of force, a display that no one in the capital, however brave or foolish, could ignore.

When she was about five hundred yards from the gates, Damira pulled up her mount. Shagonar and Syzyan rode up next to her. She motioned to the herald, who took a deep breath and shouted, "His Loftiness Emperor Shagonar Ortan is offering you one last chance for clemency. Surrender the city now."

The only answer was a hail of flaming arrows. None of them came close. They buried their heads in the dusty, bare ground fifty yards from Damira's horse. Her amulets screamed in her ears.

Kill them. Destroy them.

Swallowing hard, she motioned once more to the herald.

"Is that your answer?" he shouted.

Kill them. Destroy the city.

A figure on the top of the gates stepped forward. "We will never surrender. These are the words of Prime Konamei Ultark the Third."

The pressure in Damira's head intensified. The voices of the amulets grew louder. She clenched her fist.

"Dami, let's answer with our own arrows, shall we?" Without waiting for a response, Syzyan motioned to his aide.

She tried to breathe calmly, fighting the stinging in her hands and feet. She wouldn't give in, not yet. Syzyan always had to try his way first. But in the end, she'd do what she needed to do.

A volley of arrows shot toward the walls of the city. They exploded in fiery light. Several stones fell and part of a wall crumbled. A few soldiers fell with the rubble, their screams ending with the thud of their bodies on the rocky ground below.

The herald shouted again. "Surrender now."

"Never!"

Syzyan's archers released another round of arrows. More explosions. More screams. Damira leaned over her mare's withers, squeezing her eyes shut. Black dots danced in front of her, ripples in the air intensifying the ache in her skull. If only she could banish the pain.

Again, the herald roared their challenge. "Surrender, or you will try the patience of His Loftiness."

The shouted answer was a vulgar suggestion of what Shagonar could do while he waited.

Shagonar chuckled. "I like that one, whoever he is."

Damira's breath grew labored as stinging pain shot from her blackened toes to her knees. Enough. Enough of the pain. No more insults. She would not be mocked.

Straightening in her saddle, Damira held her gloved hand high, the soft leather hiding her blackened, withered skin. The amulets flashed red in the sun.

"No, Dami."

She heard the words as if from a distance, unsure if Shagonar or Syzyan had uttered them. It didn't matter. If she stopped now, the pain would kill her. And the hapless Prime Konamei would mock them as weak. The amulets heated, their power massing. She focused on the gates, on the guards on top, on the Prime Konamei and his herald. She let the power flow from her, slowly, slowly. The easing of the pain brought tears to her eyes. This would feel so good.

Once the power had seeped into the men on the gates and the gates themselves, she pushed.

In a heartbeat, the men and the gates were red mist. In a few heartbeats more, a gust of wind made the mist dissipate in the icy air.

With a few deep breaths, Damira relaxed. At last. No pain. She knew the respite wouldn't last, but at least she'd appeased the amulets for now.

When she raised her hand again, Shagonar touched her arm. "No, Dami. Let's wait. See what they say."

Lowering her hand, she nodded. They sat on their mares in silence, letting the wind ruffle their hair and their flags, and carry the faint wails of the grieving and frightened residents of Anbodu to them like the calls of far-off birds.

They didn't have to wait long. Five people walked out of the ruined gates, all with outstretched hands. When they were thirty paces away, they halted.

A gray-haired man stepped forward. "We are the konameis of Anbodu," he said. "We surrender the city to you and beg you to have mercy on our people."

"Of course," Shagonar said. "Lead us to the Prime Konamei's residence. From there, we will discuss our terms. If you comply, you will have nothing to fear. I don't think you want my wife to use her power again."

The man shuddered. "Please, no more. We guarantee your safety and will take you to the Prime Konamei."

Syzyan dispatched an officer to the camp with the news that the siege of Anbodu was over. "Tell Jianjun Volmar to prepare the invasion force. We'll march north in three days."

Damira smiled. Syzyan might think they were going to face Kaberco and whatever rabble of an army he'd cobbled together, but she knew her real prey. She would find Tereka. And destroy her and her dragonflies.

Then finally, she would have peace. She'd rule both countries, and no one else would live in fear of war bands or attackers. No one would suffer the tragic losses that still tore at her soul. Maybe then her scorpions would relent. Perhaps they'd be less bloodthirsty. Maybe she'd be able to control them better.

She didn't know how much more pain she could stand. And she didn't like how she felt after she did the amulets' bidding—a mixture of relief, exaltation, and the sense that she'd soiled herself. Somehow, she'd have to find a way to be free.

52

Kaberco paced back and forth in his private workroom. What was wrong with that miserable excuse of a Prime Konamei? If only the wind would blow some news his way.

Four days had passed since he'd sent a bird asking for guidance. He cursed. Four days of Juquila's quotidian visits full of thinly veiled sneers about his incompetence and not-so-subtle probes for information. She'd hinted that she was aware he had visitors in his house. How had she ferreted that out? By all that kept them safe, there was no end to the woman's deviousness. At least she hadn't shown up yet today. He'd run out of ways to deflect her questions without raising her suspicions.

His lips twitched. If she only knew who he was sheltering. Her niece, who'd been taken. One of the traders who'd been freed in the jailbreak. A prisoner who'd escaped the copper mines. Not to mention the three he'd sent away, the two fugitives and Iskra, the girl whose rebellion had sparked so many events.

He snorted. If Juquila ever learned the identity of even one of his guests, she'd have him taken. Yavaros would gladly sign the order. The other two konameis wouldn't make so much as a peep in protest.

Tension clamped his stomach. He needed answers, and he needed them now.

Like the Prime Konamei, the Riskers hadn't responded to his message. That wasn't surprising. He wouldn't blame them if they refused to help. Most likely, they were consulting their mythical sky-god. He rolled his eyes. Who knew how long that would take?

A soft rap at his door pulled him from his thoughts. "Yes?"

The door opened to admit a tall, brown-skinned man with shrewd blue eyes. Caphtor, his second in command. "If you please, a bird came. I thought it best to bring you the message straight away."

At last. Kaberco let out a breath. His muscles relaxed like a loosened bowstring. "Thank you." He took the sealed message, which bore an ornate red and black seal with a scorpion stamped on it. He frowned. "This isn't from the Prime Konamei."

"I know," Caphtor said. "But it was one of his birds. The leg band was gold, etched with the Prime Konamei's crest."

Tracing his finger over the seal, Kaberco pulled his eyebrows together. A scorpion. That could mean only one thing. This message was from the invader. But how had they gotten hold of one of the Prime Konamei's birds?

He broke the scorpion seal and skimmed the message. He blinked. Then he read it again. He rubbed his eyes. This couldn't be true.

Caphtor coughed. "If you please, what does it say?"

Kaberco opened his mouth, then closed it. He dragged a breath into his lungs. A glance at the door assured him Caphtor had shut it on his way in.

"It claims that Anbodu has fallen. The siege is over," he said, keeping his voice low. "The Prime Konamei is dead. This Shagonar is giving us one week to surrender. They are prepared to be lenient if we do. If not, they will be merciless."

"But the—" Caphtor made a strangled noise in his throat. "That cannot be."

"That was my first thought." Kaberco bit his lip. "But if it's not true, how did they get the bird?"

"They could have stolen it."

"True. But that means they have partial control of the city. Even if the Prime Konamei isn't dead."

"Can we believe this?"

Kaberco studied the signature. His eyes widened. "This gets better and better. Take a guess who they used as a scribe."

Caphtor held his hands up. "The ephor?"

"It is signed: 'As dictated to me, Tirk Sabidur.'" Kaberco snorted. "What is he doing with these invaders?"

"Tirk? You mean Juquila's clerk?"

"Yes." Kaberco tapped the name. "The first thing is to obtain a sample of his writing. Let's see if this is real or a clever forgery."

"Why would someone forge a clerk's signature?"

"To make me think Juquila is playing one of her power games?"

"Well, that would be nothing new. But why would she plant her nephew in the enemy's camp?"

"If she thought it would benefit her in some way, she would." Kaberco laid the message on the table. "Fetch a ledger from the syndic's office. Tell them I want to match it to my own accounts, to make sure there is no error on my part." Before Caphtor could dart out the door, Kaberco called him back. "I suppose I don't have to tell you to not breathe a word of this to anyone. Not Yavaros, not Juquila, no one. We can't risk panic until we're confident this news is real."

Caphtor nodded and slipped out. After the door closed behind him, Kaberco rummaged through his collection of maps. He selected one and spread it over his worktable. He traced a route from Anbodu, heading north. If Shagonar marched his army in that direction, he'd have to travel through the fields between the forest to the west and the mountains to the east. He'd most likely stop to take North Rivash.

His mouth went dry. North Rivash was at least three days march from Trofmose. Kaberco doubted he could get there in time to save the town. He cursed and slammed his fist into the table. He wasn't sure he'd get an army together in time to save Shinroo, let alone Trofmose. Why hadn't those Riskers responded?

With a sigh, he scrutinized the map. What spot would give him the best chance for victory? Perhaps just west of North Rivash, where the forest crept closer to the mountains. He could attack from the cover of the trees on either side. A large army couldn't advance all at once through that hilly land. He pulled an inkwell and parchment to himself and made notes about terrain, supplies, and weapons.

Nearly half an hour passed before Caphtor returned. Kaberco looked up with a frown. "What took you?"

"If you please, the syndic's office was in an uproar."

"Oh?" This was unlike Juquila, who prided herself on the smooth operation of her domain. "What happened? Did Juquila bully a trader into tears again?"

"No, if you please. She's gone."

Kaberco felt his eyebrows crawl up his forehead. "Explain."

"Yesterday, a bird arrived from the syndic of North Rivash. Juquila left immediately and hasn't been seen since."

Dropping his gaze to the map, Kaberco fixated on North Rivash. Just a day and a half north of Anbodu.

"There's more. Her son is missing, too."

"Which one?" He asked the question, sure he knew the answer.

"Meluz."

"Meluz." Juquila's oldest child, who'd been zealously working his way up the ranks of Kaberco's guardsmen. "Find out if any more of her family is missing. She has four other children. And check on that sister of hers."

Caphtor nodded. "Should I bring them in to see you?"

Kaberco rubbed his chin. No sense frightening the younger children. "No, just the older girl who works for Yavaros. And Juquila's sister." He waved a hand in dismissal. "Peace and safety."

Drumming his fingers on the table, Kaberco struggled to keep his breathing steady. His pulse pounded in his head. Why did he have the sense that events were spinning out of his control?

He searched through the papers on his table, seeking the message from the invader. He re-read the words. One week to prepare.

His fingers slackened, and he dropped the thin paper. It fell right-side down, revealing tiny, scrawled letters on the back.

With the paper held close to his eyes, Kaberco squinted to read the miniature script. By the time he'd finished reading half of it, his nostrils were flaring, his face was hot, and his hands were shaking. If the other message had been surprising and dismaying, this one was infuriating. Only with a great effort did he restrain himself from bellowing and throwing a chair out the window.

"*Empress Damira, wielder of 3 scorpion Amulets of Power, knows Tereka carries dragonfly Ams of Pr. D also knows that T is the Desired One of prophecy, even though she craves that title for herself. She has sworn to destroy T. Please warn T. Only the dragonflies can defeat and destroy the scorpions. TS.*"

What nonsense was this? Unlike the precise script of the ultimatum, the postscript was scribbled, as if the writer had hurried. Tirk had taken quite a risk to warn Tereka. Kaberco didn't think the Empress would be pleased if she knew the contents of this surreptitious message.

But if Tirk believed Tereka was the Desired One, then she couldn't be his sister. Kaberco narrowed his eyes. Tirk shouldn't know anything about that old prophecy, anyway. Unless Tereka, or perhaps Tarkio, had told him.

Tereka thought she'd pulled one over on him, conveniently not mentioning the amulets she carried. Had he known, he'd have killed her then and there. And the Desired One? She hadn't lied when she said she wanted to oust the Prime Konamei. Yes, she'd been abused by their system. But to use an outlawed myth to overthrow it was despicable, a deception perpetrated for her own gain. He'd been a fool not to question her about her ambitions. He'd assumed she had nothing to do with that ancient myth, even though she fit some pieces of the prophecy. He'd been right to hunt Iskra down all those years ago. A mixed-blood child couldn't be allowed to live.

Now, he knew he couldn't trust Tereka. He would execute her before anyone else learned he'd even toyed with the idea of working with her. She was too dangerous to be an ally.

He perused Tirk's message again. So, the scorpion amulets were real, the supposed source of Damira's power. Perhaps there was something to these tales of magical items. *And if the Empress has powerful amulets, maybe having some of our own will be useful.*

His eyes unfocused, he stared out the window. No. Even the mention of magic amulets had been outlawed long ago, and with good reason. It was bad enough to work with Riskers who used such things. He folded up the missive and slid it into a pocket.

A muttered curse escaped his lips. He'd never trusted Juquila. He'd half expected her to play traitor, if that was what her disappearance meant. But he'd thought he could trust Tereka and her promises of support and cooperation, at least until they'd dealt with the Emperor. The betrayal cut deep, all the more because she'd fooled him. So much for his ability to read people. A small part of him didn't blame Tereka for keeping her own secrets, after all the suffering he brought to her. But the rest of him was furious. Her subterfuge could get him taken.

With a jerk, he stood up from his table. Tereka had deceived him for four long days. It was time to end her once and for all.

53

Tereka stood at the window, staring at the square below. They'd arrived in Trofmose four days earlier. Four long days. She sneered at the monument to Prosperity that stood in the square's center. The smiling bronze women of the statue held large baskets overflowing with bread, vegetables, and fruit, a mockery of the thin gruel, watery stew and pasties people usually ate.

Her gaze traveled to the lined-up caravans. She'd always loved going on trading runs. They promised a little adventure, a chance to see something new, and a few days free of the fear of Juquila finding a new opportunity to harass her.

She shuddered at the memory of her time in Kaberco's jail. And now here she was, his guest rather than his prisoner.

So far, Kaberco had treated them well. From the start, he provided comfortable rooms, had hot meals brought to them, and even supplied sedative drinks for Iskra. Of course, that could be because he didn't want a screaming woman to flee his private rooms and burst into the offices below. Tereka chuckled at the thought. That would be quite a scene for Kaberco to explain away.

Early the first morning, he'd personally escorted Tereka

and her friends to his stables. Five guardsmen were already mounted, with two additional horses saddled.

Relio extended a hand to Savinnia and helped her to mount. He looked up at her, the corners of his mouth drooping. "Savinnia." He paused. "Savinnia. I'm sorry. For everything. You deserved much better." He abruptly turned and stumped back to the house.

Tereka gaped at him. Did Relio really regret the way he used Savinnia as a toy when they were prisoners? That was a change she never thought she'd see. Savinnia was staring after him, her chin hanging loose.

Still lost in thought, she allowed Alikse gave her a quick hug. When he stepped back, he ran his fingers over his throat and gave her a firm nod. She understood his meaning. He'd die protecting Savinnia and Iskra, even if it meant cracking a few necks. He lifted the sedated Iskra to sit in front of Savinnia. Once Iskra was settled, he mounted his own horse.

"One day to Gishin, an hour or more to get to the Riskers. They should be there by evening," Kaberco said. "Then just a day or two to return." He gave his guardsmen a hard stare. "Ride fast but be careful of our guests."

Tereka watched the lead guardsman closely. She detected only affirmation in the nod he gave Kaberco.

"Understood," he said. "Peace and safety."

She longed to go with them, to return to the warm embrace of her grandparents, to see her mother healed. And to escape the strain of allying with a man she'd long thought of as an enemy. With Kemet as her only companion, she walked back to their quarters.

Kaberco seemed to relax once Iskra was on her way. His story of helping relatives of one of the southern ephors was a good one, she had to admit. And the bit about hiding Iskra with cousins just in case the war crept this far north was brilliant. The trauma of escaping an invasion could explain Iskra's mental state. Fear of the war was a plausible, if weak, reason. The story was good enough as long as Kaberco's men didn't ask too many questions.

But that was three days ago. With each day, Kaberco grew testier, barely managing to be polite when he questioned them over and over about their dealings with the Emperor and his wife. His nostrils flared like sails under a wind every time the scorpion amulets were mentioned. Once, he snapped his quill, spilling jets of ink on the paper in front of him. He cursed so thoroughly that even Relio was impressed.

The ephor's mood made her, Relio, and Kemet nervous. If Kaberco turned on them, they wouldn't be able to fight their way out.

All of them, Kaberco included, knew the Prime Konamei's reply would determine their next course of action. Whether that action would lead to death or victory, none of them could say. Endless speculation had only tightened the band of tension around Tereka's head.

More than one bird had been sent. Kaberco swore he'd sent the first the night Tereka and her friends had arrived. He had no explanation for the delay, which seemed to make him more agitated.

If that wasn't bad enough, they'd had no word from the Riskers. Tereka counted the distance over and over. Trofmose was just over half a day's ride to Gishin, going hard. So with Iskra, maybe more like a full day. Then it was a short walk up the mountain to the Riskers. Even if Alikse carried Iskra, the hike would only take an hour, maybe a little more.

Picking at her fingernails, Tereka wondered what could have gone wrong. Right now, she'd welcome any diversion. A raucous fight between Sebezh and Tirk would be just the thing. Or a few quiet moments with Naco. A sigh seeped from between her lips. How she missed him.

She glanced at Kemet. He'd gone moody and silent, brooding about something. Relio paced like a horse that sensed a warboar on the prowl. His conversation consisted of little more than curses, broken only by demands for wine. Thankfully, Kaberco refused to give them more than a bottle a day. She did not want to deal with a drunk Relio.

Footfalls made her whirl in place. The door crashed open and Kaberco burst into the room, his face dark and his teeth bared. He slammed the door shut behind him and pounced on Tereka. Grabbing her by the throat, he pushed her against the wall, forcing her up so her feet dangled. "I trusted you."

54

Tereka's eyes bulged. She struggled to breathe. Pressure mounted in her head, the blood pounded against her skull.

Kaberco shook her and her head banged against the wall. "When were you going to tell me?" He flung her to the floor.

Slowly, she lifted her chin and rubbed her bruised throat. "Tell you what?" The pain made every word an agony.

"Don't play with me." Kaberco snarled the words.

Relio stepped to Tereka's side, stooped, and pulled her to her feet. "Girly will talk better if you don't choke the life out of her." He helped Tereka to a divan. "What do you want to know?"

Gulping back the pain in her throat, Tereka stared at Relio. He'd made a bold move, interceding for her when it could make him the target of Kaberco's wrath. No wonder he'd earned the respect of prisoners and guards alike.

"Did you know about her magic amulets?" Kaberco shouted.

"Oh." Tereka bit her lip. How had he found out? Had the Riskers told his messengers? There was no way of knowing.

She answered for Relio. "They did. They all saw me use them."

"Use them how?"

Kaberco's snarl made her shiver.

"To heal a few times. To find water in the desert, and for protection and help when I needed it most." Her bruised throat rasped out the words. Relio handed her a cup of water and she gulped it down.

"You're going to have to do better than that," Kaberco said with a sneer.

Relio explained how she'd healed him of a near-fatal wound in the prison camp, then launched into the tale of how they'd fought the pirates. Kaberco stood with his arms crossed, frowning. When Relio got to the part where Tereka found an amulet of power that led them to water and weapons, Kaberco's scowl turned into an incredulous look. Kemet sat motionless with his lips pressed into a thin line.

A vein pulsed on Kaberco's temple. "So you have Amulets of Power. That makes you the Desired One, doesn't it?"

Tereka rubbed her hand on the back of her head and tugged on her hair. Just mentioning the Desired One was enough to get someone taken. The fact that Kaberco brought it up meant he was rattled. And a rattled Kaberco could be dangerous for her.

Before she could answer, someone knocked at the door. It opened to reveal Caphtor, Kaberco's second. "If you please, the guardsmen you sent to the Riskers have returned. With a messenger."

Kaberco glared at the man. "What are you waiting for? Send him in."

Caphtor stood back and Da strode into the room.

Flying from her seat, Tereka threw her arms around him. "Da." She buried her face in his chest. "I didn't expect you."

"Neither did I," Kaberco said, his voice grating and cold. "Tarkio, you have some explaining to do."

Da raised an eyebrow. "Oh?"

"He's asking about the amulets and the Desired One."

With a nod, Da slid an arm around Tereka's shoulders. "It's a long story. Tereka, your grandparents send their greetings. Your friends do as well." He turned toward the scowling Kaberco. "But, if you please, don't you want to know the Riskers' response to your letter?"

"Later. Now, I want the truth," snapped Kaberco. "Convince me why I shouldn't call my guards and tell them you tried to kill me. You'd be dead in less than five heartbeats."

Tereka looked at him, then Relio, whose eyes were narrowed. Then Kemet, who couldn't hide his shaking hands. She leaned against Da. If she told Kaberco the whole truth, he'd slaughter them all. But without the truth, he'd kill them, anyway.

Kaberco pointed a finger at Da. "If she's the Desired One, then she's not your daughter. Are you telling me you've lied all these years?"

Heat surged through her veins, fueled by her anger at Kaberco's persecution of her parents and his unjust treatment of her. "What did you want him to do? Talk about something that could get him and his whole family taken?" Tereka asked. "The prophecy—the myth that was outlawed—says the Desired One will be born to a Risker and a villager." She pointed an accusing finger at Kaberco. "You knew my mother. You tracked her down when she fled Gishin to marry a Risker."

"You're Iskra's daughter? That's impossible. She told me you were dead. You're Tarkio's daughter."

"Am I? Do I look anything like him?"

Kaberco frowned, his eyes darting from Tereka's golden tan face and blue eyes to Tarkio's coppery skin and brown eyes. When he sighed, she continued. "My Risker father was a green-eyed man who was a talented archer. He passed his skill to me." She waved a hand at her friends. "Ask any of them. Or give me a bow and I'll show you."

She straightened, moving out from under Da's arm. "My father died at your hands before I took my first steps. You captured my mother, turned her over to a brute, then sent her to prison long before I spoke my first words. My parents were willing to die to protect me from you." She sucked in a deep breath, seeking to steady her shaking voice. "And I was conceived in a year that began with a double eclipse around the time the fields started to ripen for harvest."

"Coincidence." Kaberco shook his head. "I suppose Tarkio filled your mind with this story."

"No, I heard it first from my Risker relatives." Tereka reached for her bag of dragonflies. "I have an inheritance from my parents." She pulled out the two small amulets and laid them on the table. "These belonged to them." She shook the other three into her hand and held them up. "These are the three Amulets of Power. Amulets that will find the Desired One when they are needed most." She glared at Kaberco. "My mother found the first just before you killed my father. Relio told you how the second amulet found me."

"When did you find the third?" Da asked.

"Right before Kaberco caught us."

"Doesn't seem to have done you much good," Kaberco said.

"You didn't kill me outright, did you?" She tipped her chin up. "With these, I can tap into the power of the sky-god."

Kaberco laughed. "That I'd like to see."

She pointed at his right hand. "When we were on the way here, you complained of an old injury. A bone in your thumb that hadn't set properly."

He held up his right hand, crooked thumb extended. "So?"

Tereka stepped toward him, heart pounding. *If ever I needed the power, I need it now. Please.* She held the amulets over his hand. "Heal him, sky-god."

The green and purple light flashed, illuminating Kaberco's hand. His eyes bulged, and he stared at his thumb. He flexed and relaxed his fingers. "The pain is gone. The bone is straight. What did you do?"

"The sky-god healed you." Sweat trickled down her neck despite the chill in the room.

"What evil is this?" Kaberco backed away.

"No evil," she said. "Just truth."

Balling his hand into a fist, Kaberco said, "This can't be real. I refuse to accept it."

"Refuse to accept what?" Tereka asked. "That the Riskers' magic amulets have a power you can't control? That the Prime Konamei and his ancestors have forced us all to believe lies simply to hold on to their power? Or perhaps you're angry because, despite all your words about safety and fairness, you've supported a corrupt regime and failed to keep us safe." She paused for breath. "And instead of allowing the worship of the sky-god, you made safety your god. All that did was make everyone afraid of everything."

Kaberco's olive skin turned a mottled purple. He stood panting as if he'd been chasing bandits up a steep mountain slope.

Tereka held her breath. She wasn't sure if Kaberco would kill her or Da first.

With a groan, Kaberco dropped into a chair. He rubbed his face with his hands. He let out a long sigh and stared at Tereka. "During your trial, I saw a flash of Iskra in you. She once asked me the same question. 'Safe and fair for whom?' Little did you know how your words rankled."

Tereka locked her startled eyes on his face. "Is that why you voted to condemn me?"

He bowed his head, his shoulders slumping. "You and your mother. You both confronted me with a truth I didn't want to face. You voiced the words I've often thought, but never dare to utter." He pressed his hand to his mouth. "This regime has been corrupt for a long time. And I— At first, I sought power to make conditions better. But always, I needed more, so I'd be safe. So I wouldn't be the one taken. I did horrible things to keep myself secure." He looked down at his hands. "It nearly broke me to see what happened to Iskra."

Words surged into Tereka's mouth, biting comments about how badly he'd broken her mother, how she'd never learned the name her parents had given her, how his cowardice had turned her into a fugitive. A torrent of curses stuck in her tight throat. She coughed and drew breath to shout her ire at the man who'd caused such agony in her life.

Da put his arm around Tereka's shoulders. "Kaberco, if you please." His tone was gentle but firm. "The past is the past. We have an invader to confront. We'll have time for restitution later."

Tereka relaxed just the slightest bit. How well Da understood her. His words were as much for her as for Kaberco. "Da's right. We'll talk about all this later."

"Good." Da patted her shoulder. "Kaberco, shall I share with you what the Riskers have to say?"

Kaberco winced. "That we wanted to be separate from them, so we're on our own?"

"No. Not anymore. They would have said that a week ago. But this Emperor Shagonar's wife, Damira, I think she's called, bears scorpion amulets. She razed a Risker camp, turning everything and everyone into mist. All but two who were in the fields were killed."

They all gasped except Relio, who muttered, "Better them than us."

Glaring at him, Tereka shouted. "They're people. My people."

"Tereka," Da said softly. "I'm so sorry. Your uncle Lilio happened to be there. He's dead."

She dropped her chin to her chest, her eyes damp and stinging.

"We had no word of this," Kaberco said.

"The news only reached Zafrad five days ago. The next day, the letters from you and Tereka arrived. The Riskers' word is this: They will fight on the side of the Desired One, the one that bears the three Amulets of Power. She is the only one who can defeat the bearer of the three scorpion Amulets of Power. They already believe Tereka to be that person. They pledge to use their amulets in the struggle and suggest that you ally with her as well, if she is willing."

"Why wouldn't she be?" Kaberco asked.

"Because of what you did to her parents." Da spoke sharply, then softened his tone. "Tereka, your grandmother is doing all she can for Iskra. Cillia's already healed most of the physical wounds. But the other scars, the internal ones? She doesn't know. Iskra may never be completely lucid."

"My mother is insane because of you," Tereka said, squarely facing Kaberco. "Because you hounded her like an animal. All because she wanted the truth. Don't assume that can be brushed aside like last year's dead leaves."

Kaberco bowed his head. "I can never make up for the years your mother suffered, or for what you missed in not knowing her." He tilted his chin up to meet Tereka's gaze. "I promise I will fight to the death with you against the invaders, and if we prevail, no one will suffer like that again. We'll make a new treaty with the Riskers and welcome them as friends and allies."

"If they'll have you," put in Relio, causing Tereka to snort and Kaberco's nostrils to flare.

"You never imagined the Riskers would prefer to have nothing to do with the villagers, did you?" Tereka chuckled. "But don't worry. They'll want to help rebuild. That's just who they are."

"But first, we need a plan to defeat the invaders," Kaberco said.

Tereka pulled her eyebrows together. "I don't know how to use the amulets to fight."

"I can help with that," Da said. "Your grandmother heard from a few more elders from the south. One recalled some ancient lore about the dragonflies. You need to get the three drag-onflies close to the scorpions, and the sky-god will do the rest."

"How close?"

Da made a face. "Cillia said no one was sure. Their best guess was near enough to touch. What they did know was that if you kill the empress before the amulets are destroyed, they will belong to you."

"That would be good, right?"

Da shook his head. "If you haven't trained to master them, they'll control you. I don't think you want to become their tool."

Tereka shuddered. "Absolutely not. But if I can't kill her, how do I destroy the amulets without her turning me into mist?"

"That's why you need an army to distract her." Da looked at Kaberco, who rolled his eyes.

"That's about all my army will be good for," he said. "Except for a few traders and—" He sighed, then reluctantly said, "the Riskers."

Tereka's stomach writhed. "The amulets are supposed to offer protection…"

"That's right," Da said. "And they offer guidance and amplify your abilities."

Would her amulets be powerful enough to keep her from being misted? She swallowed the sour taste in her mouth. "Did the elders say when I should do this?"

"No, but they said to inquire of the sky-god every step of the way."

"Right." Tereka fingered her amulets and closed her eyes. *Sky-god? I don't even know what to ask.*

A sudden thought slipped into her mind. *Now.*

She opened her eyes. "We need to move quickly. The sooner we confront Damira, the better." She gulped. The fate of the country hung on her. The amulets had protected her in the past. She'd seen them heal and guide. But why did she feel like an alloe rat preparing to challenge a warboar?

55

Damira stretched her legs out, careful to not disturb the rabbit slumbering on her lap. Six days had passed since she destroyed the gates of Anbodu. That had taken care of the stinging pain in her fingers and the throbbing in her head. But it had left her with four withered toes on her left foot. Her right foot and lower leg were blackened and shriveled, as if they'd been burnt.

She wiped the sweat from her forehead. The yurt was stuffy, the air close. A few days after Shagonar took control of Anbodu, they'd taken part of their army north, settling just south of North Rivash. This late in the year, winter should have arrived. Why was it so hot? Why was there no breeze?

At least soon, her suffering would end once they conquered the whole land. All the agony would have been worth the price she'd paid. She could set the amulets aside. Her body would heal. And she and Shagonar and Syzyan could have the happy lives they'd dreamed of long ago.

The door opened, admitting a puff of fresh air and a soldier. "I beg your pardon, Your Loftiness. I am seeking Jianjun Syzyan."

"I believe he is meeting with the other jianjuns. What do you need him for?"

"We captured some northern spies."

At last, something to do besides wait and endure her stinging fingers and toes. Damira raised her chin. "Send them in."

"But, Your Loftiness, shouldn't your brother—"

Damira stared down her nose. "He's got many other things to do, while I sit here sipping tea. I'll speak to them. Now."

The man gulped and backed out of the yurt. *Durak.* He'd probably gone easy on these spies, whoever they were.

She settled back in her chair and pulled silk gloves onto her hands, hiding the blackened, shriveled fingers. Idly, she stroked her rabbit's fur, wondering if these spies had any news worth hearing.

The officer returned shortly thereafter, with two women and a young man. Damira dismissed the soldier with a jerk of her chin.

All three spies were tall. The youth was brown-skinned with dark hair. The women's faces were a darker brown. One wore a turban, while the other's head was uncovered revealing the flaming red hair of Uzhasovia. Interesting, that despite all the intermarrying they did in Tlefas, occasionally people looked like they were of only one blood. These two women could have passed for Uzhasovians.

They resembled each other, so they were most likely relatives. Sisters, perhaps. The one was pretty enough. Even the mandated blunt haircut didn't diminish her looks, although she wore a discontented look on her face and had a deep furrow between her eyebrows.

The other was a different story. She was a beauty, with sensuous lips, large dark eyes, and a figure that even the shapeless village clothing couldn't hide. The look in her eyes said she expected attention and admiration, and she held her turbaned head high. This could be interesting. The turban meant she was either the wife of a konamei or a konamei herself. From her bearing, Damira guessed the latter.

Without a word, Damira scrutinized the newcomers for so long they began to fidget. "Who are you and why do you spy on my troops?" she finally asked.

The turbaned one lifted her chin. "If you please, we are not spies. We come to share information, not steal it."

Sell information was more like it, Damira thought. But she would see. "Your names?"

"I am Juquila Kurosawa, and this is my sister, Groa Sabidur. My son, Meluz Kurosawa."

Damira frowned. Kurosawa was an Uzhasovian name. But Sabidur? That was Vernian, and vaguely familiar. "And?"

Juquila motioned to her sister. "She's a market vendor, married to a trader. I am syndic of Trofmose. My son was a member of the Prime Konamei's guard."

Oh. This was getting very interesting. Trofmose, the seat of that irritating chulu fly, Kaberco. "What do you have to say for yourselves?"

"If you please, our ephor Kaberco allied with a young woman, an escaped prisoner."

Pain throbbed in Damira's head. This woman was wasting her time. Who cared about a convict? "And?"

"And they are going to join with the Riskers against you."

Damira lowered her eyes. That would be inconvenient, but not impossible to overcome. In any case, the Riskers wouldn't defy her. Not after word spread about what she did to one of their camps.

Kill them.

A vein throbbed in her scalp. Maybe she should do as the amulets urged. It would be easier. "Why would Kaberco ally with a convict?"

"Well…"

This woman was hedging. Obviously, she wanted some

kind of reward for her information. If she was a syndic, what kind of position would she want? Time to find out. "Why have you come to me? Why no loyalty to your ephor? What do you expect to gain?"

When Juquila blinked, Damira smiled to herself. *This one thinks she's the only one who can play games. But she can't deal with someone who calls her out.*

After a few heartbeats, Juquila responded, "Kaberco is going to get us all killed. He's raising an army but to oppose you is suicidal. He has no chance. I thought I would try to save my people."

Damira curled her lip. *No, Juquila, you're trying to save your own position and power.* "So, you're telling me that Kaberco, the only one with the stones to stand up and defend his people, has allied with barbarians and convicts? There must be a reason."

Kill them.

Forcing the amulets' whispers from her mind, Damira studied Juquila's face. When she didn't respond, Damira frowned. "What is so special about this convict? Do you know her? What is her name?"

"Tereka. Tereka Sabidur." Groa spit the words out as if they were poison on her tongue.

Tereka. Heat rushed through Damira's veins and curses swirled through her mind. *I should have killed the girl when I had the chance.* She shouldn't have listened to Syzyan and Shagonar.

Kill her.

She didn't know if the amulets meant Tereka or Juquila, but she agreed—both needed to die. Sabidur. If she wasn't mistaken, Sabidur was Tirk's surname as well.

Plucking a bell from a side table, Damira rang to bring a soldier into the yurt. She waved him to her and whispered her command. He strode out without a backward look.

"Now. Just how do you know this convict, this Tereka?" Damira made her words smooth. She noted the angry look on

Groa's face. There was a story there, she was sure of it, but she didn't know how hard she wanted to work to get it out of them.

After a long pause, Juquila answered, "She's not important."

"Just some slut's brat," Groa said.

Groa wasn't just angry. Was that jealousy Damira sensed? She rubbed her hand over her mouth. "You know," she said, "I can tell when people lie to me."

Something flickered in Groa's eyes and she shuffled a step back, hunching her shoulders. Good, Damira thought. *She's learned to fear me.*

Juquila stepped forward. "We heard you were powerful, if you please. Which is why we are sure Kaberco could never defeat you."

Damira was beginning to think these three had nothing to tell her. Just a trio of opportunists who decided to choose a side before it was too late. Well, she couldn't fault them for that. But did they have to be so tiresome? And where was that sentry with Tirk?

As if on cue, a panting Tirk was shoved into the yurt. The soldier must have made him run the entire way. He stepped toward Damira, then stopped. "Mam? Aunt Juquila?"

So. Tereka's relatives. Damira pressed her lips together. Why hadn't they acknowledged the relationship? "You are Tirk's mother. Is that correct, Groa?"

The woman flinched and bowed her head. "Yes, if you please."

"Do you have other children?"

Groa responded with a quaver in her voice. "Yes, one son. He's nine."

Tirk twitched at the response. Interesting, Damira thought. *I wonder why.* "And where is he?"

"I left him in Trofmose with his cousins. It seemed to be the safest place for him."

"No other children?"

"No."

"Are you lying to me?"

Kill her.

Putting a hand to her face as if to ward off Damira's gaze, Groa cowered. "No, if you please."

"Tirk told me he has a sister." Damira curled her lip. "One of you is lying. Is it him? Or you?"

"If you please," said Juquila. "Let me explain. My sister gave birth to twins, Tirk and a girl who was sickly. About the time the girl died, my sister's husband brought home a road child, the spawn of some dalliance, no doubt. He convinced my sister to raise it as her own."

"What?" Meluz had wide eyes, and his jaw was slightly slack. Tirk, while startled, seemed more disappointed than shocked.

Juquila went on. "The girl is nothing but a troublemaker. She tried to be a trader and failed. She falsified documents and was taken. Less than a month later, she broke out of prison and has been on the run ever since."

Damira's eyes flicked between the faces of Juquila, Tirk, Meluz, and Groa. Tirk's face reddened and he clenched his hands. He wasn't comfortable with his aunt's words. Meluz looked as stunned as if someone had told him there was a third moon in the sky. Groa had her eyes down, whether in shame or something else, Damira couldn't tell. But Juquila had spoken with her eyes on Damira's, full of confidence, as if she believed everything she said.

But was Juquila lying? Her story had only a few details in common with what Tereka and Tirk had told Damira. She had to know the truth. She sent a sliver of her power into Juquila's mind.

Kill her.

If she wasn't careful, she would. Very cautiously, she let her power sift through Juquila's thoughts. Yes, she believed

Tereka was the trader's daughter. If that were true, the only way Tereka could be the Desired One would be if her mother was a Risker. But even that didn't fit the prophecy. She was about to probe a little further when she heard Shagonar's voice outside the yurt.

She tensed, waiting. When her husband didn't enter the yurt, she expelled the breath she'd been holding and assumed he'd walked past.

She pulled back from Juquila's mind and turned to Meluz. "Is what your aunt saying about Tereka true?"

"I never knew any of that."

"Are you sure?" Damira sent a beam of hot red light at one of his hands.

He yelped and jumped back. The smell of burning flesh filled the yurt.

Juquila flashed a glare at Damira. "How dare you?"

"Because I can," Damira said. She returned Juquila's glare with one of her own before refocusing on Meluz. "I ask you again."

Meluz held his uninjured hand out to her. "If you please, I always believed Tereka to be my cousin."

"None of our children knew the truth," Juquila said, stepping in front of her son. "Had word gotten out that we lied about Tereka being Groa's daughter, we all could have been taken."

That could be true, and it made sense, Damira thought. "If he knows nothing, why did you bring him?"

"If you please," Juquila said, "I feared that Kaberco would punish him, once he discovered that I'd left. And we wanted protection on the road."

Damira sneered, certain that in Juquila's mind, protection for herself was more important than shielding her son.

"Take Tirk and his cousin to Tirk's yurt," Damira said to the soldier standing by the door. She thought maybe Farnaz could get more of the story out of them, now that they were both rattled. She pointed at the women. "Chain these two in a prison yurt. I'll deal with them tomorrow."

She suppressed a smile when Juquila's long eyelashes flipped wide. Obviously, that one had expected far better treatment.

Fondling her rabbit's ears, Damira leaned back in her chair. When she learned all the newcomers had to tell her, she'd decide if she should kill them. If she did, it would placate the amulets for a time. And get rid of people who might be trouble in the future.

56

In the hours since Damira had sent Juquila away, the pain in her head had intensified, creating an ever-tightening band of tension. She considered taking a rock and bashing it onto her skull. That would hurt less.

The shriveled leg ached and stung. She thought she'd go mad from the pain. She needed something to ease it. Maybe ask one of the healers? But she couldn't show the blackened leg and toes to anyone. Shagonar and Syzyan would find out and resume nagging her to use the amulets less, a nagging that was as irritating as raindrops falling through the smoke hole in the top of the yurt.

No, no one could know how much damage the amulets had inflicted on her body. She'd given up allowing anyone to attend her in the bath and she wore silk leggings with socks to bed. Only under the cover of darkness would she remove them.

She let out a huff. When would this nightmare be over? Her amulets insisted Tereka was the culprit. Defeat her and the pain would go away.

But she needed to be sure. She rang a bell, and a guard stepped into her yurt. "Bring me the prisoner called Tirk."

The man bowed his head. "Yes, Your Loftiness."

After he left, she hobbled to the brazier and poured herself a cup of tea. She limped back to her seat and lowered herself to the cushion. Sweat trickled down her neck. *Oh, to be able to move without pain.* She took a sip, allowing the warmth to roll down her dry throat. *Soon. Just destroy Tereka and this will all be over.*

By the time the guard shoved Tirk into the yurt, she'd finished her tea. "Your Loftiness, will that be all?" the sentry asked.

"Yes." She dismissed him with a wave, and he backed out of the yurt.

Setting down her teacup, Damira smiled at Tirk. His hands were gripped together, his eyes wide, and his shoulders drooped. Good. He's afraid. Maybe now he'll talk.

"So, we didn't finish our little chat earlier. Who is this Meluz to you?"

"Meluz? He's my cousin."

"Does he know your sister?"

Tirk shook his head. "My aunt never allowed Tereka to associate with her children. She said she didn't want them polluted by the spawn of a whore."

If that were true, Meluz would have nothing to add. No sense bothering with him. "Your aunt made many interesting statements about your sister. Was she telling the truth?"

Damira nearly laughed at the expression on Tirk's face. His eyes darted from one side of the yurt to the other. He wrapped his arms around himself and took a step back. He looked like a rabbit cowering before a hungry sand wolf.

"Come now," she said. "It's a simple question."

"My sister was a trader, that is true. Apprenticed to our da." He bit his lip. "But she wasn't a failure."

"Then why would your aunt say so? She's the syndic. I would think she'd be a good one to judge."

"If you please, I was her clerk. Tereka traded well. Except she fought."

"With other traders?"

"No, bandits."

Damira ran a hand through her hair. This idiot wasn't making any sense. "What's wrong with fighting bandits?"

"It's against the rules."

"Oh, I see." Damira leaned back. "Fighting bandits who are trying to kill you is unsafe." She didn't attempt to keep the sarcasm from her voice.

Tirk nodded vigorously. "And you can impede the guards, who are supposed to fight them off."

No wonder it had been so easy to subdue the south. No one, other than the guardsmen and a handful of traders, knew how to use weapons, let alone had the will for combat. Damira tapped her fingers against her lips. "What's this about falsified documents?"

His face reddening, Tirk stared at the floor. "Aunt Juquila wanted to teach Tereka a lesson, so she had me create some false receipts and we took her to the questor. He found her guilty." He looked up at Damira. "They told me all she'd get was a fine. But they had her taken."

Peering into the boy's eyes, she read sadness, shame, and indignation. This story was most likely the truth. And it matched what Tereka herself had said. *So now I know.* Juquila was an accomplished liar, willing to sacrifice even a niece if it suited her purposes. How despicable.

Still, Tirk seemed to be hiding something. "Is that all? Your sister, or rather, your half-sister, is just a simple trader who was framed by a conniving aunt and a coward of a half-brother?"

After a flinch and a long pause, Tirk nodded. "That's right."

Kill him.

She felt the familiar sting of her amulets. Clenching her

teeth, she battled the urge to give in, to get respite from the pain. She needed answers, not a dead prisoner. "Are you certain?"

His throat bobbed. "Yes. You asked me all this before."

"I'm not so sure I got the truth from you then." She raised a hand and let the power flow to her fingers. The warmth intensified into a sting, begging to be released. She sent a little of the power to his mind. Time to sift through the lies and discover the truth. "Who was Tereka's mother?"

He hunched his shoulders, cowering before her, and turned as if to flee.

She shot burning light at him. The flesh on his arm sizzled, and he dropped to his knees with a scream.

Now. Slowly, carefully, she peered into his thoughts.

The door to the yurt crashed open. "Dami, what—"

Syzyan. She pulled back from Tirk's mind and swallowed her vexation. "Yes?"

"I heard screams." He glanced from her to Tirk.

"I was interrogating him. It's not my fault he's been lying to us."

Her brother took a deep breath and closed the door to the yurt. "Dami," he said in the tone he used to soothe a frenzied mare. "We can question him in other ways."

He was the one who needed to calm himself. She glared at him. "But we need the truth."

"Yes, we do. But don't you think withholding food and water will do the same? By morning, he'll be begging to tell us everything he knows."

Damira tipped her head to the side and pretended to consider his words. "Yes, Syz, we'll do it your way." She waved a hand at Tirk, who was still lying on the floor. "Can you have the guard take him away?"

Syzyan pulled Tirk up and put an arm under his shoulders. "Get some rest, Dami. I think you're pushing yourself too hard."

She smiled. That was Syzyan, always the big brother telling her what to do.

As she watched him help Tirk out of the yurt, she decided the interruption didn't matter. She'd seen enough. Even if she hadn't discovered all Tirk knew, he seemed to think that his mother and aunt knew more about Tereka than they let on.

Fine. She'd probe their minds in the morning.

57

In the cold stillness just before dawn, stinging pain woke Damira. Fire coursed up and down her entire left leg.

She lay still, listening to the sounds of the camp at night. A guard tramping by on his rounds. A banner flapping on top of her yurt. A horse whinnying in the distance.

Kill them.

Damira didn't know which was worse—the relentless stings and aches or the incessant, murderous voices in her head. She squeezed her eyes shut, then opened them. Sticky sweat made her nightclothes cling to her limbs. Shagonar's even breathing told her he was fast asleep.

How she envied him. He wasn't wracked with pain. Using the amulets had taken a toll on him, but nothing like the shriveling of fingers and toes she endured.

He'd urged her to stop, as had Syzyan. But where Syzyan tried to impose his will on her, Shagonar understood why she insisted that she carry on until all their enemies were dead. He hadn't forgotten the anguish of witnessing the destruction of their entire clan.

But she couldn't think about putting the amulets aside for long. Somehow, they knew when she wanted to be rid of them. The headaches would intensify into flaming agony, only subsiding when she gave in to the amulets' demands to hurt or destroy.

She eased herself off the sleeping mat. Stifling a moan, she pulled on her leggings and tunic. Fumbling in the dark, she found her soft leather slippers and gloves. She wrapped a cloak around herself and limped out of the yurt. There was only one way to ease her pain.

And to silence the nagging in her mind. She had to know.

The four guards at the door snapped to attention when she slipped out of the yurt. "Do you require anything, Your Loftiness?" the leader asked.

Damira shook her head, assuming he could see her in the moonlight. "No." She pointed at her foot. "I pulled something in my leg earlier and it throbs. Probably a little walking will ease the stiffness." When one stepped forward, she waved a hand in dismissal. "I don't need an escort."

As she walked away, she tried to minimize her limp. The chilly night air lifted her hair, tossing it around her face. An old memory flashed in her mind. She was riding on the steppe with Syzyan and Shagonar late one night, reveling in the light of two full moons. They'd been just children then, heedless of the dangers. And how they'd been punished for their recklessness. A few days later, their fathers were dead, killed by Izolliyan raiders. She never wanted to feel that pain and fear again. The stinging in her limbs was a small price to pay.

Outside the prison yurt, the quartet of guards stood tall. *Good. Even in the late watches of the night, they're disciplined.* "The morning comes well, does it not?" she said.

The guards put their hands together and bowed. "Your Loftiness. The morning comes well."

The oldest of them asked, "Do you require anything?"

"No," she answered. "Have our prisoners given any trouble?"

"Not that we couldn't handle."

"Oh?"

"One demanded bathing water and a laundress. When we refused, she attempted to seduce the Arban-u Darga."

"Unsuccessfully?"

"Of course."

Damira stifled her laugh. Oh, that Juquila was entertaining. It was a shame she was too much of a snake to be allowed to live. "I'm going to have a word with them. See that no one disturbs us. For any reason."

The guards inclined their heads as she strode into the yurt.

Inside, the red coals of the brazier offered a dim light. Soft breathing told Damira that both women were asleep. She shook her head. Laundry. Even in chains, Juquila demanded comforts. The nerve of the woman. She was lucky she was housed in a yurt, not tossed into an open pit with other prisoners.

Sending a tendril of her power into the brazier, Damira brought the flames to life. She hobbled to the lone wooden chair and sat. "You should wake up now."

One of the sleeping forms roused, her chains clanking. "What, Juquila?"

"I'm not Juquila, and I'm telling you to wake up."

"Who? What?" The woman jerked upright.

Damira laughed. "Have you forgotten me so quickly?" She kept her tone mocking rather than harsh.

Groa reached over and shook her sister. "Juquila, wake up."

Juquila sat up and rubbed her eyes. In the light of the flames, Damira noted that while Groa's hair was cut short at chin level with bangs, Juquila's was long and flowing, something that wasn't visible when she wore her turban. Interesting. Another benefit of power in Tlefas and more evidence of the lies and corruption of its rulers. It was a good thing they came to liberate these people.

"Who's here?" Juquila asked.

"As I asked your sister, have you forgotten me so quickly?"

"Your Loftiness," Juquila said. "Why are you here? And at this hour? If you please."

Kill them.

Damira swallowed hard. Not yet. "I know you lied about your niece. She never falsified documents. You did that." Even in the dim light, she could see Juquila flinch. "Why did you do that?"

"Because she was a hooligan."

"Seems like a lot of trouble to go to for a rebellious girl. You couldn't control her another way?"

"She was a danger to safety and fairness and she wasn't contributing to the building of our peaceful and prosperous society. She had to be removed."

Even in chains, the woman still spouted the Prime Konamei's drivel, the dreck they used to keep people in line. Damira grimaced, her leg stinging and her head pounding. Who did Juquila think she was talking to?

Kill them.

"Are you sure that's the only reason?"

A guarded expression crept over Juquila's brown face. "Yes."

Damira narrowed her eyes. "You're lying." She raised a finger. Red light flashed, burning a hole the size of a horse's hoof in the shoulder of Juquila's tunic. The woman yelped and clapped a hand over the burn.

With a smirk, Damira asked, "Are you sure there's nothing else you want to tell me?" When Juquila didn't respond, she lifted her hand. "Anything?"

"Why are you treating me this way?" Juquila's voice was steady, almost imperious. Her chin was lifted.

Impressive. Juquila showed more courage than most men on the receiving end of the amulets' power, but her bravery was useless. "Because I know you're lying." *And you're making my head ache.* "Would you like to learn what I do to liars?"

Kill her.

Juquila flinched. "Tereka's father was a malcontent and a troublemaker for years. He needed to be suppressed. Striking through Tereka seemed like the best way to do it."

Groa recoiled as if she'd been struck.

"And what do you say, Groa?" Damira asked in a gentle tone. "Is your husband a troublemaker?"

"Yes." The word came in a trembling voice.

"So, you allowed your sister to sentence a girl to be taken, a child you raised, simply because you were angry with her father? That seems rather cold to me."

"If you please," Juquila said. "From an early age, it was clear that Tarkio's spawn was no good. Tereka had to be taken. Safety and fairness need to be preserved at all costs."

Damira studied the two women's faces. They were ruthless, to be sure. And willing to sacrifice even their nearest for their own gains. Probably the syndic knew more than the other. She sent another beam of light at Juquila, this time singeing her ear, smiling when the woman screamed. "Tell me," Damira said, "all you know of Kaberco and his plans."

Juquila's whimpers ceased, and she frowned, clearly startled by the abrupt change in subject. "I told you. He's allying with the Riskers."

"Oh, come now. Surely a syndic would have been cleverer. You told me all you know without asking anything in return?" Damira clicked her tongue. "Perhaps you have forgotten." She flicked her fingers.

Clutching her leg, Juquila fell to her knees. A moan seeped from her lips.

"How about you?" Damira turned to Groa. "And what do you know?"

Groa gasped and shrank back. "Please, don't hurt me. I'll tell you anything."

"See that you do. And make sure it's the truth. Now, your sister says Tereka isn't your daughter. Is she?"

"No, if you please."

"Is she your husband's child?"

"No."

Juquila's head jerked up, her eyes wide and startled.

Damira sucked air between her teeth. That news seemed to be a surprise to Juquila. "Then whose child is she?"

"I'm not entirely certain."

Intriguing that Groa had never told her sister this part of the story. Damira rubbed her stinging fingers. "Tell me what you think, sure or not."

"My husband brought her home when she was an infant. He told me a tale of a village girl who'd run off with a Risker. He claimed Kaberco had killed them both." Her voice took on an angry note. "And he persuaded me to raise her as my own."

"You raised a Risker's brat?" Juquila asked. "How could you?" Her words dripped with reproach.

One wave of Damira's finger and Juquila shut her mouth with a snap. She wrapped her arms around herself.

Kill her.

The scowl on Groa's face, coupled with the anger in her tone, spoke of resentment long held. Which meant Groa was telling the truth. Tereka was the child of a Risker and a villager. "What can you tell me about the Risker?" Damira asked.

Groa shook her head. "Not much, and I didn't want to know. One barbarian is the same as another."

"Your husband never said anything about the father?"

"Oh, he'd spoken of him. They'd apparently been great friends." Groa snorted. "Had I known he was so thick with savages, I never would have married him."

Kill her.

Damira rubbed her stinging knee. "Tell me everything your husband ever said about his barbarian friend. Anything at all. No matter how trivial."

When Groa didn't immediately respond, Damira frowned. "Unless you'd rather end up like your sister."

The woman began babbling, all kinds of mixed-up stories about Tarkio and his friend Xico tumbling from her mouth. Tales of hunting warboars and tracking rabbits, harvesting honey, and teasing Xico's sisters.

But the main points were that Xico had green eyes and was a skilled archer. Two more facts that pointed to Tereka as the fulfillment of the prophecy.

Now, what to do with Groa and her sister? If they told all they knew, then word that Tereka was the Desired One would spread. That information needed to be suppressed at all costs.

She pushed her power into Juquila's mind. Pain and fear were uppermost. And a loathing of Kaberco, but not much about his plans. She raised her hand, then dropped it. Shagonar and Syzyan wouldn't like it if she misted Juquila and her sister. Maybe she could accuse them of something as an excuse?

Kill them.

Damira nearly screamed at the piercing pain in her head and the burn in her knee. If this kept up, she wouldn't be able to walk.

With a twitch of her hand, she misted Groa.

Juquila screamed. "Have mercy, I beg you."

"Mercy? That was merciful. For you, I have something better." She slid a wisp of her power into Juquila's leg and pushed. Juquila's scream masked her moan of relief as the stinging pain in her toes ebbed.

As soon as Juquila's screams had subsided into a groan, Damira studied her handiwork. The woman's right leg was twisted, bent between her knee and hip.

Tipping her head, Damira considered this result. It was possible to mist a portion of a bone and leave the rest of the limb intact. That could be useful in the future.

"What have I done to deserve this?" Juquila stroked her lifeless leg.

"What, indeed." Damira pushed power into Juquila's arm. It twisted and went limp. Another bone turned to mist. The woman writhed on the floor.

When Juquila's whimpers and moans faded, Damira pushed her power into Juquila's collarbone. The woman's shoulders hunched together. Her breath came in ragged pants.

"This is what I do to those who seek to manipulate me," Damira said as casually as if she were telling Juquila she'd like some cakes with her tea. "Do you not think this is fair?"

Juquila's eyes were so wide Damira could see the whites.

"Do you not have anything to say for yourself?" she asked.

"What have I done?" Juquila muttered.

Damira misted the top of Juquila's skull and grinned as the woman's eyes rolled up. With one last shove of power, Juquila became red mist that settled in a damp spot on the floor.

The relief was palpable. The pain in Damira's knee vanished and the pounding in her head diminished to a dull ache. Time to get back to her own yurt before Shagonar woke up.

She stood up and took a few steps to the door. She halted, staring at her feet in surprise. No stinging, no limp. Was that all it took to rid herself of the stinging agony? A little torture, a little misting, and she was free of pain? Should she mist Tirk and Meluz as well? No, they'd serve another purpose, at least for the time being. They'd bait the trap she was about to set for Tereka.

58

The next morning, Damira sipped her tea and nibbled on sweet cakes. She flexed her fingers, reveling in the absence of pain. It had been years since she'd felt so vibrant. Misting the two spies had brought more relief than she expected.

A thought intruded into her contentment, accusing her of enjoying her acts of torture. She shoved it away. She'd only given those women what they deserved.

Once she misted Tereka, all her problems would dissipate, she was sure of it. She wiggled her fingers. Maybe the stinging would wane from them, too, now that she discovered a way to banish it for a few hours. Or even better, her shriveled foot would heal. What a joy to be able to walk without pain again.

The yurt's door opened to admit Shagonar and Syzyan. Both wore scowls and stalked over to stand in front of her.

"What?" she asked.

"How could you, Dami?" Syzyan's tone was accusing and angry.

She tipped her head up to look at him. "Why don't you sit down and tell me what this is about?"

Syzyan huffed and strode to the opposite side of the yurt.

Shagonar sat on the chair next to Damira's. He looked at her, the corners of his mouth drooping, sadness dulling his eyes. "What did you do?"

"What are you talking about?"

With a few steps, Syzyan stalked to her and waved a finger in her face. "Don't act like you don't know. Those women who came yesterday. The ones you tortured in the night."

Damira widened her eyes. She could pretend to not understand him, but decided telling the truth would be better. The guards had probably already told their superiors about her early morning visit to the spies' yurt. They had to report it when they realized the prisoners were gone, lest they be accused of allowing the women to escape. The only surprising thing was how quickly the news had reached her brother. "I couldn't sleep."

Shagonar shot a look at Syzyan, then faced Damira. "Why not?"

She shrugged. "Just restless. And you were sleeping like a rock. I thought a little stroll would help." There. If they thought using her amulets gave her too much pain to walk, that should take care of it.

"And you visited the people you assumed were spies?"

"Well, yes. I had a few questions. Since they were nagging at my mind, I decided to ask. Then I could put my doubts behind me and go to sleep."

Syzyan frowned. "What did you ask?" His face was a bland mask, the expression he used when he interrogated officers he suspected of mistreating their men.

How dare he suspect her. He'd be sorry he ever doubted her when he learned what the spies had revealed. "All kinds of things. Our former friend Tereka is the daughter of a Risker and a villager. A green-eyed Risker who was a skilled archer." When they didn't respond, she continued. "Don't you see? She fits the prophecy."

Shagonar drummed his fingers on the carved arm of his chair. "So it seems. Can you believe them?"

"That's why I had to dig into their minds. They told me such a jumble of truth and lies I couldn't be sure." She tried to look into Shagonar's eyes, but he was staring at the floor. A muscle in his jaw twitched.

"Dami, I understand you were trying to help." Syzyan's tone softened as he spoke. "But did you have to mist them?"

"Of course, I did. If anyone were to learn that Tereka could be the Desired One, they'd flock to her. We'd be surrounded by enemies."

"But if she is the Desired One..." Syzyan let his words trail off.

Kill him.

Swallowing hard, Damira leaned toward her brother. "Syz, listen. Maybe she is, or maybe it's just an odd coincidence. But you know as well as I do, we can't take any chances. We can't trust anyone. Too many oppose our goal of lasting peace. I'm the only one who can ensure we achieve it. No one else. Then there will be no more war."

"Dami—"

"Come now, Syz. Who have we ever been able to trust but each other? Not Iktul, not Nishio, not anyone. I hold the power. I can bring peace and make it stick. This Tereka, who knows what she'd do? We can't take the risk." She huffed. "And since she lied to us about having dragonfly amulets, we know we can't trust her."

Syzyan dropped into a chair and put his head in his hands. Damira swiveled toward Shagonar and jerked her head toward her brother. "What's wrong with him?"

Shagonar raised his head. "I think he wants the girl you used to be back." His voice was strained and husky. "As do I."

His words cut through her, piercing and burning like a flash of lightning. Did Shagonar no longer love her? Her chest tightened, and she struggled to breathe.

Destroy them.

The amulets were becoming more insistent. But Shagonar and Syzyan? She couldn't live without either of them. "I'm sorry. I guess I panicked when they told me about Tereka."

"You promised not to mist anyone else." Shagonar raised his eyes to meet hers.

She studied her husband's face. "I promised not to torture our own men. Did you mean that mercy to extend to spies?"

His gaze flickered, as if he was hiding something. What was he up to?

Before he could respond, the door opened. A Jagun-u Darga strode in. "Your Loftiness, I bring news."

"Out with it," Shagonar said.

"Our scouts tell us an army approaches from the north."

"See?" Damira said. "I knew they'd be coming soon."

"How big of an army?" Syzyan asked.

"Maybe about twenty-five or thirty arbatus. Almost all on foot."

Damira pursed her lips. Less than three hundred men. A fraction of their own forces.

"When will they be here?" Shagonar asked.

"Less than a day, maybe."

"Summon the jianjuns to my yurt," Syzyan said. "I'll meet with them shortly." He rubbed his chin, frowning as the man closed the door behind him. "Kaberco moved faster than I anticipated. Even if we move now, our armies will clash in the narrowest spot between the forest and the mountains. Clever of him to choose that location. It makes our greater numbers less of an advantage."

"What does it matter?" Damira asked. "In a narrow place, our explosives can easily deal with one hundred foot soldiers. And if any survive, our horsemen can take care of the rest." *And if Syz blows up Tereka, then she'll be dead and I won't be forced to mist her. As gratifying as that would be.* She snorted. "For that matter, a few of our amulet wielders could do the job themselves."

"True," Shagonar said. "But perhaps we should try to negotiate with them. Maybe Kaberco will listen to reason and abandon his hopeless resistance."

"Why would we offer him anything?" Damira snorted. There was no point in delaying the inevitable.

"Because, Dami," Shagonar said, "if we can get Kaberco on our side, he'd be a good choice to govern the north. He's already popular."

"And an effective leader," put in Syzyan. "I agree. Once he and his army approach, we'll send an offer of clemency if they surrender. If Tereka is with him, then he'll know Dami can mist people. Kaberco won't go into a battle he knows is suicide."

Damira clenched her stinging fingers together. Syzyan could make his plans, but she'd concoct some of her own. She had four hostages. She'd use them to make sure Tereka didn't survive.

59

T ereka huddled in her cloak, staring in the direction of North Rivash. Scudding clouds in a gray sky broke the weak sunlight into pieces. She shivered in the barren chill of a dying autumn after the leaves had fallen and blown away. But the goosebumps on her arms and the shivers down her spine weren't caused by the wind alone.

Kaberco had gathered his army, such as it was, and marched them south. Kemet had done his job well and had managed to recruit nearly fifty traders, all of whom were experienced bandit fighters. Not the best soldiers, Tereka thought, but probably equal to the guardsmen Kaberco commanded.

Alikse and Savinnia had met them south of Shinroo, along with the Riskers who'd agreed to fight alongside them. They, at least, were skilled archers and brave defenders of their lands. Tereka hoped they hadn't rallied to her cause only to be slaughtered.

A hand on her shoulder pulled her out of her gloomy imaginings. Da stood beside her, with Relio and Alikse. All of them wore somber expressions.

Kaberco stalked over and pointed. "Two hours' march will bring us to the narrow spot between the woods on either side. We'll be able to see the town and our enemy's vanguard. That's where we'll stop and wait for them to come to us."

"What if they don't?" Tereka asked.

"Then we send an envoy to tell them to leave."

Relio barked out a laugh. "They're not about to pack up and go home because you told them to."

"That would be propitious, wouldn't it?" Kaberco chuckled. "No, they won't leave. I'll wager they'll send another ultimatum."

"Bah." Relio spat out a curse. "Those *yanshyri* are more likely to behead the envoy. Or mist him."

Tereka's cold hands turned icy. This could very well be her last night on earth. She'd never touch Naco, hear Cillia's voice, or see her mother again. She gripped her bow. If this was her destiny, then she couldn't shirk it. Better to face it bravely and live up to the legacy of her parents.

Da shook his head. "Maybe not. They've been patient so far. My sense is they'd rather not slaughter us. I think they'll make one more offer."

"I agree." Kaberco's tone was confident. "I'll fight this war with words as long as I can. But Tarkio's right. They'll only give us one more chance to surrender. Which means, Tereka, you'll have to move fast."

"Are you sure it won't be better to wait for the morning?" Knowing what he would say, she asked anyway, prompted by shaking knees that urged her to delay just a few heartbeats longer.

Kaberco pulled his soot-colored cloak tightly around himself, covering his black leather armor. "I know the days are short this time of year and we only have a few hours of daylight left. But I don't want my recruits to lose their nerve and slip away in the night. And I certainly don't want the

Emperor to mount a sneak attack under cover of darkness and massacre us in our sleep."

"When will you leave?" Da asked.

Tereka knew how she should reply, but the words stuck in her throat. All day, she'd felt her amulets, a wordless urging to move, to act. She swallowed the sour taste in her mouth. "As soon as Relio and Alikse are ready."

"We've been ready, girly," Relio said. "You're the one standing around gossiping with your da."

Da pulled Tereka into a hug. "I suppose I don't need to tell you to be careful."

She compelled her lips to form a grin. "What could go wrong? Aren't the amulets supposed to provide protection?"

"Just don't take them for granted," Da said. He closed his eyes for a few heartbeats. "I've mulled this over in the quiet watches of many sleepless nights. The prophecy only says you'll bring a new order. It mentions nothing about you living to see it."

Staring into Da's somber brown eyes, Tereka blinked a few times. "I never thought of that," she said. Slowly, she sought out Relio's gaze, then Alikse's. "Do you still want to go with me?"

"It's like this, girly," Relio said. "My best chance of surviving this is with you. You and those dragonflies." He winked.

"Right." Alikse snorted. "Gratitude over the fact that we owe our lives to her several times over has nothing to do with your decision."

"Well, that, too." Relio chuckled. "Besides, we can't let girly have all the fun."

Encouraged to have at least two stalwart companions supporting her, she squared her shoulders and stiffened her spine. But then a frosty hand clutched her heart. She yearned to have one other with her. Naco. Was he even still alive?

Her face suddenly hot, she clenched her fists. She'd never had a chance to find out Naco's feelings for her, or hers for him. No chance to explore where those feelings would have led. It wasn't fair.

She swallowed down her resentment. No time for that now. "Then let's go." After scooping her quiver from the ground, she attached it to her hip and slung her bow over her shoulder. Her heart thumped faster. Time to make her move. She patted Da's arm and forced her lips into a flicker of a smile. "Peace and safety."

"We'll meet the Emperor's forces in two hours, maybe less," Kaberco said. "I'll delay the battle as long as I can." He tipped his head up toward the sun. "By then, it will be late afternoon. You'll have more shadows to hide in, but so will the enemy's spies."

Da gripped Tereka's fingers, his own as cold as hers. One look at Da's ravaged face made her eyes sting. She pressed her forehead to his shoulder. He wrapped an arm around her head. "I have no words for you, except I'm sorry."

"Sorry for what?" She lifted her face. "Da, there is nothing to forgive. I am in your debt. And will always love you as my da."

He choked, then stepped back. "Then make me proud."

Kaberco coughed. "I know I have much to regret, but I promise you, if it comes to it, I will die trying to save you." He bowed his head and placed his hand over his heart. "I'm sorry we didn't ally sooner. Peace and safety."

A lump formed in her throat and she croaked out her words. "Thank you. Peace and safety."

Holding a hand in the air as a silent farewell, she turned and trotted west, Alikse and Relio at her side. They headed for the forest that hugged the edge of the North Rivash road.

When they reached the tree line, they darted between the oaks and maples, the former still clinging to their brown leaves, the latter denuded of the brilliant foliage they'd worn just a short time before. Now their leaves lay on the ground, dry and crumbling.

"You couldn't have planned this for the summer, girly?"

She rolled her eyes at Relio. "Yes, and I should have challenged the Empress to single combat, too."

"Quiet." Alikse spoke softly.

Tereka nodded. He was right. This late in the fall, there was hardly any cover in the forest save the scattered pine trees. There'd been no rain, so the leaves underfoot crackled as if heralding their presence. The Emperor most likely had scouts in the woods, scouts who wouldn't be easy to elude.

They followed a trail that weaved its way southward through the trees, all the while wondering how they would accomplish their mission. Their goals were simple—destroy the scorpion amulets and rescue Naco, Tirk, and Sebezh. How to achieve these aims was another matter.

As they walked, the sun sinking slowly to their right, her da's words echoed in Tereka's mind. Would the Desired One live to see the new order? The hair on the back of her neck prickled. She wouldn't survive if she didn't keep alert for the sound of anyone in the woods besides her and her companions.

Relio's huffing breath behind her made hearing anything else difficult. On a sudden impulse, she halted next to a large pine tree with branches that nearly swept the ground. She closed her eyes and listened. A bird sang. A gentle rustle nearby told her a small animal, perhaps an alloe rat, scampered for its den. She was preparing to move when she heard the sharp snap of a breaking branch. She whirled and stared at Relio and Alikse, who stared back with flared eyes.

Alikse pointed to the pine tree. He made a circular motion with one finger.

Right, Tereka thought. We should go behind, not under. If we're found, we'll be better able to fight our way out.

She moved to the tree, slowly placing each foot, careful to

avoid dry, fallen branches that could break. She fought back the urge to hurry, valuing silence over speed. After several torturous moments, the three squatted behind the pine, panting as if they'd run a race.

Only a few heartbeats passed before they heard footsteps crunching through the fallen leaves. Tereka eased three arrows from her quiver and readied her bow.

To her horror, the voices came from her right, from the north. How had they not noticed these people before? At first, she could barely understand their words. Then she recognized the strange pronunciation of the invaders.

"Seems odd, doesn't it?" a reedy voice asked. "Why do they have no spies in these woods?"

Tereka's throat clenched. She nocked an arrow.

The other chuckled. "Probably because they need every man to fight. They know where we are, anyway." He snorted. "This is a waste of time. Let's go back and report."

Slowly, Tereka exhaled, hoping she didn't have to kill them. Then they could make their report and no one else would give half a thought to the western woods.

The first scout spoke. "The whole thing is a waste of time. If this last holdout doesn't surrender, the Empress will mist them all, just like she did those northern spies."

Their words were lost in the blood that pounded through Tereka's head. Did that mean Tirk, Naco, and Sebezh were dead? Her eyes stung and her head spun.

Strong fingers gripped her shoulder. "Breathe, girly." Relio's whisper was as soft as the sound of a falling leaf. She sucked in a breath. The voices moved away to the south.

"You heard them," she said to Relio, her voice barely audible.

"We don't know who they were talking about. Kaberco could have sent his own spies. Or perhaps the Riskers did."

Relio was right. She looked at Alikse, who tipped his head

toward the trail heading south. She tightened her grip on her bow and arrows and stepped back onto the path.

The next hour was an agony of jumping at every crackle in the underbrush and fighting the urge to move as quickly as she could. The shadows lengthened. Tereka shivered, chilled by the cooling air and her growing fear. While the dusky light made it harder for Tereka to make out the path, they were also less likely to be spotted. She hoped more of the Empress' soldiers felt the way the two scouts did—bored and complacent. Then the sentries might not be alert.

The slow going frayed her nerves, especially because she didn't know how rapidly Kaberco had moved his forces. His small army could march more quickly on the road than she could slink noiselessly through the trees, testing each footstep, pausing with each rustle and crackle in the underbrush. Had his troops been spotted by the Emperor's scouts yet?

Faint whinnies of horses and shouts of men drifted through the trees. Tereka slowed her pace, crouching lower. The camp noises grew louder, intensifying the beating of her already-racing heart.

Soon, the lights of campfires flickered among the trees. Tereka stopped, holding her breath. They'd found the war camp.

"Now what?" Relio breathed the words into Tereka's ear.

Now what, indeed?

She peered between the trees. From the quick movements of the men, she guessed that Kaberco's advancing army had been spotted and troops were being mobilized to meet him. Good. The more activity in the camp, the less noticeable she and her companions would be.

Groups of soldiers were dismantling the first few rows of yurts and packing the pieces onto wagons. Rows of horsemen were lining up. All of them bore long bows and fat quivers of arrows. Kaberco didn't stand a chance against that force.

Which left everything up to her. She could try a stealthy

approach, making her way through the trees until she found the Empress. But did she have time?

Sky-god? What do I do?

Suddenly, the knowledge flashed through her mind like a fire lit in a dark, dense forest. "Come on," she said.

Darting from the woods, Tereka plunged into the war camp, sprinting between the yurts.

60

Tereka bolted into the center of the camp where a wide lane bisected the rows of white yurts. Slowing her pace, she turned and walked south. Relio and Alikse strode beside her, breathing hard from their sprint.

Around her, soldiers rushed, leather armor creaking. A horse whinnied. Officers shouted orders. No one paid attention to Tereka and her companions, as if they were no more than shadows on the ground.

Her amulets, she recalled, had a way to keep from being found. How she knew this was one of those times, she couldn't say, but she and her friends strode through the camp unchallenged.

As usual, Alikse remained stoically silent. Relio muttered curses. Something about fools and how he wished snakes would crawl into someone's eyeballs. Tereka didn't know the target of his cussing. It didn't matter. She was grateful for anything that distracted her from her fear.

Relio elbowed her. "Sure hope you know what you're doing, girly."

Alikse chuckled. "Of course, she doesn't."

Despite their jibes, Tereka felt a confidence in her direction she didn't understand—as if her amulets were guiding her. Just the way they had when they showed her the water and weapons they needed when she and her fellow prisoners were about to be slaughtered by pirates. *They saved us then, they'll save us now. I have to believe that.*

Resolutely, Tereka stalked past several yurts, then came to an area of tents. All had their sides looped up, allowing those inside to observe everything around them. The open tents were filled with officers working at tables, some writing, some shouting orders. The largest was well lit and she could just make out the Emperor and his Supreme Jianjun Syzyan seated at a table, listening to an officer give a report. They did not appear to think they had to prepare for a sudden retreat. Most likely, they knew how badly they outnumbered Kaberco's tiny army.

The amulets nudged Tereka to keep moving. She continued south and her amulets grew icy cold, a sign that Damira and her scorpions weren't far.

She passed the Emperor's tent and the yurt behind it, then halted so abruptly that Relio and Alikse bumped into her. In an open area between rows of yurts, the Empress stood in the light of the dying sun, a triumphant smile spreading across her face.

Empress Damira's long, dark hair had been pulled up into an elaborate knot. Her crimson tunic fluttered in the breeze, its intricate embroidery in black, gold, and white forming patterns of tiny scorpions. Her three scorpion amulets hung from a chain around her neck, the scarlet and black stones twinkling in the dim light. She grasped a bow in one hand. A quiver of red arrows hung on one hip and a curved sword in a sheath on the other. Her grin widened as she took a step toward Tereka.

Ten paces behind the Empress, four men knelt on the ground, hands held behind their heads. Sebezh, Tirk, Naco, and the fourth? Tereka squinted in the dim light. Was that her cousin Meluz? What was he doing there? Her breath hitched. Juquila must be nearby as well.

Relio nudged her.

"I see them," she said.

"They don't look good," he answered.

All four of the kneeling men bore wounds and raw gashes on their faces. Blood stained their clothing. Behind them stood four soldiers, all grasping drawn swords, the curved blades gleaming red in the setting sun.

With her stomach hardening into a painful knot, Tereka silently cursed herself. She never should have left any of her friends with this evil scorpion wielder. She might as well have killed them herself.

Naco gazed into her eyes. His lips moved, but she was too far away to hear him. He seemed to be saying, "I'm with you. Always."

"So, Tereka Sabidur," Damira purred. "You have returned."

When Tereka didn't answer, the Empress continued. "I knew you were near. My amulets told me an hour ago. I had time to prepare." She waved a hand at her prisoners. "It's good that you finally showed up. I was growing bored with their screaming. Although killing one of them might have been amusing."

Tereka's lips parted and curled back from her teeth. Her mouth was dry sand.

"Nothing to say?" Damira asked as casually if she was making an offhand inquiry about Tereka's latest meal.

"You have the poison of a snake in your mouth," Tereka said.

Relio gasped. "Not sure that's a good idea, girly."

She wasn't either, but those were the words the sky-god had put in her mouth.

Damira sneered. "And you have sharpened your tongue like a sword."

"Your throat is an open grave." Tereka's stomach clenched. Why was the sky-god prompting her to answer the Empress so bluntly?

The boom of an explosion broke through the camp noise. Tereka's heart skipped a beat and Damira chuckled. "Oh, don't look so frightened," she said. "That was just one of our exploding arrows. A little demonstration for Kaberco of what we can destroy with a single arrow. He'd be wise to surrender now."

Pacing around her prisoners, Damira tapped her lips with a gloved hand. "Which one should I kill first? Sebezh?" The man cowered and Damira grinned, her white teeth gleaming like bones in the moonlight. "No, you wouldn't miss him as much as the others." She stood behind Meluz. "This one says he's your cousin. Is that true?"

"He is."

The Empress held up a finger and waved it at Tereka. "You really shouldn't lie to me. I know he's not."

"But—"

"I had a lovely chat with the syndic of Trofmose."

Tereka gasped. "My Aunt Juquila?"

"Now, now. We all know she's no relation to you." Damira smirked. "Yes, I heard the whole story. Risker father, villager mother. A trader who convinced his wife to raise you as her own, along with her son." She stepped to stand behind Tirk, seized a handful of his hair and jerked his head back. "The only reason I haven't slit his throat is that I haven't decided if he's been lying to me, or if his mother kept him ignorant about the girl he thought was his twin sister." She released Tirk with a shake.

Staring hard at Tirk, Tereka realized he hadn't betrayed her to Damira. Whatever he'd done to her in the past, she would gladly forgive. What torment had he endured to keep silent? She tried to catch his eyes, but he resolutely stared at the ground.

"So, Tereka Sabidur, you haven't asked about your supposed aunt or supposed mother. Why is that?"

"Groa was here, too?" Tereka gulped.

"Oh, yes. She was most informative. More so than the syndic. I had such fun getting all the secrets out of her."

As cruelly as Groa had tormented Tereka, she didn't like the idea of Damira interrogating the woman. She grew queasy thinking of the methods the Empress might have used and gripped her bow tighter, trying to still her shaking hands.

"I don't suppose you'll tell me your real surname," Damira said.

"No, I don't suppose I will," Tereka answered. *No sense putting my grandparents in danger.*

"Pity. Well, no matter. Would you like to see your aunt and mother?" Damira laced the final three words with sarcasm.

"If it wouldn't be too much trouble," Tereka said. She rubbed the back of her head and tugged on her hair. What was this woman up to?

"Oh, I'm so sorry. I'm afraid it would be rather difficult. Impossible, in fact. Mist has a way of dissipating."

From the startled gasps and bulging eyes of Tirk and Meluz, Tereka understood that neither had known the fate of their mothers. Her chest tightened. Her feelings for both women were complicated, but they didn't deserve the death they'd faced.

"Enough." Damira's voice turned hard. "You, Tereka, have annoyed me and defied me long enough. Surrender to me or I'll kill them all. These four, and the two mutes beside you."

Tereka blinked rapidly. "How do I know you won't kill them later?"

"You don't. But at least you will have bought them more time. Unless you want to see them turned to mist—" Damira fingered the amulets hanging around her neck. Their red stones glinted in the silver moonlight.

Opening her mouth, Tereka was about to say no, don't kill them, she'd give herself up. But Relio growled.

"Don't do it, girly," he said.

She looked at Naco. His gaze defiant, he shook his head. She shoved a hand into her pocket and gripped her amulets.

Fight. Words of truth will break her teeth.

Her heart beating like a war drum in her ears, Tereka hoped she wasn't condemning them all to death. She faced Damira. "No. You are the one who will surrender."

61

Leading his ragtag army, Kaberco rounded a bend in the rutted road. He tightened his grip on the reins, slowing his horse's gait. For some time, he'd been able to see the flickering lights of torches between the bare trees. The enemy was near.

He hadn't realized how close. A few hundred yards in front of him, lines of mounted soldiers blocked the road. Even in the dusky light, he could observe the bows in their hands, arrows nocked on taut bowstrings.

Heart pounding, Kaberco advanced enough for his entire force to reach the straight section of the road. A glance over his shoulder told him that all fifteen rows were in place.

His mouth went dry. Fifteen rows of foot soldiers and archers against countless lines of mounted bowmen. "Whoa." He pulled on the reins, stopping his horse. The forces behind him halted, the tramp of their footsteps fading.

Clenching his jaw, he considered his options. His sword would be useless in the face of mounted archers. And his foot soldiers? All the enemy would need to do was gallop into Kaberco's lines and trample them underfoot. The battle would be over in less than half an hour.

Motionless, he waited. A tug on his stirrup drew his attention. Tarkio stood next to him, eyebrows drawn together. "Kaberco, what are your orders for the archers?"

"Let's wait. If those riders move a single step, then the archers need to start shooting. Down as many horses in the front as they can to slow the rest."

Tarkio nodded and slipped into the shadows.

Kaberco forced himself to sit tall in the saddle, to appear proud and unconcerned despite the overwhelming army gathered against him. He had one hundred villagers, counting traders. Two hundred Riskers. A few stalks of rye standing against a forest of oaks.

An explosion shook the ground and illuminated the road for a trio of heartbeats. His horse reared and he struggled to keep his seat, gripping desperately with his knees. When the animal shied and tried to turn, Kaberco pulled hard on the reins. The horse quieted, and he patted its neck, murmuring. Reassured the animal wouldn't bolt, he turned his head, assessing his loss. Officers on his left flank were shouting and a few men were screaming.

He twisted in the saddle, yelling to the commander of his left flank. "Boreje! Report!"

The man ran to him, a streak of blood dripping into his mud-brown eyes. "They shot one arrow. Only one. Ten of our men are gone. Blown to bits."

With one arrow, ten men were dead. Kaberco gulped. Thirty arrows could destroy his whole army.

Swallowing the bile in his mouth, he tried to ignore the cramping of his bowels. Had this venture been nothing more than a fool's errand? Maybe he should surrender now, before more died needlessly.

To the south, the Emperor's riders were motionless other than the occasional stamp of a horse's hoof or toss of a mane. Maybe the arrow was meant to be a message, a prelude to whatever ultimatum the Emperor would issue.

His hopes were all pinned on a young girl. Tereka. He swallowed hard, thinking of her mother, the spark that had set so many events in motion. Tereka had fanned the flame. And now, if she succeeded, her revolution would flood the country like a forest fire sweeps through dry brush. Tlefas would never be the same.

And if she failed? They'd all die.

He had no choice. He would give Tereka a little more time. How long he could hold out, he didn't know.

BLOOD PULSING IN HER EARS, Tereka fingered the amulets in her pocket, desperately wishing for their help, their strength. Or at least the courage to face the end.

Damira laughed. "You come against me with a bow and arrow? Or do you think your pathetic dragonflies can match my scorpions? What power do they have? None."

Tereka lifted her chin. "It doesn't take much to kill and destroy. The real challenge is healing. And building. What power do you possess to do those things? None that I see."

Her amulets vibrated, a sure sign of their approval. Perhaps this battle needed to be fought with words as much as magic power.

She groped for the right phrase, the right language to persuade Damira to stop the killing. "You tell people they will be safe. But from what? From rules? From menacing enemies? You are the most horrible threat of all."

"You have no idea what you're saying." Damira's face contorted into a sneer. "I saved my people from the horrors of the Endless War and brought a lasting peace. What have you ever done?"

Tereka flinched. That was a good question. What had she ever accomplished? "I sought to tell the truth, the truth that would set us all free."

"Bah. What is truth? It's what the powerful say it is. Nothing more."

"Surely, you don't believe that," Tereka said. "Stopping the Endless War was a noble goal. But why did you bring war to us? What had we ever done to you?"

Damira scowled. "You denied me aid when I needed it. Then you planned to invade our lands. We had to act. I was prepared to be merciful, but not to users of the foul dragonflies."

Tereka grabbed the hair on the back of her head and tugged. Who denied Damira aid? Tlefas was planning to invade? What was the Empress talking about?

She pointed a finger at Tereka, a blackened, shriveled finger that looked as if it had been burned. "You have caused me much pain, Tereka Sabidur. And for that, I will end you. No mercy for one such as you, a dragonfly wielder. Piece by piece, I will end you, laughing while you beg for death."

A second explosion shook the ground. With a shudder, Tereka wondered how much of Kaberco's army remained standing. She studied Damira's face, forcing herself not to let terror defeat her. Was the Empress's twisted expression due to pain? Or something else?

Hobbling to stand behind Naco, Damira said. "I can see you love him. What would you do to save him?" She seized his hair and yanked his head back.

Her knees shaking, Tereka fought the urge to vomit. "I would venture much to save those I love, rescue the innocent, and follow the sky-god."

She didn't know what she'd been expecting, but a belly laugh from the Empress wasn't it. Damira limped a few steps toward Tereka, chortling. "Sky-god? Bah. You speak empty words about a dead god. But then, I suppose one who believes she is the fulfillment of a myth will believe anything." She sneered. "And I suppose you think your words will fight your battle for you?"

"Words are far better weapons than your torture and terror." Tereka didn't know where the sentiments flowing through her dry mouth had come from, but she knew she had to keep speaking. "You have listened to the lies of your scorpions. Put down your amulets. You can be free of them."

Damira screamed, her agony and rage cutting through the cold air like an arrow seeking a target. She sent a bolt of red light at Naco. He toppled over and lay on the ground, twitching. The man guarding him leaped back. The blade of his sword trembled in his hands.

Tereka's stomach lurched and tears pricked her eyes. She took a step toward Naco. Her breath came in gasps and when Damira spoke, she could barely hear the words.

"Know this, pretender to be the Desired One. You carry dragonflies. That makes you my enemy. Forever. Instead of a quick end, I will make sure yours is slow and painful. Bone by shattered bone."

"I'm the pretender?" Tereka blinked hard. "You can't be the Desired One. You're not the child of a villager and a Risker."

"The Vernians of our land had a prophecy of the Desired One long before anyone ever settled here," Damira said.

From the way the Empress sneered, Tereka was sure Damira meant to weaken her confidence in the sky-god. She shrugged off her taunt. "Which means that long ago the sky-god knew this would happen. And that the Desired One would bring a new order to a suffering land."

Damira pointed her bow at Tereka. "I brought the new order without any help from that myth." She hurled the bow to the ground. "Enough. I didn't come to fight you with words or weapons." With a sharp jerk, she broke the chain around her neck and grasped her scorpion amulets in her hand. "Now it's time to end this." She raised her hand, the amulets glowing fiery red.

"Snakes' teeth, Dami! What are you doing?" Emperor

Shagonar raced out of the darkness and grabbed his wife's arm.

The Empress glared at him, their gazes locked as if they could burn each other with their eyes. Tereka stared, unable to turn away, to move, to breathe.

Suddenly, Tirk jumped to his feet and wrestled the sword from the soldier behind him. He held it over his head and ran for Damira.

Four, five rapid steps, and Tirk was upon her. He yelled and swung the sword. Shagonar shoved Damira and spun. The sword sliced through his neck. Blood spurted like a fountain and he crumpled to the ground, his head resting beside his limp body.

The Emperor was dead.

62

The Empress Damira gaped as Shagonar crumbled to the ground. Her eyes flared. Emptiness consumed her. He couldn't be gone. The joy of her life. Her one constant supporter. She'd never see that flirtatious grin or the gleam of mischief in his eyes. He was gone.

The pain seared her heart, more excruciating than anything the amulets had ever inflicted. The air rippled, black streaks blurring her vision. She forced herself to draw a breath. Heat rose within her, a heat that threatened to ignite her very soul.

Damira screamed, her wail of loss and wretched misery and fury piercing the air like a spear. "No!" Shagonar's quick death denied her any time for a final kiss, a final declaration of love. The one who'd deprived her must pay. She held out both hands and blasted Tirk with red light. His body flew into the air and landed at Tereka's feet with a thud. The girl screamed and jumped back.

Kill her.

This time she didn't want to fight her amulets. She was in full agreement with their demands. Gladly, she'd let the amulets have their way and inflict as much pain as possible. She would torture the girl with the cobalt blue eyes for as long as she survived.

Kill her.

Oh, yes. She let the red power stream above her head. It crackled like bolts of lightning. She smirked as everyone around her—Tereka, guards, and prisoners—cowered.

She raked her eyes over Tereka's tear-stained face. "By the time I'm done with you, you'll wish for your brother's fate." She held out her hand out. In a heartbeat, Tirk's body had turned to mist.

Damira's grin widened as she surveyed Tereka's hunched shoulders and contorted face. *Good. Now you know what it feels like. And you'll feel much more.*

Syzyan ran to Damira. "What—" His mouth sagged open. "Shag? No. It can't be."

"He's dead," Damira growled. She raised her hand and the red lightning crackled.

"Dami, stop." Syzyan tugged her arm. "Shag wouldn't have wanted this."

Kill him.

This was all Syzyan's fault. Had he not fought her, Shag-onar would still be alive. She raised her hand, intending to blast him with her red light. Then she glimpsed the horror in his eyes. He didn't see her as his much-loved sister, but as a monster out of control, something to be feared.

Kill them.

The pain in her head was intense and growing. Her skull was about to crack open as if a blacksmith had struck it with his hammer. Someone had to die or she wouldn't be able to bear it. Syzyan was shouting words she couldn't, wouldn't comprehend.

She held her hand aloft, her three amulets dangling from her fist. Now she'd end them all.

TEARS ROLLED down Tereka's face. Tirk's blackened head and the gaping hole in his abdomen gave her no way to deny the truth—he was dead. A sob burst from her mouth. A few heartbeats later, the Empress misted him. The strength ebbed from Tereka's limbs and her knees wobbled.

As from a distance, she heard Relio yelling. "Girly! Do something!" A string of curses followed, ending in a choked gurgle. Relio dropped to his knees. He clutched his throat and his face turned purple.

Alikse charged the empress. With another flick of her hand, he collapsed next to Relio, his face crimson and his eyes bugging out as he clawed at whatever invisible cord tightened around his throat.

"Don't worry," Damira said, smirking at Tereka. "I won't let them die right away."

The Empress tossed her head and stalked toward Sebezh and Meluz, still kneeling with their hands behind their heads. The soldiers behind them backed away as she approached.

In a few heartbeats, the Empress's power would strangle Relio and Alikse to death. How could she stop her without killing her? Swallowing the bitter taste of terror, Tereka pulled three arrows from her quiver. With a fluid motion, she nocked the first and raised the bow.

Sky-god, please.

She released the arrow.

The bolt struck Damira's right heel. She cursed and turned, her mouth twisted into a scowl. The amulets in her hand glowed scarlet, as if they were blood illuminated from within.

Tereka nocked a second arrow. Released it.

The shot went cleanly through Damira's hand. The Empress yelped and dropped her amulets.

Flinging her bow to the ground, Tereka sprinted toward

the gleaming amulets. She scooped up the nearest two. They were burning hot and stung her hand.

A sense of despair washed over her. Screaming voices commanded her to sink to her knees and yield to Damira. Her mind seethed with warped, misty visions of Naco pulled limb from limb, the Empress swinging his arm like a club, smashing Relio's head like a grape.

Jutting her chin in the air, Tereka stiffened her wobbling knees. "No!" she yelled. With trembling fingers, she pulled her amulets from her pocket. Taking a deep breath, she clasped her hands, holding the dragonflies and scorpions together.

For a moment, everything went still, as if the entire camp —soldiers, horses, and the cold breezes of the evening—held their breath. A beam of purple light flashed from the sky.

Smoke rose from the scorpions. Tereka hurled them away while clutching the dragonflies in her stinging fingers. The scorpions lay in the dust, their red and black stones dulled to slate gray.

Damira wailed like a wounded beast. She staggered toward the third amulet.

Tereka dove for it, snatching it from Damira's grasp. Damira flailed her arms, struck Tereka's face, and scratched her forearm.

Stinging pain ran up the arm. Tereka shoved the Empress, knocking her to her knees.

The commanding voices shrieked obscenities in Tereka's head. They showed her a world of drab darkness, where joy and light and love were only taunting memories. And instead of death, the voices promised her an eternity of excruciating torture. She cowered and a whimper escaped her throat.

Grabbing Tereka's legs, Damira dug her fingernails into the flesh. Tereka kicked her, then lost her balance when the Empress let go, and toppled to the ground. Damira flung herself on Tereka, clawing at the hand that held the final scorpion.

The voices growled in Tereka's head, their thundering commands threatening to split her skull.

The sky-god has abandoned you. We are all there is.

The blood whooshed in Tereka's ears and black streaks rippled in the air. Her grip on the scorpion loosened.

Submit. Or die.

Damira seized her wrist and twisted it.

The pain wrested Tereka's attention away from the voices. Tereka didn't know much about the scorpions, but she was sure of one thing. They were liars. She had to destroy the last scorpion before it killed her.

Another voice was yelling, begging Damira to stop. "Please, Dami!" Was that the Jianjun?

The Empress flung a stone at Syzyan. He yelped and went silent. She swung her arm back and hit Tereka in the face.

Tereka gasped. She twisted and put her foot on Damira's head, shoving the Empress away. With a sob, she brought the hand that held her dragonflies against the scorpion. A flash of purple light lit Damira's contorted face and wide, panicked eyes. The light intensified and spread like a wave of purple fire flooding over the camp, the battlefield and beyond, lighting up the entire sky. When it faded, Tereka flung the third amulet to lie in the dust with the others.

An unearthly howl cut the air, a sound like a pack of tormented warboars. Red and black mist rose from the ashes of the scorpion amulets. A heartbeat later it vanished with the breeze.

Panting, Tereka watched the scorpion amulets crumble into little mounds of sooty ash as if they'd been consumed by a raging inferno. The only sound was her own ragged breaths, sucking air into her lungs. Tereka tottered to her feet.

A hand on her back steadied her. "Girly?" Relio's voice rasped as if he'd been screaming for hours.

Had she ever hated Relio? Feared him? Never again. While he'd been horrible as commander of a prison brigade, the past few months had changed him. He and Alikse were the only two who'd stuck with her when all the others were scattered or dead. Including Naco.

Sobs competed with her jagged breaths. Naco was gone. Anguish mixed with rage. For a heartbeat, she understood Damira's outburst after the Emperor's death. A dark hole opened in her soul, an empty place that would never be filled, now that Naco was no more.

"Come on, girly. Finish the job."

She took a step and winced, the wounds left by Damira's fingernails stinging and burning. "I can't."

Alikse slid a hand under her arm. "You can. I'll help you."

He supported her as she stumbled to Damira, who lay huddled on the ground, motionless. Syzyan knelt beside her, clutching one of her hands to his heart.

Tereka stared. What had happened to Damira? Her confident beauty had withered like fallen fruit under a summer sun. The Empress had become a twisted, burnt shell, shriveling into itself.

"Syz." Tereka could barely hear the word Damira whispered before her body collapsed in a puff of dust.

Syzyan let out a sob. He slapped his hands on his knees, his chest heaving with his labored breathing. He rubbed his eyes, leaving a smudge of black where the ashes of his sister mixed with his tears and sweat.

Tereka turned to Relio, whose wide eyes mirrored her own. It was hard to believe, but the Empress was dead. Defeated.

A noise called her attention to Syzyan, now standing. He squared his shoulders. Tereka looked into his eyes, clutching her amulets. Her heart raced as she waited for his words.

"Your Loftiness, my Emperor and his Empress are dead. As Supreme Jianjun of his armies, I offer peace." His throat bobbed. "We will help you rebuild. May you show us mercy." He laid his right hand on his heart and bowed his head.

She sagged against Relio. Was it really over?

"I don't think we should trust him, girly. Maybe end him as well?"

Tereka didn't want any more killing. In her few dealings with him, Syzyan had always seemed like the voice of reason.

A messenger darted up to him. "Jianjun, what are we to do? All of our amulets have turned to dust."

Syzyan looked the man in the eye. "Our scorpions were defeated by more powerful amulets. Tell my jianjuns to lay down their arms. Send an envoy to Kaberco, telling him we would like to negotiate a truce, and are currently discussing terms with Tereka Sabidur. Invite him to join us, or, if he would prefer, send an emissary."

Gaping at the jianjun, Tereka realized she had no idea what terms she wanted. Blinking hard, she struggled to comprehend that she had survived her encounter with Damira and whatever unholy power fueled her scorpions. Her eyes pricked. Tirk and Naco hadn't made it. Her knees wobbled and she pressed a hand to her mouth. *Naco. No. He can't be gone.* There was no joy in this victory if Naco wasn't there to share it with her. "Um, Relio, can you and Kaberco start without me?" She turned to the general. "Jianjun—"

He cut her off. "Please. Loftiness. I am Jianjun of a defeated army and am no longer worthy of the title. Call me Syzyan."

"Please. Do not call me Loftiness." She looked in his grief-filled eyes and spoke gently. "I don't blame you for your sister's actions and the evil she did while possessed by those scorpions. You did what you could to stop her." She glanced at Relio and Alikse. "You ask for mercy. I grant it freely. I don't know what Kaberco will say."

Without waiting for an answer, she staggered to the damp spot that was all that was left of Tirk, unable to contain her tears any longer. He'd been faithful to the end, her twin who wasn't her twin.

Sebezh and Meluz were still seated on the ground, their shoulders slumped and their jaws slack. Neither seemed to be able to focus their eyes on anything. For once, Sebezh's arrogance seemed to have abandoned him.

A few feet away, Naco's body lay still and lifeless.

63

A lump rose in Tereka's throat. At least Naco hadn't been misted.

With a sob, Tereka ran to him and flung herself to her knees. "Naco." A trickle of blood ran out of the corner of his mouth. One leg was bent at an odd angle above his knee. His tunic was soaked with blood.

"What are you waiting for, girly? Get to work."

She looked over her shoulder. Relio had followed her. "What do you mean?"

"He's not dead. Not yet, anyway."

Her eyes widened. Then she saw the faint movement of his chest. Naco was breathing, slowly and shallowly, as if each breath would be his last. Gently, she picked up his hand. His fingers still held a trace of warmth.

Holding her breath, she laid one amulet on his forehead and gripped the other two, one in each hand. "Oh, sky-god. Please."

A gentle vibration answered her plea. She passed the amulets over Naco's injuries. His chest rose. "Quick, help me with his leg," she said.

At Tereka's direction, Alikse and Relio straightened Naco's

broken leg. With a snap, it pulled itself back together. After a gentle flash of purple light, Naco's breathing strengthened. His eyelids fluttered and opened.

His tawny eyes met Tereka's. "Where's the Empress? Why aren't you fighting?"

She stared, then chuckled. "We won." Clutching her amulets, she laid her head on his chest and sobbed. His hand gently stroked her hair.

Dimly, she heard Relio's voice. "Girly, Syzyan, Alikse, and I will meet Kaberco in the Emperor's tent. We'll take Sebezh and the other one with us."

A moment later, Naco's arms wrapped around her. "I always believed in you."

Pulling back, she shoved the amulets into her pocket. "You mean, about the Desired One?"

He struggled to sit up. She knelt before him, peering into his face.

"Yes," he said. "Even when you didn't believe, when you resisted. And I understood. You wanted to choose your own life. Accepting your destiny as the Desired One was like being assigned a profession or marriage against your will."

Had she heard that right? The shouts of officers and the tramping of soldiers and their horses made it hard to hear. "That was exactly it," she said. "How did you know?"

"I guess because I felt the same way about copper mining." He gave her a wry smile.

She clutched him to her and laughed. "I was never fond of mining, either."

"Tereka." His voice was serious. "Whatever you do, I'm with you. Always."

"That's what you were trying to tell me when I found you with the Empress."

He nodded.

"But why didn't you ever say anything before? Like all winter?"

"What, that I love you?"

For a heartbeat, she'd thought he was going to deny it. Now she could barely believe he'd uttered the words out loud.

"How could I?" he said, his gaze earnest. "To start with, I was a penniless, escaped prisoner. I only had a place to live because your family took us in."

"That was hardly your fault."

"No, but that's who I am. And you are the Desired One. How could I interfere with your destiny? I had to wait until you fulfilled the prophecy, or at least most of it. And now you have."

"I don't see how you loving me would have interfered."

"Maybe it wouldn't have," he said. "I had no way of knowing. Besides, if you and I had taken up together, that would have left Savinnia at Relio's mercy. Or Sebezh's. I couldn't do that to her." He pulled in a shaky breath. "She could barely sleep as it was, even when I slept outside your room. Don't think I don't know how often one or both of you woke up screaming from nightmares, shouting about the prison." He shook his head. "Torn between my love for you and my duty to my sister, I didn't know what to do. It was better for all of us to not speak about it."

She pursed her lips. Something about his reasoning didn't make sense.

He ran a finger gently down her cheek. "Up on that mountain, under the stars and the light of two moons, what would have happened had I spoken?"

Her face flushed under his touch. Somehow, she understood him. Not that she agreed entirely, but... "Instead, you made me doubt myself."

"No, you already doubted." He stroked her hair. "But I'll make it up to you."

"How?"

"Will you let me show you? Every day, for the rest of our lives?"

Her breath caught. "Naco, do you mean…"

"Why do you think I insisted on being the Empress's hostage? Had you stayed, she would have killed you. I didn't want to live if you perished." His arms tightened around her and his voice shook. "I didn't dare hope we'd both survive."

She snorted. "We have a way of doing that, don't we?"

"So?"

"Are you sure?" She frowned. "I'm the Desired One, as you say. I can't choose my life, my direction. Where will I live? What will I do? What will you do?"

"We can figure all that out later. The important thing is that you know I love you." He laced his fingers into her hair, cupping the back of her head in his hand. "Whatever your calling, wherever it takes you, I'll be there with you. Always." His eyes searched hers. "If you'll have me."

She looked down, unable to meet the intensity of his gaze. A gentle warmth filled her, a sense of well-being she'd rarely felt. "I love you, too."

"No buts?"

"None." She tipped her head back and snickered. "Who would have thought I'd meet the love of my life in prison?"

"Or that I'd lose my heart to an outlaw?" He leaned closer to her. "But I don't want to talk anymore." Before she could say another word, he pressed his lips to hers.

Tingling warmth raced through her body down to her toes. She tightened her arms around his broad shoulders, leaning into his kiss. There was nothing, no one, but her and Naco.

A horse's whinny brought her back to reality. She broke the kiss and rested her forehead against his. "Naco, I could stay here with you all night, but—"

"You have a peace to negotiate." He climbed to his feet, hissing softly.

"Your leg!"

"It's healed, but a few of the burns still hurt." He rubbed his chest. "Please don't worry. The pain is fading."

Hand in hand, they walked to the Emperor's tent. As they stepped inside, a tall, brown-skinned man stood up. When Tereka recognized Da's strong chin and nose in the torchlight, she ran to him and flung herself into his embrace.

He held her close, her sobs muffled against his shoulder.

"I wish I didn't have to tell you this, Da. Tirk is gone."

His arms tightened around her. "I know." His voice cracked and his body shook.

Tereka didn't know how long they stood holding each other. When the first grief had passed, she pulled back. Da's stricken eyes met hers. She gulped back a sob and jerked her chin toward Meluz. "Do you know he came with Juquila and Groa?"

"Yes, he told me." He turned to Meluz. "Where are they?"

His eyes welling, Meluz shuddered. "The Empress misted them."

"I am so very sorry," Da said.

How sorry was he? Tereka wondered. Juquila had been his enemy for decades. Groa had tossed him out like so much trash. But he'd had two sons with her. That had to count for something.

"Meluz," Da asked, "Where is my son?"

"Aito is with my sisters. In Trofmose."

Da's tight face relaxed. "Then he should be fine, for now." He rubbed his chin. "So, Tereka, what do you want us to do?"

"Me?"

"You're the Desired One. You ended the old order. It's up to you to establish the new one."

64

Tereka wasn't sure about many things, but one fact stood out. Kaberco was an efficient leader. In less than an hour, he organized brigades that recorded the names of the dead, collected their armor and weapons, and cremated the remains.

Meanwhile, Jianjun Syzyan set a few of his brigades to rebuilding the yurts that had been dismantled before the battle began and ensured there was room in the healing yurts for Kaberco's wounded. He also commanded that yurts be built for Kaberco's army on the north side of the camp. With a pained expression on his face, he had Shagonar's remains taken to the yurt the emperor had shared with Damira.

Once the two armies were busy tending their wounded, preparing meals, and arranging accommodations for the night, Syzyan joined Kaberco and Tereka in what had been the Emperor's command tent.

"Please, sit." Kaberco gestured to a cushion near the brazier, where he and Tereka warmed their hands over the flames. "Let's make this quick before it gets even colder." He shivered under his black cloak.

Syzyan sank onto a cushion, the lines around his eyes

more pronounced than usual. "Thank you for not putting me in chains."

"I couldn't do that," Tereka said.

"You would have every right. I led an invasion of your land."

"Because your sister was driven by the scorpions."

He nodded. "Yes. They prompted her to concoct a lie that you were about to invade. That was enough for us to act to forestall you. When I learned the truth, it became unbearable. I wanted a military victory but not because we attacked you based on a falsehood. I'll live with the shame that I betrayed my own sister for the rest of my days."

"How did you do that?" Kaberco asked.

"I had Tirk send a warning to Tereka. Didn't you receive it?"

Kaberco and Tereka exchanged wry smiles. He'd nearly killed her when he received the message. But the confrontation it prompted had brought about their alliance. Tereka extended a hand to Syzyan. "Thank you. You have no idea how that completely changed our minds about what to do."

Gently squeezing her hand, he said, "I should have done more, and sooner."

"That doesn't matter now," Kaberco said. "Let's get to it, shall we? First, when will your forces leave Anbodu?"

With that, the negotiations began. Tereka's mouth went dry every time Kaberco or Syzyan deferred to her. Surely, they knew she couldn't lead as effectively as either of them. Thankfully, they knew the major points to include, such as how long the agreement would hold and under what circumstances it could be broken. She couldn't imagine any of them would ever want to resume the war but didn't argue the point. In less than half an hour, the three of them had agreed on a temporary truce.

Syzyan dispatched a pair of messengers to his army camped outside of Anbodu. They were to extract their forces from the city and await the arrival of the Desired One in two days. Then a conference would be held to settle on terms for a lasting peace.

Tereka pursed her lips as Syzyan dictated his message to the scribe. Now, there was no escape—she had to claim her role as the Desired One. Her stomach writhed. She didn't want to rule Tlefas. Wrapping her arms around herself, she considered all the country had been through and how its citizens deserved a fair and just ruler. She could give them that much. Whether she'd be efficient, decisive, and strong enough to maintain order was another question.

At least she didn't have to think about wielding power right away. Instead, she spent the rest of the early evening hours healing wounded men with her amulets.

When she'd done all she could, she sought out her friends. She found Naco, along with Relio, Alikse, Sebezh, and Meluz in Farnaz's yurt. Except for Farnaz, who was seated on a cushion near the brazier, they'd all fallen asleep.

Sitting next to Farnaz, Tereka studied his downturned face for a long moment. "I'm sorry."

He stared at her, his dark eyes bleak. "I am too. About my aunt and uncle, and your brother."

The mention of Tirk's death brought tears to Tereka's eyes. She blinked them away. "How is your father?"

"I don't know. He's doing what he always does, burying himself in the concerns of his army. He'll be at it all night. That's why he told me to sleep here, so he wouldn't keep me awake."

So much pain for everyone. She put a hand on his arm. "You might want to check on him later. Make sure he's eaten."

Farnaz sighed. "He's lost so much. His sister and my uncle were his only family for years." His bleak expression tore at Tereka's heart.

Before she could think of words to comfort him, Farnaz

said, "My father assigned the yurt next to this one for you and your da, and had food sent for you."

"Thank you." Feeling the weariness of the day, she took her leave. She blew a kiss at the slumbering Naco and waved a hand at the others, none of whom stirred as she left the yurt.

While she'd been inside, guards had been posted at the yurt's entrance. When they saw her, they put two fingers of their right hands to their temples, then lowered their arms and held them horizontally across their chests and bowed their heads. "Loftiness," they murmured in unison.

Surprised, she nearly asked them who they were talking to. *Oh, they're calling me Loftiness.*

She nodded to them and walked to the next yurt. The guards greeted her with the same salute and "Loftiness." Suppressing her irritation, she dipped her chin. This adulation or whatever it was couldn't go on. She opened the door to the yurt and froze, one foot on the threshold.

Instead of Da, Syzyan was inside. He knelt by the brazier, cradling the Empress's rabbit in his arms. A tear trickled down his tanned cheek and dripped onto the animal's black fur, where it glinted like a diamond in the firelight. She looked away, unable to witness his grief and anguish. Silently, she backed out of the yurt and gently closed the door.

"Loftiness?" one of the guards asked.

"I'm afraid I've come to the wrong yurt. I was looking for my father."

"Yes, Loftiness." The guard pointed to a nearby yurt. "He is there."

With a muttered, "Thank you," she darted for the yurt. What she wanted more than anything was to have some time away from all the people and acclaim and just be with Da.

A few heartbeats later, she was in his arms, sobbing on his shoulder.

"I know." He murmured the words over and over. "I know."

She stepped back, wiping the tears from her face. "Tirk braved torture for me, even to the end. And I couldn't save him."

Da pressed a hand to his mouth. Deep wrinkles formed around his eyes as he squeezed them shut. "I was so angry at him for what he did to you. He lost his way, and I lost my son." He dropped onto a cushion by the brazier. "He found his way back and then I lost him again."

Tereka sat next to him and leaned her head on his chest. Da draped an arm around her and they sat without speaking for a long time, the only sound the crackling of the flames. They began to share memories of Tirk, the boy he'd been, the confused youth he became, and the man he grew into.

Neither had much appetite for the food servants had left. Instead, they sipped tea and cried together over Tirk and even a little over Juquila and Groa. No one, they agreed, deserved to be misted.

They talked late into the night, mostly about Tereka's future and her plans for Tlefas. And whether or not the people would accept or rebel against her rule.

Even when she laid herself to sleep, worries about ruling continued to plague her. Would peace be possible between the Riskers and the villagers, after centuries of mistrust and hatred? And with the Razdelians, after the unprovoked invasion? Would the people of Tlefas accept as a ruler a girl of mixed blood? If they protested, her reign could be over before it started.

Clutching the bag that contained her amulets, she murmured, "What do I do?"

A thought sprang to her mind, and she sat up. *That just might work.* Feeling a weight lift from her shoulders, she lay back down. *I'll talk to Da in the morning.* She turned to lie on her side and tucked a hand under her cheek. If the sky-god gave her the idea, Da would surely go along with it. But would anyone else?

65

Tereka's breath made puffs of steam in the chilly morning air. The weak autumn sun had barely risen as she rode, following the herald who announced her as the Desired One.

Her feelings chased each other like fallen leaves under a capricious breeze. At times, triumph made her want to sing or shout, anything to express her elation that the scorpion amulets had been destroyed and the Razdelians had agreed to peace. That no one would ever be tortured or misted again. And that she was no longer an outlaw with a price on her head.

Then joy danced with the exultation within her, a joy that made her heart race and warmth shoot down to her toes, the joy of the promised future with Naco.

After a handful of glorious moments, her mood would shift, and she'd ache for Tirk. And for Da, who'd lost his oldest son. From deep inside, a flicker of the scared, abused child she'd been rose within her. She wasn't worthy of all the acclaim, Da's approval, or Naco's love. She was a nameless orphan, a despised stepchild. A heartbeat or two later, her natural courage would assert itself and her stomach would flutter as she anticipated the changes that she'd bring to Tlefas for the good of all the people.

All these conflicting emotions made the tension grip her head like a too-tight helmet. She held her chin up with great effort. Her people needed to see a strong, confident leader, no matter what she felt inside.

Despite the doubts that caused her hands to sweat, she had to appear assured and capable. Kaberco had told her they would meet with the konament of Anbodu, where she would establish her reign. She'd have to convince them to accept her. The thought of ruling made her stomach heave and her skin crawl.

A day and a half later, she spotted the spires of Anbodu piercing the air like spears. Tereka's heart stuttered as they approached the twisted, ruined gates of the capital. Her moment was approaching far too quickly.

Several arbatus of Razdelian soldiers were hard at work, sorting out the rubble, separating the stones into piles, and pulling out the metal. Syzyan, it seemed, was making good on his pledge to help repair the damage to the city.

When the herald reached the gates, he called, "Welcome the Desired One!"

He was answered by a rousing cheer. Even though Kaberco had told her his plans for her entry into the capital, how he and Syzyan had sent a brigade or two of men to get the cheering started, her stomach fluttered and her skin tingled. She wasn't sure how she felt about all the adulation.

Setting her mouth into a smile, Tereka stiffened her spine and sat tall in the saddle. She sucked in a deep breath and urged her horse to follow the herald. As she rode, she waved at the crowds who lined the streets. Kaberco and Syzyan rode in her wake.

Her chest tightened as she surveyed the city. If she wanted more evidence of the Prime Konamei's corruption, she need look no further. The streets were paved with smooth stones, with no gaps or uneven places. No dirt lanes littered with puddles and potholes like in the provincial towns. The houses of Anbodu weren't the wood shacks of the villages. Instead, they were snug stone structures that appeared well kept rather than neglected and run down. Every time she'd traded in Anbodu, the disparity had rankled. The people in the capital lived far better than the rest of the country. She pressed her lips together. That would have to change.

As they approached the Prime Konamei's residence, the streets widened. Trees lined the sides of the roads as if standing guard in front of houses. Instead of one-story dwellings, many rose two or three stories high, the upper windows arched, with carved stone surrounding the glass. Tereka shook her head. In all of Trofmose, only Kaberco had glass windows. Here it seemed just about everyone did, even those who dwelled in tiny cottages.

Still following the herald, she rode through an archway into the courtyard of the Prime Konamei's castle. She tipped her head back, surveying the high towers that flanked the square residence. What a farce, the idea that everyone in Tlefas was to live on the same level to ensure fairness. How many had suffered for it, she wondered.

She pushed her shoulders back and kept a tight smile fixed on her face. A row of five gray-clad people stood near the massive arched doorway to the house. The two women wore gray turbans. Each of the five wore a chain draped over their shoulders, each a different material: gold, silver, bronze, wood, and wool. They were the Konament of Anbodu.

Tereka slid from her horse and handed the reins to a waiting groom. Kaberco and Syzyan joined her. "Shall we?" Kaberco asked.

The tips of her fingers turned to ice. Kaberco had insisted that she lead. It had been easy to agree when they were in a yurt far away. Now, she was having a hard time keeping her knees from shaking.

With a firm nod to Kaberco, she strode to the Konament members. "I am Tereka Sabidur, the Desired One. Whom do I have the pleasure of meeting?" Her voice was steady and confident, and she hoped none of her nervousness was obvious.

The konameis introduced themselves. "If you please," said the ephor, a gaunt man with a pale, freckled face and deep-set eyes. He gave Tereka a smile she assumed was meant to be ingratiating but struck her as insincere. "We have the large meeting room ready."

"Lead on," Tereka said. Out of the corner of her eye, she caught an approving nod from Kaberco.

The ephor ushered them into the castle. Stone floors in the entry gave way to polished wood in a long room with high ceilings and tall glazed windows. Brightly colored tapestries depicting scenes from Tlefas' history covered the walls. A fire blazed in a massive fireplace big enough inside for even Kaberco to stand upright. Five banners hung over the fire-place, each representing one of the five offices of the kona-ment. The elaborately carved mantle held jeweled vases full of fresh flowers.

Surveying the room, Tereka could not help but frown. She'd known the Prime Konamei had lied that everyone lived the same. Her time in Kaberco's house had told her that much. But this was beyond a few extra comforts. Fresh flowers in winter in the middle of a war? That was flagrant opulence.

A silver teapot stood on a sideboard, delicate cups and saucers waiting to be filled. Platters of pasties, apples, and pears covered the rest of the sideboard. Tereka shook her head. If the Prime Konamei was able to have fresh fruit this late in the year, then the entire country should as well. One more wrong to be righted.

A wood table that could easily seat twenty dominated the center of the room. Tereka counted sixteen high-backed chairs set around it. Two ornate gold candelabras stood on its polished surface. Blank sheets of parchment, inkwells, and quills sat in front of every place. Tereka hesitated. She and Kaberco had discussed seating arrangements for the meeting. Still, it felt odd to take the Prime Konamei's seat at the head of the table.

With a firm step, she strode to the elaborately carved chair. A thick green cushion rested on its seat. Sheaves of grain, scales, leaves, and flowers were carved into its arms and back, the symbols of a safe, fair, and prosperous society. *If only the rulers had tried to live up to those ideals instead of hoarding power and wealth for themselves.* She perched on the chair, half expecting someone to tell her she had no right to sit there.

As agreed, Kaberco sat on her right and Syzyan on her left. The five Konament members took the seats to Kaberco's right, while on the opposite side, Farnaz and four of Syzyan's jianjuns sat to Syzyan's left. Da settled into a chair at the foot of the table, flanked by Naco and Relio. Ten of Kaberco's guardsmen stood at intervals around the room. Alikse positioned himself on a stool behind Tereka.

She'd balked at that idea, saying Alikse deserved to sit at the table. But Kaberco had insisted. They didn't know if the konameis of Anbodu would yield to her. Better to have someone close to her on guard. Just in case.

Letting her gaze travel around the table, she took in the odd assembly. The remnants of her band from prison. Kaberco and Syzyan, enemies turned allies. The konament members who she hoped would be friends rather than adversaries, partners rather than obstacles. And Da, who'd always been her strongest support even when she didn't realize it.

Only then did she notice the side table where two men and two women sat, all wearing the village gray. Two wore the black bands of the ephor's clerks around their shoulders, the others, the crimson bands of the questor's clerks. Their eyes were locked on her face, their pens poised ready to record her every word.

Her heart beat like a battle drum and she took a slow breath to fill her lungs. "We are here to make peace between ourselves and the people of Razdelia," she said.

"Peace?" The ephor scowled at Syzyan. "They invaded our land. For no reason. Attacked our city, killed our people, and destroyed our gates. Slaughtered our Prime Konamei. They should all be thrown into the salt mines." He curled his mouth in a sneer. "Along with the rest of you upstarts."

66

Tereka gave the ephor a cool gaze, clenching her teeth to keep the dismay from her face. Echoes of Juquila's taunts rang in her mind. *Nameless, useless spawn.* No. She would not let old insults define her.

Alikse stood and stepped closer to her. Relio was cursing under his breath while Kaberco's countenance was impassive.

She knew what he wanted her to do. With a lift of her chin, she raked her eyes over the konameis. "Upstarts? Have you forgotten who removed the threat to your lives, to your very existence?" Slowly, she allowed the corners of her mouth to twist upward. She snorted. "What would have happened if my band of upstarts hadn't rescued you?"

The questor, syndic, and adile slumped. The ludi pressed his lips together. Only the gray-haired ephor remained defiant.

"And yes," Tereka said, "The Razdelians did what you say. All at the instigation of a leader who was possessed by the scorpion amulets. You yourselves saw their destructive power. And now the Empress who wielded them is dead." She pointed at Syzyan. "Her brother did what he could to dissuade her. In the end, he provided us with valuable information."

"So, he's a traitor?" The ephor curled his lip.

"No," Syzyan said. "My sister, the Emperor, and I had a grand vision for Razdelia, a vision of a land free of the Endless War where our people could live in peace. We achieved our dream because Damira could wield the amulets with more power than any man." His voice cracked. "But I didn't understand they were rotting her from within until it was far too late. Out of love for my sister, I couldn't allow her to become a monster, a tyrant who ruled by terror. Which is why I helped your Desired One defeat her."

"That doesn't absolve you of your crimes." The ephor's voice grew harsh.

"Enough." Tereka spoke quietly but firmly. "What are you suggesting? That we put him on trial? For what? Being a danger to safety, fairness, and prosperity?" Her final words dripped with sarcasm.

Which the nodding ephor and questor completely missed. Relio's smirk and Naco's grin told her they had caught her meaning. She scoffed. "Also, you seem to have forgotten that Razdelia's army of fifty thousand disciplined soldiers is camped outside the city. What do you think they'll do if we execute their general?"

Tereka flicked her eyebrows up in a silent challenge and waited until the ephor dropped his gaze. "You raise fair points," she continued. "But that is why we're here. To negotiate terms. Not one of us wants any more war. This meeting is our best chance to forge a lasting peace."

She extended a hand to Kaberco, who passed her a sheaf of documents. "The ephor of Trofmose and I have discussed this."

"Why him?" asked the questor.

"Because he was the only one brave enough to resist hiding behind stone walls. The only one who didn't capitulate, even when cornered. The only one willing to stand with me in battle," Tereka said. "Now, Supreme Jianjun Syzyan Yurga has pledged peace with Tlefas. He and his people are interested in trade, not conquest."

She looked around the table at the frowning konameis. "I spent several weeks in their war camp. I saw how they live. They produce many things that will benefit Tlefas."

The syndic leaned forward. "Expanding trade could be useful to build prosperity."

The adile nodded. "Trade would be better than war."

Resting against the high wooden back of her chair, Tereka nodded. She'd done what she needed to do. They were talking. It might take weeks, but there would be a treaty. Best to allow them to say whatever they wanted now and worry about the details later.

She repressed a smile. Kaberco had told her that was how he dealt with his konameis. Let them wear themselves out, then press for the most critical points. And while they're wrangling among themselves, think about more important things. Her gaze roamed around the table as she wondered what her friends would do once the peace was made. The sound of her name jolted her back to the present.

The questor was speaking. "If you please, when would you like to be installed as Prime Konamei?"

Tereka sat up as if stuck with a pin. "About that."

All heads turned to her.

"I don't intend to be the Prime Konamei."

She nearly laughed at the wide eyes, slack jaws, and puzzled faces that surrounded her. Over the gasps and mutters, the ephor spoke. "You want to be queen?" He scowled. "Prime Konamei not good enough for you? A monarchy would certainly be a new order." He crossed his arms. "But I don't think it would be any safer or fairer than the old one."

"No. Not queen." She swallowed hard and fixed her eyes

on Da, seated at the foot of the table directly opposite her. "I don't intend to rule at all."

Several voices spoke at once. "But you must."

"You are the Desired One."

"Or are you?"

This last was from the smarmy ephor. Without taking her eyes from him, she slowly pulled out her dragonfly amulets and laid them on the table, the three Amulets of Power in the center flanked by the two smaller ones. "As you see, I bear the amulets spoken of in the prophecy. Some of you saw with your own eyes how I destroyed the scorpions." She blinked a few times, letting her words sink in. "Yes, the power of the sky-god flows through me. And yes, I am the Desired One of the prophecy. But—"

Tereka glanced at Naco, who smiled, and Da, who nodded. "The prophecy says the Desired One will bring a new order to the land. I have done that, or will have, once we sign the treaty." She scanned the faces of her listeners, some scowling, others thoughtful. "We will trade with our neighbors to the east. We will no longer call the Riskers barbarians but embrace them as relatives and friends. And we will end the rules that keep us cowering in fear. That is the new order I bring."

Widening her gaze to take in all five konameis, she contin-ued. "But I will not rule you. I will not make the mistake of Empress Damira, who wielded the power of the amulets and ruled alongside the Emperor. That was too much power for any one person."

Syzyan let out a deep sigh. "You are wise, far wiser than I was."

The ephor pointed at Syzyan. "What will happen to him in his own country? They should execute him."

"That, my friend, is a matter for my fellow Razdelians to decide," Syzyan said. "My jianjuns and I intend to take that question up with the Emperor's council when we return home." He turned to Tereka. "Speaking of which, we have a favor to ask of you. Perhaps it could be added to the treaty."

"What favor?" She eyed him warily.

"After you destroyed my sister's amulets, those among us who bore lesser amulets noticed they had turned to ash as if their existence was bound to the Three. As far as we can tell, no scorpion amulets remain."

"Which is a relief," put in Farnaz. "No one will ever be tempted to use them again."

"We need to be certain," Syzyan said. "Destroying the amulets won't rid the world of the power behind them."

He was right, Tereka thought. But conquering the evil power was a task for the sky-god. She shuddered. She certainly couldn't defeat those voices she'd heard shrieking death and despair.

Syzyan leaned toward Tereka. "If we discover some of the scorpions have survived, will you come to Razdelia and destroy them? Or allow us to send them to you for destruction?"

"Of course." She trained a steely gaze on the ephor. "Do you not agree that such a request means they truly want peace with us? Why else would they give up their most powerful weapons?"

Before he could respond, she held up a hand. "You didn't permit me to finish. Once there is a new order in the land, the prophecy will be fulfilled. My role will be over."

"But—"

She cut the ephor off. "The prophecy did not say the Desired One would rule over the new order, just bring it about." Sweat dampened her palms. She could trust only one person with the power. If he refused it, she might have to keep it.

And that, she thought, could be dangerous. If she'd learned anything from Damira, it was the peril of wielding amulets and holding political power. The temptation to assert her own will could trap her just as Damira had been ensnared.

Looking slowly around the room, she met the eyes of each person seated at the table. "The man I have in mind will be the fair, competent, and brave ruler Tlefas deserves. He has my full respect and trust."

Tereka dropped her eyes and used the next heartbeat to gather her courage before lifting her chin. "Kaberco Gougin," she said. "Will you become the Prime Konamei?"

His hazel eyes flared open, and he blinked several times. She hadn't thought it was possible to stun him into silence, but she'd done it.

"Me? But we've been enemies—"

"True, but everything you did was through blind allegiance to a corrupt regime. You always did what you believed was right and made every effort to be fair to all. Except, of course, in my case. And my mother's." She swallowed the lump in her throat that formed when she thought of Iskra. "Your actions these past few weeks have proved to me that you understand the wrongs you've committed. I believe you sincerely regret them. And Tlefas has no one else with your courage, your sense of fairness, and your strength."

As she looked into his eyes, his gaze wavered. A muscle twitched in his jaw. He nodded. "I accept."

"Will you all affirm Kaberco as my successor?" She surveyed the faces around the table. "The one who held the north, in the face of all odds? Who led the last stand against the invasion, and who can admit to having made a mistake?"

Relio snorted and there were a few chuckles.

Tereka's chest lightened, and she took an easy breath. "Since none of you opposed him, then it's settled. Kaberco Gougin is the new Prime Konamei." She folded her hands and rested them on the table. "Now, let's talk about terms."

67

The following afternoon, Tereka's eyelids drooped, and she stifled a yawn. She lounged in her conference room chair, the heat from the fireplace feeding her drowsiness.

The negotiations had dragged on all the previous day to the present, replete with droning speeches about tedious details of trade and travel that delayed the treaty process.

Boring as the endless speechifying was, it was better than angry outbursts or fistfights. Tereka had thought at least one of the members of Anbodu's konament would strike Kaberco for insisting that, other than certain temporary trade concessions, Razdelia would pay no reparations.

"Do you not understand that Razdclia could fragment now that its emperor is dead?" Kaberco fastened his fierce hazel eyes on the ephor. "It is to our benefit that the Razdelians stay united and at peace with each other. We want trade goods to come here, not refugees or mercenaries."

Somehow, between Syzyan's diplomacy and Kaberco's force of will, they agreed on terms that satisfied everyone, even the ephor, who tried to maintain every shred of his power as well as the repressive rules of Tlefas.

When the final item had been agreed on, Tereka leaned back with a deep sigh. She had achieved what she'd labored and sacrificed for. A new order. A new Prime Konamei who would rule justly.

She slumped in her seat, twisting her hands together, paying little attention as Kaberco closed the meeting. Her tongue stuck to the roof of her mouth. She should be feeling satisfied and complete. But something bothered her and she couldn't quite place it.

The new Prime Konamei ordered four scribes to write out twelve copies of the treaty. They huddled at a worktable, their quills busily penning the words as their chief dictated from her notes.

"While they work," Tereka said, "let's install you as Prime Konamei."

Kaberco nodded. "Tarkio, Syzyan, Farnaz, Naco, Relio and Alikse can serve as witnesses. Six should be enough."

He led the way to the room where they'd haggled out the treaty's terms and stood with his back to the massive fireplace, resting his hand on the pommel of his sword. The five konameis entered the chamber, the ephor bearing the jeweled Sword of Safety. The questor carried the Scales of Fairness in Justice and the syndic, the Scales of Fairness in Trade. The adile carried a loaf of bread to symbolize prosperity, while the ludi bore the Book of Doings and Decrees of the Prime Konameis. They placed the items on the table in front of Kaberco.

The ephor said, "We ask you to serve as the Prime Konamei, to ensure peace, safety, fairness, and prosperity."

"I will," Kaberco replied.

That was Tereka's cue. She stood on her tiptoes and draped the chain of the Prime Konamei over Kaberco's shoulders, a chain formed of links that alternated between gold, silver, bronze, wood, and wool.

For a few heartbeats, the only sound in the room was the

scratching of the scribe's pen as he recorded the event in the book of Doings and Decrees.

Tereka breathed a sigh of relief, the weight of the duty she'd carried leaving her as she exhaled. She'd fulfilled her role as Desired One and turned the burden of rule over to someone who could bear it well, although what he would do with his power remained to be seen.

The new Prime Konamei dismissed the konament of Anbodu, telling them to see to their own affairs. "I'll have you summoned when the scribes are ready for us to sign the treaty." He waited until the konameis left the room. "If you please, all of you, sit. I have some matters to discuss with you."

After they arranged themselves around the table, Kaberco rested his hands its polished surface. "Thank you for trusting me. I know you had reason not to." He rubbed his palms together. "But since you did entrust me with this position, I ask you. What will you do for the peace and safety of Tlefas?"

Relio gasped and Alikse's eyes flashed open wide. Tereka compressed her lips, stifling a smile. Naco was staring at the ceiling, his lips twitching. Kaberco hadn't taken him by surprise with his request.

When no one answered, Kaberco unfolded a piece of parchment. "You can't expect me to do this on my own." He raised his eyebrows. "Right? Well. First things first. I have a few vacancies in the konament in Trofmose. Any suggestions?"

"Wouldn't Caphtor be the logical person for ephor?" Da asked.

"Yes, that one is clear," Kaberco said. "I was thinking about the syndic." He chuckled. "Which reminds me."

He shuffled his documents and pulled out a missive. "This arrived from Caphtor this morning." He unrolled the paper. "According to him, Trofmose is jubilant that I was chosen to be the Prime Konamei." He rifled through the papers again. "Yavaros and the adile both wrote effusive letters of support, only outdone by Kulooq's effort. Listen:

" '*To Prime Konamei Kaberco Gougin,*
'*Greetings from your humble servant Kulooq, Ludi of Trofmose.*' "

Kaberco snickered. "As if I would forget who he was. Nice touch, though, dropping his surname to appear like he wasn't giving himself airs."

Squinting at the paper, he continued. " '*I congratulate you on your impressive feats of bravery and brilliance in defeating an over-whelming force.*' Which means they all expected me to be killed in battle." He smirked. " '*Congratulations on ascending to the exalted position of the Prime Konamei. May your reign be long, safe, fair, and prosperous more than any other. I have always served you loyally and am ever at your service and, along with the other konameis of Trofmose, look forward to a fruitful and equitable partnership.*' "

Tereka relaxed back into her chair. Oversight of the fractious and conniving konameis rested on Kaberco's head, not hers. She didn't envy him in the least.

With a sneer, Kaberco tossed the letter aside. "Had Juquila been able to take him to her bed a few more times, Kulooq would have backed her in any bid to overthrow me." He snorted. "He was the only one who even hinted about Juquila's absence. None of them expressed any regret about her death." His tone grew solemn. "That doesn't answer the question they all had, but were afraid to ask. With both Juquila and Tirk dead, who is to be syndic? One of her junior clerks?" He looked from Tereka to Da.

Da shrugged. "Perhaps one of the traders would do. It would be a welcome change from having the vendors in control."

"I'm glad you feel that way," Kaberco said with a smile. "I'd like to name you."

"Me?" Da shook his head. "No."

"Why not, Da?" Tereka asked. "You're trusted by all, known to be fair and honest and wise. I think you're the perfect choice."

Her father pressed his lips together. "I recently lost my

oldest son. Can't I spend some time with my surviving son and my daughter?"

"I'd like to spend time with my wife," Kaberco answered. "But there's no telling when that will happen. She's still trying to convince our children that they want to leave Trofmose. A hard task, since she doesn't want to herself. Who knows how long it will take her to make the move."

Tereka flashed an amused glance at Da, who chuckled.

Relio snickered. "Managing a realm can be easier than managing a wife. I wish you luck."

His grin fading, Da said, "If you please, Kaberco, find someone else."

"If not you, then who?" asked Kaberco.

"Waukomis?" Tereka suggested. "Or even Kemet?"

Da shook his head. "I spoke with them this morning. They asked if I knew who would replace Juquila. They had an interesting suggestion, and I think they're right." He displayed his teeth in a wide grin. "Who else but Yeroblat?"

Of course. Tereka nodded. The jovial trader was well-liked and only resembled Juquila in one aspect—he was efficient. He'd be a fair syndic. "I agree."

"Then that settles Trofmose," Kaberco said. "I've received birds from Litavye and some of the other southern towns. As long as I promise to abolish the practice of taking and the most restrictive rules, they will accept me as the Prime Konamei. The center of the country, grateful that the war ended before their territory was damaged, also has agreed."

Another bit of tension eased from Tereka's weary muscles. She hadn't expected the other regions to rebel, but it was a relief to know that they wouldn't. For a heartbeat, she felt sorry for Kaberco, who would have to hold the country together without resorting to fear and threats.

Kaberco, however, didn't seem to be concerned. He plucked a document from his pile and spread it out. "Fewer restrictions, more trade goods, and the comforts the Riskers and Razdelians can bring will keep the people satisfied, at least for now." He tapped his fingers on the table. "The next item is my own staff. I've offered Poales and Savinnia positions, and they've both accepted."

Tereka pulled her eyebrows together. He hadn't asked her to work for him. Did that mean that he'd valued her only as the Desired One, and now she was of no more use to him than last week's stew?

"Savinnia?" Naco asked. "What do you want with her?"

Choosing to meet the protective older brother's challenging tone with a quiet voice, Kaberco explained. "Tereka tells me she was a questor's clerk before she was taken." He dipped his quill into the inkwell. "I've decided that the konament of Anbodu will only have jurisdiction over the city and the region. I will have my own konament to handle national and international matters."

"That's wise," Da said. His face took on a thoughtful expression.

"So, you would make Savinnia questor?" Naco asked.

"Not right away," Kaberco said. "I've appointed her senior clerk. The man I want for questor is old. When he can no longer serve, Savinnia—or one of the other clerks—should be ready to take over. We'll decide when the time comes."

Naco rubbed his chin and nodded. "My sister will serve you well."

"Good," said Kaberco. "Eltolad from Tyov will make a fine ephor. I'll move the adile from Litavye here, so the south will feel one of their own holds some power."

"What about the ludi?" Da asked.

"The ludi of Paamiat should do," Kaberco said. "I want someone from a remote area that's been neglected. Someone who will help the small villages and make sure they get their fair share."

"That leaves the syndic," said Relio.

Tereka tipped her head to the side. Maybe that's what Kaberco had in mind for her.

"You don't suppose I'll name you?" Kaberco asked, grinning at Relio.

"No, but you should ask girly's da. He's the one. An honest trader, knows the Riskers."

Da shook his head. "I don't want to be syndic of anything."

Kaberco fixed his eyes on the man. "Come to think of it, Tarkio, you'd be perfect. Everyone who deals with you trusts you." When Da hesitated, Kaberco went on. "I need someone incorruptible and scrupulously fair."

While Tereka agreed her da would be great for the job, she couldn't help but feel a pang. She'd love to be syndic. She'd correct Juquila's abuses and make sure all the traders and vendors were treated justly.

"But," continued Kaberco, "I've offered the job to Poales."

"Poales?" Tereka asked. With an effort, she kept the corners of her mouth from drooping.

"Yes." Kaberco nodded. "For the same reasons I thought of your father. The Riskers know and trust him. He also—or so I've been told—has dealt with the pirates. He might be able to do something about that scourge as well."

Da smiled. "I think he's a wise choice."

As much as she didn't like it, Tereka had to agree.

"Very well, Tarkio," Kaberco said. "Even though you've wriggled out of becoming a syndic, don't congratulate yourself. I have another idea in mind for you."

Now, what was Kaberco up to? Tereka struggled to hide her impatience.

"I already told you—" Da began.

"I'm forming a special commission to hear the cases of people who've been taken," Kaberco interrupted. "We can start with the liberated miners and the household servants of the ephors and the Prime Konamei. And any others we find. I want to know who was justly sentenced, and who—" He broke off, his face reddening.

"Who was a victim of corrupt officials who sought to protect their own power," Naco finished quietly.

Kaberco winced. "Yes. Tarkio, I can think of no one better than you to lead the commission."

Da let out a sigh. "I could give you a year, two at the most. But I need a few weeks to retrieve my son and take care of some other business."

Tereka gawked at him. Why the time limit? And what other business? From the way Da folded his arms across his chest, she knew there was no point in asking him now. She'd have to pry the secret out of him later.

"Thank you." The corners of Kaberco's mouth twitched. "I think the commission should have three members. Would you accept Relio as one of them?"

Relio's eyes bulged, and he muttered a curse.

"You're the perfect choice," Tereka said. "The prisoners will trust you to get them justice."

Naco and Alikse nodded. "I agree," they both said.

Relio's mouth opened, but no sound came out.

"Since I hear no objection, consider yourself appointed," Kaberco said. "In the case of people who were taken for expressing unpopular opinions, we'll offer some form of compensation. The same for those who were sentenced too harshly for petty crimes. For those who committed serious crimes, the commission will decide if the time they've spent in the mines or other servitude was long enough, or if they need to serve longer."

If Tereka had harbored any doubts about Kaberco, they vanished like dust under a gentle rain. He intended to make amends for the past, and his first actions proved his determination to do so.

Except for the Riskers. He hadn't mentioned them. It

hadn't escaped her that they hadn't been invited to negotiate the treaty with Razdelia, even though they'd suffered losses in the war. It had been bothering her all day.

With a deep sigh, Relio leaned back in his chair. "I'd be delighted to serve on the commission."

Kaberco gave him a clipped nod. "Tarkio, you can choose the third at your leisure." He gestured to his scribe. "Send birds to Eltolad, along with the ludi of Paamiat and the adile of Litavye, inviting them to serve. Also to Yeroblat, appointing him syndic, and to Caphtor appointing him ephor." He pursed his lips. "I've decided to allow Meluz to continue as a guardsman. He tells me he had no idea what his mother was plotting, and I'm inclined to believe him." He let out a breath. "I told him he was on probation and sent a bird to Caphtor explaining the situation. It's his problem now." He looked around the room. "Does anyone have any questions?"

"Thank you." Relio leaned forward. "All I expected was my freedom. This is…" He shrugged. "But what about Naco and Alikse? Are you just going to turn them loose?"

"Alikse accepted a position yesterday," Kaberco replied.

Tereka stared at Alikse. Did Kaberco have a use for everyone but her? "What position?"

"I'm a member of Kaberco's personal bodyguard."

She had to admit it made sense. Alikse was quiet, observant, and easily overlooked. And could kill a man with his bare hands. But what about Naco? Her breath caught, afraid Kaberco would send him to the far south, or even Razdelia. And what about her? She needed something to do when she wasn't destroying stray scorpion amulets.

Why had she ceded so much power to Kaberco without extracting a few promises first? She folded her hands in her lap. She wouldn't publicly oppose Kaberco, not this soon in his reign. But if she was dissatisfied with the positions he came up with for Naco and her, she'd have a private word with him later.

"Regarding Naco, I thought I'd best consult with Tereka." Kaberco leaned toward her. "Would you be my emissary to the Riskers, to establish how we can work with them? And since it's a big job, I'll need two emissaries. If you two think you can work together." He winked.

The tension in her neck eased and Tereka laughed. Kaberco hadn't forgotten the Riskers. Naco reached for her hand under the table. His gaze met hers and he nodded. "We accept," they said in unison.

As Naco squeezed her hand, she realized Kaberco was right. He'd given them an enormous task. Centuries of mistrust on both sides had festered into deep-seated prejudice, even loathing. But reconciling the two groups was a job worth doing. Relief flooded her. She had a purpose and the prospect of a fulfilling life ahead.

"Girly's the right one for the job," Relio said. He nodded to her before turning back to Kaberco. "That takes care of everyone except that *yanshyr* Sebezh."

Kaberco scowled. "Tereka doesn't want him punished, so we're allowing him to live in Anbodu for now. You will, of course, look into his case and discover why he was taken in the first place."

Relio narrowed his eyes, then grinned. "I'd be delighted to send that *kassil* back to the mines."

"Only if he deserves it," Kaberco said.

"Of course, your Primeness."

Tereka couldn't restrain her snort over Relio's impudence. The thought of Sebezh returning to the copper mines didn't depress her mood in the least.

"One more thing, if I may," Syzyan said.

"Please." Kaberco waved his hand, palm up.

"My army will leave in a few days." He tipped his head to Kaberco. "Thank you for giving us our emperor's body. I intend to cremate him in our traditional way when we return to Otrechia." His throat bobbed. "I would ask that you accept my son as ambassador from Razdelia."

"Father, why me?" Farnaz asked.

"The country might turn on me for allowing Damira to get out of control. I wouldn't blame them. I blame myself. If I have to be sacrificed for peace, so be it. I'm not sure what life will be like without Dami and Shag."

His palpable grief made Tereka's eyes sting. "But what of your son? And your family?" Tereka asked.

"My wife died years ago, as did my daughter. Farnaz is all I have left. I want to be sure he'll be safe and not get caught up in any mob revenge."

"Yes, of course." Kaberco nodded. "Write me an official letter about his appointment. He'll be protected here. I'll see to that."

Syzyan smiled sadly. "My jianjuns and I hope that we can keep Razdelia from splitting apart again. That your treaty with us, and the memories of the Endless War, will persuade the regional leaders to cooperate with us. I'm not optimistic, but who knows? Perhaps the sky-god will look on us with favor." He put a hand on Farnaz's shoulder. "Besides, if I'm reading things right, you're very interested in a certain questor's senior clerk." A smile flickered on his face. "That is, if Naco approves."

Farnaz's face reddened.

Tereka pressed her lips together to restrain her grin. Savinnia would be delighted that Farnaz hadn't returned to Razdelia.

"Kaberco, if you please," Tereka said, "I'd like to visit my mother before I begin my duties."

He rubbed his chin. "What about this? You and Naco go to Zafrad, but take the route through the mountains to the Risker camps. Now that winter's upon us, you won't be able to get to Altiad, but you can stop at the other northern settlements. Invite the elders to a conference to renegotiate the old treaty. When you're ready, you can visit the southern camps."

Her face broke into a smile. "Thank you, Kaberco. I'll only stay a week—"

"Take a month," Kaberco said. "We won't hold the conference until spring, anyway."

"If you please, Kaberco," Da said, "I'll leave tomorrow. I'll collect my son and meet Tereka at her grandparents' home. We'll return together, if that's acceptable to you."

Tereka's heart swelled. A month with her mother in her grandparents' home, with Naco and Da. And she'd finally be reunited with her younger brother. She blinked away the tears joy brought to her eyes.

"Yes, of course. And if you would, take a few guards and the official documents appointing Caphtor and Yeroblat." Kaberco looked over Da's head. The chief scribe had risen from her seat. "If you please," Kaberco said to one of his guards, "summon my konameis. We have a treaty to sign."

68

A frosty morning wind tugged Tereka's cloak, making her shiver as she waited in the courtyard. The shortest day of the year would soon be upon them. It wasn't the best weather for riding through the mountains. But now that the new order was in place, she could hardly bear to wait one more heartbeat. She yearned to be at her mother's side.

Kaberco saw them off, his black cloak fluttering. He stood tall and solid, strong jaw set, his hazel eyes resolute. Tereka clasped his hand. "Thank you."

"Thank you." He gripped her hand in both of his. "Not many would have forgiven such offenses."

"You need to make it up to me with the way you rule."

He laughed. "I plan to. My first act will be to ban the wearing of turbans and all regulations on how people cut their hair. I can only imagine the commotion when the female konameis and the wives of the others show off their long hair."

"Indeed."

Relio saluted her in the Razdelian manner, two fingers to

his temple, then an arm across his chest and a curt bow of the head. "Ride safely, Tereka."

Her jaw went slack. Had her ears deceived her? Had Relio called her by her name?

With a chuckle, Alikse gathered her into a hug as Relio smirked. She turned to Savinnia, who gave her a long embrace. "I hope your mother has recovered," she whispered in Tereka's ear.

She'd miss them, her companions from prison and exile. And while she'd see many of them again, it wouldn't be the same, now that they were no longer dependent on each other to survive. One corner of her mouth twitched upward. Who would have thought that her band of outlaw fugitives would end up helping to rule the country?

Da encircled her with his arms. "I'll see you in a week or so, my dear girl." He sprang onto his horse and rode out of the courtyard, surrounded by ten of Kaberco's guardsmen.

Tereka mounted her chestnut mare and nodded to Naco, who was already seated on a brown stallion. "Shall we?" She nudged her horse's sides with her heels and rode toward the courtyard's gates, Naco at her side, followed by four of Kaberco's guards.

Syzyan and Farnaz stood near the gates, the wind ruffling their dark hair. They gave her the Razdelian salute, keeping their heads bowed as she passed. She returned it, suddenly somber. How she hoped Syzyan wasn't returning home only to be put to death.

He'd only shrugged when she asked him what he expected on his return. "I'll tell them the truth. My sister was possessed by evil amulets. The Desired One destroyed the amulets and told us to make peace. And so we did." He rubbed a hand over his forehead. "While this could end very badly for me, I don't think it will. The people are grateful that they haven't had war for the last eighteen years. This invasion didn't cost them much, and we gained a trading partner. But we'll have to see."

The Jianjun crossed her mind many times over the next twelve days as she and her companions rode through the mountains, knowing he and his army were on a similar trek. The steepness of the winding trails astounded her. No wonder their journey would take more than a week following this route, when it was a matter of a few days on the roads through the flatlands. And to think Iskra and Xico had done this trip on foot, her mother pregnant the whole time. Her admiration for her parents' courage and stamina rose.

Along the way, they visited the twenty Risker camps nestled in mountain valleys or perched on slopes. Their reactions to tidings of a new order were not free from skepticism and doubt, but overall, the change was welcome. All the elders promised to send an envoy to Kaberco's summit to renegotiate the treaty.

After the last camp, they parted ways with their guards, who were to ride to Gishin, send a bird to Kaberco reporting on their mission, and return home to Trofmose. Tereka and Naco rode on alone. Now there would be no more delays. She'd finally be reunited with her mother. Her heart sped up, and she wished she could fly.

With a click of her tongue, she urged her mare forward. Just a day and a half riding over snow-dusted mountain trails, and they'd be in Zafrad.

Early the next afternoon, they let the horses pick their way down a steep slope into a spacious valley. The Riskers guarding the pass looked familiar to her, although she didn't remember their names. They recognized her, however, telling her that Osip's granddaughter and her friend were always welcome.

She led Naco through the wide snow-covered meadow that flanked the camp, the fifty stone houses coming into view.

Winter sunlight glinted off their glass windows as if they were welcoming beacons.

When they reached the outskirts, she dismounted. "We'll walk the horses from here."

Naco slid from his horse. "Lead on."

As they ambled through the camp, the plucked notes of a harp danced in the air. The scent of burning wood and roasting meat tickled Tereka's nose. Painted doors of the snug houses were vivid against the snowy ground, the reds and blues and greens vibrant in contrast to the white of the snow-covered roofs. Barren window boxes hung under windows, waiting for the spring to be filled with flowers.

Barren. Empty. Suddenly, that was how Tereka felt. Blank, like a night sky after clouds had rolled in. Her throat constricted and her mouth was dry as though filled with dust.

Her steps slowed.

Naco touched her arm. "What's wrong?"

"Nothing."

"Nothing? For days, all you've wanted to do was see your mother. Now that we're almost there, you're dawdling like you're going to your execution."

She swallowed the lump in her throat. "What if she's worse? Or will never get better?"

He rubbed her shoulder. "She might have improved."

"I keep hoping. But it's more than that. Maybe I'm selfish." She sighed. "Ever since I found out that I wasn't Groa's daughter, I've never known who I am. Then to learn that Da wasn't my father, but a Risker was? Well, you can imagine."

Naco nodded. "I can."

"And what made it worse? No one knew what my parents named me. When I found my mother, I thought I'd finally know. But she barely remembers her own name."

They fell into silence, the only sound the rush of wind and the flapping of their cloaks. "What will you do if you never find out?" Naco asked.

Tereka shook her head. "I don't want to think about it."

"You should," Naco said. "There's no point in letting that rule your life. You'll have to accept not knowing if you're going to have any peace."

Biting back an angry retort, Tereka stared at the packed snow of the path in front of her. He didn't understand. But then, he'd always known who he was and who he belonged to. He was a much-loved son, not a nameless orphan who'd been taunted and abused. She couldn't explain why learning her real name was so important to her. Why she believed that if she knew the name her parents had given her, she wouldn't be haunted by Juquila's insults, and that the sting would have gone from *Useless Spawn*. And why not knowing gnawed at her happiness like an alloe rat chewed its way through a crust of bread.

"Accept not knowing?" She shook her head. "I'm not sure I can." Shoulders slumping, she shuffled to the violet door of Osip's house and raised her hand to knock.

And froze in place. As long as she stayed outside, she'd have hope. She wasn't ready to lose it. Not yet.

69

Tereka took a deep breath of the bracing mountain air. No sense letting her fearful villager side rule her. She was a Risker, or at least half a Risker. She wasn't sure where she belonged, but she knew which side gave her courage.

She gripped her fist tight and clenched her teeth. Before she could rap on the door, it flew open.

"How long are you going to lurk on the doorstep?" a deep voice boomed. A heartbeat later, Osip engulfed her in a fierce hug.

"Move aside, old man, and let someone else see the girl." Cillia drew Tereka into a warm embrace.

"So, you brought Naco with you?" Osip said. He clapped Naco on the back. "Come with me, my boy, and we'll put your horses up." He took the reins of the mare. "Follow me."

Cillia dragged Tereka into the house and pulled the girl's damp cloak from her. *Mmm.* Tereka inhaled. How she'd missed the smell of her grandparents' house. Simmering stew. Freshly baked bread. Pungent herbs. All mixed with the crisp odor of pine logs burning in the fireplace. The tension ebbed from her spine and she let her shoulders relax.

"And what about me?"

Tereka spun and threw herself into Da's arms. "You're here."

"Of course I am." He jerked his chin toward the sideboard. "Let me help you."

He held up a pitcher. Tereka held her hands over the basin and moaned as he poured warm water over her frozen fingers.

Da handed her a towel. "When you're done, come sit with us."

She wiped her hands and turned her eyes to the long table in the center of the room, covered with platters of roasted venison, fresh bread, diced herbs, and squash. Piles of little cakes filled with hopberry jam and honey nestled in baskets. Two candelabras with five lavender beeswax candles each offset the dreary winter sky outside.

Then she noticed Iskra, who sat near the end of one of the table's long sides.

While still thin, Iskra no longer looked skeletal. The wild glint in her gray eyes had vanished, replaced by a wariness that wavered into fear but didn't quite descend into panic. A few glints of gold shined in the stubble of her newly grown, dirty blonde hair.

Tereka's stomach fluttered as hope stirred within. She raised her eyebrows and looked at her grandmother.

Cillia tilted her head in affirmation. "Yes, she's doing much better. Why don't you sit by her?"

Tereka slid onto the bench next to Iskra. Da sat across from her with a boy of about ten whose black hair, coppery skin, and large eyes were startlingly like Tirk's. Tears stung Tereka's eyes. The boy had to be her brother, Aito. She smiled at him. "Peace and safety."

The boy frowned. "Peace and safety," he mumbled.

A lump formed in Tereka's throat and pain constricted her heart. Groa must have filled his head with stories about his wicked sister. The little boy who'd called her Terter was gone forever.

The door opened and Osip and Naco entered, bringing a draft of cold, fresh air. They shed their cloaks and boots. After they washed their hands, Osip flapped the towel in Tereka's direction. "Go on," he said to Naco. "Sit by the girl."

Naco grinned and slid into the seat next to Tereka. Her skin tingled as his shoulder brushed against hers.

Cillia set a tureen of steaming chicken stew on the table and handed around plates. Tereka smiled at the ring of autumn leaves painted on the edges. Maybe now the villagers could have pretty dishes, too.

Osip poured wine for all but Aito and raised his glass. "To the sky-god."

After repeating the toast, Tereka sipped the wine. Its fruity taste warmed her, along with the heat radiating from the huge brick oven and her grandparents' loving welcome.

"For you, dearie?" Cillia asked Iskra, picking up a ladle. Without waiting for a reply, she scooped stew onto Iskra's plate. Iskra smiled vaguely and picked up her spoon. Cillia held her hand out for Tereka's plate.

"If Riskers eat like this every day," Naco said, "I don't think I'll ever leave."

Tereka reached for his hand under the table. She didn't want to leave this haven of warmth and peace, either.

Her grandparents spent most of the time they weren't chewing to pump Naco for details of Tereka's exploits.

A muscle twitched in Osip's face as Naco told of Tereka's standoff with Damira. "I always knew you had it in you," her grandfather said. "I'm so proud of how you handled it all. Every bit of it."

Before Tereka could collect her thoughts enough to reply, the door flew open. Her uncle Tikul burst into the house, followed by his wife, Zamora. The door slammed shut behind them. "Sorry, Mam," Tikul said. "The wind caught me off guard."

"No matter," Cillia said. "Will you join us?" she added after a round of exuberant greetings were exchanged.

"Thank you, but no. We ate earlier," Tikul said. He sat next to Aito, who scooted away from him. Tikul grinned. "Have you heard about your da going warboar hunting?"

The boy's eyes widened. "Da? Hunting warboars? That's not safe."

"No, it's not," Da said.

"Let me tell you about it." Mischief twinkled in Tikul's blue eyes. He gave Tereka a wink. "You'll want to hear this, too."

Zamora rolled her eyes and sat next to her husband. "How he loves this story."

As she took a second plate of stew from Cillia, Tereka's eyes darted between Da and her uncle. She'd never heard of any warboar hunt.

"My da traded with Tarkio's da for years," Tikul said. "One day he brought your da here. You were what, nine?"

Da tore a piece of bread from the loaf and dipped it in his stew. "More like twelve."

"Anyway, my da told me and my little brother to entertain him," Tikul continued. "Xico thought hunting warboars would be just the thing."

Tereka's heart skipped a beat. Xico. Her father.

"So, we went into the woods…"

She let the sounds of Tikul's animated voice and Da's calmer tones wash over her, savoring every word of the story. Cillia and Osip shook their heads ruefully as Tikul spun out the tale of a warboar chasing the boys through the forest. Iskra stared dreamily into space, repeating Xico's name every time it was mentioned.

The tightness in Tereka's chest eased, and she found herself laughing more heartily than she had in years. Even if

Iskra's memories didn't return, Tereka would have years to ask
Tikul to tell her of her father. Maybe she'd get to know the
boy Xico had been.

Aito's wary expression faded as the tale rolled on. From
time to time, a smile flittered across his face. Perhaps one day
he'd warm up to her.

After Tikul finished his story, complete with corrections
from Da, Cillia refilled teacups and handed around the cakes.
Tikul took one and waved it at Da. "So, Tarkio. Are you still
leaving in the morning?"

"You're leaving?" Tereka asked. "But I just got here."

"I waited for you," Da said. "And I'll be back in a few
days. I have business in Mikkeliad that I don't want to put off
any longer."

Tereka tipped her head to the side. Why was Da going
there? What urgent business could he have?

Cillia stood up. "Tereka, would you be so kind as to
help me?"

"Of course." Tereka jumped to her feet.

"I think we need more wine. Will you come with me?"

Eyeing her grandmother, Tereka wondered what this was
about. Surely, she could carry a few bottles herself. She
followed Cillia into the lean-to off the kitchen.

Once inside, Cillia closed the door and gave her a small
smile that didn't reach her vivid green eyes. "I want to talk
about your mother."

Tereka's stomach clenched. "She's not, she's—"

"She's fine. I mean, her physical wounds are healing. She's
sleeping well, and no longer wakes up screaming. But her
memories are not returning the way I'd hoped. She knows me
and Osip now, but she has no memory of ever meeting Tikul
or Zamora, or my girls. I think we should try healing her with
your amulets. Just don't get your hopes up."

Cillia pulled a bottle of wine from a rack on the wall. "I'm not sure she'll recover her mind after what she went through. Maybe it's better that she doesn't."

That might be true. Tereka sighed. She'd so longed for her mother to remember her, to tell her of her early days, when she had both parents to love her. Maybe Naco was right. She'd have to accept she'd never have the answers to her questions.

By the time they returned to the kitchen, Osip had put Tikul and Da to work washing dishes. Aito laughed and cheered as Tikul splashed as much water on Da as he did in the sink.

When they finished, Zamora announced she was taking Aito to her house, where her younger children were waiting for their share of Cillia's honey cakes.

Da nodded. "Go, son. I'm sure they'll let you help eat the cakes."

Once Zamora and Aito had left, Tereka couldn't help but notice the looks exchanged between Osip, Cillia, and Da.

Cillia bent in front of Iskra. "Dearie, would you like to take a walk with Tereka and me? We won't have many more nice days like this until spring." Iskra stood and silently fetched her cloak.

Tereka looked at Naco. "Will you join us?"

"No, he won't." Da leaned forward. "I want to have a talk with him, as do your grandfather and uncle." His voice was stern, but smile lines feathered around the corners of his eyes.

Naco gaped at him for a moment before a slow grin spread across his coppery face. "It will be my pleasure."

Answering his smile with one of her own, Tereka's face burned and her heart swelled within her.

"After that," Osip said, "I want to have a chat with your da."

Da raised his eyebrows.

Osip chuckled. "You're not fooling anyone. Going to Mikkeliad indeed. Remember, even though you've been pining for her ever since the first day you set eyes on her, you've been widowed less than a month. And Veressa lost the husband she loved a few short weeks before that. She's always valued your friendship but give her time to figure out if she'll ever feel any more for you. *Samatale?*"

His brown face flushed, but Da's smile didn't waver. "*Samatale.*"

So that was why Da only agreed to serve Kaberco for a year or two. He fully intended to court Veressa. And this was the one secret he'd been keeping from Tereka, the one he promised had nothing to do with her. She put a hand to her mouth to hide her grin.

"All right then, women folk, be off with you." Osip pointed to the door. "We have a lot of talking to do here."

Tereka squeezed Naco's hand. She rose, smirked at Da, and dropped a kiss on the top of Osip's head. Once she'd flung on her cloak, she grabbed her bow and quiver. With a final glance over her shoulder at Naco's grin, she strolled out after Cillia and Iskra.

Cillia led the way to a trail through a knot of pine trees, their dark green limbs half obscured under shining mounds of snow. When they were out of sight of the camp, she stopped. "Do you want to try?"

Pulling out her three Amulets of Power, Tereka held them in front of Iskra, who touched one of the glowing purple stones. "Oh, pretty."

The green and purple stones flashed in the sunlight. Tereka put one hand on Iskra's head and murmured to the sky-god. The stones warmed in her hand. Her heart quivered and stumbled over a few beats. She stepped back and peered into Iskra's face.

Iskra's expression was as vague as ever. She tipped her head to the side. "Do I know you?" she asked Tereka.

A lump formed in Tereka's throat as she shoved the amulets into their pouch. Her last hope was gone. She'd never have her mother back. "Yes, we've met. A few times."

Pointing down the trail, Iskra asked, "What's that way?"

"A lake where we swim in the summer," Cillia said. "I'll show you." She led the way down the sloping trail to a lake rimmed with cliffs on one side and pebbly beaches on the other. An outcropping of rock jutted up from the shore about twenty feet above the surface of the gray water.

"You swim in that?" Tereka asked.

"Only in summer. It's fed by streams and a few warm springs, so it's lovely. Your mother enjoyed it."

"My mother?"

"Xico taught her to swim here. She jumped off that rock with him."

That towering rock? Tereka tried and failed to imagine her mother climbing up that high.

"Xico." Iskra repeated the name. "Xico. He loved me."

Cillia patted her shoulder. "That he did. And he married you."

Iskra held out her arm and pulled the sleeve of her dress back, exposing her wrist. She traced the scars of the X's she'd carved into her flesh. "Xico." She looked at the rock. "We swam here."

"You did." Cillia's eyes widened and Tereka stiffened. Was her mother starting to remember the past?

"What happened to my baby?" Iskra said.

Tereka's heart stopped. This was the first Iskra had ever mentioned her.

Answering slowly as if measuring her words, Cillia replied, "You had a baby, a girl."

"Where is she?"

Iskra asked the question so calmly that Tereka found the courage to answer. "I am your baby."

Iskra laughed. "Oh, no, my baby is small. She can't walk or talk."

"That was many years ago," Tereka said. "I've grown up."

Staring into Tereka's face, Iskra said, "You have blue eyes. Xico's were green."

"That's right," said Cillia. "But look. The shape of the eyes is the same, and she has Xico's chin. Her skin is the same golden tan as his and if her hair was a shade darker, it would be his. But her nose is yours. She is your daughter." Cillia took a shaky breath. "She's my son Xico's daughter."

"It's been that long?" Iskra rubbed her forehead. "So many memories are a blur." She ran a finger down Tereka's cheek, tracing the track of a rolling tear. "Why do you cry?"

Tereka struggled to speak. "I never thought I'd find you."

"How did you lose me?"

She didn't know what to say to that. She shot a look at Cillia, wordlessly begging her grandmother for help.

"Your baby—Tereka here—was less than a year old when you were separated," Cillia explained.

Iskra shook her head. "Why does she call you Tereka?"

"Because that's the name they gave me. No one knew what you and Xico called me. Do you remember?"

Tereka held her breath. Iskra paused so long she had to let it out, her hopes dissipating. *She doesn't know.*

Tipping her head to the side, Iskra said, "I'm not sure about many things, but I know this." She rubbed the back of her head and tugged on her short hair. "Xico chose it. When he told me what it meant, I had to agree."

Her heart racing, Tereka asked her question. "What is it?" Goosebumps prickled Tereka's forearms and her hands tingled. At last, she'd know her name.

"Xinua." Iskra smiled, her gaze locked on Tereka's face. "Beloved blessing from the sky-god."

I hope you enjoyed reading **Flood of the Fire** as much as I enjoyed writing it!

If you'd like to receive updates about upcoming releases, book recommendations, bonus content, and sneak peeks of my work, please subscribe to my newsletter at:

https://subscribe.evelynpuerto.com/

If you enjoyed this book, I would be deeply grateful if you would leave an honest review on BookBub, Goodreads or my shopify store.

Book reviews mean a ton to a self-published author like myself. More reviews help my books get better visibility and perform better in search algorithms. Your review will help others find my books and will make my day!

Even one sentence giving your opinion of the book will help a lot. Thank you!

ACKNOWLEDGMENTS

First, a big thank you to you, my readers, for spending time in the world of Tlefas I created ten years ago. I'm especially grateful to those of you who read **Flight of the Spark**, **Flicker of the Flame** and **Sting of the Scorpion** and patiently waited while I wrapped up the final book of the series. It's been a bittersweet time for me to end the journey in Tlefas after so many years. Finishing **Flood of the Fire** was like saying good-bye to old friends like Tarkio, Tereka, and Naco. I think I'll miss writing Juquila the most!

Special thanks to Joe Bunting and the gang over at the Write Practice. Lyn Blair, John King, Antonio Roberts, Robert Harrell, Lori Palmer and many others faithfully read and critiqued early versions of this book. Your feedback was priceless, as was your encouragement and enthusiasm about this story.

My editor Elizabeth Doyle offered valuable suggestions and pointed out inconsistencies that no one else, including me, noticed. Thank you for helping me keep everything straight and for providing the inspiration for Damira's rabbit.

Sebastian Breit of Foreign Worlds Cartography did an outstanding job taking my old sketches of Tlefas and turning them into a wonderful map.

Most of all I'm grateful to my husband Tony, whose support, encouragement and love keep me going when I can't find the words. And thank you for patiently listening to me ramble on about my imaginary people.

And lastly, thanks be to God, who gave me what ability I have to string words together into a story.

ABOUT THE AUTHOR

Evelyn Puerto entered the world around the time of the unveiling of the microchip, the introduction of Japanese cars to the US, and postage stamps that cost four cents. Her Saturday morning friends were Mighty Mouse, Dudley Do-Right and the Jetsons.

Growing up, school was merely an interruption of her exploration of the worlds of Grimm's Fairy Tales, Louisa May Alcott and, later, JRR Tolkien.

When she married late in life, inherited three stepdaughters, a pair of step-grandsons, and a psychotic cat. Currently she writes from South Carolina.

She's the author of the award-winning **Beyond the Rapids**, and is now an emerging author of fantasy. **Flight of the Spark,** the first book in her Outlawed Myth series, won a Readers' Favorite Silver Medal.

To read more of her short fiction or to subscribe to her newsletter, visit www.evelynpuerto.com.

- tiktok.com/@evelyn.puerto.aut
- instagram.com/theevelynpuerto
- bookbub.com/profile/evelyn-puerto
- facebook.com/Author.Evelyn.Puerto

Other books by Evelyn Puerto

The Outlawed Myth Series

Flight of the Spark (now available in audio)
Flicker of the Flame
Sting of the Scorpion
Flood of the Fire

The Royal Mages Series

The Girl Who Broke the Dark
The Girl Who Wrote on Water
The Girl Who Shattered the Sea

www.ingramcontent.com/pod-product-compliance
Lightning Source LLC
Chambersburg PA
CBHW031026030726
47497CB00004B/1020